Trudi Pacter, a former Fleet Street journalist, has been chronicling the lives of the rich and famous for twenty years. She is the highly acclaimed author of two previous novels, *Kiss and Tell* and *Screen Kisses*. She lives in London with her husband, Baronet Sir Nigel Seely, and is currently working on her next novel, *Living Doll*.

TRUDI PACTER

The Sleeping Partner

GraftonBooks

A Division of HarperCollins*Publishers*

GraftonBooks
A Division of HarperCollins*Publishers*
77–85 Fulham Palace Road,
Hammersmith, London W6 8JB

Published in paperback by GraftonBooks 1991
9 8 7 6 5 4 3 2 1

First published in Great Britain by
GraftonBooks 1991

ISBN 0-586-21186-1

Printed in Great Britain by
HarperCollinsManufacturing Glasgow

Set in Sabon

For Nigel, an advertising legend
in his own lunchtime

1

When she woke she knew something was wrong with the world. For a start the pillow under her head was not her own. It was hard and bouncy and smelt of hotels. Expensive hotels. Her eyes opened with a start. Frances knew exactly where she was and what was happening.

She was in Claridges Hotel on the morning of her wedding. Two thoughts chased each other round the cotton wool of her mind. Should she go and find her mother? Or should she pretend she was still asleep and let her mother find her? She was tempted to settle for the soft option. Then she pulled herself together.

If I'm going into battle, she thought, I might as well be on the offensive. She sat up quickly, swinging her legs onto the soft, thick carpet. Then she stood up, stretched and stepped out of her nightie.

Naked, with her hair tousled and her eyes half closed from sleep, Frances Buckingham still looked like the flower of English womanhood. There was something fragile and unawakened about her that put you in mind of a colt or a new-born kitten. Her limbs were long and elegantly shaped. Her breasts were buds tipped with the palest pink, and her entire body seemed to be covered with fine blonde down which matched the fall of her hair. Only her mouth gave her away. In repose it made her look like an angel. Then she smiled, and the story changed. For Frances Buckingham had the come-hither grin of a chorus girl.

That day, the moment Frances was out of bed she made for the bathroom and threw herself under the shower. Holding her breath, she turned the water on to cold and as the jets bounced and stung her skin she started to come awake. She wished she hadn't. The day stretching ahead of her began to resemble an obstacle race. There was the hairdresser, the manicurist, the girl to do her make-up. And there was the biggest obstacle of all: her mother.

The image of her floated into her mind. Solid, expensively finished and looking like the Queen. With the image of her mother came others. Her flatmate sitting up in bed, feverish with flu. Sorry to miss the wedding. Her father elegant in his morning suit, impatient to get going. Archie, the man she was going to marry. She wondered how he felt about it.

Impatiently, Frances turned off the shower and shook herself – like a cat after a shower of rain. There's no use wondering how Archie feels about things, she told herself grimly. Archie will feel how Archie's expected to feel. And once more a feeling of wrongness threatened to overtake her.

She made it as far as the drawing-room of her suite to find her mother ordering breakfast. Freshly squeezed juice, toast, marmalade, coffee, eggs, bacon. She started to feel queasy.

'You might have asked me,' she started to say. Then she stopped herself. Since when did her mother consult her on anything?

She walked across the over-decorated room with its phoney antiques and gilded mirrors. Normally the sight of a room like this, self-consciously expensive and shouting out new money, cheered her up. Today it irritated her. Her elder sister had been married from Claridges with her mother looking over her shoulder and the rest of the family roaring approval. Now it was her turn.

A flunkey arrived at the door wheeling a linen-covered trolley set with bone china and glinting crystal glasses containing the fruit juice. From a heated drawer underneath the starched cloth he produced the breakfast. Frances wasn't going to eat it, and she suspected her mother wasn't going to either. She calculated that for the same money she could have had a delicious dinner anywhere along the King's Road. For the second time that morning she wondered how she had got into all this.

Archie wasn't like the other boys she went out with. For a start he was five years older than she was. Twenty-seven, a grown up man. Not her type at all. Then there was his job as a junior partner at a city stockbrokers. She'd been used to drama students with private incomes or Cambridge graduates who did something vague at Christie's. 'Junior partner' had a serious, settled sound to it. If he hadn't been so good looking, Frances would have told Archie to get lost the minute she set eyes on him. As it was, it was the last thing she did. Instead she let him take her to the opera where she fell asleep, any number of cocktail parties where she got tipsy, and two rather formal dinners at the Savoy where she didn't eat.

It didn't seem to put him off. Archie went on ringing her up and inviting her to things and Frances went on going because she thought he might ask her to bed. Instead he asked her to marry him.

She was astounded.

'You don't have to do that,' she told him. 'Why don't we go away for the weekend instead?'

But Archie refused to be drawn. Frances Buckingham was the second daughter of a Baron. A minor Baron, but a Baron, nonetheless. So no matter how pretty she was, or how available, he wasn't playing. Girls like Frances were created for one reason only. To be married to men like him in order to produce heirs. So Frances could turn that teasing, tempting smile of hers on him as much as she liked and she wouldn't succeed in leading him anywhere but the altar.

Frances's reverie was broken by the sound of her mother's voice, clipped and disapproving.

'Don't you think you'd better have something to eat,' she said, 'before the hairdresser arrives?'

Frances went reluctantly over to the breakfast trolley and poured herself a cup of coffee. Then she nibbled on a tiny triangle of toast while her mother droned on about wedding presents. To date she had received a canteen of Georgian silver from her grandmother, what seemed like half of the stock of the White House from relations she hardly knew existed, a Cartier clip from her future mother-in-law and from her parents the deeds to a house in Wiltshire.

It was the house that stuck in Frances's throat. It wasn't that she didn't want it. Who wouldn't be grateful for a manor house in its own grounds a stone's throw from Bath? She just wished she had had some say in where she was going to live. But then she stopped having a say in anything six months ago, when she finally agreed to marry Archie.

In the beginning she hadn't wanted to marry him at all, but she didn't want to say goodbye to him either. So she played for time.

'Don't rush me,' she told him. 'I want to know you better.' Archie took her to see his parents. And then Frances was truly lost, for they were nothing like any family she had ever known. She had been told the Brunsdons had only had money for two generations and she had expected vulgarity and flashiness. Instead she found generosity.

Archie's father, Reggie, had a large house in Leicestershire on the borders of the Pytchley Hunt. It was like all the other country houses Frances had ever visited, only more so. The carpets were in better repair, the pictures were in proper frames, and so well restored you could easily read the signatures. Stubbs and Ferneley in the dining-room, Landseer in the drawing-room and in the bedrooms Modigliani and Picasso. It was the bedroom pictures that fascinated Frances most. Real people didn't put modern pictures in their country houses. Not in the bedrooms and certainly not in the bathrooms.

It wasn't just their choice of pictures that made the Brunsdons different though. It was their whole attitude. Frances had been brought up in an atmosphere of true British restraint. The heating was never turned on until the middle of December, and then it was turned on low. Her mother wore fake emeralds and kept the real ones in the bank. And they never took holidays. The Buckinghams were rich but they behaved as if any day their fortune might be snatched away from them.

Archie's parents didn't seem to worry about their money. All they worried about was enjoying themselves. When Frances went down to Leicestershire for the weekend there was too much food on the table, too many guests for drinks, and Reggie was far too nice to the servants. Frances took to him instantly. He had married for the second time to a French ski champion, Jeanne-Marie. The three of them would hunt together most weekends. These expeditions caused the first sour note between Frances and Archie, for Archie had been badly scared by a horse while he was at school and he refused to have anything more to do with them. Frances's love for horses pleased him not at all. He always refused to talk to her for an hour before she went out and an hour after she came back. There would be no stables in their Wiltshire house. Frances knew that, and for a moment she regarded her mother with exasperation. Why did she always have to go along with everything Archie wanted?

Frances went to get herself more coffee just as the buzzer sounded in the suite. Fiona Buckingham got to her feet.

'That will be the girl to do your hair,' she said to her daughter. 'Go into the bedroom and I'll send her through.'

Frances snuggled deeper into the fluffy towelling dressing-gown. It's begun, she thought. Now there's no turning back.

11

Nearly forty-five minutes later Frances's fine blonde hair was piled on top of her head in a carefully constructed swirl. She had never worn it like this before and she knew she never would again. It was a bride's style, designed to go with a headdress and a veil. She glanced at her watch. In an hour and a half she would be standing in church wearing that veil. Without warning her stomach gave a sickening lurch.

The hairdresser looked concerned. 'Are you alright?' she asked. 'For a moment you looked pale.'

Frances smiled weakly. 'Nothing the make-up lady won't cure.'

The woman from Elizabeth Arden knew exactly how a bride should look on her wedding day. Radiant, dewy and above all innocent. She had been applying the look for the past twenty years now and so practised was her hand she could have made an angel out of a streetwalker. When she saw Frances scrubbed and faintly scented from her bath, she knew there would be no tax on her skills. This was a virgin if ever she saw one. The child looked so innocent, so butter-wouldn't-melt-in-her-mouth that she was tempted to ask her if her mother had explained the facts of life.

Archie had taken Frances to bed four hours after they became formally engaged. When it was over she wondered why she had agreed to marry him in the first place. I've been conned, she thought as she lay beside her sleeping fiancé. Then she looked at his Byronic profile and the way his hair curled around the bottom of his ears, and she forgave him. It's bound to get better, she decided. After that build-up it's got to.

They had kissed each other goodnight the first time they dated, but that's all they did until Archie proposed marriage and was turned down. Then he went into action. The next time he took Frances out, Archie invited himself to her flat for coffee.

She remembered how excited she felt that first time. They

had never been properly alone together before. Frances had looked at Archie's handsome, somehow formal face and felt a surge of pure lust. At last, she thought, I'll find out if you feel as good as you look.

He did. His breath tasted fresh, as if he had been sucking mints all night. His mouth on hers was moist and open, and his tongue probed and made demands. They were on the sofa in her over-furnished, over-pictured drawing-room. The gas log fire was burning brightly in the grate, and Archie's hand was starting to undo the buttons on her blouse. Frances twisted her body so that it lay more comfortably under his. I've been good, she thought, and I've been patient. For four weeks now I've been listening to you talk about Eton and Sandhurst. I've even sat all the way through the opera. Now it's my turn to have some fun.

She felt a familiar quickening of her pulse as his hands found her breasts. You know what you're doing, she thought. His fingers traced a pattern round her nipples. Then he replaced his fingers with his mouth. And she stopped thinking.

Frances had trodden this path before. Twice before. But neither of her lovers had she lusted after the way she did Archie. He had a way of touching her skin that brought her to the moment of orgasm. And when his hand started to move past her knee and onwards up her thigh, she realised she was sopping wet. With mounting excitement she started to undo the top of his trousers, but he stopped her.

'Not now,' he said gently, 'not yet.'

She lay back on the sofa. Her skirt was up round her waist now, and she could see as well as feel his fingers moving slowly, lightly upwards. She thought she would die of excitement. Every time his hand made contact with skin, a small electric charge went through her. Slowly, with great deliberation, he took hold of the top of her panties. Then before she realised it he was sliding them down her legs.

For a moment she felt ashamed. Her other encounters had always been in the dark. She had never displayed herself in front of a man like this. Then she looked into his face and saw his hunger. And in that moment she knew she had to possess him, or be possessed by him.

Once more his hand caressed her thigh and with an awful fascination she watched as he parted her legs. He started to play with her, teasing the fine blonde hair, gently probing the folds beneath it with his fingers until he found her centre. For a moment the world stood still. Then suddenly, without warning, he was gone.

With a start Frances opened her eyes and saw Archie standing a small distance away from the sofa. She felt the way she thought a fish would feel when it landed belly up on a river bank.

'What happened?' she said weakly. 'What on earth went wrong?'

He smiled, and for a moment the handsome face looked sad.

'Nothing went wrong,' he told her. 'I stopped before anything could happen.'

She sat up and pushed her skirt down around her knees.

'Are you mad?' she asked him.

Once more the handsome face looked sad. Almost apologetic.

'Not mad,' he said, 'just careful. What we nearly did just now wasn't worthy of you. I know it felt right. But believe me it wouldn't have felt right to either of us in the morning.'

Her cheeks were burning now.

'Speak for yourself,' Frances said. 'I don't need a wedding ring to make me feel clean. I don't have those kind of hang-ups.'

Archie sat down beside her and took her hand. 'Then you'll have to be patient with me,' he said, 'because I do.'

Nothing Frances could say, nothing she could do would make him change his mind. Archie Brunsdon was immune to flattery. Impervious to seduction. He wasn't giving an inch unless she promised to marry him. After ten days and two more encounters on the sofa, Frances melted. She would be honoured, she said, to become Archie's wife. He had produced an engagement ring on the spot, and Frances wondered how he could be so sure of her. Later that night in bed, she wondered again. For Archie's love-making never lived up to his foreplay. It was like a shaggy dog story with a weak punchline. Once he had roused her to unknown heights of passion, Archie plunged himself inside her and was spent in seconds. No matter how patient she was, how many times they went to bed together, the story was always the same. Archie simply couldn't stay the course. After a month or so Frances thought of calling the whole thing off, but by then it was too late. Over four hundred people had been invited to the wedding. St Paul's Church in Knightsbridge had been booked. The honeymoon was planned, and Frances's parents had put a down payment on the large house in Wiltshire.

Frances stood stock still in her bedroom at Claridges and stared at herself in the full-length mirror. She was dressed in the wedding-gown that Worth had made for her. The tight bodice showed the world that she had a hand-span waist and a rich father, for it was hand embroidered with thousands of tiny pearls sewn in elaborate patterns. The skirt was made of the same lace resting over layer upon layer of fine net. On her head was a garland of silk flowers with diamond hearts supporting a filmy veil. I'm caught, thought Frances. I'm cooked and trussed up and ready.

For a moment her eyes left her reflection and looked out of the window. Below her the rush-hour traffic snarled down Brook Street and into the heart of the shopping centre. People were hurrying to meetings, buying shoes or just having tea. The world was turning but Frances wasn't turning with it – and in her heart she knew she never would again.

She turned her back abruptly on the mirror and made her way through to the drawing-room. Her mother was there waiting for her. Frances smiled as brightly as she could.

'Lead me to the slaughter,' she said.

2

Gerald Buckingham was waiting for his daughter in the hired Daimler. How distinguished he looks, Frances thought, and how formal in his black morning coat and pale grey waistcoat. He helped her into the back of the car and gave her a message from her flatmate Sophie.

'She's running a temperature of 103,' he said looking apologetic, 'but she sends love and wishes you tons of luck. We all do,' he added.

Frances smiled weakly and squeezed his hand. 'I know,' she said.

She stared out of the window watching their progress down Piccadilly, round Hyde Park Corner and finally into the leafy white Georgian squares of Belgravia.

Her father turned to her.

'Nearly there,' he said reassuringly. As they swung their way round Wilton Crescent the church came into view. St Paul's was a yellow brick perpendicular church built in the early nineteenth century. By anyone's standards it was a beautiful building with its shallow stone courtyard and towering spire. As if to prove it, most of the Royal Family had, at some time or another, graced it with their presence.

As the car pulled up outside, Frances could see that a sizeable crowd had gathered outside. Nannies with their small charges and tourists in garish dresses stood and gawped as her father pushed, pulled and finally half carried her out of the Daimler. With a start she noticed a battery of newspaper photographers. Thank the Lord I don't have a train, she thought. Then I really would have looked awkward.

17

The train, or rather the absence of it, was her one small rebellion. Her mother had chosen her wedding dress the way she had chosen her house in Wiltshire – without consulting her.

When it came to the final fitting in Paris, Frances decided to make a stand.

'I don't want the train,' she had said. 'It's heavy and old fashioned. I'll have enough to think about on the day without dragging that behind me.'

There was fury from the French couturier and bullying from her mother, but Frances was adamant.

'You can either see the train at St Paul's,' she said tartly, 'or you can see me. We won't be there together.'

Everyone backed down and Frances was left with one small victory, one statement of independence. The strength it gave her carried her through the elaborate wedding preparations, the night in Claridges with her parents, the attentions of the make-up lady.

Only now, standing outside the tall elegant place of worship in Knightsbridge did Frances's courage desert her. None of this is anything to do with me, she told herself. It's a ritual, that's all. A medieval rite that gives Archie permission to sleep with me in the same bed tonight. The thought failed to comfort her and she noticed that her legs were trembling as she walked towards the carved stone arches which led into the church.

Suddenly she found she was surrounded on all sides. The dressmaker hurried towards her, fluffing out her skirts, adjusting her veil, straightening the cumbersome diamond studded headdress. Her sister and a matronly woman she recognised as a distant cousin were busy organising the bridesmaids. Then everything went quiet and Frances realised that the church bells had stopped ringing.

The jitters that had made her legs tremble came back to her. I can't do it, she thought in a rush of panic. I've come this far and I just can't go any further. Her father came forward and took her arm and she was carried into the vestry of the church.

The air smelled of incense and sweat and a hundred different French perfumes. Frances breathed it in and peered through her veil at the surroundings. The first thing she noticed were the hats. There were hundreds of them dotted among the rows and rows of pews. Expensive fabrications made of silk and chiffon and decorated with ridiculously artificial-looking flowers.

Some of the occupants of the pews turned round to stare at her and Frances realised that her entire world had turned out to see her on this day. There were cousins and schoolfriends, Archie's two brothers, even the man who looked after her father's estate. She peered through to the end of the church for a glimpse of her husband to be. For a reason that was unknown to her it suddenly became very important that she should see Archie, as if the sight of his face, his body, his very presence would give her the reassurance she needed to go through with the marriage.

Then she saw him.

He was standing to one side at the foot of the altar. Frances had expected him to look nervous, a reflection of the way she was feeling herself. But he looked nothing of the sort. She started to turn away and gather herself together for the final long walk up the aisle, when he swivelled round and looked back at her.

For a second she stared into his eyes. And in that fleeting moment Frances learned everything she needed to know about the life she would have with Archie Brunsdon. She saw a quiet country existence spreading out in front of her. She would organise formal dinner parties and run the servants the way her mother had done before her. She would bear sons, she knew that, and she would be insulated from them by an army of nannies. She would see her husband for dinner every night across a sea of polished

19

wood. And every night they would lie in bed together, and Archie would make love to her – without love.

Frances felt panic rise in her throat. Then instinctively, without thinking, she let go of her father's arm, drew her skirts around her and turned, throwing back her veil and pushing her way past the bridesmaids out into the bright summer day. The crowds on either side of her stood stock still. Whether it was in shock or confusion Frances never knew, for once she was outside she broke into a run and everything around her became a blur. As she ran out of the entrance of the church, her heel caught in a flagstone nearly tipping her off balance. It was at that moment that she became aware of the flashbulbs popping around her.

The tears started to gather in the corners of her eyes. She pulled herself together. I must survive this, she told herself firmly. Afterwards I'll cry.

She knelt down and rescued her shoe. Then resolutely, with her head high, she marched into Wilton Place. The first thing she saw was a taxi on its way out of the Berkeley Hotel. With a cry of relief she stopped it, threw herself into the back and shouted the address of her flatmate to the driver.

The newspapers had a field day. 'Peer's Daughter Bolts' announced the *Evening Standard*. The *Times* was more restrained. 'Sir Gerald Buckingham in family scandal.' But it was left to the *Sun* to have the last word. 'Naughty Frances does a runner,' it screamed.

The *Sun* summed up the situation perfectly. At least that's what Archie's father, Reggie, said. It was Reggie who came to Frances's rescue. He packed her off to his villa in Antibes until the fuss died down, then he tried to sort things out. It was clear, he explained to Gerald Buckingham, that Frances had had a classic attack of wedding nerves. It could happen to anyone. Why not give the girl another chance? A quiet wedding was what she needed – away from all the brouhaha. As luck would have it, he knew of a *curé* in the South of France who would settle the thing in a matter of weeks, possibly days if he paid enough to the church restoration fund.

Sir Gerald was unconvinced. 'What about Archie?' he asked. 'He couldn't have been overjoyed at being made to look a prize ass. Perhaps he won't want to marry Frances.'

Reggie Brunsdon looked thoughtful.

'Leave Archie to me,' he said.

Archie was understandably furious. He didn't have a sense of humour at the best of times, and times were not looking good. He sulked in his flat in the Barbican for a week. Venturing out only to go to his office in the city. After two days of being pursued by reporters he didn't even do that.

Reggie finally tracked him down at an out of the way point-to-point in Gloucestershire. Like Frances, he had decided to go to ground until the story moved off the news pages.

When Reggie finally found his son he took him off to a nearby pub where he plied him with whisky and sympathy. Archie didn't seem to want sympathy, though. As far as he was concerned the whole matter of Frances Buckingham was past history. She was a nice enough girl, quite good enough to become his wife. However, she had been put to the test and had fallen at the first fence.

'But the girl had been under pressure,' Reggie reasoned. 'That mother of hers is not the easiest of women. And what with buying a house and all the preparations, I expect she leaned on Frances a bit too heavily. The creature lost her nerve. Anyone can see that.'

Archie wasn't interested. At the mention of Frances's name a scowl threatened to distort his perfect features.

'If she couldn't manage a simple thing like getting married, what will she do when it comes to having babies, or putting on a dinner party?'

He took a pull on his whisky and soda. 'No, Frances simply wasn't cut out for what I had in mind. I don't want you or anyone else to mention her again.'

'Look I know you must be very hurt,' said Reggie as gently as he could, 'but you must have loved the girl. You can't just turn it off because she's done something wrong.'

The scowl deepened. 'I can turn it off,' said Archie, 'I just have turned it off. Weren't you listening to me?'

You really are a pompous arse, Reggie thought, looking at his son in despair. Maybe Frances was right when she ran away from you. He sighed. The boy was his son, his sole heir. The least thing he could do was to make sure he married a reasonable girl. He turned to Archie.

'You'll get over that business at St Paul's,' he said wearily. 'It's only your pride that's suffered. But if you don't do the right thing and marry Frances, then you could have real problems.'

Archie stiffened. 'What sort of problems?'

'Inheritance problems,' Reggie said quietly.

There was a small silence during which Archie signalled to the bartender for another whisky. When it came he swallowed it in one. Then he faced his father.

'Okay,' he said coldly. 'Tell the Buckinghams to wheel in the bitch. I'll marry her if that's what you all want, but it won't be a pleasure.'

Frances was less easily persuaded. First her sister arrived in Antibes to talk her round. When she failed, her mother went into battle. Neither of them made any impression at all.

A month later, when Frances arrived back in England, her father took her out to lunch at his club. When he first saw her sitting at the tiny circular bar in the Women's Annexe at Bucks, he hardly recognised her. The Mediterranean sun had baked her pale skin the colour of butterscotch. She had had her hair cut off to her shoulders.

The real difference in her though, went beyond the surface. She looked, he thought, more definite than she ever had before. A lot of her meekness had gone, and there was a set to her shoulders he didn't like at all.

Over drinks he kept the conversation to neutral topics. The weather in Antibes, what parties she was going to that season. Finally he came to the point.

'I want to get this marriage thing with Archie clear in my mind,' he said. 'Are you going to go through with it or not?'

Frances glanced round the cubicle the club had erected around their table. Normally the glass partitions isolating the guests from each other irritated her. Now she welcomed the privacy.

She looked her father in the eye. 'Daddy,' she said, 'I just can't do it.'

Sir Gerald was exasperated.

'Why not, you seemed keen enough on him before all this business.'

'I wasn't keen on him,' Frances said stubbornly. 'You were keen on him. Mummy was keen on him. I sort of got pushed into all this when I wasn't looking.'

Sir Gerald wiped his mouth with a clean linen napkin, then discarded it.

'You're being childish,' he said coldly. 'When young Brunsdon asked you to marry him, you were the one who said yes. From what I can gather from your sister, marriage wasn't the only thing you said yes to.'

Frances squared her shoulders. If her father wanted a showdown, it was fine with her.

'If you're talking about Archie and I going to bed,' she said thinly, 'then you're right. We did. But this is 1974, Daddy. Nowadays you don't have to get married if you do that.'

'Maybe you don't in your book, Frances. But where I come from it's different. Either you marry Archie or . . .'

Frances leaned forward on the table, 'Or what, Daddy?'

Sir Gerald called for the waitress to take the plates away. Then when the table was quite clear, he turned to his daughter.

'If you refuse to marry Archie,' he said, 'I'll cut off your allowance. Then how will you manage to pay the rent on that flat of yours?'

Frances smiled sweetly and got up to leave.

'I'll manage the way everyone else manages.' She stepped out of the booth they were sitting in and headed for the door.

'I'll go out and find myself a job.'

3

After a frustrating week of calling friends and visiting employment agencies Frances realised she was going to have difficulty paying the rent. Eating and clothing herself were expenses she didn't dare think about. She simply wasn't equipped to work. Her expensive private school had taught her how to sew and how to cook. She could hold her own at Ascot; she knew how to conduct herself in the presence of royalty; on the dance floor she had no equal. But she couldn't type, and it was this simple skill that stood between Frances and poverty. Secretarial work was the only work that paid. There were other jobs available. She could have worked in an art gallery or an antique shop. High-class stationers and trendy boutiques were full of girls like her, but there was no money in any of them. They were for amusement only, a way of passing the time in between parties and meeting Mr Right. If you wanted to pay the rent, you typed at sixty words a minute and took shorthand at one hundred and twenty.

After two weeks of wearing out her shoe leather, Frances lowered her sights. She started applying for waitress jobs. You got paid less than you would in an office, but you got paid. She drew a blank there as well – she had no experience, and restaurant owners seeing her expensive clothes, her well kept hair, her perfect make-up thought she was playing games.

It was only when one of them called her bluff that she finally got a break. She had gone to see Antonio who owned a trattoria off Oxford Street. It was a restaurant that owed much to the Sixties. White-lacquered shutters, tangled green plants, bright patterned tiles on the floor.

The kitchen where she saw the owner was a different story. Half of it was taken up by the ovens and cooking surfaces. Around her a dozen different sauces and stews perfumed and flavoured the air. It was the other half of the kitchen though, that held her attention. It contained the sink, and as she sat there, greasy pots, dirty dishes and a tangle of cutlery were dumped by a series of waiters who moved off as fast as they could.

Antonio, a small dark Italian, looked at them with distaste. Then he looked at Frances.

'So you want to become one of them,' he said. 'Why?'

'The money,' said Frances, who was beyond pretence. 'Why else?'

Antonio shrugged. 'It's none of my business, but you look as if you have enough money to me.'

This was the fourth restaurant Frances had seen that day. Her feet hurt and her earrings pinched. She was getting a headache.

'I ran out of money three weeks ago,' she said flatly. 'So if you've got a job I'll take it. And if you haven't I'll go and find someone who has.'

She got up to leave, but the Italian motioned her to sit down.

'How serious are you,' he said, 'about needing the money?'

She looked at him. 'Very serious. Why, have you got something?'

He nodded. 'But not anything you had in mind.'

She got up for the second time. 'I did say, I'd take any job that paid me.'

There was a silence. Then Antonio motioned over to the sink.

'I need someone to wash up,' he said. 'I pay £25 for a six-day week. If you want to work overtime, I'll give you another £1.50 an hour.'

Frances did a rapid calculation. £25 just covered her rent.

'How much overtime will you give me?' she asked.

The restaurateur looked surprised. 'As much as you can do. Why do you ask?'

'Because I need to eat,' she said.

Frances started work the following day. She arrived at Antonio's just before lunch and left sometime after midnight. For the first few days she didn't enjoy the work. Then she became organised. The main problems she encountered were the filth and the attitude of the waiters. They were in the habit of dumping the dirty dishes wherever there was a free surface.

And if there wasn't a free surface, they piled them on the floor. When Frances had cleared and cleaned the area thoroughly she found she had room for manoeuvre. The kitchens looked out onto a tiny paved courtyard, and if she threw open the connecting door there was an additional space where the dishes could be left.

At first the waiters were surly and refused to cooperate, so Frances took the dishes out herself. She didn't argue with them and she didn't sulk. She just got on with what she had to do, and in the end they all came round.

Within two months she was one of the boys, and within three Antonio gave her lunch and dinner when she came in every day. Her appearance began to change.

She started to leave off the heavy make-up that had always been her social armour. She braided her hair behind her back to keep it out of the steam. And she took to wearing jeans. She felt younger than she ever had before. She also felt more tired.

In the beginning she tried to keep up with her friends. On the one day she had off every week she crammed in all the parties and good times she had missed, until she started to feel out of place.

It was the women who set her apart. Before she earned her own living, she thought nothing of spending £500 on a new dress for Ascot. Now she didn't have £500 for a new dress, or anything else, and she had ceased to care about Ascot.

'What on earth is the point,' she said to Sophie, 'of standing around in a car park eating boiled salmon and talking about racing? I don't care about racing.'

Her flatmate gave her a warning glance. 'A lot of people feel that way,' she said, 'but it's better if you keep it to yourself. You don't want people to think there's something odd about you.'

But there was something odd about her. Frances began to have opinions. Not her father's views – that would have been expected, even acceptable. Frances's opinions came from her own head, and she talked about her job. People stopped asking her to parties. She wasn't amusing any more. Not to the bright young things who inhabited Knightsbridge and the shires. And she was looking so shabby these days. Not like the old Frances at all . . .

It didn't hurt as much as she expected. Somewhere along the way she had ceased to need approval. For now she knew her own worth. She could measure it in overtime. In cash.

And finally in promotion.

After six months of washing up, Frances was allowed to wait on tables. The other waiters took it in turns to show her the ropes and she learnt fast. After a few weeks in the restaurant, her tiredness started to recede and she earned more. Now she was taking home £50 a week, every week. Her old allowance had been £200 a week. She never compared her old life with her new one, though. She saw no point in making herself unhappy. Then one day Sophie, her flatmate, spotted an ad in the *Evening News*. 'Calling all beauties,' it said. '*The Macho Club promises to pay £250 a week to any girl who can* come up to its standards. *Only the fairest in the land need apply.*'

'It's some beauty contest,' Frances said when she saw it. 'I'm not interested in being looked over by a crowd of dirty old men.'

Sophie laughed. 'That's what you think. Haven't you heard of the Macho Club?'

Frances looked vague. 'I don't think so. No, hang on a minute. Isn't it something like the Playboy – only home grown.'

'Exactly,' said Sophie. 'It's run by a character called Richard Gregory. From what I hear he's a bit of a King's Road cowboy, but that shouldn't concern you. The point is, Macho isn't looking for beauty queens. It's looking for waitresses for the club. Obviously you've got to have a reasonable figure and you can't get away with looking like an old bat.' She grinned and gave Frances a quick once over. 'I'd say if you washed your hair and put on a bit of make-up, you might just be in with a chance.'

4

Richard Gregory sat up in bed and ran a hand through his thick tallow blond hair, then he checked whose face was on the pillow beside him. The check was almost a reflex action. A nervous tic. Richard could never be quite certain who he was going to find next to him in the morning.

Since his last regular girl went on her way, there had been a parade of consolation prizes: the girl who came to cut his hair; a horse-faced heiress who wanted to put money into his clubs; a sexy black rock singer. Not forgetting the Dollies from the Macho. In times of stress they could always be relied on to lend a shoulder and most of the other parts of their anatomy.

That morning when Richard looked to see who was sharing his space, he came up with no-one. Whoever had helped him rumple the bedclothes the night before had disappeared into thin air. Then he scented coffee on the air and fried bacon, and he knew where she'd got to.

'Make mine two eggs,' he shouted through the open door. 'I like them sunny-side up, and don't cloud the yolks.'

He racked his brains. Who did he know that cooked breakfast? The girls he took to bed weren't that industrious, or that domestic. His mind went over the previous evening. He had gone over to the club and had a drink. He always did that. Then he had gone to Abner Morris's party at the Penthouse Club.

He sighed at the eccentricity of his American partner.

Most guys who had a half interest in a club like the Macho would entertain on their own premises. But not Abner. He liked to keep an eye on the competition, so when he threw a party he called Bob Guccione or Victor Lownes and got them to organise it for him.

It had been a hell of a bash. Bob was out of town that night, but his staff more than compensated and between them they had managed to round up every available piece of talent in the country. There were country girls and city girls, girls from the jet set who were just visiting and girls from the suburbs who hadn't told their mothers where they were going. But wherever they came from, they had one thing in common. They had passed Abner's test. When he walked into the Penthouse that night, Richard knew he could expect to meet beauties who were looking for action. Abner's test was like the old-fashioned morals clause but in reverse. Any girl with pretensions to respectability was automatically disqualified.

When he walked into the dark cavernous club he went straight to the bar and ordered a whisky. He needed a drink to get his bearings and work out a plan. He was going to end up with someone in the room, that was for certain. But who? To his eye they all looked the same. Any man who looked at as many girls as Richard would always have that problem.

Richard Gregory had started life as a photographer in the Sixties. He had been good. The *National Geographic* had commissioned him, so had *Life* magazine, and even *Tatler* had hired him to cover society parties.

By the time he was twenty-six Richard had won two awards, and had his first exhibition at the Hamilton Gallery. He had only one problem: he was bored. Success had come too easily to him and now he needed a new challenge, something to put a bit of excitement in his life. Then the *Sun* hired him to photograph their new 'page three girl' and his whole life changed.

Her name was Suzy and she had the largest, whitest breasts he had ever set eyes on. For some reason they startled him. He had photographed nudes in his career,

31

but they were arty, tasteful nudes, seen through mist and draperies. The *Sun* didn't want any drapery to get in the way of Suzy. So he photographed her straight. When she came into his studio, Richard instructed Suzy to take her top off and stand against a white background. Then he ran off a couple of Polaroids to see what effect he was getting. When he saw them he was appalled. Suzy looked dead, though her breasts were in focus. Huge and tilted and bouncing all over the place. Suzy's face and Suzy's breasts were living separate lives. The *Sun* would never buy the pictures.

Richard decided to liven her up and sent Harry, his assistant, out to the off-licence to buy a bottle of wine. Then he set out the glasses and asked the girl to make herself at home.

Before he could stop her, the girl removed the rest of her clothes.

'What did you do that for?' he asked, surprised.

Suzy surveyed him out of shrewd blue eyes. 'To get in the mood for this session. You're not going to get anything interesting if I don't feel sexy. And I can't feel sexy in half my clothes.'

Richard took the point and opened the bottle his assistant brought back. After a few glasses of wine, all three of them started to feel happier.

'Do you feel like having another go at these pictures?' Richard asked his model.

She pouted. 'I'm not in the mood yet.' She put down her glass and thought for a moment. 'I'll tell you what. Why don't you put on some music and send out for another bottle. That should do the trick.'

Once more Harry went round to the off-licence, and Richard sorted out a tape of Frank Sinatra and put it on his cassette player. He also went and got himself a bottle of mineral water. If Suzy ever did get in the mood for this session, he wanted to be sober enough to take pictures.

Half way through the second bottle of Chianti, Suzy started to relax. She stopped sitting bolt upright on a chair with her legs crossed and went across to the leather sofa at the back of the studio.

Once there she settled into a semi-reclining position and Richard was reminded of the 'Venus de Milo'. She was a big girl. Soft and rounded and dimpled. Richard fought down the irresistible urge to fondle the great and bouncy breasts she was presenting to him.

'Suzy,' he said irritably. 'Sit up, will you? You're giving both of us ideas.'

The girl smiled and widened her eyes. 'If you're getting the ideas I think you are, then you'll have the pictures you want. Sex always puts me in the right mood.'

He was beside her before his assistant could put down his drink.

'Do you want me to send Harry out of the room?' he asked.

Again she smiled. 'Please yourself. Personally I always find the more the merrier.'

They took it in turns to make love to Suzy on the battered brown leather couch. Richard went first, burying himself in the mountains of her breasts, losing himself in flesh. Then Harry got to know her. Finally Richard called a halt.

'We're here for a picture session,' he said ruefully. 'Not an orgy.'

The orgy had the right effect. The pictures Richard took of Suzy caught her at her most joyous.

She looked like a girl who had just got out of bed and who couldn't wait to resume exactly where she left off.

When the shot appeared in the *Sun*, Richard was besieged by offers from the girlie magazines. They all wanted their models to look like Suzy. Richard gave up the *National Geographic* and *Life* instantly and started taking pictures of nudes.

*　　*　　*

It had to stop, of course. Richard couldn't go on working as Britain's top glamour photographer for ever. He was earning too much money and having too much fun. What he needed was something more permanent, more serious in his life.

After some thought, he decided to launch his own glamour magazine. A small merchant bank in the city lent him the money to do it and on the day it hit the stands, *Macho* was a sell-out. In its first six months the magazine overtook both *Playboy* and *Penthouse*, and that was just in England. A year later Richard found an American distributor. A year after that he found Abner Morris.

Abner's main business was tobacco. He presided over the giant conglomerate, American Tobacco, providing filter tips, cigars and pipe tobacco for most of the Western world. Running the company took up most of his time, but he had a weakness for women, so when he ran into Richard he saw a way of pandering to his needs.

Abner suggested they go into the nightclub business together. He would put up the money, if Richard would provide the girls, and when Abner told him how much money, Richard agreed fast. All that happened in 1972. Two or three years had passed since then and there were now Macho clubs in New York, Washington and London.

Like Playboy, the success of Macho was due almost entirely to the half-naked girls who served the drinks and waited on the tables. They were called Dollies, sometimes Dolly birds, and they were strictly off-limits to all the club members who leched after them.

For the men who employed them, it was a different story, which is how every young woman, everywhere he went, started to look the same to Richard Gregory.

Richard leaned against the bar of the Penthouse Club and finished his drink. Then he let his eyes roam around the beautiful women displaying themselves in the room.

I must be suffering from some sort of indigestion, he thought. There isn't one girl here tonight I want to take home with me.

A group of three girls, their arms linked around each other, joined him. They were high on something other than strong drink. They were laughing uncontrollably and nothing he could say would send them away. In the end Richard decided to go with the flow. If he was going to be taken over by three bimbos tonight, so be it. He ordered another double scotch and resigned himself to the inevitable.

The four of them got back to his apartment at around three in the morning. The girls were still high and Richard was floating on an ocean of booze and feeling no pain at all. When they all went to bed together he lost consciousness. They could have made love to him all night, they could have done it in unison. They could have set it to music and Richard wouldn't have known anything about it.

Damn, he thought, I had it made and I missed out. He threw back the coverlets, got out of bed, and made his way through to the kitchen. There was no way he was going to miss out a second time.

The moment he saw them, sitting round his kitchen table he knew he was not going to win. Last night he had been picked up by three ravers, but that was last night. This morning they had disintegrated into a coffee clutch.

Richard went over to the stove and helped himself to some coffee from the percolator. Then he cleared his throat. One of the girls turned round to see where the noise was coming from. Richard took a closer look at all of them and realised that any glamour they might have had in the Penthouse Club had disappeared with the first rays of dawn. They had all washed their faces, and two of them were wearing curlers. Even if they'd offered to abandon their breakfast and come back to bed, he doubted if he could whip up any enthusiasm.

The moment had gone, and with it, his faith in the female sex.

He looked at his watch. It was nearly half-past nine.

'It's been fun knowing you all,' he said, 'but the time has come for us to say farewell.'

The girls didn't seem to mind. They went on talking while they went from room to room gathering their things around them. When the last one had finally departed, Richard heaved a sigh of relief. Women, he thought. If I didn't make my living out of them, I'd take a vow of chastity.

5

The headquarters of the Macho organisation were sprawled along the edges of Knightsbridge. When Richard Gregory had founded the empire he had bought two run-down houses and renovated them. The result was a slick, black-fronted building that fronted one of the leafy squares opposite Hyde Park.

'Richard's taste in buildings is the same as his taste in photos. Stylish.'

This last bit of information was imparted to Frances and a group of five other girls by a bleached blonde in leather trousers and a tight black sweater. She had turned up at eleven in the morning expecting to be shown into a restaurant kitchen not unlike the one she worked in at Antonio's. Instead, a doorman had ushered her through into a club room that put her in mind of a grown-up Aladdin's cave. The ceiling was high and moulded in the manner of the Victorian houses in that part of Knightsbridge, but there the resemblance to any house she had seen came to an end. The whole of the huge room Frances was standing in was covered in a thick squashy carpet. What fascinated her about it was not its tobacco colour, or the depth of its pile, but the fact that it wasn't confined to the floor.

The soft pile extended up the walls like a giant furry animal giving the interior a womb-like appearance. The whole area was dominated by a long floodlit bar, all brass and studded brown leather. This was repeated on the arm chairs and squashy sofas grouped around tiny circular tables. The centre of the room was occupied by a dance floor.

At night with all the floodlights on Frances imagined

that the club could have looked exotic, even luxurious. Now, with the morning light showing up the cheapness of the brass fittings and the remains of last night's paper streamers still on the carpet, it looked seedy. The blonde didn't add any class to the scenario. She had seated herself at the bar, where she proceeded to chain smoke her way through a pack of cigarettes. Between puffs, she informed Frances and the others that if they were offered jobs, they would be known as 'Dolly Birds', Macho's official term for their waitresses. Each of them would be given a pet name, and they would have to wear a costume.

'Don't you mean a uniform,' said Frances.

'You can call it what you like,' said the girl. 'You're the one who has to look good in it.'

Five minutes later when she was struggling her way into her outfit, Frances realised what the blonde had meant. They had been shown through into a cramped changing-room where each of them had been given a low-cut body suit. With the body suit went a tiny mini skirt and a pair of high black plastic boots. The secret of the costume, though, lay in the corset that fitted inside the suit. It was boned from diaphragm to hip, pulling in the waist and jutting out the breasts.

Frances looked at herself in astonishment. She had never been particularly aware of her body before. She knew she was slim and developed enough to wear a bra, but the woman who confronted her in the full-length mirror had voluptuous curves and a deep cleavage. Her eyes travelled down her length and she saw there was something about the cut of the skimpy costume that made her legs look longer. Almost indecently so.

Embarrassed, she grabbed the tiny skirt and fastened it round her waist, but it swung open all the way down one side and only made her look more undressed. In desperation Frances climbed into the boots. They had spiky heels and came up to the middle of her thighs.

Christ, she thought, I look like the original dirty post-card.

All the other girls were ready now and together the six of them trooped back into the club. The blonde told them to line up on the dance floor, and Frances noticed that somebody had turned on the spotlights. She had visions of a band starting up and all of them high-kicking their way through a dance routine. She smothered a giggle. After this build-up, she thought, whatever happens next had better be good.

What happened next was Richard Gregory. Macho's owner, Frances observed, was a tall tow-headed man in tight jeans and a battered leather jacket. He was very pale, even under the artificial light, and he wore the look of a man surprised by nothing. Frances put him at around thirty-five.

Thirty-five going on nineteen. She was intrigued.

Then as she regarded this man, her fascination went sour, for Richard was inspecting the line-up like an Arab potentate, on the look-out for new members to add to his harem. He lifted chins, peered down cleavages, measured waists and patted buttocks. When he came to Frances, she backed away.

'Sorry,' she said, 'but you can count me out of your plans.'

For the first time that morning Richard looked interested.

'Why?' he asked her.

'Because I don't like being pawed,' she told him. 'Not even for £250 a week.'

The remark stopped him dead in his tracks. He was used to girls deferring to him. If he wanted to run his hands over the merchandise, he did because it was his right. Clearly this new girl didn't think so.

He smiled and started to walk round her, inspecting her from every angle. He realised that when he started to look at her, she wasn't like any of the others at all. For a start she wasn't wearing much make-up, and her hair hung straight and freshly washed around her shoulders. I bet it's her natural colour, he thought. It's not bright enough to be a bleach job.

She had a good figure too. The boobs weren't enormous, but they weren't small either, and with that tiny waist she didn't need to carry any more on top.

'Have I seen you somewhere before?' he asked her.

'I don't think so,' Frances said, shaking her head. 'Unless we ran into each other at Ascot or a charity dance.'

The voice told him all he wanted to know about her. Even if she hadn't said she was on the deb circuit, he would have known just by listening to her. Her vowels gave her away. He screwed his face up. What was a classy production like her doing in the Macho Club? He looked her over again and he knew he had met her before. He was convinced of it. Nobody could forget a face like that. Suddenly he had it. He'd seen this girl in the *Sun*. Not on page three, but blasted right across the front page. He started to laugh.

'You're naughty Frances!' he exclaimed. 'The bird who left some poor bastard standing at the altar.'

He looked at her with a certain admiration. 'Why the hell did you do it?'

He had caught her off-balance. Frances had put the debacle of her wedding day firmly out of her mind. None of her friends had dared raise the subject, and nobody had recognised her. Until today.

Now the whole thing came flooding back. And with it the terror and the fury she had felt on that day at St Paul's.

'I did it,' she said, 'because I didn't want to marry the stuffed shirt who was waiting at the altar.'

Richard Gregory grinned, and Frances noticed the washed-out green of his eyes.

'He might have been a stuffed shirt,' he said, 'but he looked as though he had a bob or two. I would have thought a girl like you was interested in the kind of life he could have given you.'

Frances drew herself up to her full height and for a moment she forgot the skimpy, revealing costume she was wearing.

'Then you got me wrong, didn't you?' she said snappily. 'I'm not for sale – either to a husband who wants to take me for granted, or to an employer who wants to take advantage of me.'

She turned on her heel and started to make for the changing-room.

It was at that moment Richard Gregory made up his mind. I'm going to have her, he thought, but it's not going to be for a night, or even a couple of weeks, she's too good for that. Too classy, too different from the others. This girl I'm going to take my time with, and when she's finally mine, I doubt if I'll even look at anybody else for at least a year.

He surveyed Frances's back view disappearing into the changing-rooms. Then he called out her name.

'Naughty Frances,' he shouted. 'Come back here this minute. I haven't finished with you yet.'

Frances wasn't used to people speaking to her like that. It was vulgar. Unspeakably common. Every ounce of her reason told her to ignore this man. Only her instincts worked against her. Without fully understanding what she was doing, Frances turned round and came back to the tiny dance floor.

'What do you want from me?' she asked.

Richard stood stock still for several minutes considering. Then he started to appraise her.

With the others he had used his hands. With Frances he used his eyes. He started with her breasts, blatantly stripping away the revealing costume, and as he did so,

Frances felt her nipples harden. Stop it, she said to herself. Can't you see what he's doing. The man's a libertine. A dirty lecher. He eats women like me for breakfast. Yet despite herself she went on standing where she was, unable to move.

Then slowly, agonisingly slowly, Richard Gregory's gaze travelled downwards. His eyes caressed her waist and in her mind Frances felt the tiny skirt falling away. Then his eyes stopped their journey and came to rest at a point exactly between her legs. Frances started to feel aroused, and she beat back the feeling – without success. It was Richard who finally broke the silence.

'Little girl,' he said. 'Never ask me a question like that again.'

The next day a crate of champagne arrived at Frances's flat in the Fulham Road. When she opened it, she found it was vintage Bollinger. She also found a note. It was from Richard Gregory.

> *Beautiful naughty Frances,* he wrote, *if I promise not to take advantage of you, will you come and be one of my Dolly Birds? Do say yes,*
> *Richard.*

Frances was both furious and flattered at the same time. Furious because he hadn't bothered to explain himself or apologise for the way he behaved. Flattered because no-one had ever sent her vintage Bollinger before.

Against her better judgement Frances rang the tired blonde she had met at the Macho Club. Her name was Doris and when she got put through Frances informed her she would like to join the payroll.

'So Richard got in touch,' Doris said flatly.

'Yes, he sent me a crate of champagne, actually.'

There was a silence.

'Was it vintage Bollinger?' Doris enquired.

Frances was surprised. 'How did you know?'

There was laughter on the other end of the line.

'I've been working here for five years now. After that long you get to know a man's habits.'

Frances started at the club the following week. In her first month she saw Richard Gregory just twice. The first time he was having lunch in the club with Michael Caine and a small white-haired man she thought might be his agent.

The next time she saw him he was drinking highballs at the bar in the early hours of the morning. He was accompanied by a wafer-thin brunette in a gold lamé dress. Her hair hung like an expensive silk curtain half-way down her back and Frances noticed she was wearing real diamonds.

'Who's the girl with Richard?' she asked one of the other waitresses when she came back to the kitchen.

Dolly Barbara gave her a knowing look from under fake black lashes.

'You mean Amber,' she said, 'the latest conquest. She's a fashion model from New York. A big star we're told. Not that that's going to do her any good. I reckon she'll be on the way out in a couple of months.'

Frances was intrigued.

'You're taking a cynical view aren't you? She's absolutely lovely. Why won't she last?'

Barbara smiled and started piling bowls of chilli onto her tray.

'I'm not saying she won't last,' she said. 'Some of Richard's girls manage to stay around for a full year. But I wouldn't put money on this one. She looks like she might not do as she's told.'

'Is that important?'

'With Richard I'd say so. He takes his pleasure very seriously.'

She lifted up the heavy tray and pointed herself in the direction of the restaurant. Frances stopped her.

'How do you know all this?'

The girl giggled. And Frances noticed her teeth were covered in tiny nicotine stains.

'How does any of us know?' she replied. 'I've been to bed with him of course.'

Over the next few months Frances discovered that one or two of the Dollies were regular bedmates of Richard's. In a way it was as if these girls inhabited a different world to her own. She would come to work on time, change into her uncomfortable costume, and allow herself to be leered at by the salesmen and executives who used the club. Her day usually lasted from seven in the evening till well past midnight when she staggered home exhausted.

Richard's girls didn't live like her at all. They seemed to start work whenever they chose to, and they always arrived from a long lunch at some impossibly glamorous place like the Clermont or Scotts. Sometimes Frances would overhear whispered conversations about a party Richard had organised in Paris or New York. She realised that the Macho Club wasn't one club at all, but two. There was a nightclub that she worked in that looked wicked but was as ordinary and workmanlike as any West End restaurant. Then there was this other club, a secret élite that consisted of Richard Gregory and his friends, and one or two of the Dollies.

When Frances discovered the existence of this other club, she discovered something else as well. Every single girl who worked in the Macho wanted to be chosen by Richard.

When he came into the club they followed him around like puppies: running to get his drinks, hanging on his every word with vast adoring eyes. And because they behaved like pets, he treated them that way.

When Frances first saw Richard tweaking and patting the Dollies, she had been furious with him. Now she was furious with them as well.

'How can you let him behave like that?' she demanded.

But they just looked at her as if she was mad, and in the end she dropped it. If the other waitresses wanted to be used by Richard and his friends, it was their lookout. As far as she was concerned, she was earning £250 a week for being a waitress. It was fifty per cent more than she could make anywhere else. And all she had to do for the money was put on a pair of fishnet tights and totter around in kinky boots all night.

She couldn't exactly tell her old friends what she was doing. But until her family decided to forgive her, it was as good a way as any of making ends meet.

6

Louise Tragos stood stock still on the sidewalk and hefted the heavy folio from one arm to the other. She had carried the large oblong leather-covered holdall half way across New York City. It had been up and down elevators, across the subway and in and out of most of the top ad agencies in Manhattan.

Inside it was her life's work. Or to be precise the first three years of her working life. There were trade ads for foot powder, and a mentholated cigarette brand, a couple of regional magazine covers and finished artwork for a new dogfood label that never got past test market. It wasn't a glittering start to a career, but the Maria Goldblatt Design Consultancy wasn't a very high-profile outfit.

None of this bothered Louise. Sure, she was in a hurry to get to the top. Wasn't everybody? But she had to be able to walk before she could run and Maria Goldblatt was as good a place as any to learn. At any rate, that's what Louise had been told by her tutor at Art College.

'Every art director on Madison Avenue started out in a small design shop,' she had said. 'Ron Travisano did it, George Lois did it and look where they got. No, Louise, you do your apprenticeship for three or four years, then the big agencies will open their doors to you.'

The heavy weight of the leather folio was threatening to pull her arm out of its socket, and if Louise had had the strength to shake her fist at her old teacher, she would have done. For none of the twenty agencies she had seen so far had shown any sign of opening their doors. They had picked over her trade ads and shaken their heads when they saw her magazine covers.

'It shows promise,' was the highest praise she got. But Louise couldn't live on promises. She had to eat. Her first smell of a job had come that morning from Judy Wald, the top Madison Avenue headhunter. She had left her name on the books without really expecting to hear from them. Then out of the blue she got a call at the office. 'Benton and Bowles are looking for someone to do mechanicals,' one of Judy's girls told her. 'I know it's not what you're looking for, but it's a start. And B & B are a top agency.'

They fixed an interview for her after work and Louise took the afternoon off to review the contents of her wardrobe. She was still living with her parents in the Kingsbridge section of the Bronx. As she sat in the room she shared with her sister she tried to figure out how she should present herself to Benton and Bowles. Then she made a promise to herself. The minute I start to earn a decent salary, she vowed, I'm going to get out of here.

Both her parents were Greek, immigrants from Athens thirty years ago. Their real name was Tragosas. The first thing Louise had done when she started work was to shorten her surname to Tragos. She wasn't ashamed of her roots or her family. Quite the reverse. However, she was ambitious, and she knew the first rule for success in New York was to fit in. Tragos was a name you could pronounce. A name that didn't impose itself on you. It sounded foreign, sure, but it sounded like it had been around for a few years in New York. Louise didn't want anyone to think she'd just come off the boat.

Now standing on the sidewalk, she was certain she could have fooled anyone. The suit she had put on for her interview was grey flannel with a tiny white chalk stripe in it. It was straight and severe and hid her long, sexy legs. The coat that went with it had a tiny Peter Pan collar and a row of buttons that did right up to the neck. It had cost Louise two weeks' salary in the Bloomingdales' sale but she didn't begrudge the expense, for in this finery she didn't look Greek any more. She might have black hair and brown eyes, her face might have come straight off an Etruscan vase, but looking at her nobody could tell she lived in Kingsbridge. She could have been a bank teller from Gramercy Park, or a wages clerk from Massepequa.

It was this image of clean-living America that Louise carried with her to the interview at Benton and Bowles. It lost her the job.

Michael Peters, the head of Benton and Bowles art department, was looking forward to meeting Louise. Junior art directors who could cut out type and paste it into just the right position on the page were in short supply. Most of the good people preferred to work in television, but this agency still produced print ads and made a lot of money from them. He sat behind his desk and prayed Louise had the right experience.

Louise was beyond prayers. The moment she walked into the imposing marble lobby with its bank of elevators and liveried porters she knew this was where she wanted to work.

It wasn't any chintzy little shop living on two-bit clients. In here they handled tobacco accounts and detergents. Millions of dollars were spent every week placing full colour ads in *Time* and *Cosmopolitan*. Most of their commercials ran on network television – prime time.

With something approaching awe Louise made her way through the pastel-carpeted reception area and announced her name to the girl on duty. This was up-town with a vengeance. Louise was glad she looked the part.

She started to have doubts about herself after five minutes. As she sat waiting for Michael Peters to call her in, her eyes roamed around Benton and Bowles reception, and what she saw was a group of creative guys – art directors and copywriters – on their way out for a drink. None of them was wearing grey flannel. In fact none of them was even wearing a suit. With a sinking heart, she realised that every one of them looked like they belonged in Kingsbridge. They were wearing faded Levis cut tight across the crotch, T-shirts with this month's slogan across the front, leather jackets, and their hair was wild and freaky.

The temptation came over Louise to turn tail and run. Then the receptionist beckoned her through, and it was too late. When she walked into Michael Peters' office, her face was roughly the same colour as her suit.

The office didn't do anything to make her feel part of things. Everywhere she looked she saw chaos. There were papers piled high, on the desk, on the table by the window. Even on the chairs and the floor. All over the walls Peters had pinned ads roughly torn out from magazines. Half-finished lay-outs.

I should have come in my working clothes, she thought bitterly. This man might just have mistaken me for an art director.

The interview proceeded slowly. Peters asked Louise about her background – her years in art school, the accounts she had worked on at the design consultancy.

She answered every question as fully as she could, but her heart wasn't in it. Louise hated herself for the blunder she had made, and because she hated herself, the resentment spilled over to the man who was interviewing her. She frowned and scowled, contorting her dark heavy features into a mask of unfriendliness. As she described the work she had done she took hold of a tendril of her black curly hair and twisted it around her finger. She communicated nervousness, hostility, incompetence. Michael Peters didn't even ask her to take her work out of her leather briefcase. Instead he told her he would be in touch and showed her the door.

She went straight home and took off the grey flannel suit. Then she hung it up ... on her sister's side of the wardrobe. She would never put it on her back again.

She had just blown the best chance she had of getting into Madison Avenue. All because she was ashamed of the way she looked. She wondered if she would ever get herself right.

In Kingsbridge, where she grew up, everybody on the block was Irish. Her friends in school had pale fine complexions and eyes the colour of mist. From the word go Louise looked different. She was darker and heavier than the other girls, and it didn't help that her mother made her wear traditional clothes. Long skirts, thick stockings, shawls with fringes. Yet Louise carried her head high – until the day someone called her 'greaseball'.

In that moment all the fine traditions of her ancestry counted for nothing. The icons, the burning incense that hung in the corridors of their apartment, the Greek Orthodox Church of St Spyridon where she took communion, her reverence for every male member of her family were suddenly out-moded and foreign. The taunt didn't drive her towards the Irish community. They were a minority, like her. Micks instead of greaseballs. Louise had her sights on better things. She was going to be an American.

The first thing Louise did was to dress like an American. Out went the shawls with fringes to be replaced with tight jeans that showed her legs and her waist, and T-shirts that showed not only her breasts, but her nipples as well. Her father had a fit. She would go to the devil, he said. No nice Greek boy would ever marry her now. That suited Louise down to the ground. She had no intention of raising a brood of Evzones in the slums; that was for her sisters to do. Louise had her sights firmly set on Manhattan.

Her passport out of the Bronx was a college education.

At school Louise had always been fascinated by graphic images. She could pick up a piece of chalk and doodle a picture of any one of her classmates on the blackboard, and she would get a likeness. It became a party trick, a way of grabbing attention. Louise's thumbnail sketches of a family friend, someone's pet parrot or the school bully earned her instant popularity.

One of her teachers took her aside.

'You have a talent, Louise,' she said. 'Did you ever think of doing anything with it?'

Then the teacher told her about the Pratt Institute in Brooklyn. If Louise worked, really worked, she might just pass the entrance exams, and if she was lucky she could win a scholarship.

'How could I use a career in art?' Louise asked. 'I don't want to be a full-time painter.'

'You could go into advertising,' her teacher replied. Louise didn't need to hear any more. Advertising conjured up images of penthouses in skyscraper buildings. Fast cars and expense accounts. The Manhattan skyline.

She grinned at her teacher. 'Point me at it,' she said.

The talent Louise showed got her to the Pratt Institute, and her drive got her out of it. In the middle of her second year she was offered a job at the Goldblatt Consultancy, and she grabbed it. She was twenty years old. By Greek standards an old woman. It was time to get out and make something of herself, so she learned how to make coffee at the Goldblatt shop. Then, after six months they taught her how to use paste and a scalpel.

Within the year Louise was cutting out type and placing it on the page with the precision of an expert. She learned about typography and print orders, and when she had mastered the technical side of the job, she started to have ideas. She had always communicated visually, in images: the smile on an old man's face; a hungry child; a sunlit breakfast table. They told her more about the world in which she lived than words ever did. Bit by bit Louise learned how to make these images work for her.

She discovered that if she presented things right, she could make people want them. She could persuade people to buy an ordinary dress by putting it on a beautiful girl.

A cut-price dog food looked covetable in a crystal bowl; if she placed a pedigree pooch next to the bowl, she could make the dog food sell right off the page.

Other people's products were easy to move, because she knew exactly who it was she wanted to buy them. Her own product, Louise Tragos, was a more difficult proposition. She knew she wanted to look beautiful, elegant, desirable. But who for? The only buyers in her sights had been the boys in her neighbourhood and they had liked her, of that there had been no doubt. The problem was would the high-flyers in Manhattan feel the same way?

Every night when Louise went home she examined her reflection in the mirror. She saw a tall girl with a full bosom and long straight legs. Of her face, she had no opinion. It was her grandmother's face and her mother's. They all had black eyes shaped like almonds, high cheekbones, wide mobile mouths. Louise sighed. There was nothing she could do to change her face. There was no cosmetic made that would make the slightest impression on it.

Not even a new hairstyle made her look any different, and after trying half a dozen different styles, she finally let it do what it wanted. The morning she had gone to see Benton and Bowles, it had curled and snaked over her shoulders.

She smiled. At least I looked like an art director from the neck up, she thought. Maybe next time, I'll bring the rest of me into line. The disastrous interview had taught her one thing at least: how to present herself for a job on Madison Avenue. If I ever get another chance, Louise vowed, I'll let it all hang out.

Six weeks later Judy Wald called again. Acker and Stein had a vacancy for a junior art director. Not a paste-up artist or someone to do mechanicals. The agency wanted an art director to work on campaigns. This time Louise Tragos was ready for them.

7

Acker and Stein on the eightieth floor of the Seagrams Building had been in business for over thirty years. It showed in its style – affluent, fat cat and dull. The agency owed its fortunes to a Minnesota soap powder manufacturer and a brand of mentholated cigarettes. For each client it produced the sort of safe advertising that hadn't changed its character in a dozen or more years.

Acker and Stein got away with it because the products were both leaders in their fields. When Louise turned up for her interview she knew all this, but she didn't kick against it. As far as she was concerned, she needed a job in Madison Avenue. If Acker and Stein had one on offer, she wasn't going to turn it down.

The agency was exactly the way she had pictured it. Acres of grey carpet punctuated by smoked glass partitions. The creative department consisted of a long thin corridor, off which there were small cubicles. In each worked a copywriter/art director team who dreamed up the ads. At the top of the corridor was an office that could have doubled as a boardroom. The furniture was Thirties' style and fashioned in walnut. One wall was covered entirely by a glass-fronted bookcase. There was a long table where meetings were held, and at the end of the room was a large imposing desk where the creative director sat.

Louise thought he didn't look very creative. He was a small bearded man of around fifty, in a well-tailored city suit. For a moment she regretted the way she had dressed for the meeting. But only for a moment.

Benton and Bowles was a fat cat agency, she reminded

herself – and look at the way their art directors got themselves up!

Louise was wearing a short tight skirt in black leather. With it she had teamed a loose satin shirt and all the silver necklaces she possessed. She knew she jangled when she walked, and she didn't care. It was a look that was in vogue that season. Art directors, trendy art directors in big agencies, were meant to be in vogue, she reasoned.

With as much confidence as she could muster, Louise produced her leather-covered folio.

'I brought along some samples of my work,' she announced to the man sitting in front of her.

He smiled and nodded. 'Show me,' he said.

Louise took the pages out of their binding and started to lay them along his desk. She started with the magazine covers, then the trade ads. Finally she produced the dog food label.

With each sample of her work, she explained what she had done and why she had done it. With a certain surprise, she found she was embroidering her experiences. She invented bigger problems than had existed at the time, and the solutions she came up with sounded earth shattering – as if she had invented the wheel, rather than pinched a second-hand idea.

Suddenly Louise understood that she was presenting her work this way because she despised the agency, but she couldn't stop herself. Christ, she thought, as she wound up her presentation. I've really blown it this time.

The creative director looked at her out of small glittering eyes.

'Tell me your name again?' he asked.

Louise cleared her throat.

'Tragos. Louise Tragos.'

In the close carpeted office the name sounded even more foreign than it was. I should have changed it, Louise thought, panic rising. I should have called myself Peters or Green.

She looked across at the grey-bearded man and saw he was still nodding and smiling.

'How much did you say you wanted?' he said.

Louise swallowed. Hard. This was the one question she wasn't prepared for. If he had asked her what grades she got at Pratt, or how she felt about the new Schlitz campaign, she could have told him in detail. But a salary – that hadn't even crossed her mind.

The creative director stopped smiling.

'You do expect to get paid for the job, don't you?' he said curiously.

Louise did a rapid calculation. At the consultancy she was paid fifteen thousand dollars a year, enough to eat and pay her fares. If she was to rent her own flat in the city she would need much more. She took a gamble.

'I'd be prepared to come to Acker and Stein for thirty thousand,' she said.

The man didn't change his expression.

'Then you have a job with us,' he said calmly. 'I'll arrange for you to see your group head. He'll fill you in with all the details.'

Louise couldn't believe it.

She'd been turned down all over town. Now in an agency she didn't like, at an interview she thought she'd blown, she'd hit the jackpot.

She scrambled to her feet and shook the creative director's hand. Then she gathered up her work, slipped it back into the folio and headed for the door. As she reached it, the man called out her name. She stopped walking, worried that for some reason he had changed his mind.

'About your salary,' he said. 'Normally we pay our juniors a minimum of forty thousand a year. I'm delighted you're so modest in your requirements.'

8

The creative department was located on the fourteenth floor at the back of the building. Traditional advertising agencies with blue-chip clients liked to hide the people who actually made the ads. They knew they had to house the group of eccentrics who dreamed up the slogans, drew the pictures, but they didn't want to pass the time of day with them, and they certainly didn't want to show them to the client.

Acker and Stein followed this ruling to the letter. When Joe Rivers, the man who had hired Louise, showed her to her room, she felt she was entering a segregated zone. Where the rest of the agency was lushly carpeted, the creative department had wooden floors. The expensive abstract pictures were replaced by posters and roughed up ads. Even the secretaries were somehow less polished, less put together than the girls she had seen sitting in the lobby.

Joe told Louise she would be sharing her room with Mike Calder, her writer and opposite number, and when she got there she found him waiting for her. He was a tiny man dressed in flared trousers and a rollneck sweater. He reminded Louise of an exotic garden gnome.

However, it was the room itself that drew her attention. Either Mike or the previous art director had painted the walls a violent shade of purple. The floorboards were polished to a glaze, and in the centre of the tiny cubicle was a white fluffy flokati rug.

'How do you like it?' Mike asked when Joe finally took his leave of them.

Louise suppressed a smile.

'It's — very homes and gardens,' she said, cautiously, 'though you might do something about the walls.'

The tiny man lit a cigarillo.

'Be my guest,' he said. 'This room is your home too now. Your working home, at least. We should both feel good about it.' He looked at her enquiringly. 'Did you ever work with a writer before?'

Louise shook her head.

'Then you're going to love it. If you get an idea, even half an idea, I take it away, toss it around and hand it back to you with a little bit added on. Then you work at it some more and hand it back to me. When we're doing an ad we live in each other's heads. Or we should do.'

'You make it sound a bit like an arranged marriage,' Louise said.

Mike puffed on the thin black cigar.

'It is a bit. Only we get off on ideas, rather than sex.'

Louise looked up at the cork board running along one of the walls. On it were pinned posters and press ads torn out from newspapers and magazines.

'You're talking about this kind of thing.'

Mike looked at her and pursed his lips. He walked over to the cork wall and jabbed his cigar at one of the ads.

It was a full page picture of a little black boy. He must have been about four or five and he was very cute with a big 'piccaninny' smile. Underneath the slogan read: You don't have to be Jewish to love Levy's ryebread.

Mike looked at her, the scowl still on his face.

'You like this?' he asked.

Louise wondered if it was a rhetorical question. 'Of course I like it. Who wouldn't? It's absolutely brilliant.'

Mike walked over to the window and stared out over Manhattan. Finally he sighed and turned round to face her.

'I didn't write it,' he said. 'A girl at another agency created that little award winner.'

Mike gestured to the rest of the work pinned along the wall.

There was a Volkswagen masquerading as a Beetle, a group of aeroplanes painted in surrealistic colours, a gorilla operating an office copier.

'I didn't write any of this,' he said bitterly. 'I couldn't have done. Not in this agency.'

Louise looked at her new partner with something approaching scorn.

'Now I suppose you're going to tell me you're a frustrated genius, and Acker and Stein is strangling your talent. Well if we're going to work together, you can do me a big favour and stop whining. I don't need you to tell me this place is dull. I knew that from the moment I signed on for my salary. That doesn't mean to say you have to give up and stop trying, does it?

'Listen, Mike, where I come from people earn their living on the subways and sweeping the streets. Nobody ever comes uptown. Certainly nobody I ever knew set foot in a ritzy office like this one. So if I can come this far in five short years, don't tell me you can't create a great campaign and get this agency to run it. Because you can.'

Mike stubbed out his cigarillo.

'Are you asking me,' he queried, 'or are you telling me?'

Louise stared at him.

'I'm telling you,' she said.

Then she reached up to the cork board and started taking down all the brightly coloured award winners. When she had finished what she was doing she crumpled them all into a heap and stuffed them into the wastepaper basket.

'The next things to go up there,' she said with an edge to her voice, 'will be our work. And it had better be good.'

Louise didn't try to change the world. Not overnight. For she knew their big spending clients – soap powder manufacturers, the pet food kings – would never change direction, unless they were in trouble. Instead she directed her efforts at little concerns. A series of ads for garden furniture in trade magazines, a face cream testing out in Idaho. This kind of business was handled at a low level by junior executives.

When the firm tried to resist her selling ideas, Louise used her charm. When that failed, she used her brain. On one occasion she lost her temper. But only once.

She was beginning to acquire a reputation around the agency for making things work. The schemes she dreamed up and Mike put into words were starting to move the merchandise: the small garden furniture company sold the whole of its line in one season; the face cream did business in Idaho and started looking further afield.

After six months, the cork board in Louise's office started to look crammed. More importantly, it started to look exciting. It was at that point that Joe Rivers called her into his office.

His furniture looked as pompous as ever and as phoney, but Joe looked as if he was trying to move with the times. He was wearing a suit made out of blue denim.

'To what do I owe the pleasure?' she asked Joe once he was seated behind the mahogany desk.

Rivers smiled.

'United Foods,' he said shortly. 'The company is launching a new spaghetti and I'm thinking of putting you to work on it.'

Louise looked confused.

'I don't get it,' she said. 'United Foods has got its own writer. What do they want with me getting in on the act?'

Joe Rivers started to feel uncomfortable. Why does this woman always have to ask questions, he thought. Most of the other writers would give their eye teeth for an assignment like this. This kid starts out looking for snags.

Aloud he said: 'Why don't you let me worry about the United Foods writers. The way I see it, a new brand needs an exciting new idea. You seem to have cornered the market in ideas.'

'Yes,' Louise said, still worried. 'But United Foods is a great big stodgy piece of business. Senior honchos work on it. Very WASP, very East Coast honchos. They're not going to want me, some crazy from the Bronx, telling them how to think. They'll veto everything I put up. It'll be a complete waste of time.'

Joe Rivers contemplated his fingernails. He needed this woman. He needed her brains, her inventiveness, but how to motivate her? He thought back on what Mike Calder had told him about his first meeting with her. 'She doesn't like to lose,' the copywriter had said. 'One day she'll hurt herself on that ambition of hers.' Joe decided to put it to the test.

He leaned forward across the desk and started to shake his head.

'It's very sad,' he said. 'It's the worst shame I've ever seen.'

Louise sat up in her chair.

'What on earth are you talking about?'

The creative chief looked mournful.

'You,' he said. 'You're not even twenty-four yet and already the business is getting to you. What happened in the last six months to frighten you? When I hired you, you were ready to take on all comers.'

Louise stiffened, and when she spoke next, her voice was dangerously low.

'Nothing happened, and I'm not frightened. I just don't want to waste my time, that's all.'

She'd taken the bait.

'I decided to put you into this situation,' Joe Rivers said, 'because I happen to believe you can out-think every writer who has ever worked on United Foods. I also believe you can get the executives on your side if you put your mind to it. It's up to you — if you think it's going to be a waste of time, then it probably will be. I don't want you on the project if you're not up to it.'

There was a silence while Louise considered. Logic told her she was being set up. No-one in their right mind took on United Foods, not single handed. On the other hand, what if she got away with it? What if she came up with something so clever, so original that they had to buy it? The idea was irresistible and she threw caution to the winds.

'I'm up to your spaghetti project,' she said sharply. 'Give me the brief before I change my mind.'

Louise met with the account group the following day. They were as bad as she feared: grey suited, tanned from boating in the Hamptons. She hated them all on sight. The man she reserved all her aggression for, though, was the leader of the pack, Brian Elder. If the others looked as if they came from the East Coast, he looked as if he owned it.

Everything about him, the handsome upper crust face, the thick blond hair that curled around his collar, the Cary Grant accent, told Louise that this man came from old money.

The meeting was held in Elder's office. The moment Louise walked through the door she felt vulnerable. Joe Rivers's headquarters she could cope with. The room she was standing in was a different story. All the furniture was antique, from the Sheraton table to the French Empire desk next to it. Someone who knew what they were doing had arranged this room; someone who knew more than she did.

Elder had sat her down in a wing-backed leather chair right next to him. From where she was sitting Louise could smell his lemon-scented aftershave. It frightened her and turned her on all at the same time.

For nearly an hour she sat and listened to the account

director tell the meeting about spaghetti. Finally he got down to the brand itself.

'It's an up-market pasta,' he said, 'selling at a premium price. We have to find a way of persuading the housewife that our spaghetti is worth more than everyone else's. Otherwise why would she be paying more for it?'

Louise looked down at the tips of her pointed Italian boots.

'You've got a good point there,' she murmured half to herself.

Elder stopped what he was saying and inclined his expensive blond head in her direction.

'Did you say something?' he enquired.

Louise felt ridiculous, like a naughty girl at the back of the classroom. Her cheeks started to redden.

'I was just thinking to myself,' she mumbled.

Elder raised an eyebrow. 'Well can it. I've got precious little time as it is, without having to stop for inter-ruptions.'

He meant it. In the middle of his summing up, his tall, impossibly beautiful secretary put her head round the door.

'Your car is outside, Mr Elder,' she whispered.

The account supremo looked at his watch and cursed under his breath. Then he walked into the adjoining office and came back in a camel coloured overcoat. There was something soft and expensive about the stuff it was made of and Louise guessed it had probably set him back over a thousand dollars.

She felt unaccountably depressed. She and Brian Elder might work in the same office, but they could have come from different planets. How could a man like him even begin to understand why a housewife went out and bought a pack of spaghetti? The Brian Elders of this life didn't eat spaghetti when they went home at night, and if they did she bet their wives didn't cook it for them. Some fancy cook would prepare it as part of an Italian gourmet feast, or he might indulge in it after a heavy game of squash at the country club. She sighed. The next couple of months were going to be tougher than she had anticipated.

Because of agency policy, Louise and Mike weren't the only creative team on the project. A United Foods writer, Bill Peck, had also been put to work on the business. He was the least of their problems since he was a company hack. If he had any talent at all, it was the talent to ingratiate himself. His work was solid and dull and based on research and the food manufacturer loved it because it was safe. If Bill was selling a cake or a line of hamburgers, he wouldn't try to excite your taste buds, or even make you laugh. He would tell you the product was good value, and if there wasn't a price benefit, he would dig up a tried and tested campaign and justify running it again.

Even in an agency as old fashioned as Acker and Stein, Bill was something of a joke. Louise took pity on him. On their second meeting when they were due to show rough ideas to the account team, Louise let Bill take precedence over her.

He didn't do too badly. Brian Elder liked two of his ideas and suggested the best one be developed and taken through to a finished campaign. Louise suppressed a smile. Bill's slogan for the spaghetti was 'A taste of Italy'. She had seen it used two years ago by a rival agency for a tomato sauce. Then she shrugged. Maybe the account supremo knew Peck was a no-hoper and was just being kind. She shuffled through the roughs on her drawing-board and prepared to present her work.

Elder shot down every single one of her ideas. Some of them he wouldn't even discuss.

He just shook his head and put his thumbs down. Louise wondered if he was doing it on purpose. She knew she wasn't showing him her best work; that would come as they worked together, but she also knew that she had made a respectable start. There was a glimmer there, a spark here. If she and Mike had time to work them up, or even discuss them, they could have been onto something good. Instead they were killed. Vetoed. Destroyed. Elder was going out of his way to be as difficult as he could.

That night Louise went home and cooked herself a pot of spaghetti. When everything else failed, Louise always went back to the goods she was trying to sell. All the time she was working on her campaign for face cream, she had rubbed it into her skin every night, and in some strange way it gave her a greater sense of it. The cream ceased to be a product on a shelf. It was something she used, something that lived on her dressing table. She felt real emotions about it. In effect she became the consumer as well as the salesman.

Now, as she took her basket of shopping up the five floors to her tiny apartment, she searched her mind for some new approach to the pasta problem.

Louise had moved into the two-room walk-up in Gramercy Park just eight weeks previously. She had been saving up for the down-payment on cheap rental ever since she started work at the agency and seven days after she had it she found the apartment in Gramercy Park. It wasn't anything to boast about. The tiny sitting-room had a kitchenette at one end of it, and the bedroom was just big enough to sleep in and hang her clothes. If she was honest with herself she had just as much room and considerably more comfort in her parents' house, but that was in the Bronx, and she was on her way out of there.

Louise was not ashamed of being Greek or of coming from immigrant stock. She was what she was. Nevertheless, she wanted better for herself than the life her parents had had. She continued to dream of wearing designer clothes, of eating in fine restaurants. The walk-up in Gramercy Park was her first step towards those ambitions. To her it was the longest step she would take in her entire life for she knew she wasn't just moving a few blocks closer to work. She was moving out of one world and into another.

Louise spent all evening preparing the spaghetti. She made it with meat sauce, with tomato sauce. She threw clams into it, she even tried it with plain butter and lemon juice.

When she finally got into bed she felt weary, slightly sick, and the whole apartment smelled of garlic. She had a hundred thoughts about the pasta but not one good idea. Yet in the morning, when she woke up, the slogan was on her lips.

Rossi Pasta . . . Spaghetti like Mama used to make.

I must have dreamed it, Louise marvelled as she stood under the shower. Maybe when I get into the office, it won't sound so good.

But when she repeated it to Mike, he thought it had magic, and when she'd sketched half-a-dozen different lay-outs, they were both convinced they had something that worked. Every Italian mama she had ever dreamed of smiled out from her sketch pad: they were cooking spaghetti over steaming stoves, hanging it out to dry in the Mediterranean sunshine, serving it to fat bambinos.

A week later Louise marched into Elder's office convinced she had a proposition. He had assembled all his executives for the presentation of her work. When Louise went into her pitch, she spoke with the confidence of her three years in the agency business. At the end of it, Brian Elder came round to where she was standing and looked over her shoulder at the lay-outs. There was a faint smile on his face and he looked genuinely interested.

'I'd like to know how you came to this line, "Like Mama used to make",' he asked her. He wasn't really asking Louise at all, he was addressing the meeting.

What the hell is he up to? Louise wondered. Then she pulled herself together – she had nothing to lose. So she told Brian about her cookery session in Gramercy Park. He listened attentively, the tiny smile lifting the corners of his mouth. Then he told her what he thought of her campaign.

At first Louise wasn't quite sure of what he was saying since he used so many figures and statistics that the words had little meaning to her. Then he finally came to the point.

'I've heard cornier lines,' he said, 'but not much cornier. It's the kind of work I would expect from a trainee at art college. But I forgot, you've only just come out of college, haven't you?'

He picked up the lay-out nearest to him. It showed a fat Italian mama leaning over a pot of spaghetti.

The account supremo held it up, so the entire meeting could see what he had in his hands. Then slowly, deliberately he tore the rough ad in two halves, letting them flutter to the ground. Then he turned on his heel and walked out of the meeting.

Mike was on his feet and helping Louise stack the lay-outs as soon as Elder was out of the room.

'Don't cry,' he muttered to her, 'not in front of this group. Don't give them the satisfaction.'

Then he addressed the meeting. 'The show's over for today,' he said. 'You can all go back to your offices.' He turned and put his arm round Louise.

'Come on,' he whispered. 'Let's get out of here.'

Louise walked down the carpeted corridor in a kind of daze. So this was it. The end of her career in advertising. The original water colours in their gilt frames seemed to mock her from the walls. They belonged to an expensive, exclusive world. A world where she didn't belong. Brian Elder's world.

Even back at her office she didn't feel safe.

She knew she wouldn't be staying there for too much longer. The man who had just destroyed her work would see to that.

Louise was filled with dread. She had been on Madison Avenue for just seven months, she had had her own apartment for two. Now it was all coming to an end. Before she knew it she'd be back in the Bronx. She wondered what kind of work she'd find there. The family will be pleased, she thought bitterly. Mama always said I'd come to no good in the city. So deep was her despair that the phone on her desk had been ringing for a full sixty seconds before she heard it. Abstractedly Louise picked it up. Brian Elder was on the line.

'I think you and I should talk,' he said curtly.

Louise remembered the patronising way he had listened to her when she tried to explain her ads and the way her mind worked.

'What's the point?' she asked dully. 'We never seem to get anywhere.'

Elder chuckled. 'Maybe we pick the wrong place to discuss things. I know my office can sometimes be intimidating. What if I bought you a drink somewhere instead?'

Now Louise was totally thrown. One moment Elder was trying to fire her, the next he was suggesting they have a drink. She suspected he was trying to trick her.

'Where were you thinking of taking me for a drink?' she asked.

Elder suggested they meet at a French restaurant nearby. Louise occasionally went there for lunch – it was pricey but it was fun, and much in favour with the arty crowd. She accepted the invitation – what did she have to lose?

When she got to the restaurant she saw that the advertising supremo had arrived before her. He had commandeered a table outside and was working his way through a pitcher of martini. He smiled when he saw Louise coming towards him, then he stood up while she settled herself into one of the wicker chairs.

Although she never normally touched martini, Louise took the glass that he proffered. It might make me brave, she thought. She took a sip and winced as the liquor burned the back of her throat.

'What's the reason for all this?' she asked him. 'You must have better ways of spending an evening.'

Elder smiled and stretched his long, expensively suited legs out in front of him.

'I thought it was time we got to know each other,' he told her. 'Before we actually came to blows.'

So he wasn't going to fire her. He couldn't be, otherwise why would he want to know her better? Though she felt relief, Louise was still unconvinced. The man hated her work, that she knew. She glanced at the Ivy League suit, the four hundred dollar shoes, the million dollar suntan. They weren't exactly social equals either. So why did he want to know her?

She let him talk about the agency, nodding and smiling at the company jokes while she got his measure. She learned that Elder lived in Westchester and was a member of the local golf club. He had a wife and two sons who were being expensively educated in Switzerland.

'What made you choose this place to buy me a drink?' Louise asked curiously.

Elder smiled and signalled the waiter for another round of martinis.

'It's a couple of blocks away from my apartment. I thought we could have supper there later if you weren't doing anything.'

'I'd like that,' Louise said. 'I'm looking forward to meeting your wife.'

A veil came over his light blue eyes, like a pond freezing over.

'Veronica isn't in town,' he said abruptly. 'There will just be the two of us.'

Louise leaned back in the wide wicker chair. So that was what it was all about. Sex with the office help. A perk of the job.

'Is it just supper you had in mind, or was it something else?'

Elder looked her over, not like a would-be lover, or even an employee. He priced her like a piece of merchandise and Louise was aware that her clothes were strictly working-girl.

'What I had in mind,' he said slowly, 'was for you to stay the night. Does that bother you?'

He said it coldly, without emotion. Instead of feeling indignant or outraged, Louise felt something quite different – she felt frightened. Suddenly she wanted to put as much distance between herself and this tough man as she possibly could. Excuses flooded into her mind: her mother expected her home, she had arranged to meet a girlfriend. None of them was in the least convincing. In the end she said,

'I have to be somewhere else later on.'

Elder didn't change his expression.

'Then you have a choice,' he told her. 'You can come back with me and protect your future, or you can keep your date with whoever it is and take your chances. I know which one I'd choose.'

Louise's instinct was to grab her bag and make a run for it, but something stopped her. Another terror rose inside her, a terror far worse than her fear of Brian Elder. She recognised it, welcomed it like an old friend. For it was her fear of going back to the Bronx. In her mind's eye she could see the drab streets with their smell of poverty, endlessly grey, endlessly cold.

She closed her eyes, and when she opened them, she saw Brian Elder sitting in front of her. Waiting. She took a deep breath.

'I've decided to choose the future,' she said. 'Whatever it brings.'

9

Brian Elder lived in one of the blocks overlooking the Park. One of the blocks with a striped canopy coming down over the pavement. The lobby, Louise noticed, had dark red carpets, and a doorman. Unless you actually lived there, you couldn't walk into the elevator unattended. Louise looked at Brian Elder with his burnished blond hair and his handmade shoes. How well you insulate yourself, she thought bitterly. How well your money protects you from the world.

The elevator deposited them on the fifteenth floor, and as they walked towards Elder's apartment, Louise made a silent promise to herself.

One day I will live like you, she vowed. One day I will have more money and more power than you ever dreamed of. And when that day comes I will make you pay for everything you do to me tonight.

The main sitting-room had a view of the trees and the sky through a huge picture window at one end of it. Framed by velvet curtains it was not unlike the French impressionist paintings that decorated the walls. The only other place Louise had seen pictures like that was in the Metropolitan Museum of Art and she knew she was meant to feel out of her depth. Why else would he have brought her into this showpiece with the pricey antiques and Persian carpets if he didn't intend to overawe her? Why not take her straight into the bedroom? That's what she was there for. But Brian Elder liked to savour his pleasures, to take them at his leisure. He poured himself a drink and left the bar at her disposal. Then he picked up the phone and ordered a take-away for two: salt beef, bagels, herrings in sour cream.

When he put down the receiver, he looked pleased with himself.

'No-one can call me a bad host,' he said proudly. 'I know just the sort of thing you people like to eat.'

We're all the same to him, Louise thought. Jews, Greeks, Poles. We're immigrants. Foreigners. Lesser mortals. The knowledge instead of enraging her, hardly touched her. Just as the grand drawing-room failed to impress. It was as if her anger had somehow separated her from this situation. Taking away all emotion and all feeling.

Louise noticed she hadn't got herself a drink and realised she no longer needed one. Somewhere inside her, she had found a reserve of strength she never knew existed, and as she waited for the food to arrive, she felt calm. Almost relaxed.

As they had done earlier on, they talked about the office and Louise discovered that the chairman of United Foods was an old friend of Brian Elder's family. So that's where his power lies she thought. That's why he sits on the board of Acker and Stein. The guy owns a hundred million dollars' worth of business. She filed the fact away in her memory. One day she would use it against him.

The takeaway arrived and Louise found to her surprise she was hungry. She glanced at her watch. It was nine o'clock.

She figured he would make his move over the coffee. She wasn't wrong. Sometime after ten, Brian got out of his chair and yawned. Then he tipped the contents of his brandy balloon down his throat and looked at Louise expectantly.

'Time for bed,' he said.

Louise got up and smoothed her skirt over her hips. It was a calculated gesture, designed to arouse. She had made her mind up that tonight would be no rape scene. If she played the bruised innocent she knew she would lose, and losing was something she refused to contemplate.

She had worked out that the bedroom was somewhere down the hall. With the poise of an actress, she walked ahead of him leading the way. Instinct told her to behave as if she'd seen it all before, lived it all before.

When they got to the room where he slept, she closed the door behind them and turned to him.

'What do you want me to do?' she asked.

Elder looked at her and she was reminded of a furtive little boy.

'Take your clothes off,' he said. He pointed to a chair by the side of the bed. 'You can leave them over there.'

Louise did as he told her, unbuttoning her blouse, loosening her jeans, peeling off her tights. Finally she stood in her bra and bikini pants.

'Would you like to do the rest?' she asked.

Brian Elder was still dressed in his shirt and pants. The top button of his collar was undone and he had loosened his tie. Otherwise he was immaculate, unruffled.

'It's not time for me to touch you yet,' he said. 'You don't look right.'

She was baffled.

'How do you want me to look?'

He walked over to the closet and took out a hanger. On it was an outfit for a maid in a French farce. It was made of black silky material with a boned top and a tiny short skirt. Attached to it was a white pinafore.

Brian handed it to her.

'Take off the rest of what you're wearing and put this on.'

Louise suppressed her astonishment. The grand drawing-room she was prepared for. Even the Jewish takeaway she understood. But dressing-up games were beyond her experience.

As she put the costume on, she dredged her memory for any clue to this eccentricity.

She glanced at the man watching her and there was

something about the look on his face that she had seen once before. He had looked exactly like this when he had torn up her precious ad. The one she had presented to a room of executives. He had wanted to humiliate her then and he had succeeded. In a fraction of a second, she realised what the whole thing was about.

She spun around on bare feet, lowering her eyes.

'Do you have anything else for me to put on,' she paused, 'Sir . . .'

He reached back into the wardrobe and came back with a pair of high, shiny shoes, a garter belt and black, sheer stockings. Wordlessly she took the items from him and put them on. Then she stood by the bed and waited. He walked over to the bed and turned her round so that her back was to him. Then before she knew what was happening he had bent her over the edge of the bed. With one hand he pushed her skirt up around her waist, then he started to slap her bare backside.

At first his touch was light, almost delicate. Then the blows came faster, and harder until the pain was almost too much to bear. He turned Louise over on her back and as he did so, she saw his flies were undone.

For an instant the insanity of the scenario hit Louise. She was spreadeagled across a stranger's bed with her skirt rucked up and only a garter belt to cover her nakedness.

Automatically she struggled to get up but Elder pushed her back, parting her legs, feeling for the opening between them.

'You're a dirty little slut,' he said almost conversationally. 'And I'm going to give you what you deserve.'

He rammed his cock into her, pushing it up as far as it would go. Despite herself, Louise cried out in pain and surprise. He withdrew and thrust into her harder, and harder still. And then the strangest thing happened. She began to feel excited. Sprawled beneath Brian Elder, Louise recognised herself for what she was. A Greek girl from the Bronx. A nothing, a nobody being pleasured by her master.

Now her loins felt a new urgency, and as the orgasm began to build inside her, she felt another sensation. Elder's hand was stroking her buttocks, caressing the welts and the bruises. Then his fingers moved to the entrance at the back of her. Exploring then jabbing. All at once pain and pleasure joined together in one giant rollercoaster. From somewhere far away Louise heard herself screaming into the darkness.

'Hurt me Brian,' she begged, 'hurt me! Oh please hurt me . . .'

A week later Joe Rivers called Louise into his office.

'Congratulations,' he said. 'I handed you a tough assignment, and you came through for me.'

Louise looked at him as if he were crazy.

'I don't know what you're talking about.'

Rivers sighed and pulled out a crumpled pack of cigarettes. He took his time selecting one, tapping down the tobacco.

'I don't understand you, Louise,' he said. 'You get the biggest breakthrough of your career and you behave as if nothing has happened.'

Louise started to become annoyed.

'If I had a breakthrough, nobody told me about it. Would you mind explaining to me what this is all about?'

'Rossi Pasta is what it's about.' He looked at Louise, 'Didn't Brian tell you?'

Louise was shaken momentarily.

She hadn't heard a word from Brian Elder since the night at his apartment. She put it down to experience. The guy obviously wanted to get his rocks off while his wife was out of town, and she suspected she was one of many girls he liked playing games with. Louise didn't like herself for going along with Elder, but when she came in the next

74

morning and found she still had a job, she breathed a sigh of relief and tried to forget about it.

Rossi Pasta was one of her failures. A job consigned to the wastepaper basket. So what was Joe doing talking about a breakthrough?

'Are you sure you've got the right person?' she asked. 'Bill Peck was working on Rossi Pasta as well. I've got a feeling he's the one who had the breakthrough.'

The creative chief shook his head. 'I don't think so,' he said, 'unless it was Peck who came up with "Spaghetti like Mama used to make".'

Louise did a double take. That was the line Brian dismissed as corny, the product of a college kid.

'From what I recall,' she ventured, 'Brian wasn't all that enamoured with that approach. Something must have happened to change his mind.'

As soon as the words were out of her mouth, she regretted them. She knew damn well what had happened, all she hoped was nobody else did. Nervously she looked at Joe. Any time now, she thought, he's going to call me a whore, a calculating strumpet. He did nothing of the kind. Instead he sat down at his desk, stubbed out his cigarette and picked up a letter sitting in front of him. Even upside-down Louise could see the United Foods logo on top of the page.

'This is from Rossi's marketing director,' said Joe shortly. 'He says he likes the "Mama used to make" slogan so much, he's thinking of backing it with a thirty-second TV commercial.'

He looked at her appraisingly.

'It seems to me,' he said, 'that Brian Elder was having you on. If he hated the advertising so much, he wouldn't have shown it to United Foods, much less sold it to them.

'Relax, kid. Take a couple of days off. You've done a terrific job on United Foods – a better job than you know.'

The Rossi Pasta campaign broke on network television

at the beginning of the New Year. It took off from the word go.

It wasn't one of the great advertising ideas, but the cornball approach worked with American housewives, and the less time they had to spend in the kitchen, the more Rossi spaghetti they bought. They all imagined that some cute old lady in Italy had given it her blessing, some magic ingredient that made it taste as if they had spent hours over a hot stove.

In two months, the sales virtually doubled, and the factory in New Jersey went on overtime to keep up with production. United Foods had had an overwhelming success with a new product and Brian Elder was rewarded with an increased advertising budget and a major brand of tomato sauce. He started spending more time with Louise. The kid had an uncanny talent for getting inside the mind of the consumer. She knew what they wanted out there on the street and she knew how to motivate them to spend money. He gave her a lead on a dying brand of diet biscuit. She mounted a slick television campaign and put it back on its feet in six months. He put her to work on a canned soup in test market. It went national within the year.

Yet Elder was sparing in his praise of Louise Tragos. Their relationship had been carefully established right from the start.

He was the master. The dominant force. Louise was his handmaiden, there to dance to his bidding, to kiss his feet, to submit to his punishment.

Louise acted her part to the letter. She knew Elder was using her and claiming credit for her success. She also knew that without him there would be no success.

Once or twice a week, Louise went up to Elder's apartment overlooking the Park and played his sex games. Sometimes he liked to lock her in a dark cupboard and leave her there while he went out to dinner. Occasionally he beat her with a cane. Whatever the pain, whatever the humiliation, Louise suffered it without complaint. She was Greek, and the Greeks were used to being conquered. The Turks had done it twice. The Albanians once, pillaging and plundering as they went. In the end her countrymen had risen up against their oppressors and driven them out for ever. The same fate awaited Brian Elder. But when Louise cast him out, it wouldn't just be from her bed. It would be from Acker and Stein itself. Louise's intention was to deprive Brian Elder of his livelihood.

10

At the end of summer, Frances received an invitation from Richard Gregory. Would she be free to spend a weekend at his castle in Scotland?

Frances had known about the castle, of course. The chosen Macho girls went up there regularly and returned with movie stars and businessmen who would take them to gambling clubs and expensive restaurants. Now it was her turn, and she wondered how on earth she had been chosen.

Ever since that one moment when he had mentally stripped off her clothes at the Macho Club audition, Frances had had little to do with Richard. He was attractive, she admitted that to herself, but he was dangerous too and she had no intention of joining a harem. Only now there seemed little alternative. As soon as she could, she tried to get out of it. She went and had a word with Doris, the bleached blonde she had first met when she joined the organisation. The Playboy Clubs, on which Macho was modelled, had bunny mothers to run their show. The Macho had Doris, who doubled as Richard's secretary.

When she heard that Frances wasn't interested in Richard's invitation, she was horrified.

'But all the other Dollies would give their arms to go to the castle,' she told Frances.

Frances was unimpressed.

'Fine,' she said. 'Why don't you ask one of them instead?'

Doris was worried. Normally Richard left it to her to decide which of the girls was going to spend the weekend in Scotland. This time he had specifically asked for Frances, which is why she had been sent a formal invitation. Doris wondered what had got into the girl.

'You're not unhappy with the job, are you?' she asked. 'I mean, Richard or one of the others hasn't done anything to upset you?'

Frances smiled. 'No,' she said. 'It's nothing like that. I just don't want to go to see Richard in Scotland, that's all.' She paused, worried she might have sounded rude. 'I mean,' she said weakly, 'I do have other things to do.'

Doris lit a cigarette and searched her memory for what she knew of this difficult Dolly. Then understanding began to dawn.

'Weren't you a deb or something?' she asked. Then she started to laugh. 'Of course, I remember reading about you. Naughty Frances.'

Frances began to feel uncomfortable.

'I don't see what that's got to do with my not going to Scotland.'

The blonde gave her an old-fashioned look.

'I do,' she said. 'You probably think you're too good to spend time with someone like Richard.'

It was true, of course, and both the women knew it, but it put Frances on the spot. If she agreed with Doris, then the knowledge that she thought she was superior to the man who employed her would go right back to him.

The consequences didn't bear thinking about, so she bent over backwards to deny it, and found herself being talked into going to Scotland.

As she heard herself agreeing, Frances studied the tired blonde. Was it relief she saw in her eyes? Or was it a glimmer of victory? Then she thought, the hell with it. She'd met richer men than Richard Gregory – and better looking ones. She was more than a match for him.

On the plane up to Glasgow, Frances recognised the New York model she had seen with Richard in the Macho Club.

79

She was dressed in a dark mink coat over pale blonde cashmere. Sitting beside her was another familiar face. Dolly Barbara. She looked cleaner than she did in the club, less dishevelled. Frances peered closely as the tiny blonde laughed at something her companion had said. Then she leaned back in her seat, satisfied. Barbara had been to the dentist and had the nicotine stains removed from her teeth. This weekend clearly meant something special to her.

Frances wondered who else would be there. Doris had already told her that a couple of important American businessmen had been invited. 'They like to stay in Scotland, because of the golf,' Richard's secretary had informed her. Frances smiled inwardly. They like to stay in Scotland because of the likes of Dolly Barbara, she thought.

Well I just hope one of them hasn't got any plans for me, because he'll be disappointed.

Two long black limousines were waiting for the women at the airport. Frances spotted the Americans immediately. They both had paunches from too many expense account martinis. Although they were well into middle age, there was a boyishness about them. An eager-beaver look that advertised their openness to fun and games. What really distinguished them as Americans, though, was their clothing. They wore loud tartan trousers that could have only been bought in New York, and one of them was wearing a deerstalker. The American's idea of British country wear. Frances suppressed a giggle, and introduced herself. The older of the two Americans looked surprised.

'I wasn't told about any Frances Buckingham,' he said. 'My list said Dolly Barbara, Dolly Frances and Lila, the model.'

Realisation dawned on his face. 'Hey, you wouldn't be Dolly Frances, would you?'

Frances was spared any reply by the approach of the other girls. They were accompanied by a tall, elegant, greying man who she immediately recognised as Paul

Mason, a television actor. They all piled into the limousines, ready for the two-hour journey to the castle.

Frances found she was travelling with Paul Mason and Lila, who sat in the front seat. For some unknown reason she formed an instant dislike for the girl. There was something languid about her manner that she found patronising. It was as if Lila was telling everyone: I'm beautiful, rich men seek my company and this weekend, I'm the queen of the castle. Within the space of half an hour, Lila had managed to let drop that she had signed a million-dollar contract with a cosmetic company and was to be on the cover of September's *Vogue*.

Frances concentrated her attention on the television star who was sitting with her on the back seat. She was glad she made the effort for despite his matinée idol looks, Mason was a surprisingly modest man. His face had hardly been off the small screen that summer, yet he seemed pathetically grateful that he was working at all. Frances felt that the girl in the front seat could do with a bit of his humility. Her opinion was reinforced as they swung into the castle drive.

'I hope Richard has sent his butler to meet us,' Lila drawled. 'I've brought three big suitcases with me, and I can't be expected to carry them all in myself.'

Frances's irritation disappeared as she saw the castle rear up in front of her. It was the sort of edifice she had read about in fairy tales – tall turrets and silver stone disappearing into the mist that surrounded it. Because the castle had no drawbridge, Frances imagined it had been built in the time of Queen Victoria, probably by a rich merchant who wanted something a bit grander than a manor house.

She leaned forward in her seat as they came up alongside it and she saw that it had been built in Victorian gothic style, with slits for windows in the upper towers. Frances longed to go inside. She knew that nightclub money could afford to buy a fantasy castle, but did Richard Gregory have the taste or the style to make it look right? Or had he hired some ghastly interior decorator to fill it full of reproduction junk?

Five minutes later she discovered the Macho boss had both taste and style. As the butler led them through a vast central hall Frances saw a couple of old masters she remembered hanging in Agnew's, Persian rugs and the kind of dark-stained glossy wood furniture that could only be the real thing. As she climbed the staircase to the gallery that ran all the way round the hall, Frances sensed the ghosts of unseen ancestors. Then she pulled herself together. The only ancestors Richard Gregory had were still haunting the Mile End Road. Further proof that the castle was bought with new money came when she reached her bedroom. The whole room was taken up with a modern four poster. It was draped on all sides with a kind of filmy fabric, and it had a little ceiling, draped like an Arabian tent.

Frances smiled. I bet the bathroom's a revelation, she thought, starting towards it. The whole room was tiled in turquoise and gold mosaic. There were two washbasins that reminded her of the bathrooms of grand hotels, and the bath was shaped like a pink conch shell. She was debating whether or not to try it, when the phone rang in the bedroom.

When she picked it up, she found Richard Gregory on the other end.

'So you finally got here,' he said. 'How was the journey?'

'Fine,' Frances said, keeping her voice in neutral.

Richard Gregory didn't waste any more time on politeness. 'In that case,' he said, 'you'll be more than ready for a drink. We're all meeting in the Jacuzzi at six. That gives us time to have a glass of champagne and get changed afterwards for dinner.'

Frances searched wildly for an excuse not to go – any excuse.

'I haven't got a swimming costume,' she said feebly.

'No problem. You'll find one in your wardrobe.'

There was a silence. Then she said, 'Actually I'm feeling a bit tired. Would you mind if I had a rest and caught up with you later?'

She could almost hear the smile in his voice.

'What's the matter, are you frightened I'll jump on you?'

'No, of course I'm not,' Frances said crossly.

'Then stop behaving like a teenage virgin and come down here at once. There's a lift to the basement, you can't miss it.'

He replaced the receiver before she could say anything else.

Defeated, Frances walked over to the wardrobe where she found a skimpy bikini and a one-piece. She put on the one-piece and looked at herself in the bathroom mirror. She could have been wearing her costume at the Macho Club. Since the whole thing seemed designed to accentuate her sexuality. The legs were cut almost up to her waist, and the top half pushed her bosom forward into an indecent cleavage.

Irritated she took it off. I'll go for the bikini, she decided. I may show a bit too much flesh, but at least it will be my flesh on display.

When she reached the Jacuzzi some moments later, she was glad she'd worn her towelling bathrobe, for the whole place looked like an elaborate setting for an orgy. The room must have run the length of the castle, and Frances judged that originally it must have been a wine cellar. There was a dampness about the overheated air, clamminess that put her in mind of a tropical storm.

Richard had kept the lights down here to a minimum and Frances was just able to make out the three interlocking pools of the Jacuzzi. Each one of them was the size of a small swimming bath, full of bubbling, steaming water. There was one main bath, with two smaller pools on either side, and Richard had set up a bar on an island in the centre of the big bath. As Frances drew up she saw the other Dollies and the American guests on one side of the Jacuzzi, while Richard and Paul Mason were in a huddle on the other.

Richard waved to her. 'Come on in,' he said, 'the water's lovely.'

Frances raised her eyes to the glass he was holding out and as she did, she saw the mural. It wasn't quite pornography, but it was a near thing. Naked girls with impossibly large breasts sprinted around the walls, hotly pursued by leering, lustful satyrs. Frances stood stock still, taking in the scene. Christ, she thought, what have I got myself into?

From the moment Richard Gregory saw Frances standing on the edge of the pool he wondered what she had on under the towelling robe. Was it the sexy one-piece or the skimpy bikini? He had arranged for both of them to be waiting for her when she arrived. Whichever she chose he was sure to get a better look at her.

Richard had taken his time going after the new girl. More time than he thought he would, because of Lila. She was a diversion, of course. Nothing more. Now he was getting bored with the New York model girl and as he did, Frances came back to the top of his list.

He glanced up from his conversation expecting to see her stripped for action and coming for the drink he had offered, but she wasn't. She was still standing huddled in her dressing-gown looking nervous. If she had been any other girl, he would have been annoyed, but there was something vulnerable about Frances that made him feel protective.

Poor kid, he thought. She must be petrified. He decided to rescue her. Grabbing a bottle of Bollinger and two glasses he made his way out of the pool.

When Frances saw him coming towards her she backed away. He's going to make a grab at me, she panicked, I know his type. But Richard Gregory climbed up the marble steps and splashed over to where she was standing.

'Come and sit down,' he said, indicating a wooden bench. 'You look as if you need to get used to all this.'

She smiled weakly. 'I don't think I ever will,' she said.

Undressed, Richard had a better body than Frances had imagined. His shoulders were broad, like the shoulders of a boxer and when he moved he rippled. He works out, she thought, and as she noticed, she approved. She saw he was smiling.

'What's so funny?' she asked.

'You are,' he said. 'You're the first bird ever to come down here and keep her bathrobe on. You must be sweltering in that.'

She grinned and slipped it off her shoulders.

'Sorry,' she said. 'I felt a bit shy.'

He handed her a glass of champagne.

'I like that,' he told her, 'though you've nothing to be shy about.'

Her body was better than he had dreamed. The Macho costume with its bones and clever seaming hid a multitude of sins, but this girl had nothing to hide, her flesh had a kind of sheen to it. She was terribly white, almost translucent, so that he was aware of her bones and her fragile construction. She's like a lovely piece of porcelain, he thought, and he fought down the urge to touch her.

Careful Richard, he said to himself. You don't want to frighten her off, not when you've got this far. With an effort he looked away from her. Then he made his face neutral and his voice stern.

'You know your problem,' he said. 'You're still half living in that upper-class little world of yours. I've watched you working in the club. You're polite to the customers and you just tolerate the other girls, but your heart isn't in it.'

Frances felt angry. 'You didn't drag me all the way up to Scotland just to tell me that did you?'

Richard leaned back and took a sip of his wine.

'No I didn't,' he said.

'Then why the hell am I here?'

He looked at her properly now, appraisingly – the way he had viewed her at that first audition.

'You interest me,' Richard said finally. 'I wanted to know what makes a girl like you – a girl with everything – turn her back on the high life and come and work in a tacky joint like the Macho.'

Frances sat up straight.

'I didn't know you thought the Macho was tacky.'

'Well it's not the Ritz is it, or the Royal Enclosure?'

Richard started to laugh. 'You don't think I have any illusions about the kind of operation I run, do you? I'm not pretending to offer a fancy lifestyle. I run a nightclub that charges twice as much as any other because it has pretty half-naked girls walking around in it. Every time I sell a bottle of Beaujolais or a well-done steak, I sell the promise of a good time in bed.'

'So that's why you make us wear those vulgar costumes,' Frances said.

Richard nodded. 'And that's why you earn twice as much in the Macho as you could anywhere else. But you still haven't answered my question. If your family's got so much money and class, why did you come and work with us?'

Frances shrugged. 'It was a question of having to. You know I left my fiancé standing at the church, and my family wasn't all that understanding about it. They wanted me to toe the line and go through with the wedding. I had other ideas, so they cut off my allowance.'

'You still could have found something better than the Macho,' Richard insisted.

'No, I couldn't,' Frances replied frankly.

Then she leaned over and helped herself to another

glass of champagne, and as she did she felt herself start to relax. Richard Gregory wasn't as bad as she'd feared. He had an honesty she hadn't expected and something in her responded to that. She found herself telling him about her attempts to survive without her family. Sitting here with this man she didn't feel ashamed of it anymore.

'It took me a long time before I even got to be a waitress,' Frances confessed.

Richard laughed and looked at her with admiration.

'You're a tough little thing, aren't you,' he said. 'Tougher than you look. But you're still rather prim. I'll have to see what I can do about that.'

11

For Frances, dinner in the country always conformed to a certain style dictated by the surroundings. If the day had been spent hunting in one of the horsey counties – Leicestershire or Cheshire – you usually dressed up. If you were simply hacking in Somerset, you wore jeans. Tennis weekends called for cotton dresses, shooting parties demanded dinner jackets.

Now as Frances rummaged through the contents of her suitcase she was totally confused. She had just spent the best part of the afternoon in a Jacuzzi. What you wore after that kind of sporting event was not chronicled in the books on etiquette.

In the end she settled for suede trousers and a loose silk shirt. When she let her hair down it came nearly to her waist and she decided to leave it that way. She felt it fitted in with the mood of the party.

As soon as she walked into the dining-room, she realised she'd got it wrong. The men were all in dinner jackets. Her eyes took in the dinner table adorned with old crystal, monogrammed silver and lilies out of season. Then she looked at the other girls. Dolly Barbara was all tricked out in gold lamé and paste costume jewellery. But there was nothing of the high street about Lila. Her simple white silk jersey gown looked as if it had walked out of the Milan collections. What held Frances's eye though, was that Lila wore the dress straight. There was no jewellery – fake or otherwise – to confuse its lines. There was no underwear either.

To give the model girl her due, the dress was so sheer and so clinging that even a bra strap would have shown through, but Frances didn't feel like making excuses for Lila.

She was about to turn tail and change when a tall, spare, greying man came striding into the room. Frances had no idea who he was, but everyone else clearly did, for all conversation in the room stopped. The men stood up a little straighter, and the women started to preen.

Frances held out her hand.

'We haven't met,' she said boldly. 'I'm Frances Buckingham.'

The man was obviously not used to women coming forward by themselves. He halted in his tracks and looked her up and down. For an uncomfortable moment Frances was reminded of certain breeders she had seen at bloodstock sales. At last he took her hand and instead of shaking it, he kissed it.

'The name's Abner Morris,' he said softly. 'I own this joint.'

The voice was cultivated, East Coast American and there was a confidence about it that told her he had a great deal of money. Her mind raced back over what she knew about the Macho organisation. Hadn't one of the girls said something about an American backer?

Richard came towards them.

'Abner,' he said, 'I wasn't expecting you. What time did you get in?'

The American grinned. It was a sensual smile that spoke of indolence and good times.

'About an hour ago,' he explained. 'I heard you were all in the Jacuzzi but I settled for a nap instead. I'm here for the next couple of days so I guess I'll find my way down there eventually.'

He turned to Frances, 'You're new around here, aren't you?'

It was a statement rather than a question and Frances stiffened.

'Is that important?' she asked.

Again the lazy, sensual smile crossed his face.

'It's not important if you don't intend to come again, but if you do, you'd better get to know the rules.'

He took her arm and led her to the table.

'The first rule is I get to sit beside the prettiest girl at dinner.'

Abner Morris was surprisingly easy to talk to. Frances was used to small talk at dinner parties and her private school had taught her to embroider the trivial, but what Abner Morris wanted to talk about was himself and for the next two and a half hours he did just that.

Despite herself, Frances was fascinated. She hadn't met many Americans and she certainly hadn't met one like Abner.

The son of an East Coast banker, he grew up with all the privileges money could buy. He played polo, he went to Harvard and he married the daughter of one of the bank's chief stockholders. After that he kicked over the traces. Abner's life changed on a plane journey from New York to San Francisco, and the reason it changed was the stewardess on the flight.

She was blonde, she was pert and she was a long-standing member of the 'mile high' club. Abner discovered this midway across the Rockies. After that there was no going back. When the plane arrived in San Francisco, the stewardess checked into Abner's hotel. Three weeks after that, Abner left his wife and his young family.

At the age of twenty-six he had found sex and from that moment on it was to be the force that governed his entire life. His father threw him out, of course, and not just for business reasons. As far as he was concerned, his son had broken all the rules a gentleman lived by. Until he mended his ways and went crawling back to his wife, he wanted nothing more to do with him. Abner never saw his father again.

Instead he went to work for a going-nowhere tobacco company in St Louis. The old man who ran the business was impressed with Abner's Harvard degree and banking credentials. His instincts were spot on. In three years Abner had turned the company round. In four years they were making a profit. And the owner, who had no son to inherit from him, retired leaving twenty per cent of the shares to Abner. It wasn't long before the American Tobacco Company came into the picture, scooping up the company and making Abner his first million. The first thing he did was get rid of the airline stewardess. Abner was on his way to the top now and he didn't want any dependants. It was a canny decision. American Tobacco, sensing his flair for business, kept him pretty much in orbit for the next ten years.

During that time he built up three existing companies in the corporate empire and organised the takeover of half a dozen others. By the time he was in his early thirties his personal fortune stood at three million dollars. He quadrupled that when he went into the Miami property market.

Abner's property interests might have taken him away from American Tobacco if it hadn't been for Wilbur Evans. Evans had been running the show for more than a dozen years and would have gone on running it for longer but for an untimely car crash that put him in a wheelchair. When he heard that Abner was thinking of leaving American Tobacco, he delegated half his responsibilities to him. Then he raised his salary and cut him in on share options. When Wilbur Evans died, Abner stepped into his shoes and at the age of forty, found he was one of the richest men in the United States.

His career in big business did nothing to quench his appetite for girls, if anything he needed women more and he needed variety. When he was stressed he sought the company of stupid women, off-duty he needed the stimulation of brighter companions, women who could talk about music and painting and the latest gossip on Wall Street. There was only one problem. Abner didn't have the time or the energy to seek new women out all the time. He needed someone else to do that for him.

So he found Richard Gregory and discovered that his women problems were at an end.

When they met, Richard was running the hugely successful *Macho* magazine. Both *Penthouse* and *Playboy* were already diversifying into clubs and Abner suggested *Macho* should follow their lead. He backed his suggestion with money and business expertise, and in exchange he asked for a hefty share of the action and a ready supply of girls. Handpicked beautiful girls who had been road-tested by Richard himself.

Abner grinned, remembering Richard's eager acceptance of his terms.

'We've been in business together for four years now,' he told Frances, 'and things have never gone better. We've opened seven clubs in Europe – and that's not counting England. We opened up in New York eighteen months ago and right now I've got my eye on Miami and L.A.'

Frances looked at him out of the corners of her eyes.

'How about the girl situation,' she asked him. 'Does Richard still pick them out for you?'

Abner tipped his chair back and looked pleased with himself.

'You bet,' he said, 'and every time he comes up with a winner.'

Frances allowed herself time to study the man. She looked him over the way he had appraised her earlier that evening. She saw a handsome forty-five-year-old with sleek hair, greying around the temples. He was expensively suited, impeccably manicured. You've been spoon-fed for too long, she thought. You need a little jolt to remind you what the real world is all about.

She turned to him, putting on her best debutante's smile.

'If you're looking for winners,' she said, 'I wouldn't waste any more time on me.'

Abner raised an eyebrow. 'Why not?'

'Because men aren't really my thing,' she told him. She looked slowly across the table. Letting her eyes rest on Dolly Barbara, wilting slightly in her gold lamé.

'Men aren't her thing either,' she said.

12

'Have you any idea of what you put poor Dolly Barbara through last night?' said Richard, pouring Frances out a second cup of coffee.

'I do wish you wouldn't call the girls those silly names,' Frances told him crossly. 'Dolly Barbara, Dolly this, Dolly that . . . I'm sure they've got perfectly good names of their own. Why don't you use them?'

They were sitting alone in the conservatory at the back of the house. Nobody had managed to struggle out of bed yet, and from where she was, Frances could see a long sweep of valley covered in early morning frost. There was a lake nestling right at the bottom of the escarpment and all around it in the water weeds she could make out the movement of pheasant and moorhens. Her watch told her it was nine-thirty, but she knew the landscape had been awake since dawn. She longed to be out walking in it, instead of sitting in the stuffy greenhouse drinking coffee.

'You're in a bad mood this morning,' Richard observed, turning to her. 'What got into you?'

Frances pulled a face.

'It's not what got into me, it's who. Your friend Abner seems to think women are like commodities, meant for buying or selling. He doesn't see us as people at all.'

'So you thought pretending to be a dyke might make you more real to him?'

She took a sip of her coffee.

'I didn't do it for that reason,' she said. 'I did it to wipe that smug expression off his face. He just seemed too pleased with himself.'

Richard looked irritated.

'In future when you decide to take my American boss down a peg, you might check with me first. You managed to make quite a fool of him last night.'

Frances smiled. 'How did I do that?'

Richard put his coffee cup down with a crash.

'You know perfectly well what you did. I can forgive you pretending to like girls, but you didn't have to bring Barbara into your act.'

She started to get worried.

'What's so important about Barbara?'

Richard sighed and prayed for patience. 'What's important about Barbara,' he said carefully, 'is that she is available, and when Abner turned up out of the blue I had a quiet word with her before dinner and made sure she'd be putting herself out for him.'

Now it was Frances's turn to look furious.

'But that's disgusting. Worse than that – it's immoral.'

Richard rounded on her. 'Would you mind explaining to me what's immoral about the arrangement? Barbara's a perfectly ordinary girl, not very bright, not even all that nice but what she most wants to do in the world is to have a good time and sleep with as many men as she can before she starts to lose her looks. All I'm doing is helping her achieve those ambitions.'

Frances looked around her at the lush tropical plants growing in the hothouse where they were eating breakfast and for a moment she felt claustrophobic.

'You're not helping Barbara achieve her ambitions,' she exploded. 'You're using her.'

'I'm not the only one around here who's using Barbara,' said Richard softly. 'If you remember you passed her off as a lesbian last night. You even hinted you were having a relationship with her yourself, and what did you do that for? To make a point. To put Abner Morris in his place. That's why you did it. So don't go preaching at me about protecting the morals of young women. At least I didn't try to change her habits.'

There was a silence while Richard's words sank in. Finally Frances summoned the courage to meet his eyes.

'You win,' she said. 'I'm sorry about Barbara.'

But Richard wasn't letting her off the hook.

'It's not me you should be apologising to,' he said. 'Barbara's the one who suffered. After you went to bed last night, Abner decided to hit the bourbon and when he was well and truly drunk, he decided to have a go at Barbara. Abner's used to getting what he wants and when he comes here he expects a willing enthusiastic bimbo at his disposal. The fact that he thought Barbara was less than willing filled him with fury. He was rude about the way she looked, the way she spoke, even the way she was sipping her drink.'

Frances was horrified.

'How did it all end up?' she asked.

'With Barbara in tears,' Richard said quietly. 'Abner started making remarks about her sexual preferences and that completely finished her. The poor girl's been involved in scenes where several people play – they all have, but that doesn't make her a dyke.'

Frances stopped him.

'You're talking about orgies,' she said, her voice on edge.

Richard smiled tightly.

'I'm talking about sexual happenings between consenting adults. Believe me a lot of people go for that kind of thing. Anyway, in the end I sent everyone else off to bed and sorted out the situation myself. I realised what had gone wrong when Abner told me what you said to him over dinner.'

Frances looked up and as she did she saw Abner walk into the room. He was wearing a paisley dressing-gown over silk pyjamas and from the look of him, he seemed to have enjoyed a restful night.

'Richard told me you were selling me a load of horseshit last night,' he said pleasantly. 'Were you?'

Frances was completely confused. Richard she could cope with, but this brash American was another story. As she thought, Richard got up and left them together.

'Don't you think you'd better explain yourself?' Abner said softly.

He had taken hold of her lightly but firmly under the elbow.

As calmly as she could, Frances said, 'I only did it to tease. It was late and I'd had a lot of wine. I didn't mean to upset you.'

The American reflected for a moment.

'You didn't upset me,' he said. 'You made me mad as hell. I don't like being made to look like an asshole. Not by a woman.'

'You mean a man could have got away with it?'

It was a flip remark and Frances had said it without thinking. The instant the words were out of her mouth, she regretted them. She felt Abner stiffen.

'Your problem,' he said, 'is you're too cute for your own good. I told Richard he was crazy to employ a smartass like you, but he didn't seem to agree with me.'

Frances studied the American's face for a moment and she didn't like what she saw in it.

'You told Richard to get rid of me?' she asked.

He nodded. 'But he wasn't buying it. Not last night at any rate.'

He looked her over, taking in the soft blonde hair that hung down her back, the fragile bone structure, the tiny, almost Victorian waist.

'You're a pretty thing,' he said. 'There's a touch too much breeding for me, but I can see why Richard goes for your type.'

He laughed shortly.

'Let me give you a bit of advice,' he said. 'Be careful with

13

Richard and Frances became friends. Not in any dramatic way, but the next time Richard came into the club, Frances put herself out to be pleasant. After all, the guy had stopped her from being fired in Scotland. The least she could do was give him the time of day.

In the beginning she worried that he might want payment in kind, but he gave no sign of it. He always seemed to be on his way to meet Lila and when she wasn't in town, he didn't lack for female company. There was a Hollywood actress, a minor royal, a rising young dress designer. They all seemed to worship him.

Frances found herself wondering what his secret was. He was rich, but she had known richer men who had failed to fascinate her. She wondered if it was something to do with the way Richard looked. There was something untidy about him, not unkempt exactly, but tousled. It made her and every other female itch to smooth him out and put him to rights. But was that all of it, or did Richard have something else? Frances realised she was thinking about him too much yet she couldn't stop herself, and when he casually asked her to have dinner with him she didn't think twice before accepting.

He took her to the Clermont, the members only gambling club perched above Annabel's in Berkeley Square. Despite herself, Frances was impressed.

The membership in the Clermont was strictly limited to the rich, the well connected and the lucky.

Jet setting, backgammon hustlers inhabited the downstairs room and Frances recognised one or two of them from the society pages. Glamorously tanned, they stood around the green baize boards in tight little groups.

Richard seemed to know most of them, just as he seemed to understand the game, though refused to play.

'I'm here for pleasure tonight,' he laughed, 'not business.'

Then he put his hand on Frances's arm and steered her towards the bar. A bottle of Bollinger appeared in front of them and as the barman filled the crystal flutes, Frances turned to Richard.

'What was all that about not being here for business,' she asked. 'I didn't know you were a professional.'

He crooked an eyebrow.

'Once upon a time, before the magazine took off, this was how I supported myself.'

Frances was surprised. 'You're not telling me you belonged to that happy little group we just passed through.'

Richard took hold of his champagne glass and twirled it around in his fingers.

Finally he said, 'I don't belong to groups, or organisations unless I own them, but I like to live high. So for five or six years I had a loose friendly arrangement with most of the high rollers on the circuit. It's just possible, if you concentrate hard enough, to make a decent living out of a backgammon board. But it's a tough living, and nobody lasts very long. In the end Macho seemed a better option.'

A waiter came over bearing two leather-bound menus. Frances took one of them, but as she started to open it, Richard stopped her.

'Do you like caviar?' he asked her.

Frances remembered Christmas and grand cocktail parties where her father allowed her a tiny spoonful on a triangle of toast.

'I adore what I've had of it,' she said, 'but it's hardly dinner.'

Richard smiled. 'It is the way I eat it.'

He took the menu out of her hands and gave it back to the waiter.

'I'll have my usual,' he said, 'with a bottle of the Russian vodka. On ice.'

Richard led Frances through to a glass conservatory at the back of the gaming hall. It was a small room on several levels, full of round tables. Some of the tables had leather banquettes and Richard sat Frances down at one of them.

The vodka arrived as soon as they did and the waiter poured them both a measure in tiny glittering glass thimbles.

'You're meant to drink it with the caviar,' said Richard, 'but I can never wait that long.'

When dinner finally arrived, Frances was light headed. Then she saw the impossibly high mound of grey-blue eggs sitting on a bowl of cracked ice. She knew that even if she hadn't consumed three tots of neat vodka, her head would be swimming. She had simply never seen that much Beluga caviar in the whole of her life.

With no ceremony at all, Richard reached over and dug his spoon deep into the dark, sticky mass. Then he deposited a pile of the eggs on both their plates and offered Frances a cut lemon wedge covered with butter muslin.

'A lot of people I know spoon it up with just a squeeze of lemon.'

He indicated a cluster of glass dishes containing raw onion, and chopped up hard-boiled egg.

'I like to mix mine with this junk and pile it on toast. You can do what you like.'

Frances tried it every way, and when they had worked their way through one bowl, Richard signalled the waiter and ordered another.

He saw the surprise on Frances's face and laughed out loud.

'In that room you just walked through,' he said, 'men are winning and losing hundreds of thousands of pounds. The restaurant here serves caviar to most of those punters for free and still makes a profit. So stop worrying will you? I brought you here to enjoy yourself.'

Frances began to catch Richard's mood, and as she did, she relaxed. What a fuss I make about doing the right thing, she thought. Life isn't about that at all. She looked across at her companion and noticed that in a subtle way he seemed to have changed. He was still tousled in the casual expensive way he favoured, only now the face didn't frighten her any more.

I want to know you better, she thought.

Then she thought about his other women. She paused and took a sip of vodka. As she did, she saw Richard looking at her over the rim of the glass. It was an intense look. The message unmistakable. To hell with it, she decided. I'll take my chances.

They drove through the streets of London in Richard's open-topped Aston Martin and although the night was chilly Frances felt no pain at all. She felt deliciously fuzzy.

'Where are you taking me?' she asked as they went down into the Piccadilly underpass.

Richard's eyes glowed green in the dark and she felt her heart beating in her ears.

'I'm taking you home,' he said softly. 'It's not my style to get women drunk and take advantage of them.'

Frances started to protest, but he stopped her.

'There'll be other nights,' he promised.

A month passed. Then six weeks, but Richard didn't ask Frances to have dinner with him again. Whenever she saw him in the club he seemed busy and distracted. There was always a girl, sometimes two, claiming his attention. Once or twice he bought her a drink, and for the brief half-hours that they were together, the friendship they had started resumed its rhythm. They talked about nothing in particular, but there was an intimacy about the conversations that promised more. Except there was never any time. Frances felt spurned, then angry, and finally foolish. I'm no better than any of those pathetic Dollies in the club, she told herself. The idiots that follow him around with doe eyes.

She resolved to find herself another job. She had worked at the Macho for nearly nine months now and knew what she was doing. She wrote off to Playboy asking if they had any vacancies, then she scribbled out an identical application to Penthouse.

A month later she received a letter from Serena Williams at Playboy. There was a vacancy in the Park Lane Club for a cocktail waitress. The salary was slightly more than Frances was getting at the Macho, so she picked up the phone and made a date to see Serena the following week. Two days after that, Richard invited her to spend the weekend in Scotland.

This time she didn't attempt to get out of it. Richard Gregory, the castle in Scotland, the Mayfair club scene were all familiar territory. She knew they were minefields for the stupid and the innocent. She'd seen the corruption, and she'd managed to hold herself aloof from it.

When she arrived at the castle in Scotland she realised she was alone, for there was no sign of anyone else at all. No visiting Americans, no off-duty Dollies, not even Richard put in an appearance.

'Where has everyone got to?' Frances asked the butler on duty as she warmed herself in front of the great log fire in the main hall. All the latest glossies lay out invitingly on the long oak settle. The brocade cushions had been newly plumped up on the sofas. Without the sexual parade and the constant jibing competition between the men there was something womblike about the house, as if it was stretching out great comfortable arms and inviting her to relax.

The butler came towards her bearing the glass of white wine she had asked for. Frances noticed a freshly opened bottle of Pouilly Fumé on the dresser.

'Nobody else is expected tonight, Madam,' the servant informed her. 'The rest of the party is arriving in the morning.'

Frances was surprised.

'But Richard told me to be sure to come up on Friday night.'

The butler smiled a practised, professional smile.

'Yes, Madam,' he said. 'The people Mr Gregory was expecting have decided to spend the night in Paris, though Mr Gregory didn't know until this morning when he told me.'

Frances gazed at the fire roaring in the grate, sending the shadows dancing around the walls. Everything glowed in this warm rosy light. A feeling of contentment drifted over her.

'I don't mind spending this evening on my own,' she said. 'Not in the least.'

'At what time will you be wanting dinner, Madam?' the butler asked her.

Frances glanced at her watch. It was gone seven-thirty. If she had a quick snack now, it would give her all evening to explore the house. The problem was, she wasn't hungry. She decided to start off in the Jacuzzi and have dinner in her dressing-gown in her room. After that she could throw on her jeans and see the rest of the house.

She told the butler what she'd decided to do and set out to her room. This time she'd remembered to pack a swimsuit, and she planned to wear it even though she was alone.

When she had climbed into the one-piece black singlet, she made her way down in the lift that took her to the heated basement and walked into the steamy tropical room. The mechanism that operated the Jacuzzi was turned off, and the three circular pools gleamed softly in the subdued light. She saw steam rising from the still surface of the water. Inviting her, beckoning her to come in.

Frances cast her eyes round the walls at the mural expecting to feel shock, or at least distaste. Then the strangest thing happened. She felt herself being drawn into it.

In her mind's eye she became one of the shameless naked girls cavorting in front of her. Her eye caught her reflection in the mirror opposite her and she saw she was covered from neck to hip in black constricting lycra. Her hands reached to the top of it and started peeling it down her body.

Now her breasts were like the breasts on the girls all around her. Naked and free. She threw the swimsuit onto the tiled ledge in front of her, and as she did, she felt lightened, as if she had shed, not just an article of clothing, but an entire skin. She called her name out loud and heard it bounce and reverberate off the empty walls. She was alone in a fantasy kingdom of swirling mists and warm blue water.

Frances pressed a button set into the wall by the side of the pool nearest to her and all at once the water sprang into life. She stared down into the bubbling, churning depths and the invitation was too much for her. Slowly, she waded down the steps of the marble Jacuzzi and felt a sensation like nothing she had ever experienced before. It was as if a thousand fingers were walking all over her. They insinuated themselves into her folds and crevices, invading her most private parts, caressing and soothing, filling her with pleasure. Frances floated across the pool until she found a ledge set into the wall. She discovered if she sat down all but the top of her shoulders was submerged, and she lowered herself into the pool spreading her long blonde hair on the shimmering surface.

She had been there for nearly half an hour, when she

heard footsteps and the sound of a door opening. She raised her head, still half in a dream, and saw Richard.

For a second she thought she was imagining it, and she called out to him, announcing her presence.

His voice came back, reassuringly real. 'Don't worry. There's nobody here but me. The others are coming tomorrow.'

He was wearing a towelling dressing-gown, tied in the middle, and she noticed he was smiling.

'What's so funny?' she asked, nonplussed.

Richard's eyes went to her discarded swimsuit by the side of the pool.

'I see you've lost some of that upper-class modesty,' he said. 'Does the same thing apply to your inhibitions?'

'That depends what you have in mind,' Frances replied.

Richard took off the towelling robe and Frances saw that he hadn't bothered to put on swimming trunks. Get a hold of yourself, she told herself sternly. Pick yourself up and leave now while you still can. But even as she lectured herself, she knew it was too late. The warm water had suffused her with a weakness, a languor she didn't even begin to understand. As Richard entered the pool and started moving towards her, Frances felt her body open as if in welcome.

Richard didn't say anything. Instead he stood in front of her, his eyes not moving from her face. Then lightly, almost casually, he tilted her chin and started kissing her on the mouth. They were soft kisses, exploring kisses, and Frances was aware of her nakedness, and the fact that he hadn't touched her.

Everything happened in a kind of slow motion.

Slowly, with increasing urgency, he put his tongue in her mouth and as he did she felt his hands on her breasts, teasing the nipples. Then his hands were all over her, soft and fluttering like the ripples in the Jacuzzi. Confusion and desire mingled together and Frances wasn't sure whether it

106

was the water that was caressing her or Richard's fingers. She was still sitting on the ledge, her back against the wall of the pool, her knees pressed firmly together. Then she felt her feet leave the bottom and as they floated out from under her, her legs parted. The water pushed against her, massaging and flowing into the opening between her legs. Then she felt Richard's fingers at her entrance and she knew she was lost.

She reached towards him and felt his cock hard in her hands. She looked at him in alarm.

'You're not going to,' she said, 'not here. It's not possible.'

In answer to her question, Richard put one knee on the tiled ledge, leaning in towards her, and Frances knew she had been wrong. He entered her gently, carefully at first. Then, as he found his way, he thrust into her in one strong movement that knocked her breath away. In some strange way their bodies seemed to fuse and melt together, forming a seal against the water around them. The effect was to sharpen the sensation Frances felt, heightening her pleasure. It was as if her body was a great suction machine, drawing Richard inside her, so that he penetrated her depths, touching secret places inside her she didn't know existed. As he pushed into her, the core of her came awake.

It was as if her sex had been lying dormant all the years of her womanhood. Now it stirred hungrily inside her and grew, gaining momentum, until it flowed and shuddered into a climax.

Afterwards Richard lifted her gently out of the water and wrapped her in his dressing-gown. When Frances looked up at him, she thought she saw concern in his eyes.

'I didn't mean to do that,' he said.

She laughed shortly. 'Don't be ridiculous,' she said. 'A man like you eats little girls like me for breakfast.' She made a face. 'Or in this case, high tea.'

Richard sighed. 'I can't seem to win with you.'

Frances pulled the robe closer around her and sat on a bench.

'On the contrary,' she replied. 'On today's performance I'd say it was game, set and match.'

Richard walked over to the pool. When he turned to her Frances could see the anger on his face.

'I think it's time to get a couple of things straight,' Richard told her. 'First, I don't have a problem finding girls to go to bed with me. In the second place,' he said, 'I meant it when I said I didn't mean to make love to you. I wanted to all right, from the first moment I set eyes on you in that terrible costume. But I decided I wasn't going to do anything about it. When I got to know you, you see, I realised you were better than a casual lay.'

Frances looked at him with a new understanding.

'Is that why you took me home after we had dinner together?'

He nodded.

Frances got up from the bench, shrugging the robe off her shoulders until it fell into a heap at her feet. Then she came towards him, her body still soft and rosy from the pool.

'Are you still frightened to touch me?' she asked.

They made love for the rest of the evening, always with Richard in the lead. He roused Frances in subtle ways, ways that were new to her, and each time he allowed her to take her pleasure without thinking of himself. It was as if he was there for her only and she marvelled at his skill and his patience.

At the end of it she looked at him with something approaching humility.

'Thank you,' she said. 'I'll never forget today. Not as long as I live.'

Richard stroked her damp hair out of her eyes and held her close.

'That sounds very final,' he said gently. 'You make me feel like a treasured memory.'

Frances pulled away from him. 'I'm not a child. And I'm not a fool either. I know the way you live, Richard Gregory – with a different girl every night. So you'll have to be a memory for me, because I'm not prepared to join the harem.'

He smiled and shook his head.

'Nobody asked you to join any harem.'

'Then what do you have in mind?' Frances asked.

'I want us to be together,' Richard told her. 'Exclusively together. Something happened between us today. I'm too old and too cynical to call it love, but whatever it was it was a damn sight more fun than anything else in a very long time.'

Frances looked at him in disbelief.

'You mean you won't see Lila any more, or the honourable what's-her-name?'

Richard stroked her cheek.

'Not if you move in with me,' he said softly. 'I don't think any of them will want to know me after that.'

Frances made a mental note to call Serena Williams the moment she got back to London. Richard wouldn't like it at all if she joined Playboy.

14

Two weeks before her twenty-sixth birthday, Louise Tragos became a force to be reckoned with. What propelled her into the spotlight was a series of posters she dreamed up for a frozen vegetable. The idea was stunning and so simple that every other writer and art director in New York wondered why they hadn't thought of it first.

Each poster showed a shot of a mouth-watering vegetable, with a question. 'If you can see what's wrong with this, your standards are up to ours.' Nobody who saw the ads could pass them by. They just had to figure out what *was* wrong with a perfect piece of asparagus? A golden corn on the cob? An unblemished string bean? And while they stood wondering their eyes picked the name on the pack. And they were hooked.

If Louise had been a screen actress, she would have won an Oscar for the work she did. Instead she got an equivalent accolade from her own industry. She was awarded a Clio. Suddenly she was in demand. Headhunters who had ignored her calls now pestered her with jobs, writers from other agencies asked her out to lunch and the movers and shakers at Acker and Stein started to take her seriously. She was ready for them all, for the last three years had changed her.

She had come to Madison Avenue empty-handed except for her talent and her illusions. The affair with Brian Elder had robbed her of her illusions, but there had been compensations: a vastly increased salary, a big new apartment with a view of the river and, best of all, a new persona. A new surface to show the world.

From the word go, Louise had resented the way she

looked. Her nose was too heavy. Her hips too wide. Her hair too wild. People who ruled the world didn't look like Louise Tragos, they looked like Grace Kelly or Jackie Kennedy. Her training told her that any look could be bought and now she was earning enough money, Louise set about buying it. She dieted, she visited expensive hairdressers, she bought the latest designer clothes. When she'd saved up enough dollars she had her nose changed. The plastic surgery was the biggest alteration of all and her family gave it a mixed reception. Her sisters and her cousins thought it gave her class and they dreamed of one day being able to afford the same thing for themselves. Her mother thought the surgeon had taken away more than her nose. She regarded her youngest daughter with sorrow.

'Why did you throw away your heritage?' she asked. 'Who do you want to be?'

Louise looked at her mother with impatience.

'The best damn art director on Madison Avenue.'

The older woman shook her head.

'When the doctor did the operation,' she said, 'he took away a bit of your soul too.'

Her mother was right. The girl under the glossy surface had suffered a change, but a change so subtle that she didn't notice it happening. Louise found more determination than she ever knew she had. If an idea for a TV commercial or a series of press ads eluded her, she didn't leave it in her 'In' tray and go to the movies. She stayed late at her desk until the problem was solved. Success was no longer an abstract idea, something that would happen to her one day. Success was her goal. Until she reached it she could do without visits to the movies, drinks with her friends. She could even do without love, for she had something stronger than that to propel her forward. She had her anger.

In her quiet moments, when she gave herself time to think, Louise wondered where she had found the emotion. Nothing in her childhood had prepared her for it. Her family had protected her from life's harshness. Her art had fulfilled rather than disappointed her. Then she thought about Brian Elder and the choices he had given her. She could be his part-time whore, or go back to the Bronx.

That's where I found my anger, she thought bitterly. The people in the business think I won this award, this Clio, because I worked hard. They don't know I sold myself to get it. As Louise thought about the Clio and the price she paid for it, another notion hit her.

The award could help her even the score. For now she had clout. The clout to take Brian Elder's meal ticket, United Foods, and move it out from under him, move it to another agency. A plan began to form in her mind.

The first thing Louise had to do was find herself a new job. She realised that was no longer a problem. She could take her pick of virtually any agency in New York, but she didn't want to work in just any agency. The shop she had in mind had to pass two tests. First it had to have capacity: the place she had in mind would have to have a space for a large piece of food business.

Her second criterion was tougher: the agency she picked had to be special. If she could get United to move, it wouldn't move just anywhere, it would go to an agency with a classy chairman, or it would settle for a place with a hot reputation.

Louise went over the options and one by one she threw them out. The biggest hotshots, Doyle Dane, PKL, Della Femina and Carl Ally, all had food business. Then Louise thought about chairmen and drew another blank. Most of the good ones were semi-retired, and if they were active and didn't have a food, then chances were their companies were probably too small for an account like United.

Louise was sitting in her apartment on Sunday afternoon. She had just come back from having lunch with Mike, the guy she worked with, and the evening stretched out ahead of her.

Most Sunday nights she washed her hair and caught up with her reading. In front of her on the coffee table was a stack of contact reports, plans for new products, analyses of existing campaigns and background information on the competition. Impatiently, Louise pushed aside the mountain of paper. I could do with something lighter for a change, she decided. She caught sight of an old copy of *Advertising Age* sticking out from the bottom of the pile. It took a few moments rummaging around to extricate it and she looked at the date. June 1976. Then she glanced at the front page. Jesus, she thought. This paper's three months old and I haven't got round to reading it yet. She started to flick through the old copy. Most of the news items she already knew about and she was going to throw it to one side when her attention was caught by a photograph on the back page. It was of a tall, striking-looking man with close cropped curly hair and an animated face. It was the man's eyes that held her, though, they had a passion, an intensity that reminded her of the priests of her childhood.

Who is this fanatic? Louise wondered. Then she looked at the caption underneath and smiled. So that's what Sam Kurnitz looks like. No wonder they told so many stories about him. Louise's eyes flicked down the column. What had the madman been up to three months ago? She stopped reading when she got to the second paragraph. Kurnitz had just re-signed Leiber Inc.

Louise whistled softly. The business was worth thirty million dollars and it took in pickles, catsups and a brand of coffee. So Kurnitz was in the market for another food. Louise thought quickly. Was she in the market for Kurnitz? She had to admit, he had a lot going for him. The agency he headed, Kurnitz and Greene, was medium sized and coming up. It had an equal spread of press and television accounts, and Sam's work was classy and clever. The problem was the man himself. Louise shook her head. If only he was more stable, less of a maverick.

113

Take that business with the office copiers. No other agency would have let one of its writers carry on the way Sam had done. The only reason he got away with it was because he ran the show. Louise searched her mind for the details.

Sam had written an ad demonstrating how easy it was to use a duplicating machine. To illustrate his point he had shown a monkey operating the controls, instead of a secretary. The guys working on the business had thrown the ad out.

'Think of the office workers,' they had protested, 'they'll be insulted. We can't sell it.'

Sam reacted swiftly.

'There's no such thing as can't,' he pointed out. 'What you mean is you *won't* sell it. Well if you guys won't take it to the client, I will.'

The office copiers empire was run by Jack Rubins, a bluff, self-made millionaire who spoke his mind. When Sam showed him the ad he told him exactly what he thought.

'I hate it,' he said.

Sam didn't turn a hair.

'I love it,' he said. 'It's an attention-getter. Everyone who sees this ad is going to be intrigued.'

Sam's enthusiasm was contagious. Some of the guys surrounding the office machines' magnate started nodding their heads in agreement, but Jack still wasn't buying it.

'I hate it,' he repeated.

'But you're so wrong,' said Sam assuredly. 'Office systems advertising is dull. Boring. My stuff will make everyone sit up and take notice. They'll be hot for your copiers. Take my word for it.'

The great man exhaled. 'I still hate it,' he said.

Louise pictured Jack Rubins in his office. He was a fat man with a bull neck and a tough manner but his temper was what frightened people. If he disagreed with

114

an employee then things could get rough. If he violently disagreed, then the underling might easily find himself fired. When Sam went out on a limb for his ad he was risking more than just his reputation. He was risking the agency's business.

Any other businessman would have backed down and accepted the judgement, but Sam wasn't any other business-man.

He stood up, took hold of his ad in one hand and walked over to the window.

'There must be some way I can sell you this,' he said.

Jack shook his head.

'I don't want to talk about it,' he said.

'You shouldn't have to,' retorted Sam, 'it speaks for itself.'

As he said it, he was opening the window. Then before anyone could stop him, Sam had swung his legs over the sill. Twenty storeys below him was the sidewalk. Taking a deep breath he got to his feet and edged out onto the ledge running below the window.

Jack lost some of his confidence.

'Are you going somewhere?' he asked nervously.

'Yes,' snapped Sam. 'I'm leaving.'

Nobody said a word. It was obvious to everyone in Jack's office that Sam was trying it on. But what if he wasn't? What if Jack's out of hand rejection of the advertising had driven the creative genius over the edge?

At that moment the creative genius decided to press his advantage. He grabbed hold of the window with one hand. With the other he waved the layout he was clutching.

'You make the office machines,' he roared, 'I'll make the advertising.'

The fat tycoon had had enough.

'Stop that and come in,' he said through clenched teeth. 'You've made your point. We'll run the damn thing.'

Sam's grandstanding was rewarded. His advertising put

Jack's office copiers on the map. It also picked up a couple of awards.

What if it had gone the other way, Louise wondered.

What if the millionaire client had thrown Sam out the moment he dared disagree with him? Kurnitz and Greene would have lost twelve million dollars' worth of business, and for what? A writer's whim. Sam Kurnitz's pride in his work.

Louise put the old copy of *Ad Age* back on the table. She'd been on Madison Avenue just three years and already she'd learned there was no such thing as pride in business. Sam had been around a whole lot longer and he still didn't know it. She sighed. She liked Sam's talent and despite herself, she admired his style. But there was no way she could trust her future to a man like that. It would be like committing professional suicide.

Three nights later she had dinner with Brian, and after that she changed her mind about Sam Kurnitz. She met her lover at the 21 Club, in the downstairs bar. She knew even before she saw him, Brian wanted to talk business. The 21 Club was that kind of place. For the past few years Madison Avenue's top hustlers had been gathering there. At lunchtimes the grandees talked turkey in the glittering private restaurant upstairs. In the evening after work the agency vice presidents drank in the dimly-lit bar.

It was a very masculine room, all wood panelling and studded leather armchairs. You got drunk in a place like this. Honourably drunk. Drunk in the course of business.

Brian Elder had arrived before Louise, and was already half way through his first Gibson. Louise ordered one for herself and leaned back against the heavy chrome bar.

In the three years she had known him, Brian Elder had hardly changed at all. He still wore his Ivy League suits cut a trifle too sharply and his heavy blond hair brushed his collar in a way that could never be taken seriously in real society.

At first Louise hadn't seen these flaws, but as she'd grown in sophistication, her eye had become more selective. She recognised her lover now for exactly what he was: a shallow man. A man who had failed to make the grade in a serious profession like broking, or banking, or the law. A man who had turned to his family connections in order to break into advertising.

Louise assessed him slowly in the smoke-filled bar, the way she would a layout or a fine piece of china. You have charm, she thought to herself, and you talk a good game, but if your father hadn't been to school with the chairman of United Foods, you'd be hard pushed to find yourself a job.

Brian signalled to the waiter for the large menu and when it arrived, he pushed it over to Louise.

'I thought we'd have a steak down here,' he said, 'unless you have other ideas.'

Briefly, Louise thought about the restaurant upstairs with its starched white linen and obsequious waiters. Then she looked at her Calvin Klein suit and decided against it. She could have gone to a meeting with her most important client looking like this. She could have lunched in any one of half a dozen different restaurants, but dining at the 21 required more effort than she had taken. She glanced across at the bank of tables just beyond the bar.

'A steak here suits me fine,' she said.

Half way through dinner, Brian told her what was on his mind. He had a problem with United Foods. The biggest brand, a chocolate cupcake called 'Teatime', was losing its share of the market. It was too fattening, too self-indulgent a snack for the figure-conscious housewives of the Seventies. They liked eating between meals and they all had a taste for pâtisseries, but they didn't want to be seen buying 'Teatime' cakes.

Brian had been asked to go to work on the brand. United Foods wanted the agency to redesign, repackage and rethink the cupcake.

'Somehow or other, we have to persuade the woman in the street that our cakes aren't going to make her fat,' Brian said. 'Or if they do, she won't get as fat on "Teatime" as she will on, say "Kunzle-cake".'

Louise smiled and examined her rare steak.

'United Foods are asking for a miracle, aren't they? I only have to look at a pack of "Teatime" and I automatically put on five pounds.'

Brian didn't think it was funny. 'Look,' he said. 'My job's on the line here. If the agency can't stop the rot on "Teatime", then United Foods will put it out to a competitive pitch. And whoever gets "Teatime" will get the rest of the company's business sooner or later. It always happens.'

Louise started to pay attention.

'Surely you're getting the whole thing out of perspective,' she said. 'You've been managing that piece of business for the last twelve years now. Old man Remington trusts you because of your father. He can't just up sticks and leave the agency over one brand.'

Brian frowned and Louise saw a small muscle twitch underneath his eye.

'I can't take old man Remington for granted,' he said. 'He retires at the end of the year, and when his son takes over it's a whole different ball game.'

He pushed away his plate, most of his dinner uneaten.

'Louise,' he said, 'I'm serious when I say we're in a hole. Unless you can come up with some kind of scheme we're all sunk. You, me, the entire agency.'

Louise leaned forward in her seat and took both his hands in hers.

'Don't worry, darling,' she said, 'I've thought my way out of worse binds than this one. Leave "Teatime" to me. I'll sort it out.'

But it won't do you any good, she thought. Not now. The man who stands to gain from my bright solution is Sam Kurnitz.

15

Sam Kurnitz was in a tight corner. It didn't faze him. He had been there before and he had always talked his way out of it.

He glanced across at the man he had to convince; Charlton Peters, head of 'Coast-to-Coast' airlines. There was something smug about the man, something that told you he had been going to the same barber, the same tailor, the same shoeshine boy for the last ten years of his well-ordered life. He needs shaking up a little, thought Sam. He leaned forward and gave his best advertising man's smile.

'What you need,' he said, 'is a girl.'

Peters stiffened in his seat, but before he could utter any protest, Sam went on with what he was saying.

'I'm not suggesting you go looking for any piece of ass. What I have in mind for you is a class act. Someone who could demonstrate that "Coast-to-Coast" flies the most gorgeous, the most kissable, the most caring dames that ever served an airline meal.'

Sam had the man's attention now, and he breathed a sigh of relief. For the past hour the airlines chief had thrown out everything he and his partner, Clay, had put in front of him. The sex angle was a last ditch stand, and it had worked.

Charlton Peters moistened his lips.

'Are you talking about a blonde or a brunette?' he asked.

Sam sighed. The guy didn't want an advertising agent, he wanted a pimp. He thought of telling him so, then he remembered about Coast-to-Coast's budget. They were spending six million dollars this year. The hell with it, Sam thought, if Charlton wants to blue the lot on a broad, he'd make sure it was worth his while.

'The girl I had in mind has to be a blonde,' Sam said, thinking on his feet. 'But Grace Kelly, rather than Monroe. If you're going to screw this one, you're going to have to marry her first. It's a wholesome appeal, a family appeal. That way you get both the businessman and his wife on board.'

Now Peters was excited. 'We'll call her the "Coast-to-Coast girl",' he said. 'And I'll want her on all the press material as well as the television commercials.'

'You've got it,' said Sam, 'but a girl with this kind of appeal is going to take some finding. Unless you want to use an established star.'

The airline chief was adamant. If he was going to spend six million on a dame he wanted one of his own. He had no intention of borrowing an actress from a film studio.

The meeting was interrupted by the phone. Sam's secretary was on the line.

'I've got a call from somebody called Louise Tragos,' she said. 'It's the third time she's called this morning, and she says it's urgent. What do I tell her?'

Sam considered. He'd never heard of Louise Tragos. Under normal circumstances he would have instructed his secretary to tell her to go away. Then he looked at Charlton Peters. The airline chief looked set to talk about blondes for the next two hours. There would be the history of the blonde, blondes he had known, blondes he wanted to know.

He spoke loudly into the phone.

'I'll take the call in my office,' he said. 'Make sure not to lose it.'

He stood up.

'I've got to run,' he said. 'Clay will tie up all the ends.'

He raised his hand in a salute. His partner wouldn't be pleased about him walking out, but he'd just salvaged six million dollars' worth of business. He deserved a respite.

On his way down the corridor he wondered about Louise Tragos. The name rang a bell. Hadn't she won an award recently? Then he had it. She was a Greek dame working at one of the old established agencies. He tried to visualise what she looked like and the image of clouds of black crinkly hair and long elegant legs swam into his mind. He started to grin. Louise Tragos wouldn't suit Charlton Peters and Coast-to-Coast, but she could interrupt him any time she liked.

When he reached the phone, she was still there.

'What's so urgent?' Sam asked Louise. 'My secretary just told me this is the third time you called today.'

Louise was surprised by the coolness of her reception. Most agency chiefs went out of their way to be nice to her. Her voice betrayed her resentment.

'If you're not interested in talking to me, I won't waste any more of your time.'

She heard Sam chuckle.

'Keep the temperament for your boyfriend,' he said. 'If you want to talk about business, that's another matter.'

With an effort Louise resisted putting the phone down. 'I want to talk about coming to work for you,' she said.

There was a short silence, then Sam's voice came crackling down the line.

'Good,' he said. 'How about me buying you lunch?'

'When did you have in mind?' Louise asked.

'Tomorrow,' Sam replied. 'If you're so hot to work for Kurnitz and Greene be at the Palm at twelve-thirty.'

He broke the connection before Louise had time to reply. Arrogant bastard, she thought, I could have been meeting an important client. She was tempted to ring him back. It wasn't as if he was the ideal choice. Then she thought, no, she might never get another chance to move the United Foods business, and right now Sam was her only option. Love him or hate him, she was going to have to live with him.

Louise had been to the Palm once before and hadn't liked it. The sawdust floors and locker room atmosphere were not really her style. Anyway who could eat a slab of steak at lunchtime?

It was in this mood that she arrived at the long thin restaurant on Second Avenue. Her temper was not improved by having to fight her way past a group of drunken newspapermen. Typical, she thought as she searched the booths for the man she was meeting. I just hope Sam Kurnitz knows how to treat a lady.

Louise was not disappointed. The tall, sporty-looking man who greeted her did everything he could to soften the edges of the steak house. He ordered the only bottle of drinkable wine in the place, then apologised for the lack of menu, but explained the bill of fare better than a waiter could. By the time her broiled shrimp had arrived, Louise started to relax.

Sam Kurnitz was nicer than she had expected – and funnier, telling her improbable stories about how his agency survived against all the odds. Like all the brightest creative shops, Kurnitz and Greene had been a breakaway group. Kurnitz was the creative genius, the gifted copywriter and Clay Greene was an art man with a brain for business. Six years ago they had set up in business in a Manhattan hotel suite.

Their style was casual but clever. Slick salesmen with a twist.

The twist was the work. It was outrageous, it frequently shocked, and it sold the goods. If Sam Kurnitz worked on your business it prospered. It was as simple as that.

In nine months the partners moved out of their hotel suite and into smart offices on Fifth Avenue. They were hot, and they would have gone through the roof if it hadn't been for Sam's conscience.

Sam couldn't work for clients he didn't believe in. The list was formidable. Sam wouldn't take on a tobacco account – he believed selling cigarettes was immoral. He wouldn't work for any client who told him how to think, or how to sell, and he didn't have any truck with bullshit. So instead of ranking alongside Bates, and Young and Rubican, Kurnitz and Greene remained a boutique agency. They had a hand-picked list of clients, their work won awards, and they believed in what they did.

Louise had come to lunch prepared to hate Sam Kurnitz and his high-flown ideals. She wound up admiring the man. He was living proof that you could achieve the impossible if you didn't take no for an answer. She remembered the story of Sam threatening to jump from a client's window. I don't have your sort of courage, she thought. All Brian Elder had to do was threaten me with my job and I fell into line, and into bed. She looked at the man sitting opposite her. Broad and tanned with the eyes of a fanatic. For the first time in her life, she wished she'd been better.

Then Louise remembered why she was there, and all her good intentions died. She had not come to improve herself, or her skills. She had come seeking revenge. She sighed. One day, she promised herself, when this business is over, I will be worthy of a man like you. Right now all I can think of is surviving.

She put down her wine and turned to her companion.

'I love what I hear about Kurnitz and Greene,' she said enthusiastically. 'Is there any room for me there?'

'That depends,' Sam said. 'First I want to know why you want to quit your job. From what I hear around town, you're doing well where you are.'

There was no way Louise could tell Sam the truth. Not the clear unvarnished version at any rate. So she improvised.

124

'I'm in a bind,' she said. 'If I tell you what's happening at Acker and Stein, you could use it against me. But if I don't, I'm going to be out of a job anyway.'

Sam leaned forward, putting both arms on the table.

'Trust me,' he said, and for a moment Louise felt like a friend. But only for a moment.

'United Foods,' she said, 'the account that takes up most of my time, is about to walk out of the door. I've tried to save it. Everyone on the business had done their bit, but it's no good. United wants out. Now it's only a matter of time.'

Sam started to speak.

'How much time have you got?' he asked.

Louise made a rapid calculation. The idea she had just sold to Brian, the one intended to save his job, would take a few weeks to get on television. It would start to have an effect within days. To be on the safe side, she gave it until Christmas.

She looked across at Sam.

'At the beginning of the New Year,' she said, 'United Foods will be looking around for another agency. If you take me on, you'll stand a fighting chance of getting on the shortlist.'

Sam was confused.

'If United Foods is walking out on its agency, it will be looking for a different approach, and different faces. If I hire you, I'll be going against my own interests.'

You're so clever, Louise thought. Right now you're probably writing the best ads in the city, but when it comes to the real work – the politics, the dirty in-fighting – you haven't even been born.

'Listen to me,' she said confidently. 'I'm not suggesting you put me to work on United Foods. Not in any visible way, at any rate. But who knows how the business works at head office? Who knows where the bodies are buried? Who understands what the chairman hates and what he loves?'

She was flushed now, and her eyes were sparkling. A long, thick tendril of hair had escaped from one of the combs that was holding it back and fell across her face.

Sam regarded her with the beginnings of fondness.

'You make a very beautiful spy,' he said.

Louise grinned.

'Does that mean we're in business?'

Sam signalled for the waiter to take their plates away and when the table was clear, he got down to specifics. He wanted to know how much she earned and what else she had worked on. Then he thought for a moment. Finally he said, 'I could use another writer, and you've got the right experience for what I have in mind. When do you want to start?'

Louise was on a month's notice and she told him. Then she made a mental note. She would have to kiss Brian goodbye of course. She remembered the nights she spent at his apartment, the clothes she had to put on for him, the indignities she had to endure. There wouldn't be any more of that. Not where she was going. The future that was taking shape in front of her was gentler than that – and infinitely more seductive.

She gazed at Sam, taking in the close cropped curly hair, the strong face with its glittering black eyes. She wouldn't waste too much time kissing Brian for the last time she decided. She was saving herself for better things.

16

Louise's timing was spot on. Her last campaign for United Foods was a complete disaster. In three short weeks all the work she had put in building up the business had come undone. She had no regrets. She didn't even feel guilty. Brian should have known, she told herself. When I showed him the chocolate cake idea he should have seen it was going to ruin him. Yet deep down she knew she was lying to herself. Nobody could have known what her commercials were going to do. That's how the mistake was made in the first place. Ten years ago.

The campaign had first run in Canada, and then the idea wasn't selling chocolate cake, it was selling fudge, but the problems were the same. The product was unhealthy and it was fattening. To get round the drawbacks the ad agency had sold the fudge on an entirely different platform. Happiness. They called it the 'happiness sweet', and promised laughter and a lift every time you ate it.

It worked better than anyone could have imagined, for it gave everyone with a sweet tooth an instant excuse to indulge it. I'm buying a little happiness, they would say going to the food store. There was no arguing with it since who could begrudge anyone a moment's joy in a dull day?

In the first few days sales peaked at an all-time high. They stayed that way for a week or so, then something happened: the fudge eaters started to get fat, and they started to feel sick. Husbands found they were married to lacklustre wives. Mothers saw their children turning away their dinners.

Then came the backlash. Nobody blamed the over-indulgence on greed. They said it was the fault of the fudge, that it promised happiness and caused misery. Within weeks the sales figures started to fall. Shortly after that the product was taken off the market.

The fudge disaster was hushed up. It did the manufacturer no good, and it was bad for the agency's reputation. If Louise hadn't been looking at all the available material on the confectionery market, she would never have known about it. She came across it in an out-of-print marketing manual on chocolate. When she turned up to the fudge story, she knew she was on to something.

It was no problem substituting chocolate cake for the Canadian fudge. Because Brian didn't know the story, he went for the idea and United Foods went for it too. As everyone was in such a hurry to get it on television, nobody did any checking.

The cake campaign followed the same pattern as the fudge story, and by the time sales started to fall off, Louise was already working out her notice. She told Brian she was leaving the day United Foods decided to put the agency's business up for grabs.

The goodbye scene went better than even she could have planned. They were having a nightcap at 21 – the restaurant, not the bar – and Louise had pulled out all the stops. She was wearing a new Oscar de la Renta in red chiffon. The tiny strapless top showed off her shoulders and she was aware that her skin looked luminous against the black tangle of her hair. The waiter had just brought them two snifters of Armagnac, old and French and very expensive. Brian raised his glass in a salute.

'Enjoy it while you can,' he told Louise, 'I won't be able to afford this kind of treat for much longer.'

She raised her brows in surprise.

'Why?' she asked.

Brian took a sip of the thick, golden liqueur.

'Why do you think?' he said. 'If the agency loses United

Foods I won't have a job any more.' He surveyed Louise in her extravagant red dress.

'And nor, incidentally, will you.'

Louise's lips tightened into a smile. The expression held no warmth.

'That's what you think,' she said shortly.

The remark caught Brian Elder off balance.

'Is there something I ought to know?' he asked sharply. Too sharply.

Louise leaned forward displaying an expanse of creamy white skin. From where he was sitting, Brian could just see the tops of her breasts. He wondered how quickly he could get her back to the apartment.

'I'm joining another agency,' she said. The words hit him like a slap and he felt his desire ebbing away.

'Might I ask when?' he said coldly.

This time when Louise smiled it was with genuine pleasure.

'I left today,' she said. 'At the end of the afternoon. If you bothered to visit the creative department once in a while, you would have known.'

Rage threatened to engulf Brian Elder. He wanted to pick Louise up and shake her. To tear that expensive designer creation off her body and thrash her within an inch of her life. How dare she imagine she could walk away from him and keep it a secret? Who the hell did she think she was?

Louise saw the fury on his face and she was there before him.

'I wouldn't if I were you,' she said. 'They call the cops for that kind of activity.'

The lust Brian had felt earlier was back now.

'The activity I have in mind,' he said thickly, 'is something we'll do in private. Back at the apartment.'

Louise sat up very straight, and there was something proud about her, something independent Brian hadn't seen before.

'What makes you think I'll come back with you?' she said.

He laughed harshly. 'Because you always come back. Even when I hardly knew you you just couldn't wait to take your clothes off and open your legs. You're a slut, Louise. Admit it.'

Her expression didn't change. She could have been a duchess listening to small talk.

'Not any more,' she said firmly. 'Those days are over for me now.'

'Don't be a fool,' Brian said softly. 'You know you want it as badly as I do. Now be quiet and let's get out of here. I can't wait for you much longer.'

Louise got up and took a step away from the table, gathering her skirts around her as she did so.

Then she turned to him and spoke loudly, deliberately loudly so that the tables on either side of them could hear every word.

'I'm leaving,' she said, 'on my own. If you try to stop me, I'll scream, and I don't think your reputation could handle that.' She paused.

'Don't try to call me,' she continued. 'Either at home or in my new office. I'm going away for a few weeks. When I come back I never want to see you again. Ever.'

Then she turned on her heel and walked out of his life.

17

I've been a complete fool, thought Frances for the hundredth time that day. A spineless pathetic fool. A wimp
with no mind of my own.

A vision of the pictures Richard had taken sprung up
before her eyes. She was lying on a bed, their bed, and she
was naked. The shots had been taken early in the morning
and the clear white light showed everything in sharp relief.
Her breasts, the rounded line of her hips, the tiny triangle
of blonde hair between her legs.

Why did I let him do it, Frances wailed. Yet in the
depths of her despair she knew the answer to her own
question. She had let Richard photograph her because she
was frightened of him.

He had been her lover for three years now. He had
also been her teacher. When she first moved in with
him she had known nothing of the world and he had
begun her education by teaching her to dance. He had
shown her how to boogie at Regine's in Paris, to jive
at Club 64 in New York, to bop at Louise Brown's
disco in Cannes, and finally to smooch back in London
in Annabel's.

Richard hadn't intimidated Frances then. She had done
everything he told her to, with the ease of someone born
to the life. She drank without suffering hangovers, she
dabbled in cocaine without getting dependent and she
kept going until dawn without ever getting tired.

Her sparkle, her lust for life was fuelled by one thing.
Love.

She had fallen for Richard Gregory by accident, and
against her better nature. But once she had committed

herself she had abandoned her past and her principles, without looking back.

Six months into the affair, her father had written to her asking to see her. She had been waiting for a sign from her family for over a year. When it finally came, it was too late. Forgiveness had been offered, and a re-instatement of her allowance. Frances looked at her father as if he was out of his mind.

'I have my own world now,' she had told him. 'I'm a woman not a little girl.'

He begged her to reconsider. 'This world will corrupt you,' he said. 'Come home before it's too late.'

Frances regarded her pin-striped father with his public school manners and she felt sad.

'It was too late six months ago,' she said.

Frances and Richard lived like nomads, jetting round the world to wherever Richard had a club, or wanted to have a club, and they always travelled first class. As well as learning how to dance, Frances acquired another skill. She discovered backgammon, and to her surprise she found she was good at it. She memorised odds and remembered strategies, and from somewhere she never knew existed she discovered she had courage. She could gamble without getting emotional and because of it, she frequently won.

This new accomplishment made her more interesting to Richard, and more equal. In every area they were a match for each other, except for one. She couldn't, and wouldn't, share Richard's appetite for sex.

For a long time Frances never suspected that this man she loved, this man who had rescued her, could have another side. The fear started when he showed it to her.

It began with flirting – they had always lived their lives surrounded by girls. In the clubs there were the Dollies, and in Richard's Park Lane apartment there were the models he photographed for the magazine. Frances never objected to them, they were Richard's livelihood, his stock in trade.

If he had been a farmer she would have expected to be surrounded by cattle. To her, the girls were no different – until he took two of them to bed.

Frances remembered the evening it had happened. They were all having dinner at the apartment. She, Richard, and Abner Morris who was staying for a few days. They had reached the coffee and brandy stage and the men were starting to talk business when the girls arrived. There were two of them: Angie, a blonde model, and Jade, an exotic black girl. And when Frances had let them in, she had been puzzled. She was used to someone showing up late for Abner. It was one of the perks of owning the Macho Clubs. But two somebodys? That was a new one on her.

She showed the women through to the dining-room and gave them each a drink. Half an hour later Richard asked them to come with him to the studio on the floor below. He wanted to test a photographic set-up. Frances went on talking to Abner. Since she and Richard had become an item, Frances had called a truce with Richard's American partner. Abner seemed more at ease with the arrangement than Frances did, for try as she might, she couldn't like the man. He used women too casually, picking them up and discarding them without a thought for their feelings.

Frances remembered with distaste that Richard used to road-test Abner's girls for him and she wondered who else in the organisation performed that task now.

She was pouring out a second glass of brandy when she looked at her watch. Richard had been in the studio for over an hour and she felt uneasy. She hadn't expected him to be longer than ten minutes. What could be keeping him?

She decided to go down and find out. Abner tried to stop her. Without success. There was something wrong about the situation, something she needed to know. Nervously, Frances splashed brandy into her glass. Then she pulled herself up sharp. She was being silly, she told herself. She was living with the man she loved, the man she knew better than anyone else on earth. How could there be anything wrong?

Nevertheless, Frances still took her brandy down to the studio with her and she was glad she had. For when she got there, the first thing she did was throw it down her throat in one gulp. It was the kind of scene you needed a strong drink to contemplate.

The first thing she saw was that Richard was completely naked. Then she spied the blonde. She was on her knees in front of Richard and his cock was in her mouth. But it was the black girl who had his attention. She was oiling her body. Sliding her fingers into private, intimate places.

Teasing him. Offering herself to him. They were all three of them so wrapped up in what they were doing, they didn't notice Frances was there. Then she broke the silence.

'How could you?' she said.

Richard was the first to turn round and Frances saw that his penis was erect. She felt swamped by nausea and outrage. Richard's nakedness, his sex, didn't belong here, under the white lights of the studio, in the mouth of some blonde. These were the instruments of her private pleasure.

Richard looked at her, and Frances saw the anguish on his face.

'I'm sorry,' he said.

But she didn't wait to hear explanations. She turned tail and ran.

Abner was pouring out another brandy when she came into the room. For a second he didn't recognise her. The poised confident girl who left him five minutes earlier looked as if she had just been mugged. Her hair was all over the place and there was anguish in her eyes.

Abner went over to Frances and put an arm round her shoulders.

'What happened?' he asked.

She looked at him for a long moment, wondering whether to trust him. Then she shrugged and decided he probably knew all about it anyway.

'I found Richard in the gym with the girls,' she said, 'I'll leave you to fill in the details.'

'Poor Frances,' Abner said softly. 'It must have come as quite a shock.'

Frances stiffened.

'Don't patronise me. I can do without your pity.'

Abner led her over to the sofa and made her sit down. Then he handed her his glass.

'Get some of this down,' he instructed. 'Then go and get your coat. I'm taking you out of here.'

Frances did as he instructed. In the normal course of events she wouldn't have walked down the street with the brash American, but nothing was normal this evening.

In the limousine driving down Park Lane, she turned to Abner.

'Where are we going?' she asked.

'The New Cavendish in Knightsbridge. I always keep a suite there on permanent reserve.'

Abner saw the fear come back into her eyes and he laughed.

'I'm not going to jump on you. If the time ever comes for you and I to get together, I want you fully recovered from Richard and in your right mind.'

Until that moment, it had never occurred to Abner to want Frances. She was too headstrong for him. Too high and mighty. Yet now the wind had been knocked out of her, he started to feel differently. There was something crumpled about her. Something used that stirred him.

He had decided to check her into her room and go straight back to talk to Richard, but he changed his plans. I'll stay with her for a while, he thought, find out a little more about her. She needs someone to cry to.

When they reached the hotel and the concierge had handed over the key to the suite, Abner invited himself up.

'I'll take a cup of coffee off you,' he said, 'then I'll be on my way.'

Frances nodded her acceptance of the situation. There was a curious numbness about her. A weariness that bordered on resignation. If he tries to rape me, she thought, I can always throw myself out of the window.

If sex was on Abner's mind, he didn't show it. Instead he behaved rather as a nurse would behave towards a fretful patient. Ordering coffee and toast from room service, settling Frances on the sofa in the living-room, making sure she had everything she wanted.

'You don't have to do this,' she told him. 'I'll be all right by tomorrow. I'm quite resilient you know.'

Abner shook his head.

'I don't believe you. You're in love with the guy you just walked out on. You still can't accept what happened back there is for real.'

'How do you know all this?' Frances asked.

He smiled and went over to the door to let in the maid who had arrived with the coffee.

'I've lived a long time and known a lot of women,' he said. 'The ones like you, the girls who don't put their bodies on the open market, find it very hard to believe in the world as it really is. You have such illusions about men. Such fantasies.'

Frances stared at the tall, spare American. She didn't particularly like him, but he knew things she didn't, and tonight she needed to learn about those things.

'Are you telling me that Richard never cared for me at all – that it was all just a fantasy of mine?'

'No,' Abner said gently, 'I'm not. Richard does care for you but he also likes sex, and those two things are separate issues.'

Tears started to gather in Frances's eyes.

'But we have sex together. Good sex too.'

I bet you do, Abner thought. He had a vision of Frances naked in front of him. Her skin was very white, almost transparent and he fought down the urge to seduce her. It wouldn't be difficult tonight, he thought. A little sweet-talk, some phoney sympathy, a drink or two, maybe. I'd have her skirt up and her legs open within half an hour.

He put the thought out of his mind. Her time will come, he decided. With Richard's girls it always did.

'It's not over you know,' Abner told Frances. 'When the dust's had time to settle, you and lover-boy will be back together again. But when that happens, you have to understand him better. Richard's not a little boy. He's travelled the world and it's given him a taste for the exotic. I believe it when you say you and Richard have good sex together, but good sex isn't what he wants all the time. Sometimes he wants bad sex, dirty sex, and he can't get that from you.'

Frances felt sick.

'You're telling me if I want to go on with this relationship, I have to let Richard have his orgies.'

Abner nodded. Then he got up from where he was sitting and started towards the door.

'If you know what's good for you,' he told her.

After Abner had left, Frances poured away the rest of the coffee and went to bed. There was no way she was going back to Richard. Not after tonight. 'If I know what's good for me,' she thought, bitterly recalling Abner's last words to her.

If I know what's good for me, I'll let Richard have all the black whores and the blonde bimbos he can get his hands on. Well I do know what's good for me, and it's not that. Not while I can still think straight.

The following morning Frances's mind was made up. She would check out of the hotel, pick up her things and go home to her parents. Beyond that she couldn't reason, and she decided not to. She was going to take life a step at a time.

The phone rang as she was leaving the room. Absently she picked it up. It was Richard.

'Abner told me you were pretty upset last night,' he said quietly.

There was a silence while Frances wondered what to say, but Richard didn't wait for a reply.

'I think we need to talk,' he said. 'I have to see you, darling. Just once before you walk out of my life.'

'It's too late,' Frances told him. 'Why don't you write it all down and send me a letter.' Then she banged down the receiver. Minutes later, she bumped into Richard as she walked out of the elevator.

'You didn't tell me you were actually in the hotel,' she protested.

'You didn't seem to be interested where I was,' he said.

Frances tried to push past him, but he wouldn't let her. Instead he grabbed her arm and hustled her across to a table in the corner of the lobby.

'Sit down,' he said.

And Frances sat. As soon as she started listening to Richard she knew she was lost. He didn't have a particularly good excuse for the way he behaved, but he did say that he needed her and he couldn't bear to lose her.

'But what about the other girls?' As Frances asked the question she could feel herself drowning.

'Those girls meant nothing. They catered to another side of me. A side I wish I didn't have,' Richard explained.

Frances remembered what Abner had told her. The man she loved had a taste for the exotic, the perverted. Bad sex, he had called it. Frances wondered if she could live with it.

'That other side of yours,' she asked, 'has it always been there? Even when I started seeing you?'

Richard sighed.

'Yes,' he admitted. 'But it didn't get in the way of us, and it needn't. We can go on just the way we always did. I'll never push it under your nose again. I promise.'

It wasn't much of a promise, but she loved him so she went along with it. It's not the end of the world, Frances persuaded herself. It's not as if he has a permanent mistress. It's not as if he doesn't care for me.

The fear started after that. Frances expected apologies and excuses. She thought Richard would promise to be true to her. Only he didn't. All he said was he would go elsewhere for his pleasures.

Frances tried not to let it interfere with their life together, but every time Richard took her in his arms she wondered who else had been there, and when, and how. She became obsessively jealous. The Dollies and the models she had hardly noticed before suddenly became rivals. Which one of you, Frances wondered, will steal Richard from me? Which one will satisfy him the way I no longer can?

One night she became desperate.

'Show me one of your games,' she asked Richard. 'Include me. Let me please you.'

He introduced her to blind man's buff. They were to make love, as usual, only she would wear a blindfold. Frances went along with it, relieved there were no black models, no willing blondes.

Everything was the same as usual – except for one thing. The people having dinner with them didn't go home when Richard took her to bed. They stayed on in the apartment drinking and talking.

When he led her to the bedroom she made no comment. She said she wanted to play a game. If part of it meant making love while there were still guests in the drawing room, so be it. Nervously she got undressed, folding everything and putting it away, spinning out the time, postponing the inevitable. Richard produced the blind-fold from a drawer. When Frances saw it, she smiled in relief. She had imagined a leather mask, something from a medieval torture chamber. Instead Richard was holding a silk paisley scarf. She remembered seeing him wearing it at the weekend and thinking how ordinary it was. Frances went up to him and let him fasten it around her eyes. This is going to be a doddle, she thought.

Then she stood perfectly still. Her first sensation was one of surprise, for the blindfold was more than a ritual, it actually cut off one of her senses. She couldn't see, and although she had slept in this room for nearly three years, she had difficulty remembering where she was standing. She felt Richard's arm around her waist.

'I'm taking you to where the bed is,' he said softly. 'We'll both find it easier then.'

Frances let Richard lead her across the room and lower her onto the mattress. Then she felt his body beside hers, warm and familiar.

If this had been a normal bedtime, if she could have seen what was happening to her, she would have felt desire, but the scarf around her eyes isolated her. Frances moved towards Richard, seeking reassurance and she was assailed by the smell and taste of him. He started to kiss her, gently. Moistly. The way he always kissed her, but she was frozen inside. I'm being silly, she told herself. I must try to concentrate. She ran her hands over him, and then her lips, sliding her tongue into the folds and crevasses, finding her way to his cock. As he swelled and grew hard in her mouth, the ice inside her began to melt.

She raised her head.

'I want you,' she said.

Richard drew away from her and she felt confused, disoriented. Then Frances stretched out again searching for Richard, seeking the familiar warmth. She discovered

. . . nothing. He had left her side and she was alone in the dark.

'Richard,' she cried, but there was no answer, only the murmur of voices far away down the hall. Then Frances heard footsteps padding across the carpet and she relaxed again.

'You're back,' she said. 'What on earth were you doing?'

He said nothing. Instead she could feel him coming towards her and she opened herself. He took her without any more preliminaries, and as the heat built between them, he kissed her full and passionately on the mouth.

It was then that Frances realised she had been deceived. For the man kissing her, the man with his cock inside her was not Richard at all, but some stranger smelling of garlic and aftershave – and sex.

In the moment of realisation Frances felt such shame she wished she could have died or passed into unconsciousness. Then another quite different emotion came over her. She felt angry, and with the anger came the return of her sanity.

I let myself in for this, she thought, and I'll get myself out of it. She let her body go limp, and as she did, she felt the stranger recede inside her. She continued to do nothing. She didn't speak. She didn't move. She simply waited for the experience to be over. When it was, when her un-named lover had gone away, she sat up on the bed and unfastened the blindfold.

Richard was standing in front of her. She saw he was wearing a bathrobe and his hair was tousled.

'You were there all the time weren't you?' Frances said. 'You were watching me.'

Richard smoothed his hair back into place.

'You told me you wanted to please me,' he answered.

Frances looked at him. I wish I could hate you, she thought. I wish I could pack my bags and walk out of this house and never come back. Instead she stood up.

'I'm going to take a shower,' she told him. 'And while I'm in the bathroom I want you to get rid of your friends.' She paused. 'Next time you want to play games, I suggest you count me out.'

They started to grow further apart. They didn't quarrel or stop making love; they simply communicated less. Richard began travelling without Frances. In the beginning it hardly mattered, for he would only be gone for a day or two. Then he started taking trips to New York to see Abner and stayed away longer.

Once or twice on these trips Frances would hear what Richard was up to via one of the girls in the club, and it was over a glass of red wine that she found out there was another girl.

She wasn't anyone very important. Just a new girl who was helping out in the holidays before she finished her teacher's training course. But it rankled. How could he, Frances thought. One night I could understand. I do understand. But something more permanent, a travelling companion. I never thought he'd do that.

The fear Richard had planted in her started to grow. What if he gets tired of me, she wondered. What if he wants this exotic newcomer full time?

Although the trips got longer, Richard didn't show any signs of wanting to throw her out. Then one day, out of the blue, he asked to photograph her. In the nude, after they had made love.

Normally she would have turned him down flat. But the knowledge that she had a rival dented her confidence.

What harm can it do, Frances reasoned. There's nobody else involved. No other men. No other girls. Just Richard and I in private. It was after the pictures were taken that she realised how public it was. Then it was too late. Richard had parcelled up a set of prints and sent them off to Abner Morris in New York, and Abner had loved them.

'He wants to fly you to New York,' Richard announced. 'He's fixed up a special session for you there. With one of the top American photographers.'

Frances panicked. 'But I don't want to pose for *Macho*. I never did.'

Richard's eyes went cold.

'What's the matter?' he said. 'You're not going all prim on me again, are you?'

Frances tried to explain herself to him, then she tried reason. She tried tears but he wouldn't be moved. If she loved him, Richard said, truly loved him, then she would go to New York and do the picture session.

Frances realised that the point of no return had finally come. Either she packed her bags for New York, or she packed them for all time and the new girl would move in. She thought about the pictures Richard had taken. They were soft focus, tasteful, but they showed her breasts, her navel, her buttocks, the triangle of hair between her legs. That was what Abner Morris wanted to show the world in *Macho* magazine.

I can't do it, Frances thought. She turned to say no. Then she looked into Richard's eyes, and she was lost.

'When does Abner want to do the session?' she asked.

18

Since he had gone into partnership with Richard, Abner had given *Macho* magazine a facelift and eighteen months ago it had relocated in smart new offices on Fifth Avenue. The magazine was now glossy, brassy and virtually indistinguishable from *Penthouse* and *Playboy*. Many of the same models did the rounds of all three of the girly sheets, but the girls most in demand were the new faces, fresh flesh, unsoiled and untainted from Iowa and Orange County and Northern Canada. These models could command exorbitant fees to reveal all. Many of the more enterprising photographers would visit local beauty contests to see what they could find.

Abner liked the out-of-town girls. They had no resources, except the ones he provided. They were vulnerable and needy and dependent, and he kept them that way by accommodating them in his vast penthouse apartment, on 68th and Lexington.

Abner frequently put up five or six girls at a time and saw to it that they wanted for nothing. A stream of servants was constantly on duty, supplying everything on demand from a four-course meal to a Dior dress. If the girls wanted to see a first-run film, there was a private cinema on the premises. There was also a gym with all the latest equipment and its own instructors, a swimming pool, a sauna and a beauty parlour. Down to the last detail, Abner had made sure there was no reason for any of the girls to venture into the outside world. And they didn't. Instead they stayed and wallowed in the luxury Macho provided and turned into pampered pets. It took an inexperienced girl three days to fall in love with Abner's lifestyle. Six days to become completely hooked. After that they would do anything he asked them.

His parties were legendary. He held them at family times such as Sundays, public holidays and Christmas. He did it as a kind of challenge, to see who could resist. Very few men did. Married movie stars and heads of state all turned up without their wives, and usually incognito.

The reason they came was stronger than the lure of a few available girls. That they could get anywhere. They came and went on coming because they felt that in Abner's penthouse they had permission to break all the rules. Reformed alcoholics went there to get drunk, captains of industry got involved in rigged poker games and a much-married muscle man and father of five turned up once a week to sleep with a male model. Frances knew all about Abner's penthouse. She had visited it briefly with Richard and the one thing she was dreading, more than the picture session, was having to stay there alone. She tried to get Richard to put her up in an hotel but he wouldn't hear of it. So she resigned herself to the inevitable. With one proviso. She would only spend one night there.

In the end it was arranged that Frances flew in on the first plane, spent the afternoon with the photographer and returned to London the next day.

Abner had invited her to have dinner with him and she accepted as long as it was just the two of them. She had no intention of being paraded in front of any of his friends. If he had a senator in tow looking for a good time, or a gangster on the prowl, Frances wasn't interested. All she wanted to do was have her picture taken and get back to London and Richard.

The minute the plane landed at Kennedy Airport Frances started to miss him. During the past three years she had travelled the world, but never on her own. Richard had always been there to pour the champagne when the plane took off and hold her hand when it landed. Arriving on her own, even first class, felt wrong somehow.

Frances was met by a stretch limousine, long and black with tinted windows. The whole of the back seat was upholstered in dark brown fur and she noticed the chauffeur had opened the bar for her. There was a freshly made pitcher of martini, a magnum of champagne on ice, a bottle of bourbon.

Before, Frances would never have questioned Abner's hospitality. Now it seemed gross and over the top. She longed to be riding into town in a Checker cab like all the other international commuters. She looked out of the window searching for landmarks as they approached New York City, yet her mind wasn't paying attention. No matter what Frances did, no matter how she tried to distract herself, she kept coming back to the same thing. The photographic session. It was the one cloud on her horizon, the one obstacle there was no way round. She was going to have to take her clothes off in front of a man she didn't know.

Twenty-four hours ago she had given her word she would go through with it.

Now as the limousine swung into the mid-town traffic, she started to have second thoughts. She glanced at her watch and saw it was nearly two in the afternoon. In under an hour she was due in the studio. She wondered what kind of man the photographer would be.

His name was Elliot Burke. He had pale blond hair and he was wearing the tightest pair of blue jeans Frances had ever seen, yet he didn't worry her. Elliot had been around cameras for a very long time and it showed in the way he handled himself.

He managed to look her over without appraising her and before they started the session he insisted Frances sat down and drank a cup of coffee.

'You can't do a set of pictures like this without having some idea of the man who is taking them. You'd be too tight. Too tense.'

He set two cups down in front of an automatic kettle, then he tipped a spoonful of instant coffee into each and topped them up with boiling water.

'Here,' he said handing her a coffee, 'get this down you. It will make you feel better.'

Frances sipped the hot drink.

'You look like you've done this kind of thing often,' she said. 'Do you enjoy it?'

Elliot shrugged.

'Not much. But the pay's better than *Vogue*. It comes in handy when there isn't any advertising work about.'

'So you don't do this all the time.'

Elliot put down his cup.

'Don't look so surprised. Hardly any photographer does this full time.' He looked at her with curiosity.

'How about you,' he asked. 'Is this something you do for a living?'

Frances took a deep breath.

'I'm not a model,' she said. 'I'm doing these pictures today as a sort of favour. For a friend.'

The photographer laughed.

'He must be a very close friend.'

She thought about telling him to mind his own business but changed her mind. If I'm going to go through with this thing, she reasoned, I need all the help I can get.

So she told him about Richard. She described how she met him and how she got involved with the party scene, the Abner scene and the naked picture scene.

'So you see,' she said, 'I'm stuck. Everyone's counting on me to do this session.'

Elliot looked at her kindly.

'How about you,' he asked. 'Do you want to do it?'

'Not much,' Frances said.

Elliot walked over to where the camera was set up and started fiddling about with the lights. Then he called Frances over and stood her up against a backdrop.

'You've got what it takes,' he said slowly. 'You're tall and you're slim without being skinny. Your bones are good, your teeth don't need any work and that hair, you could do almost anything with it and it would look great.'

He stopped talking for a minute. Then he bent down and stared at her through the camera lens.

'Turn around,' he instructed her. 'Give me your profile.' Satisfied, he stood up.

'Okay, relax,' he said. 'Tell me, did you ever think of doing fashion work. Straight modelling, I mean. You'd be a natural for it.'

Frances shook her head. 'I never thought of it,' she said. Then with a sudden resolve she put the whole idea behind her.

'Would you mind telling me,' she asked him, 'where I have to go to get changed. If we don't do this session soon, I have a feeling I won't do it at all.'

Elliot smiled and indicated a cubicle at the edge of the studio floor.

'You'll find a wrap in there. When you've taken everything off, put it round you and come back here.'

She did as she was told, then shivering slightly she stepped back under the lights.

'What do you want me to do now?' she demanded.

Elliot sighed, and indicated a rug thrown in front of the backdrop.

'Take off the wrap, then spread yourself along that.' He paused. 'And try not to look as if you're about to be raped. *Macho*'s trying to sell the fantasy of the eager playmate.'

Frances undid the wrap very slowly. She was reminded of days at the English seaside. She could have been a little girl at Bognor Regis again, putting off the moment when she finally had to get into the freezing, green water.

It took her five minutes to take off the covering and when she put it down, she raised her arms in front of her body to hide herself. It was a protective gesture. Elliot did his best to ignore it.

'Get down on the rug,' he said without taking his eyes from the camera, 'and while you're arranging yourself, think about your boyfriend. Do what you did for him when he took those test shots. They were bloody sensational.'

She shuddered. She and Richard had been making love minutes before those photographs were taken. Elliot didn't know that, or if he did, she was in worse trouble than she thought. She eased herself down onto the rug keeping her legs tight together. Then she leaned back on her elbows. She was surrounded by white light. Hot and merciless and inquisitive. Though she knew there was only her and Elliot Burke in the room, she felt as if a thousand prying eyes were upon her. She felt a tremor of alarm. That's how it will be, she thought. Anyone who chooses can see me like this. Anyone with the price of a magazine in his pocket.

The photographer interrupted her thoughts.

'You're looking fine,' he said. 'Try raising your left shoulder and bringing one of your legs up a fraction.'

Frances had a vision of herself lying on the rug. In the pose Elliot had put her, her breasts swung naked and provocative and she was arching her back. She knew the camera couldn't see between her legs. Then the picture she had of herself was replaced by another. It was a photograph of an Italian girl in this month's magazine. She was lying on a rug as well and her legs were akimbo.

Frances cast her mind back to last month's picture spread. And the month before. And the month before that. Every girl, without exception, had parted her legs for the camera. It seemed to be a stock pose. A mandatory position. Frances knew beyond any doubt she would have to do the same. Slowly and with great deliberation she got

149

up from the rug. Then she picked up the wrap and put it around her.

'I can't go through with it,' she said. 'Not for you. Not for Richard. Not even to save my life. I'm not that sort of girl.'

Then without waiting to hear Elliot's answer she walked over to the changing-room and closed the door. When she came out Elliot was turning off the lights.

'I should tell you I'm sorry it didn't work out,' he said, 'but I'm not. You're a beautiful woman, Frances. You can do better than this.'

He put his hand in the pocket of his jacket and took out a card. On it was his name and telephone number.

'If you ever decide to try modelling, straight modelling I mean, then call me. If I'm not there, my service can find me.'

Frances waved the card away.

'Thank you,' she said, 'but I'm not the modelling type. I'm a wife. Or a girlfriend. That's the way I fit into the scheme of things.'

Elliot took her bag out of her hand, opened it and tucked his card into the lining.

'I appreciate what you're saying,' he told her. 'But life could change. Or you could change. If that happens, you'll know where I am.'

19

Frances had crossed Abner just once before, three years ago in Scotland. It had been a small thing, but he had reacted badly. Frances remembered how he had tried to get rid of her and she worried. What would he do, she thought, when she told him there was no picture session? She sighed and started to run a bath. She'd manage to talk her way out of the situation somehow.

It took her more than an hour to get ready and she didn't begrudge the time. She wanted to be at her best tonight. When she had finally finished with herself, she stared at her reflection in the mirror. She was wearing a dress of embroidered black lace, and it clung where it touched. Her blonde hair was straight and parted in the middle and the only jewellery she allowed herself were the diamond earrings Richard had bought her for her birthday.

I look expensive, Frances thought. The expensive property of a rich man. It was the second time that day she had regarded herself objectively. The first time she had been a centrefold. Now she was a kept woman. Neither incarnation made her feel comfortable.

Abner was waiting for her in the drawing-room. It was at the centre of his apartment and something of a showpiece. At one end by a picture window was a white grand piano. At the other was a marble fireplace. All the furniture was low and white and modern and the walls were covered with abstract paintings. Frances felt uncomfortable in the room.

Her style belonged to Queen Victoria and King George and what she was seeing now had nothing to do with that. It was a creation of the future. Of Andy Warhol. She simply didn't understand it.

Abner handed her a martini then told her about dinner. He had arranged a simple meal in his private suite. Vichyssoise, Lobster Thermidor and Strawberries Romanoff. He hoped it met with her approval.

Frances didn't know what to say. She had expected to be taken to Le Cirque or The Four Seasons. The anonymity of an international restaurant was something she had counted on. In an expense account atmosphere, surrounded by people, she could flatter and charm. A private suite was something different. For the first time she was aware of being alone with the tobacco tycoon and she wished she'd chosen a less extravagant dress. Then she fastened her mind on her immediate problems. The photographic session, or rather the lack of it.

She put on her best smile.

'Dinner alone sounds like a lovely idea,' she said.

If the drawing-room put her in mind of Andy Warhol, Abner's private dining-room reminded her of a New Orleans bordello. Everything seemed to be in shades of rose. The patterned wallpaper, the velvet curtains, the lighting. Right in the centre of the table was an arrangement of candles and flowers. It was the final touch in a room that was already too ornate. What on earth has he got in mind, she wondered.

She decided to find out. Once more she attempted a smile.

'I'm impressed with all this trouble you're taking,' she said. 'But shouldn't you save it for some other girl. Someone less attached.'

Abner helped her into her seat and poured some wine into her glass.

'Before we start talking about you and I,' he said smoothly, 'shouldn't we get this afternoon out of the way.'

Frances felt nervous.

'You mean what went on in the studio.'

'I mean what didn't go on in the studio.'

Frances racked her brains for something to say and came up with nothing. Damn, she thought. Before I walked in here, I had everything off pat. I wasn't brought up to take my clothes off, I didn't know what I was getting into, the whole thing was a mistake. In the afternoon light with her hair tied back, it all sounded perfectly reasonable. But here, surrounded by this decadence, dressed in black lace, she could never get away with it.

She looked across the table at Abner. His face was closed and very dark.

'I'm sorry,' she said with an effort. 'I just couldn't go through with it.'

Abner leaned back in his chair.

'You surprise me,' he said. 'I wouldn't have thought that would have been a problem for you.'

'Why do you say that?'

Abner didn't change expression.

'Because of what you got up to with Richard. The game with the blindfold.'

Frances felt cold in the over-heated room. 'How do you know about that?' she asked.

Abner looked at her across the rim of his wineglass. 'How do you think?'

There was a long silence while Frances wrestled with her feelings. We're not enemies, she reasoned with herself. We got off to a bad start but that was a long time ago. She summoned up her courage and returned his gaze.

'I think you've got some explaining to do,' she said.

She had expected him to soften. He had offered her a shoulder to cry on once when Richard had pushed her too far, but any resemblance between the man she had known in England and the man who confronted her now was purely coincidental. Tonight Abner Morris was playing it tough.

'What do you want me to explain?' he asked. 'The reason

you joined in with Richard's sex games? I could see that coming a mile off. The minute you decided to turn a blind eye to them it was only a matter of time before you got involved.'

Frances began to get angry and as she did some of her terror evaporated.

'I seem to remember,' she said with some heat, 'that you were the one who told me to turn a blind eye. You said yourself that Richard needed things I couldn't provide.'

Abner smiled and lit a cigarette.

'But you had to compete, didn't you? You had to show you could give as good as all the other sluts. Only you didn't have the stomach for it.'

He looked at her face, then he rang for the waiter to bring the next course.

'Don't look so injured,' he said. 'So you don't enjoy orgies. It's not the end of the world. Not in my book anyway.'

Frances stiffened.

'What's your book got to do with it?'

Abner leaned back in his chair and gave her the once-over the way he did when they first met. Only now he wasn't looking her over with a view to buy. The transaction, she realised with a sickening certainty, had already been completed.

'Didn't Richard tell you?' he questioned quietly. 'You belong to me now.'

'Since when?'

'Since you packed your bags and got on the plane to New York. It's over, Frances. The big romance is yesterday's news. I would be surprised if lover boy isn't already moving in your successor.'

She wanted to cry. To give in to all the pain she had been bottling up over the past few months when she knew it had been going wrong. But she stopped herself. She still had Abner Morris to deal with.

'So Richard's passing me down the line,' she observed. 'How neat. How very very convenient. There's only one problem. Nobody asked me how I felt about it.'

Abner came around to her side of the table.

'Look, I know you're upset and I don't blame you, but I'll make it up to you.'

Frances was furious now, her rage cleansing away everything else. She imagined Richard and Abner calmly discussing her over a nightcap.

'Frances is getting a bit restive. I can't seem to make her happy any more.'

'Don't let it worry you, old man. Send her over to me. I'll soon sort her out.'

What maddened her more than anything else was their sheer arrogance. The assumption of these two men that they could decide her future the way they planned the next issue of the magazine.

Frances looked Abner in the eye.

'How the hell do you think you're going to make anything up to me when I don't find you attractive,' she said coldly. 'Face it, Abner. You're just not my type.'

He leaned forward and put his hand around her waist. Then he pulled her towards him.

'We'll see about that,' he said.

Frances knew she should have kept her nerve. It was insane to lose control, yet something inside her exploded and as it did, the whole room seemed to go into slow motion.

She saw herself reach for the candelabra in the centre of the table. When it was in her hand, solid and heavy, she swung it up high over her shoulder and brought it crashing down onto her assailant. It connected with the back of his head, sending the candles scattering in all directions. Abner went down.

It was like one of the prize fights she had seen on television. One moment the champion was up and coming.

The next he was out for the count. Frances knelt down beside Abner, the reality of what she had done finally coming through to her. There was a trickle of blood on his forehead and his face looked very white.

Christ, Frances muttered, I hope I haven't killed him. She felt for a pulse in Abner's neck and found one. Then she thought, what now? In a few moments, or a few hours, Abner would come round and she didn't feel like being there when that happened. Unsteadily she got to her feet and walked over to the door, and out into the hall.

There was an elevator there. Frances pressed the call button and got in. Within minutes she was in the lobby of the building. From where she was standing she could see the street and suddenly she had a violent longing to be free of this place, to be free of Macho, to cut herself off from the last three years of her life.

So strong was the force propelling her forward that she quite forgot that all she was wearing was a lace cocktail dress and a pair of skimpy sandals. When she was half-way round the block she felt the cold wind against her skin and realised where she was. She stopped in the doorway of an apartment building and opened her handbag. Inside it was the card she was looking for. It gave Elliot Burke's telephone number and an address in Greenwich Village. 'Your life could change,' he had told her. 'If it does you know where to find me.'

20

Elliot Burke poured Frances a drink and listened to her story. He made up a bed in the spare room of his apartment and put her up for the night. First thing in the morning he went out and bought her a change of clothes, then he sent her on her way.

If Frances had been anyone else, he would have started her on a modelling career. She had the looks and the poise, but she wasn't anyone else. She was the girl who refused to pose for Abner Morris. The girl who had brained him when he tried to make a pass at her. If he tried to help her now, there would be no more work for *Macho* or *Penthouse* or *Playboy*. Word travelled fast in New York and Abner had friends. No, Frances would have to paddle her own canoe. All Elliot could do was dust her down and put her on the next plane home.

Elliot took his leave of Frances at eleven-thirty in the morning. In her bag was her return ticket to London and the taxi fare to Kennedy Airport. She decided to walk for a while. The craft shops and galleries of the Village were just opening their doors and most of the bars were already in business. It was a bright, crisp winter day two weeks before Christmas and the smell of festivity was in the air around her. Frances stopped off at a street vendor and bought herself a bag of roasted chestnuts, then she wandered the streets, window shopping.

For some unknown reason, she felt happier than she had done for a long time. She hummed a song that was popular on the radio and reflected on the irony of life. She should have been in tears now, weeping over the loss of her lover, the loss of her lifestyle. Somehow it didn't worry her and she realised that she didn't love Richard after all. It was over, Frances thought, the night she had found him making love to two models. She had just needed time to get used to the idea.

She glanced at her watch and discovered it was nearly lunchtime and suddenly she felt hungry. She had hardly eaten yesterday and the thought of salt beef on rye with coleslaw on the side was irresistible. What the hell, she decided, I'm not in any hurry to get anywhere.

She found a place on the sidewalk half way between a deli and a café. It was too cold to sit outside, so Frances got herself a table in the window and ordered a sandwich. While she was waiting she saw a tall man with cropped curly hair staring at her. Frances couldn't understand what he was looking at. She was in blue jeans and tennis shoes, her face was scrubbed clean of make-up and she had tied her pale blonde hair back into a ponytail.

Two tables away Sam Kurnitz felt as if he had been struck by lightning. For the tenth time he stared across at the blonde girl. It has to be a mistake, he thought. A trick of the light. But if she had been alive today, Leah would have looked like that. The image. His mind went back ten years to Israel, to his wife and his baby son playing among the olive groves of the Kibbutz. They had made their home there while he was away with the army and he remembered how Leah had objected to it.

'It's so dull there,' she protested. 'Full of farmers and country clods. What the hell will I do?'

'Behave yourself,' Sam had teased her. 'Make friends with the other women. Look after our son.'

Behind the teasing he had been deadly serious. Israel was a dangerous place, and their flat in Tel Aviv was no place for a woman on her own. The settlement in Galilee was a better bet. His son, David, would have children of his own age to play with.

They had lived there just eighteen months when the

Kibbutz suffered its first and only raid. Sam was away on manoeuvres when it happened. He came back to find a bomb site where his home had once been. Both Leah and David had been wiped out. Obliterated. Not even their bodies, not even their bones had been left to remember them by. All Sam had was the memory of a willowy blonde with haunted blue eyes and a defiant smile.

He looked at the girl in the window. She had the selfsame smile. Tough, with a hint of mockery. As if someone had bruised her, but she was damned if she was going to let it show. Suddenly he knew he had to go across and say something to her. But what? I've seen you somewhere before. You remind me of my dead wife. She'll probably call the cops.

He took a swig of his beer. You're being an idiot, he told himself. A sentimental fool. Out of the corner of his eye he saw the girl get up. In a second she'd be gone. Out of the café. Out of his life. He couldn't let it happen.

Suddenly he was on his feet and standing beside her.

'Look, you don't know me,' he said, 'but my name is Sam Kurnitz. I'm in advertising.'

Frances gave him a slightly damaged smile.

'What's that to do with me?' she asked politely.

Sam's mind raced through the possibilities. Are you free for dinner? I want to know you better. I think I've fallen in love with you. I'm going to make you a star. His mind froze for a second. I'm going to make you a star. That was it. The solution to all his problems.

He turned to her.

'Go and stand over there for a minute. In the doorway. I want to get a better look at you.'

Confused, Frances did as Sam asked, then his face broke into a grin.

'Perfect,' he said. 'You're just the girl Coast-to-Coast are looking for.'

Frances came back to where he was standing.

'Do you mind telling me what all this is about?'

Sam nodded. 'If you've got five minutes, I'd be delighted.'

Frances had five minutes. Actually she had a lifetime, but she wasn't telling that to a stranger who was trying to pick her up. No matter how handsome he was. She allowed him to persuade her to stay for a cup of coffee.

For the next half hour Sam told her about the new campaign his agency was doing for Coast-to-Coast airlines. They knew how they wanted to sell it. They even had a catchy slogan. What they didn't have was the girl. The Coast-to-Coast stewardess who was going to breathe life into the commercials. Then he'd seen Frances and knew without a shadow of a doubt that she was the one they had all been looking for.

Frances wanted to believe him. Last night she had actually been looking for a modelling assignment, but something stopped her.

During the past few years too many men had told her lies, led her along paths that ended in culs-de-sac or tears. How was she to know this plausible stranger wasn't just another con man looking to exploit her? She offered him her hand.

'It's been nice meeting you,' she said, 'and I'm tempted by what you say. More than tempted. But I'm in a hurry and I've got a plane to catch. So it has to be no.'

Before Sam could say anything else, Frances got up and hurried out of the café. Outside a yellow cab was cruising by. She hailed it, jumped in and told the driver to take her to Kennedy Airport, international departures. Then she leaned back in the seat and thought about Sam Kurnitz. As she did, she experienced a feeling of loss. If only I'd met you three years ago, she thought, things might have gone further. We might have been friends, or even lovers. She remembered the intensity in his eyes, the way the crisp black hair curled around his collar. Then she laughed at herself. What am I thinking about? I've just got out of one disaster with a man and already I'm talking myself into another.

The taxi deposited her outside the main terminal and she swung through the doors and straight into a queue. There was a plane leaving for London at five o'clock and already the tourists were crowding round the check-outs. Frances stood in line for half an hour before she got her boarding pass. Then she jostled her way past a group of students bearing back-packs into the airport bar.

I'll have one more drink on American soil, she promised herself, then I'll start thinking about reality. Already the future loomed up in front of her. She supposed she'd go home to her parents or perhaps her flatmate, Sophie, would take her back if she had a job to go to.

Gloom descended on Frances. How on earth was she going to live her life? There was no way she would work in one of the clubs again. No matter what they were paying. She'd tried that life, sampled everything it had to offer and all she had to remember it by was a sour taste. She wanted no more to do with that world. She wanted to forget she had ever inhabited it.

The man standing next to her interrupted her thoughts. 'Do you want a drink, or are you still sticking to coffee?'

Frances turned and found herself face to face with Sam. The man in the deli.

'What are you doing here?' she asked. 'I thought you said you worked in an ad agency.'

Sam grinned. 'I do. That's why I followed you here.'

Frances didn't know what to think. The man was either a first-class lecher or he really was what he claimed to be. She stood half way between hesitation and acceptance. Sam took over. He ordered a bottle of champagne, then took the drink, the glasses and Frances to a free table.

At four o'clock they had finished the first bottle and

Sam had just got up to fetch another, when Frances put a hand on his arm.

'There's no need to get me drunk,' she said.

Sam looked at her despairingly.

'How else am I going to keep you here?'

Frances sighed and tried to look patient.

'You're not,' she explained. 'My plane leaves in an hour and in about ten minutes they'll be boarding. So thank you for the champagne. It's been lovely knowing you. Maybe next time I'm in town I'll look you up.'

Sam turned round and gathered her in his arms.

'Don't go,' he pleaded. 'Please don't walk out on me.'

A thousand clever replies formed in Frances's mind and died on her lips. There was an urgency about this man, a need so real that she had no defence against it. She disentangled herself and sat down.

'You've got to be a hell of an advertising man to try this hard to find a model.'

Sam passed a hand across his hair.

'I am a hell of an adman,' he told her. 'The best. Ask anybody who works for me. They'll tell you.'

A new comprehension dawned. 'You actually own your business. You didn't tell me that.'

Sam laughed, relaxing slightly.

'Who the hell did you think I was? Some Johnny-come-lately on the make. The name is Sam Kurnitz, creative director and chief shareholder in Kurnitz and Greene. What further proof do you need that I'm on the level?'

Frances looked at him wearily.

'You don't need to prove anything to me. I'm sure you're genuine, but what makes you think you can stop me on the way home to London, tell me to drop everything and fall in with your plans?'

Sam took a deep breath.

'Do you have anything better to do?'

This is lunacy, Frances told herself. I've met this man

twice in my life. Apart from the fact that he runs an ad agency, I've no idea of who he is, I don't even know if he's married.

It was as if he could read her mind. 'I'm a widower,' Sam told her. 'I live on my own in a big empty apartment on East 56th. I'm not out to rape you or to murder you or to take advantage of you in any way.

'If you come back to the city with me, just for twenty-four hours, I'll put you up in a respectable hotel. Compliments of the firm. Then I'll take you in and introduce you to the team working on Coast-to-Coast. I'll even take you into the aeroplane. How does that sound?'

Frances regarded the tall untidy man sitting opposite her. He was wearing jeans and a sweatshirt and looked as if he never combed his hair. Yet there was something honest about him, something real that she had never encountered before. This man would never lie to her, she knew that already. He wouldn't cheat her and he wouldn't sell her short.

Before she could change her mind, she was on her feet.

'I'll give you twenty-four hours,' she said. 'Then if I feel comfortable with the situation, I'll decide what to do next.'

21

Louise bent over her lightbox and squinted hard at the transparencies. She had to hand it to the new English photographer, David Bailey, he took a great fashion shot. Now all she had to do was come up with an ad.

She sighed. It was a mixture of weariness and contentment. Her first few weeks at Kurnitz and Greene had been better than she expected. She had been given a desk in the bullpen, the room where all the work was created and she could hardly believe it. It was the best lit, the most expensively furnished, the busiest area in the entire agency.

When she registered her astonishment at this state of affairs, the other creatives who shared the space looked at her as if she was mad.

'Where did you work before you got here?' they demanded. When she told them they laughed and called her a refugee.

'Didn't anyone tell you about the creative revolution?' they asked her.

At first Louise was irritated with them. She hadn't been successful long enough to laugh at herself and she was damned if anyone else was going to do it. As the days went on, she realised that something had been going on in her business. Something that gave status and respect to people like her, the men and women who dreamed up the advertising. There were restaurants in the city that catered for them and their ilk, bars where they hung out. They even dressed a certain way – arty but expensive. Louise felt as if she had come home. For the first time in her working life she didn't have to fight to make herself understood.

Everyone in the agency knew what she was talking about. Some of them even liked what she had to say, and one or two of them, the really good ones, improved on her ideas.

Louise felt as if she had been in a deep slumber for most of her early twenties and now, like some enchanted princess, she was finally waking up. All she needed to complete the picture was the prince.

She had hardly seen Sam since she started work. He had been away filming a commercial in L.A. and when he got back he had gone straight to work on an airline campaign. It was an important piece of business for the agency. A prestige account. Louise shrugged. Let him fight his own battles, she thought. Sooner or later he'd find his way to her door.

She straightened up in her seat and saw someone else was staring at the Bailey shots. A tall, blonde girl in scruffy blue jeans and a faded anorak. She's probably a messenger from one of the studios, thought Louise, and she grinned at her.

'These are some shots, aren't they?' she said. 'I've a feeling the guy behind the camera will make his name one of these days.'

The girl smiled and Louise noticed there was something shy about her.

'Where I come from,' she said softly, 'David Bailey is already quite well known.'

When she heard the accent, Louise realised what it was about this girl. She was British. They never like to push themselves forward, she thought scornfully. A New Yorker would have told me I was patronising or out of date.

She was about to say something, when she saw Sam approach.

'So you've met Frances,' he said cheerfully. 'What do you think?'

Louise thought quickly. So she wasn't a messenger.

165

Maybe she was Sam's kid sister. Then she took another look at the woman. No, she was too blonde, too Aryan to come from Sam's parentage. Besides no man looked at his sister the way Sam was looking.

Louise decided to take no chances.

'What am I supposed to think?' she asked. 'Nobody told me what Frances is doing here.'

Sam came up behind the blonde and put an arm round her shoulders.

'Frances is our new Coast-to-Coast girl,' he said. 'She's going to do great things for the agency.'

There was something proud about the way he said it. Almost as if he had invented the girl himself. Louise narrowed her eyes. The agency isn't the only thing Frances is going to do great things for, she thought.

Frances turned towards Sam. 'I think I've taken up enough time in here,' she said. 'Everyone looks far too busy to talk to me.'

Sam walked round to where Louise was sitting.

'Are you very tied up at the moment?' he asked.

'Reasonably,' she said. 'Why?'

'Because I want to ask you a favour. I'm trying to talk Frances into doing our Coast-to-Coast commercials. And I'm making headway. Only there's a slight complication. When I ran into this girl she was on her way back to England and she wasn't keen on staying because somebody had snatched her suitcase. You're not going to believe it, but all the poor kid's got is what she's standing up in.'

Louise examined the girl, noting the pale blue eyes and the fluffy blonde hair. I've heard some tall stories, she thought, but this one takes the prize. She's either run away from college or she's had a row with her boyfriend. She looked up at Sam.

'Are you asking me to lend the girl a change of clothes? Or do you want me to take her shopping?'

There was an edge to her voice that she didn't bother to disguise. Sam stopped smiling.

'I'm not asking you to do anything,' he said. 'I wouldn't dream of taking you away from your work. What I wondered was, can you spare your assistant for a couple of hours. Frances needs somebody to show her the shops. Somebody who lives here.'

Now the whole picture started to fall into place. Sam had picked up this homeless bimbo and for unknown reasons had decided to buy her a whole new wardrobe and give her a job. Louise looked at him in despair. If I knew you better, she thought, I'd tell you there were cheaper ways of getting a fuck. Even from her. She reconsidered. Particularly from her.

She gave him her sweetest, most tolerant smile.

'I'm sorry,' she said, 'but Holly's off sick. I've got a suggestion, though. Why don't you send your secretary out shopping with Frances?'

Sam started to walk away from her desk.

'You know as well as I do,' he said crossly, 'that Ginger's rushed off her feet.' He ran his hands through his untidy black curls and looked distracted. Then he pulled himself together and seemed to come to a decision.

'I'll take her shopping myself,' he said. 'That's what I'll do. Why didn't I think of it before?'

He took hold of Frances's arm. Propelling her towards the doorway.

'If we hurry,' Louise heard him say, 'we can get across to Bergdorfs before lunch. Then if we find something decent, I'll take you down the road to the Four Seasons. You'll enjoy the Oak Room. Tell me, has anyone ever taken you there before?'

Louise turned her attention back to her lay-out pad, but try as she could, concentration eluded her. She doodled aimlessly on the blank sheet. Then she looked down and saw what she was drawing. In front of her were a series of

167

sketches of a thin girl with long pale hair. In one of them she was wearing jeans, in another a ball gown and in the last sketch Louise had drawn, she was dressed as a bride. Complete with a veil and a long train.

She put down her Pentel. I'm being foolish, she told herself. This Frances, whoever she is, is a nine-day wonder. A cheap pick-up with no place to go. Sam will forget about her the minute he's bedded her. Men always do.

But she didn't feel happy and when two of her colleagues asked her out for lunch, she made an excuse and turned them down. I'd have been better off taking Frances shopping myself, she thought grimly. At least I might have found out what she was up to.

Frances shivered, but it wasn't the December frost that was causing the tremors. It was the fact that she might be found out.

The dark girl knew she had been lying. Frances could tell from the way she looked her over. You're a phoney, the look said. Nobody took your luggage away.

From the moment she had allowed Sam to bring her back to the city a change had come over her. That morning in Greenwich Village she had started to walk away from her past. Then she had no idea who she was or who she wanted to be. By the end of the day, when Sam had checked her into a small hotel and bought her supper in Chinatown, she started to get a clearer view of herself.

The woman that she saw was the woman that Sam saw. An English lady fallen on tough times. After that the lies came naturally.

Frances told him she had been in New Jersey visiting friends and when she took the train to the city, somebody had stolen her bags. She had relegated her involvement with Macho, with Richard Gregory, with Abner Morris to the scrapheap. They belong there, she told herself. They were my one mistake. The blind alley in my life.

In her mind Frances reverted to the girl she had been, the second daughter of an English baron, sharing a flat in Fulham, marking time before she got married. When Sam asked her about her life, she told him about Archie and the dramatic way she avoided marrying him.

Told over dinner in a New York restaurant, it was an appealing story. It made Frances look young, high spirited and innocent. She thought for a moment about the last dinner she had eaten. She was wearing a black lace dress then and being passed from one man to another. No, Frances decided. She did not want any part of that experience to taint her now.

Sam took her back to her hotel later on and made no move to come to her room. The next morning a taxi collected her and took her to Sam's agency. Now he was buying her a whole new wardrobe. This latest development bothered her. She had let Richard buy her clothes, but then she had been Richard's property. She did not belong to this Sam Kurnitz. Not yet, perhaps not ever. She decided to make a stand.

Sam laughed aside her objections.

'Think of the clothes as part of your salary,' he told her. 'If you're going to be the Coast-to-Coast girl, you have to look the part.'

So they went into Bergdorfs and he dressed her in Chanel. Frances had never been put together by a man before and normally she would have rejected the experience. She knew perfectly well what suited her and what she was dressing for.

Now, because her new persona was still unformed, she had no idea how she wanted to look. So for the first time in her life she let someone else create her, and was astonished by what she saw.

The bouclé suit with its braiding and expensive gilt buttons made her look older and somehow affluent. She knew Sam saw her as a lady, but it was an American's vision of how a lady should look. Frances wondered how she could live up to it.

Sam made her keep the suit on, and when he came to pay the bill, the saleswoman complimented him on his choice.

'Your wife looks lovely,' she said.

Frances expected Sam to set the record straight. Instead, he simply smiled.

'Doesn't she just,' he replied.

He took her to the Four Seasons where he had arranged to meet his partner, Clay Greene, for lunch. The moment Frances walked into the dark, wood-panelled room, she was glad they had been to Bergdorfs.

Richard had never eaten in places like this; it was strictly a haunt for grown-ups. Businessmen in dark suits met here to sink their martinis and talk about their clients.

In an adjoining room there was an azure swimming pool but the scenario was exactly the same. Powerful men on large expense accounts talking turkey.

Clay Greene had reserved a table in the main room and was there waiting for them, half-way through his first drink.

Frances was surprised when she saw him. She had expected a slick adman in a grey flannel suit. What she got was a good-natured blimp. To say Clay was fat would have been an understatement. He was vast, house sized with three chins supporting a face that had once been boyish.

When they reached the table, he wobbled to his feet and greeted them with unrestrained enthusiasm.

'When you told me you'd found a gorgeous girl, you weren't kidding,' he said. 'Charlton Peters is going to eat you up.'

Frances looked curious.

'Who is Charlton Peters?' she asked.

Sam grinned and organised a round of drinks.

'The man who's paying for this lunch, your suit and our new advertising campaign. A couple of weeks ago, I promised to find him the classiest dame in New York, and if Clay's face is anything to go by, I seem to have succeeded.'

They ate steak for lunch, followed by strawberries out of season and French cheese.

'Do you always live like this?' Frances asked them, curious. Clay roared with laughter.

'Of course we do,' he said. 'Self indulgence is one of the few compensations of being in our business. That and the girls.'

Sam punched him playfully. 'I wouldn't let Tiffany hear you say that.'

He turned to Frances. 'Tiffany is Clay's wife. Maybe if you decide to stay here, you'll meet her.'

How cosy, Frances thought. Here I am dressed in thousands of dollars' worth of Chanel, sitting in one of the smartest restaurants in New York, talking to the chairman of the board about his wife. Her mind went back to the day before when she was spending her last few dollars on a salt-beef sandwich. It already seemed like a different world.

22

That night Sam cooked Frances dinner in his apartment high above the Hudson River. The first thing she thought when she walked into his vast drawing-room was that she had never seen such anonymous luxury.

The place bore all the marks of an interior designer: the thick carpet, the low white furniture, the old masters that looked as if they had been painted yesterday. To order. I'd do it differently, she thought. I'd put curtains across that plate glass window. And replace the modern junk with some real furniture. Then she stopped herself. This isn't my apartment, she thought, and Sam isn't my husband. He's my employer. Only he didn't act like an employer, or even an agency chief. He fussed around her, fetching drinks and bowls of olives. Asking her what dressing she wanted on her salad. Despite all her good intentions, Frances started to feel at home.

She was wearing her jeans and sneakers again and she hadn't bothered to make her face up or pin her hair back. Something in her resisted being made over. She knew one day she would have to settle for an identity, but right now she was still exploring herself and the possibilities in front of her. She looked at Sam relaxing on the sofa across from her. He was drinking a beer and talking about the latest movies on in town and Frances was surprised at how comfortable she felt. All the other men, the men she had known before him, had frightened her and set her on edge. This man did neither, and she knew with a certainty and a confidence she had never felt before that they would be lovers before the evening was out.

I want to know you, Frances thought to herself. I want

to find out where you came from and what your father does. I want you to tell me about your wife, the girl who made you a widower.

Sam was candid with her, holding back nothing and as the night wore on Frances finally found her way to him.

He was born in Hungary, the son of a Jewish violinist. Sam's father, Alex, played in the National Symphony Orchestra until Hitler invaded. Then he fled with his family to America.

They settled in New York, in Brooklyn, and through the musicians network, Alex Kurnitz found work. First in the Met and finally when he got too old and frail, teaching. He tried to teach the violin to his son, Sam, but the boy had no ear for music. His fascination was reading. Not the usual boys' books about the war, or spy thrillers. Sam loved the classics. He also loved playing ball games – baseball, softball, basketball.

'I thought my son would grow up to be an intellectual,' his father complained. 'Instead he became an athlete.'

In spite of his father's misgivings, Sam followed in the family tradition and became a thinker. By the time he was twenty-three he had majored in English Literature. He had also completed his first novel. Then in 1967, Israel started to fight the six-day war. For Sam the time for thinking had come to an end.

There was only one thing more important to Sam than writing or basketball and that was his Jewish identity. When his parents fled from Hitler they left behind them generations of cousins and aunts who had not been so lucky. Many of the remaining Kurnitz family had been herded into concentration camps. Sam remembered seeing their photographs in family albums, sepia tinted, sad faced – forever lost. He vowed then that the Kurnitzes of the future would not meet a similar fate, and when Israel came under threat, Sam responded by enlisting in the army.

He spent five years in the Middle East, and for him

it was a time of growing up, for he realised just how cosseted and protected he had been in Brooklyn. Even the ball games he had played had been childish. The worst that could happen to you in a game of baseball was that your team lost. In war, you died, and the men who didn't lose their lives were often crippled.

Sam was wounded twice. In one skirmish on the border he was hit by a piece of shrapnel and temporarily blinded. In another engagement he was blown up and nearly lost a leg. It took him six months to recover this time, and it was while he was in hospital that he met Leah. She had come to visit her brother who was in the bed next to Sam's, and because Sam's family were all in America, she spent time with him as well.

When Leah's brother was finally sent home, she still kept coming to the hospital. By this time she had fallen in love with the young American. When Sam was able to walk without crutches, they were married and a year later, their son David was born in Jerusalem. Sam and Leah were together for three years. The happiest, most blessed years of Sam's life. When his wife and child were killed on a Kibbutz, Sam realised that his time in Israel had come to an end.

He was twenty-seven when he came back to New York. A sadder man and a tougher one. He no longer saw his future as a writer of literature. He wanted a flashier success than that, something that would blot out the memory of the past five years. He chose advertising.

Rosser Reeves at Bates spotted his potential and put him to work as a copywriter. It was there he teamed up with another young Jew, Clay Greene. The combination of Sam's words and Clay's pictures won prizes from the word go. Together they could sell the hell out of everything from frozen pizza to life insurance. It took them eighteen months to be headhunted by Doyle Dane Bernbach. A year or so after that they set up in business for themselves.

It was nearly two in the morning when Sam finally finished telling his story, yet Frances still had one question to ask him.

'Did the advertising business help you forget about Israel?' she said.

Sam passed a weary hand over his eyes.

'If you're asking if it helped me forget about Leah, the answer's no. I've been round the tracks with any number of girls in the past ten years, but no matter how hard I tried to fall in love, there was always something missing.'

Frances smiled.

'Maybe you were trying too hard,' she said.

Sam looked at her for a long moment, and in that time he saw Leah's eyes looking out of Leah's face. It's an illusion, he told himself. She's a different girl from a different continent. For pity's sake, she's not even Jewish. Yet his whole being ached to take her in his arms. To find out where the illusion ended.

He got out of his chair.

'If I try not to fall in love with you,' he said, 'will you stay with me tonight?'

Frances didn't hesitate.

'If you want me to,' she said.

Sam led her through to the bedroom, and despite all the experiences of the past three years, Frances felt shy. She sensed Sam wanted more than just a sexual encounter and she wondered if she had more to give.

She looked around her, noticing the sparse furniture, the dark outlines of the bed, the windows half open, billowing out the curtains. Then he was in front of her blotting out the room. Obscuring everything except the warmth of his breath, the touch of his skin.

Frances didn't know that kissing could be so sexy. With Sam it wasn't a prelude, it was an act in itself. Frances stood in the circle of his arms, until Sam gently pulled away from her and started unbuttoning the front of her blouse.

175

Gently he pulled her jeans down over her hips and pushing the shirt from her shoulders, he unhooked, unclasped until she stood naked in front of him.

He took her over to the bed, taking his own clothes off as he went. Then once more he folded her in his arms and covered her with his body.

As Sam's flesh touched hers, Frances felt the stirrings of hunger. Then he kissed her again, and as he did, she felt herself open.

There was no foreplay. They were both too experienced for that, and too hungry. Instead Sam found the cleft between her legs and thrust himself inside her. Her body answered him with a passion she never knew she had. Rising and falling to his rhythm, leading him, then following him until they both found what they were seeking.

They slept twined around each other and Frances woke with the taste of Sam on her lips, the smell of him on her body. He opened his eyes a split second after she did and they laughed at their timing.

They spent the next week laughing with each other and at each other. During that time Sam recreated Frances as the Coast-to-Coast girl. He had her silky blonde hair cut into a swinging bob. He brushed the shadows from her face with paint and powder and he pushed her into a succession of tailored suits and smart little dresses. Everybody from the airline chief to Clay Greene thought she was adorable.

It took six weeks to create the commercials and the artwork for the posters.

And somewhere during that time, Frances moved imperceptibly from the Gotham Hotel to Sam's apartment. They had been living together for nearly two weeks when Frances told him it was time she went back to England. Sam was appalled.

'You can't go,' he protested, 'I was just getting used to you.'

She was exasperated.

'You're used to your fridge and your baseball kit. I'm not just another possession, you know.'

Sam looked at her over his morning coffee.

'Why not?' he asked.

She turned to leave.

'Because you don't own me.'

Years before when a client had turned down an ad he had written, Sam had threatened to throw himself out of a window. Now it wasn't Sam's creation that was being turned down. It was Sam himself.

'What do I have to do to make you stay?' he asked her.

'Give me something to do,' she said. 'A job. A hobby. A reason to be here. I can't make a career out of being the Coast-to-Coast girl.'

He considered throwing himself out of the window again. Then he had a better idea.

'Would marrying me give you enough to do?' he asked.

23

Frances Buckingham plighted her troth to Sam Kurnitz at the United Nations building three weeks after Christmas. Frances's mother complained that the suddenness of her daughter's announcement gave her no time to think out what she was going to wear, or to alert the rest of the family. Frances was overjoyed. There's no way I'm going to have a repeat performance of the last wedding, she thought.

She told her mother she had been swept off her feet by an American eccentric who insisted on marrying her there and then and she didn't intend to miss the opportunity.

The explanation suited her parents as Frances knew it would. They had imagined that after Archie and Richard Gregory, no man would ever make an honest woman of their daughter. Whatever Sam Kurnitz was like, even if he had two heads, they were prepared to bless the union.

When they met Sam, they were pleasantly surprised. He was handsome, he was rich, he had one head and he had beautiful manners. Fiona Buckingham was so relieved that her daughter was going to marry a gentleman she was even prepared to forgive him for being an American. Not that anyone else who came to the wedding was forgiven for it. Sam had invited all his friends, half of his office and most of his clients.

Fiona Buckingham, who expected to dominate the occasion, found herself swamped by it. She was used to seeing men in morning coats. In Manhattan nobody wore anything like that. All the men, even the bridegroom, wore tuxedos. Shiny new tuxedos that looked as if they had come from the shop that morning. The women were just as strange. There was no family jewellery on display here. Americans seemed to have an exaggerated fondness for paste. Everywhere Fiona looked she saw great shining globs of it. At the ears, at the wrists, on the lapels. The women here look like Christmas trees, she thought. So vulgar.

Fiona Buckingham was further discomfited when the wedding party moved to the Tavern on the Green. Sam had hired the restaurant for the night and the management had gone to town with fairy lights and banks of white-coated waiters bearing jeroboams of champagne. The Englishwoman cast her mind back to other family wedding receptions. They were held at Claridges, normally at tea-time and the hotel served tea and little sandwiches along with the drinks. This touch added dignity to the occasion. Something the Tavern on the Green had great need of, she observed. She saw her daughter coming towards her and softened slightly.

She had never seen Frances look quite so happy. There was nothing contrived about it. She was hardly wearing make-up and her headdress had seen better days but there was a radiance about her, a glow that went beyond expensive trappings.

As soon as she saw her mother, Frances put her arms out, and if Fiona hadn't taken a step back she would have been smothered in a hearty embrace. As it was, mother and daughter compromised with a light, dry peck on the cheek.

She hasn't changed, Frances thought. She's still trying to be more royal than the Queen Mother. Aloud she asked,

'Do you have everything you want, Mother, or can I get you something?'

Fiona Buckingham looked impatient.

'For heaven's sake stop chasing about will you. I'm perfectly happy. All I want now is to sit down somewhere and have a conversation.'

Out of the corner of her eye, she saw a bright birdlike woman threaten to descend on Frances.

'Preferably a private conversation,' she added.

Frances took hold of her mother's arm and steered her towards an empty table. Then, resolutely, she sat down with her back to the room and gave Fiona her full attention.

'What did you think of the wedding?' she asked breathlessly. 'Didn't you think it was marvellous having it at the United Nations? And this? I've never seen such a spread. They really pulled out all the stops for us tonight.'

Fiona Buckingham compressed her lips into a thin line.

'It's a little showy,' she said coldly, 'but I daresay it's what your husband wanted.'

Frances felt hurt. In her heart she suspected her mother wouldn't understand Sam or New York, or the advertising business. But she could have tried, she thought. She could have pretended. It *is* my wedding day, after all.

She looked at her mother in despair.

'I'm sorry you don't like Sam. I know it was silly of me, but I hoped you'd get on.'

The older woman didn't change her expression. Instead she reached out across the table and helped herself to a glass of mineral water. Then without consulting Frances she poured out a second glass and pushed it towards her.

'I don't dislike the man you married,' she said quietly. 'Neither your father nor I have anything against him. If anything we're eternally grateful he did the right thing. Since that dreadful business with Archie we were both at our wits' end worrying about what was going to happen to you.'

She took a sip of her water.

'At least that's all over now. You've got someone who's going to look after you. He's not the ideal choice by any means, but as long as he makes you happy, we'll accept him.'

Frances glowered across the table at the forbidding sight of her parent. All her life she had been overawed by her. She was so grand, so aristocratic, she always knew beyond a shadow of a doubt exactly what was correct. Until tonight. And tonight, for some unknown reason, she looked out of place. She didn't look wrong. Anyone could see Fiona Buckingham was dressed for a wedding. But here, against the background of Sam's friends she looked dowdy. And old. Like a country cousin or a retired family retainer.

Frances felt rebellion grow in her heart. You might deign to accept Sam, mother dear, she thought. But there's no law in the land that says Sam has to accept you.

Frances spent her honeymoon in the Maldives, and when she wasn't snorkelling or toasting herself in the sun, she was busy making plans. Now she was married she had finally found the identity she was looking for. She was going to be a wife and a mother. The mother of all mothers.

'I want a big family,' she informed Sam one evening when they were drinking rum and water and watching the sun go down.

He smiled at her fondly.

'Isn't it a bit soon to be taking on all this responsibility?' he asked. 'We've only just settled together. Don't you want to get to know New York, make some friends, go out and have a little fun before you tie yourself down?'

Frances thought about Richard Gregory and Abner Morris and shook her head.

'I've had all the fun I can handle in one lifetime. Now I want to focus on something real. Something that means something.'

She looked at her new husband with his serious brown eyes and curly dark hair that was just beginning to go grey around the temples.

'I'm not explaining myself all that well,' she said. 'What

181

I'm trying to say is that everyone needs a centre to build their lives around. You have your work, which is more than just going out and earning a living. I know you love advertising. Every time you talk to me about it, even when you're just repeating office gossip, I get flashes of how you feel, and I want to feel that passionate about something too.'

Sam came close and put his arm round her.

'Have you thought about taking a job or studying for a career maybe? There are some terrific courses at Columbia, you know. You could learn to be a journalist, or an art restorer. Maybe even a writer, a real writer, I mean. Like I used to be.'

For a moment Frances let her mind explore the possibilities. She wasn't afraid of working. She'd proved that to herself early on. But she didn't want to work because there was no point any more. She'd already made up her mind about her future.

'Columbia's a lovely idea,' she murmured. 'I'll send our sons there.'

Sam sat up straight, as if somebody had stung him.

'No you won't,' he shouted. 'Our boys will go to Yale.'

For a second Frances looked surprised.

'I'm sorry,' she said, 'I didn't realise you felt so sensitive about your old college.'

Sam turned round to face her and for the first time Frances saw pain in his eyes. Pain and regret.

'I didn't go to Yale,' he said softly, 'my family didn't have that kind of money or those kind of connections. No, I went to Columbia like all the other kids from Brooklyn Heights but that doesn't mean that my son will go there. If I've worked for anything with this job I'm supposed to love, I've worked to give a future to my children. I want my sons to go to Yale and my daughters to go to Vassar. Then maybe, with a little bit of luck, they'll grow up with some of their mother's class.'

Frances reached out for him then and held him tight against her heart, so that he couldn't see the tears in her eyes.

'Class,' she said savagely, 'what does that give you? The right accent, the right clubs. The ability to know which knife and fork to pick up. On the scale of human values, I'd put it right near the bottom.'

Clumsily she wiped her hand across her face.

'You can buy class,' she told Sam. 'What I want for my children is something better than that. I want them to have strength. The sort of strength that comes from the inside. Strength and compassion and humour that comes from suffering.'

She pulled away from Sam and looked him in the face and the tears no longer embarrassed her.

'I want the children I have with you,' she said finally, 'to be everything you are. If they make that grade, then you can send them to any damn college you like.'

Sam's apartment had two spare bedrooms and the smaller of the two, which overlooked the park, Frances made into a nursery. She had the decorators paint the room yellow so that way she could fall pregnant with either a boy or a girl and it wouldn't matter.

Sam teased her about the room.

'Hadn't you better get pregnant before you make all these plans?' he asked.

But Frances wouldn't listen.

'I'll be pregnant soon enough,' she told him, 'and when I am, I might not feel like preparing a nursery. If I start doing things now, at least I'll be good and ready.'

She found out the name and whereabouts of every baby shop in New York and when she'd chosen a crib and a carry-cot she spent her time looking at baby clothes.

Clothes were the one item she couldn't buy for they had to be either blue or pink. Until she was three months' pregnant and had had the right tests, she wouldn't know which colour to get.

There were other ways to pass the time. Frances bought books of names and argued endlessly with Sam over what they might call the latest addition to the family. If it was a boy she wanted him to be Charles. Charles Gerald, the second name after her father. Sam wanted something more American. Warren, Frank and Woodie were the names he came up with. Whenever Sam talked about boys' names, Frances changed the subject.

'What if we have a girl?' she would query.

So it went on. Choosing, discussing, dismissing. Frances made long lists of possible names which she pinned up on the noticeboard in the kitchen. One column of names were those she favoured, the other column were Sam's. Both of them changed their minds almost daily and over the months the lists were covered with crossings out and substitutions.

Sam went through a phase of foreign names. Martine and Françoise and Horst started appearing on the kitchen noticeboard until Frances put a stop to it.

'I'll make a deal with you,' she told her husband. 'Our baby has one English name and one American name. But that's it. I want nothing to do with France or Mexico. We don't live in those places.'

She enrolled them both in a course of baby classes. The idea was that they went along and listened to a course of lectures on pregnancy, birthing and caring for the newborn child.

'I want you to be there in the delivery room when I give birth,' she told him.

Sam started to get concerned. It was four months now since Frances announced she wanted to have babies. Four months of making love every night and every morning.

184

Usually after Frances had taken her temperature and recorded it on a chart. Yet despite all that, nothing had happened. His wife was not pregnant.

That fact alone made all the lists and elaborate plans somehow redundant. Without telling her he visited his private physician and had himself checked out. The report that came back three days later reassured him. He was one hundred per cent normal, one hundred per cent capable of fathering a child.

A month later Frances started to get edgy.

'I'm only in my twenties,' she said. 'I don't know of any reason why I can't have a baby, but it just isn't happening.'

Sam told her about going to see his doctor and about the result. Then he suggested she paid him a visit herself.

For the first time Frances faced the possibility that she might not be able to have a baby. It frightened her – more than frightened her – it terrified her. Without the possibility of having a family her life seemed pointless somehow. Worse, her marriage seemed pointless. She forced herself to see Dr Goldberg. If she had a problem, then it had to be faced, faced and coped with. That had always been the way she lived her life and marriage hadn't changed her attitude.

Sam's doctor did every test Frances had ever read about and some she hadn't, and at the end of it he gave her a clean bill of health.

'Technically,' he told her, 'you could become pregnant tomorrow.'

Frances regarded him suspiciously.

'Then why aren't I?' she asked him.

The private doctor smiled and looked at her over his glasses. He had attended hundreds of young women like Frances. Nervy, impatient girls who demanded too much, both from themselves and their bodies.

He indicated towards the chair in front of his desk

185

and told Frances to sit down. Then he leaned back and considered.

'The reason you can't get pregnant,' he told her, finally, 'is that you're trying too hard. You're channelling all your hopes and all your fears into this one event. That's too much pressure, even for a splendid twenty-four-year-old body like yours.'

He smiled.

'Think of it like this. You're making your womb sit the equivalent of a college finals exam every month and your insides have got nervous. In the normal course of events, your body doesn't have to sit an exam to conceive. It's something it does naturally without thinking, without preparing, without getting tense beforehand.

'Do yourself a favour, will you? Go home and forget all about having a baby. Don't keep a temperature chart. Don't make love to your husband when both of you don't feel like it. Just relax and leave your body to its own devices. It won't fail you, I promise.'

Frances looked unconvinced.

'If I do as you say,' she asked him, 'when can I expect to conceive?'

Goldberg pulled a face. This impatient girl hadn't listened to a word he'd been saying.

'I told you, you can't expect anything. You might get pregnant tomorrow. You might have to wait another year. If you're unlucky you might have to hold on for another two years. So if I were you I'd stop thinking about it and get on with your life. There's nothing else you can do.'

Dr Goldberg's consulting rooms were five or six blocks away from the apartment and because the day was fine, Frances decided to walk home. Almost as soon as she hit the street she wished she'd hailed a taxi, for that day Manhattan seemed to be full of young mothers and their babies. They were in push carts and carry cots. Some of them were big enough to toddle and they skipped along the sidewalk, clutching onto whoever was walking them.

Frances was near to tears as they passed her by. What was it the doctor said? 'If you are unlucky you could wait as long as two years before you start a baby.' Right now two months seemed an eternity. But two years? She could be a different person in two years. She might not even want a baby by then.

She stopped herself. This is silly, she thought. In two years' time she'd still be as much in love with Sam as she was now. That she was sure of. What in the world could make her stop wanting a baby? Her mind went through the possibilities.

Sam had suggested she take a course at Columbia, maybe even get a job, and her mind ground to a halt right there. If she took a job at this moment in her life, it would have to be really something, and any job that was that interesting would lead to a full-time career. It had to. The journalism course Sam suggested would get her into magazines. If she took fine arts, which she was already half considering, she'd end up in a gallery. Once she'd taken that step, she knew she would be lost.

All her attention would be claimed by paintings and people making deals. This new world she'd ventured into would suck her in and consume her. If that happened, she'd lose her need to build a family. She'd seen it happen to other women.

As she walked along Park Avenue in the last of the summer sunshine, Frances took stock of herself. She was pretty, she knew that, and she would pass that prettiness on to any child she had. She was tough. To have come through the last few years she had to be. She knew she wasn't stupid, but she had something else as well. It was this that made her ache for a child.

She needed to teach. Everything she had experienced in her life, she wanted to pass on. If she had a son, she would show him how to endure setbacks and disappointment, as she had, so he would be strong when he went out into the world. A daughter she would raise to know compassion and have the ability to understand the minds of her enemies. For a moment Frances thought about the black-haired girl she met in Sam's office. Louise Tragos. She had been an enemy. Her instincts had told her that right from the first moment she had set eyes on her.

Which is why she played dumb and kept out of her way. Louise Tragos could think what she liked about her, but if she didn't know about her, if she gave her nothing to go on, then she couldn't hurt her.

My daughter will find enemies like Louise, Frances mused. People who take against her for no reason she can understand, and as she grows up, I'll show her how to deal with them.

As she grows up . . . The last thought hung heavily on her mind. As who grows up? she wondered. There isn't a she. There isn't any anything. Not yet. But there will be. Frances's natural optimism began to take control of her.

Two years maximum. So I have to wait two years. If that's the worst thing that's going to happen to me, I don't think there's really too much to worry about. I'm married to Sam. I'm living in a penthouse in the middle of the most exciting city in the world. Maybe it's time I started to enjoy it all.

24

It was a hell of a way to start a year. United Foods gave the agency all thirty million dollars' worth of its business, Brian Elder asked Louise to have lunch with him and Sam and Frances celebrated their first wedding anniversary.

Louise didn't know how she felt about the last event. So she put it on hold, the way she had done for the past twelve months, and concentrated her mind on business.

Her gamble on Kurnitz and Greene had paid off. The information she provided them with gave them the edge they needed for the Teatime account. They won the business and Sam's work on the chocolate cake finally managed to stop the decline.

After that it was only a matter of time before the rest of the business came into the agency. Louise had lost interest in the account a long time before that. In the past year she had managed to carve a niche for herself at Kurnitz and Greene. Her clients liked her, she looked like picking up another award and Clay Greene had started asking her out to lunch. She knew it had nothing to do with the colour of her eyes. She had the fat man's attention because he thought she was bright. A couple of times when he was in a bind over a problem, she had given him the solution and now he came to her for advice on a regular basis.

Louise's friendship with Clay advanced her up the ladder and she frequently found herself in conference with both partners, shaping ideas, working out strategies for the future. When United Foods walked in the door, both Sam and Clay turned to her yet again for help.

Instead of helping them with their problems, as they expected, she gave them one of her own. Brian Elder. He had called her and asked her to have lunch with him, and he had made it plain he was looking to move to Kurnitz and Greene.

'Wasn't he the kingpin on the United business,' said Clay, looking curious, 'the one you worked with at Acker and Stein?'

Louise nodded. She didn't think she'd hear from him again. And now here he was, turning up like a bad penny.

'Was he any good?' Clay pressed.

'I've no idea,' Louise replied truthfully. 'His family knew the owners of United Foods. Brian always seemed to do whatever he wanted with them.'

Sam looked thoughtful.

'He still didn't manage to stop the business walking out of the agency door when the advertising went bad.'

Louise thought about the last campaign she wrote for United Foods, the one that put Teatime on the skids and she started to feel guilty.

'No client man, no matter how much clout he has, can argue with bad sales figures.'

'That's not the point,' interrupted Clay. 'If this Brian Elder was any kind of man he would never have let the advertising through in the first place. That last Teatime campaign was an absolute disaster. Why didn't he spot it before it was let loose on the client?'

Louise smiled nervously. 'You're talking about Teatime . . . the happiness cake.'

'You bet that's what I'm talking about. It was one of the worst dogs I've ever seen. I just hope I never meet the guy who wrote it, because I'd have to tell him so. I couldn't help it.'

Louise thought quickly. She had been the architect of that disastrous campaign and if anyone ever told Clay the fact her stock would fall through the floor. She sighed. She no longer hated Brian Elder and the revenge she'd planned for him seemed petty and childish now, but she couldn't move him to Kurnitz and Greene, even if she'd wanted to. He knew too much about her. Professionally, as well as personally, and what he knew about her professionally could hurt her. She got to her feet.

'I'll keep my date with Brian,' she told them, 'and I'll tell him there isn't any room for him over here.'

Brian Elder had chosen Gallagher's because Louise couldn't put a price tag on it. It was one of those Irish steakhouses with wood-panelled walls and a cosy clubhouse atmosphere. The sort of place a gentleman would go to on his day off. For Brian Elder every day was a day off.

Acker and Stein had paid him off the day United Foods walked out the door. It didn't surprise him. Madison Avenue had always been short on sentiment and as this was a turning point in his career, Brian reviewed his options.

He was two years off forty, which meant he was still employable. Just. For most of his working life he had been in a blue chip agency. This last fact gave him room for manoeuvre, for although a shop like Acker and Stein would no longer consider him, there was a whole raft of agencies that would welcome a man like him. The second division.

The prospect of lowering his sights made Brian cringe, but there was one thing worse: doing without an expense account. Because he could no longer charge his lunch or his drinks he was slumming it in Gallagher's, but this state of affairs wouldn't last. All he had to do was convince Louise that Kurnitz and Greene needed him, and he'd be back at the 21. Where he belonged.

He walked up to the mahogany bar and ordered a Scotch on the rocks. Then he gazed moodily at the smoke-tinted walls and wondered where the hell Louise had got to. She was already twenty minutes late and he wasn't used to being kept waiting. Not by a woman and certainly not by Louise. He looked at his watch for the tenth time and cursed under his breath. She's doing this on purpose, he thought. She knows I'm looking for a job and she's making me grovel.

Never mind, he decided. Once I'm back in harness, once I'm calling the shots on United Foods again, things will be different. Then we'll see who's boss.

He drained his drink and ordered another from the wise-cracking bartender. That's another thing that's going to change, he thought. Where I'll be drinking in future, the help will know its place.

He saw Louise coming half way through his second Scotch. She was thinner than he remembered and there was an air of success about her he hadn't seen before. It make her look tough, he thought, almost masculine. He squared his shoulders and stood up straighter as she walked through the door.

Louise embraced him. Kissing the air ineffectually on either side of his face, gushing about how nice it was to see him again. He thought, cut it out will you, it's me you're talking to. Brian Elder. The man who fucked you in his spare time for three long years. But Brian went along with Louise's game. He had been too politely brought up to do anything else. They ordered lunch at the bar then walked through to the bustling dining-room and got down to business.

Brian wanted to know all about Kurnitz and Greene. How many big-time consumer accounts did they handle? What was the relationship between the account men and the creatives? Who was going to be responsible for all the United Foods business that had just come in?

As Louise talked Brian reflected he would have got a better picture of the agency by reading *Ad Age*. She was holding out on him. He knew her well enough to sense that, but he wondered why.

Their affair was history. He knew that. He realised it

would take a month or so to talk her back into his bed. But there was more to it than that – it was almost as if Louise had a secret she didn't want to tell him. He decided to get to the bottom of it.

Brian was too experienced a negotiator to attack her head-on. Instead he tried the oblique approach. He asked her about the work she was doing. She always liked to talk about the problems she had on the drawing-board, and nothing had changed.

For an hour they talked about broadcasting regulations and marketing strategies and finally, when they were both on the coffee, he got down to cases.

'I want to follow the United Foods business into Kurnitz and Greene,' Brian told Louise. 'You know that already, otherwise we wouldn't be sitting here. It looks to me like there could be some sort of problem with that plan. Do you mind telling me what it's all about?'

Louise hadn't expected that. Brian was never this blunt, this direct. He must be desperate, she thought. She took a sip of her coffee.

'You're good at what you do,' she said slowly. 'More than good. United Foods is something you know inside out.' She took a deep breath. 'But Kurnitz and Greene isn't for you. It's not your kind of shop at all.'

Brian looked at her steadily.

'Do you mind telling me why?'

'It's creative. It's loosey-goosey. It hasn't got the structures you're used to. You'd be like a fish out of water.'

He took a pack of cigarettes out of his jacket pocket and made a big deal of selecting one. Then he produced a lighter and lit the end. He didn't make any attempt to offer Louise anything.

'Bullshit,' he said quietly. 'I've been around long enough to know where I fit and where I don't. And it would take more than a bunch of long-haired creatives to cramp my style.'

He leaned forward across the table and looked at her hard.

'Do me a favour, Louise, will you? Tell me the real reason why you don't want me around.'

She started to panic. The campaign she'd written for Teatime had done him out of a job, and she knew he was bright enough to have figured that one out by now. She took hold of the coffee and refilled both their cups. The manoeuvre gave her the time she needed to think.

Brian knows I wrote the dog of a campaign she reasoned, but he doesn't know I did it on purpose.

Her companion cut into her reverie.

'You and I go back a long way,' he said softly. 'Is that what's bothering you?'

'You're talking about our affair,' she said.

He nodded. And at that moment Louise knew she was in the clear. It hadn't occurred to Brian that she might have double-crossed him. All he could think about was the fact that he had conquered her and that she might be ashamed of it. She stifled a smile.

If that's what you want to think, she thought. It gets me off the hook. She cast her eyes down.

'It wouldn't look good at my new office, if they thought you and I had been involved.'

'Come off it, Louise,' he said roughly, 'nobody has to know about that.'

She didn't alter her expression.

'I know about it,' she said, 'and because of that it wouldn't be comfortable having you around.'

Brian took a long drag on his Marlboro. 'So that's it,' he said. 'Because you want everyone to think you're a lady now, I don't get the job.'

The anger started to rise in him, and his face became cruel.

'The problem with you, Louise, is that you're a slut from the slums and you think that an expense account and a few designer clothes can make people forget that fact. Well they can't. Nothing can do that. You can brush me under the carpet, you can even pretend you don't come from the Bronx, but people will still know who you are. Because you'll always give yourself away. It's the little things that do it. The way you eat your steak, that ambition of yours, even the way you act in bed. You're too hungry, Louise. Too greedy. You want too much, too fast.'

He stood up and took a handful of bills from his wallet. Then he threw them on the table.

'Don't worry about me,' he said. 'I'll survive. I always do. No, if I were you I'd start worrying about yourself. It's not comfortable having an enemy like me. Not when I catch up with you – and I will catch up with you, Louise. Depend on it.'

25

Tiffany Greene put the finishing touches to her upsweep, then she sprayed it hard. Had anyone's hand come into contact with her hair, it would have felt like touching spun sugar, but that night nobody was going to touch her hair. Not even her husband. Particularly not her husband.

Tiffany was the kind of woman that could be seen lunching every day in the grand restaurants of Manhattan. If she was meeting a girlfriend she could be found in Lutèce or La Côte Basque or the Russian Tea Room. If her date was with a lover it would probably be Orsini's or the River Café. If she was just seeing her husband she made for the Oyster Bar in Grand Central Station. With a husband she could let rip and enjoy her food to the full. There were some consolations being married to Clay.

When Tiffany was feeling blue she would count these blessings. There was the house in Westchester with its acre of garden. Membership of the country club. The yacht in Monte Carlo, the charge accounts at Bloomingdales and Henri Bendel.

The masseuse, the private gym instructor. And there was rent-a-chef. For this last blessing she was truly grateful. Especially tonight.

Tonight Clay was having a business dinner. Worse, he was having an agency dinner. Tiffany groaned inwardly. She would be forced to spend the entire evening being bored by his oh-so-worthy partner Sam Kurnitz. Sam and that dreary little wife of his. Stop this, Tiffany, she told herself. Pull yourself together and think nice thoughts. It's important to be good to the girl. Make her feel wanted. She thought about Frances with her floaty blonde hair and hand-span waist. So fragile. So precious. So English. Tiffany put aside her distaste the way she put aside the dark meat of a crab or the charred bits of a barbecue. She would charm Frances because Frances was the only way she would ever get through to Sam, and get through to Sam she must.

She stood up and surveyed herself in the full-length mirror. She had dressed in Ralph Lauren tonight. A black velvet dinner suit with a short straight skirt and a fitted jacket. It was the trim that lifted the outfit into the million dollar class. The Jackie Onassis class. The designer had surpassed himself and his prices that season and added a touch of mink to the jacket. It was soft and shiny the way only good mink is. It swooped from the top of her neckline to the point of her waist.

Tiffany twirled around in the mirror checking the line of her rear, the fit of her sheer stockings, the height of her heels.

You'll do, she told herself. For this shower, you'll more than do.

She walked through to her large airy dining-room and made straight for the table. As she had requested, the best silver was on display and the good crystal. She didn't expect these colleagues of her husband to understand or appreciate it, but it was out all the same. She had certain standards to maintain.

All her life Tiffany had been setting standards. In Orange County where she grew up, she was the most stylish girl in high school. Her classmates nicknamed her 'the Jewish princess'. She didn't give a damn: as long as she got the best bits of everything on offer they could call her what they liked.

It was the same when she came to New York. Her uncle, who owned a film production company, organised her a job as a secretary in the TV department of an advertising agency. The carping started again. The girls who worked there didn't like her because her clothes were better than anyone else's. The men gave her a mixed reception. The poor ones, the ones with no prospects called her a stuck-up bitch because she didn't have any time for them, but the powerful guys in the agency liked her well enough.

For a certain kind of man, Tiffany was very good news indeed because she tried so hard. Her rich father ensured she always looked terrific. She cooked like an angel, thanks to an early *cordon bleu* course. And she fucked like a stoat. Tiffany put this talent down to sheer application, allied to a powerful sexual appetite. After a year of working at the agency, her application had earned her a reputation. She was known as the Madison Avenue bicycle.

By the time she met Clay Greene there were very few men of any consequence she hadn't been to bed with, but it wasn't getting her anywhere.

Tiffany had one goal in mind. By the time she was twenty-one she wanted to be married and married to someone who earned a great deal of money or had inherited a packet. She didn't mind which. There was only one problem. No man she knew seemed remotely interested in settling down with her. Her admirers were perfectly happy to take her to dinner, to agency parties and to bed. Not one of them took her home to meet their parents. Too late, Tiffany saw where she had gone wrong. She should have been more exclusive.

There's only one thing for it, she thought. I'm going to have to lower my sights. After she made the decision, the first suitable prospect she latched onto was Clay Greene. In the normal course of events she wouldn't have considered him. He was fat, shy and he didn't head up an agency. But he had potential. Tiffany set to work on the potential.

She didn't succeed in making Clay lose any weight, but she gave him confidence and she taught him how to be ambitious. His talent did the rest. Within three years of meeting Tiffany, Clay had set up his own business with another creative guy, Sam Kurnitz. When Clay and Sam looked like making money, Tiffany helped Clay make his final decision. She allowed him to marry her.

It was a big Jewish wedding. One of the biggest in Orange County and her father parted with the money for the celebration because she told him he was making an investment in her future. When Tiffany said investment, she meant investment, she had seen to it that every contact, every marketing guy, every businessman with money to spend on advertising was at the synagogue.

Within eighteen months, four of the prospects in her sights had placed advertising business with her husband. She'd screwed every one of them to cement the deals. It had been worth it. She and Clay were going to the top and if it took a little humping to speed them on their way, then hump she would. With pleasure and with application.

Tiffany surveyed the grand room where she was standing. The fireplace had been imported from England and was chipped out of marble. All the furniture, from the sideboard to the satinwood dining-table, was genuine antique.

This is what it means to succeed, Tiffany thought. These possessions. This Ralph Lauren suit I'm wearing. The help I hire. As if to underline her thoughts a maid in black bombazine and the regulation starched apron appeared at the door.

'Two of your guests have arrived, Madam,' she said. 'I showed them through to the bar.'

Tiffany nodded her approval and hurried after her. The focal point of the Greenes' house was their oak-panelled bar. Other residents of Westchester served drinks in their drawing-rooms, some of them had bar areas in their conservatories. Tiffany and Clay had gone one better and converted their den into a Western-style saloon.

Everything was covered in rawhide: the counter where the drinks were served, the tops of the barstools, even the martini shaker. In the corner stood an old jukebox, the kind Tex Ritter had played in the Fifties. Clay, who was playing barman, was sporting a ten-gallon hat.

Frances had a tough time keeping a straight face. She had been to the house several times but the sheer vulgarity of the Greenes never failed to amaze her. She accepted a martini from Clay and asked who else was expected for dinner. On previous occasions she had met a camp fashion designer who wanted to dress her from top to toe in black leather, a dyed-blonde model who she suspected was a part-time hooker and a Hollywood film director.

'Tonight,' Clay told her, beaming from ear to ear, 'we've got a real treat in store for you. The agency's talent has decided to pay us a visit.'

Frances smiled politely.

'How nice,' she said. 'Tell me about him.'

Clay chuckled.

'It's not him,' he said. 'This talent's a gal.' He made a gesture with his hands like a figure eight. 'She's dynamite, and not just on the drawing-board. If you get my drift.'

The polite smile on Frances's face didn't falter.

'Does the talent have a name?' she asked.

'Sure she's got a name,' said Clay. 'She's called Louise. Louise Tragos. Sam must have mentioned her.'

Something clicked into place. A memory. And with the memory a slight feeling of apprehension. Frances had met Louise a year or so ago before she and Sam were married. Her mind worried at the memory. There had to be something about the girl that made her feel so nervous. Then she had it. Louise was the dark girl with the cynical eyes who wouldn't take her shopping. Francis shuddered. I'm not going to enjoy this dinner she thought.

Louise felt the same way. She hadn't wanted to dine with the Greenes. Of all the women in the world, the one she liked least of all was Tiffany, who, in her opinion, was a parasite. Unfortunately she was also the boss's wife and when she called, Louise was at a loss for a decent excuse to get out of having dinner.

'I've decided to give you a month's notice,' Tiffany said, 'so you'll have plenty of time to plan what to wear and who to bring.'

Louise didn't tell Tiffany that she had better things to do than plan her dinner outfits or her dinner escorts. Instead she gritted her teeth and called Mike Calder.

Her former partner at Acker and Stein was invaluable at times like this. He was gay, so there were no sexual complications, he was an old friend and he could talk advertising till the cows came home. For company dinners and industry get-togethers he was her permanent escort. I wonder how he'll get along with Tiffany, she thought.

She needn't have worried. Tiffany Greene and Mike Calder might have been made for each other. They both knew the same group of people, interior designers and media celebrities, and they both fed on the same gossip. Almost as soon as they arrived, Tiffany and Mike went into a huddle and Louise was left with her two agency bosses. And Frances.

From the word go, Louise knew the woman was suspicious of her and she couldn't figure out why. Sure, once upon a time, she'd had the hots for Sam but that was in the past now. Swept under the carpet with Brian Elder and all the others who came after him. Louise discovered she could take her pick of almost any man she set her sights on. All she had to do was incline her head a little, smile a certain way and it was a foregone conclusion.

There had been a well known male model, a newspaper editor, a visiting movie star. No man had been able to resist her. Except for Sam.

She looked at the English girl clinging possessively to her husband's arm. He's all yours, honey, Louise thought. I'm sure you deserve him a damn sight more than I do.

The maid came in and announced dinner. Saved by the

gong, thought Louise. With any luck I won't have to talk to her for the rest of the evening.

Tiffany's dining-table, however, made sure that she did just that. It was circular and designed for community conversation. Nobody could talk to their neighbour without being overheard and the result was that people took it in turns to hold the stage. Clay kicked off by talking about his experiences on a dogfood commercial. Sam capped the story with an anecdote about a tame gorilla in a photographer's studio. By the time the main course came on the whole party had loosened up.

I was worried about nothing, thought Louise. Tiffany isn't that bad and Sam's silly little wife seems to be keeping her opinions to herself. She accepted another glass of Château Latour and started to relax.

The dining-room, she noticed, had been prepared in much the same way as a film set. Even though they were coming into spring a fire had been lit in the grate and the flames cast shadows across the regency striped walls. Everywhere her eyes travelled there were flowers. Roses out of season.

Louise wondered how much the party had cost the Greenes. Out of the corner of her eye, she noticed Frances admiring one of the silver game birds on the table and, she thought, what the hell, what can I lose by being friendly?

'They're beautiful aren't they?' she said smiling at the blonde girl. 'I keep meaning to buy some really good silver but I never seem to get round to it.'

Frances stiffened imperceptibly. What you mean, she thought, is you've got more important things to do than waste your time in hardware stores. That kind of thing gets left to little wives like me. She glanced at the dark girl, poised and confident in her Italian knit suit. I'll teach you to patronise me, she decided.

'I don't have a problem with silver,' she told Louise. 'The day we got married I got shelves full of the stuff.'

202

The Greek girl did her best to look interested.

'How lovely,' she said. 'I hear the English stores stock some very fine pieces.'

Everyone at the table seemed to stop talking and Frances drew her breath in. It's now or never, she thought.

'My family don't buy that kind of thing,' she said, 'they inherit it.'

Louise looked startled.

'Forgive me,' she said, 'I'd no idea you were so grand.'

Frances smiled her best smile. Her social register smile.

'How could you possibly know,' she said, 'you don't come from my world.'

Louise put her wine glass down and leaned forward and when she next spoke there was a tension in her face that Frances hadn't seen before.

'What do you mean by that?' she asked softly.

Frances started to lose her nerve.

'I'm sorry to sound snobby,' she said, 'but the society I come from is full of stuffy old families who have known each other for generations. If you were one of us, you would have understood that.'

Everyone's attention was on them now. Frances glanced around the table. Sam looked worried. Tiffany looked interested for the first time that evening, but it was Louise who held her attention. The woman looked as if she was about to explode.

'I'm not one of you,' she said in the same soft dangerous voice. 'I'm a New Yorker. A New Yorker from the wrong side of the tracks. That's what you were trying to say wasn't it?'

Frances sat up very straight in her seat and started to say something, but Sam stopped her.

'Have some more wine, Louise,' he said, 'and stop being silly. You and Frances are different, there's no denying that, but there's no point in making a fuss about it either. I married Frances for what she is and I hired you for what you are – a damn fine art director, sweetheart. One of the best in the City. I admire you for that and I respect you too. We all do.'

Louise pasted a smile on her face, picked up her glass again and the conversation went back to normal. Almost.

For a long time afterwards the Greek girl sat stock still in her seat and brooded on what Frances had said to her and as she did Brian Elder's words returned. 'You're a slut from the slums,' he had said. 'No matter what you do, you'll always give yourself away.'

And she had. The snotty English girl had seen right through her. The Italian knit suit. The fifty dollar hairdo. The St Laurent earrings. None of them made any difference. To the discerning eye she didn't belong and never would.

Louise looked at Sam with his close cropped hair and dark glittering eyes. Sam who had reminded her of her achievements, Sam who valued her for them. So you admire me, she thought. I'm glad. Before very much longer you're going to do a damn sight more than just admire me and your dear little wife has only herself to blame for that.

26

It was Kitten Catfood that gave Louise the opportunity she was looking for. She, Sam and Clay were sitting around wondering how the hell they were going to sell the stuff when she had an idea.

Normally she would have scribbled it out on a piece of paper and pushed it across to Clay. The fat man was Sam's partner after all. The two worked as a team. But something made her hesitate. The Kitten idea was hers and it was a good one. There was no point in throwing it away. Instead of scribbling it down, she gave voice to her thoughts.

Sam picked up the notion the way a pitcher catches a ball and like a pitcher, he turned it round and lobbed it straight back. For the next half hour the two of them tussled and wrestled with the idea. Half a dozen times people came into the room with pieces of artwork, dockets to sign, questions to be answered. They needn't have existed as far as Louise was concerned or Sam. They were both totally immersed in what they were doing. The idea had taken over.

Clay, who had been through the exercise dozens of times before, stood back and let it happen. He wasn't bothered about Louise taking over from him. Kitten Catfood was a bitch of a project. If Louise could make it work, she was welcome to it, and to Sam. It would do him good to work with another art director for a change.

Louise started her campaign to woo Sam as subtly as she knew how. He wasn't like any of the other men she had known. For a start, he loved his wife, but that wasn't the whole story.

What set Sam apart from the rest was the thing that had drawn her to him in the first place. His integrity. If

Sam believed in something, he put himself on the line for it. He had gone to war for Israel because he believed in his Jewishness and he frequently went to war with his clients because he believed in his talent. Louise was staggered by his attitude. Advertising, the advertising she knew, wasn't a business for saints and heroes. It was a business for rats. Rats who knifed each other in the back when they got half the chance. Despite herself, Louise admired Sam. Not for his integrity but for his toughness. She knew that to play it straight in this business and get away with it, Sam had to be tougher than even she knew. This was what she was up against. A warrior who believed in truth and justice and true love and was prepared to defend all three to the death.

There had to be a chink in his armour, though. Some weakness that would lead him off the shining path and into a cul-de-sac. A cul-de-sac with a bed in it. Until Louise could find that weakness, she played it cool. For the time being she was content to play the friendly professional. At least it kept her close to Sam.

The catfood campaign was an ambitious project. There were posters, magazine ads, press ads, trade ads and television commercials. Keeping up the volume of work occupied all her waking hours. Sam's waking hours as well. The two of them took to spending their lunch hours together and the cocktail hour before going home.

Louise had been used to advertising's watering holes — downstairs bar at the 21, the Four Seasons. Sam wasn't into any of that. He liked Charlie 'O's on the corner of 48th Street which he called the most stylish Irish pub in New York. Louise learned to admire the blow-ups of booze lovers that covered the walls of the black and white restaurant. She learned to drink saki in out-of-the-way Chinese joints and she got to know every decent deli in the city. For a lot of the time, Sam wasn't interested in sitting around in restaurants.

'My brain functions best when I'm on the move,' he told her. They would walk for hours in Central Park, munching on bagels, talking catfood, talking advertising.

Sometimes when they ran out of ideas, they would talk about themselves. Louise told Sam about her childhood in Kingsbridge. Her Greek Orthodox father who worked as a florist. Her mother who wanted her to marry a local boy and have babies. Sam was intrigued.

'Now I understand you better,' he told her. 'There is no way you could turn out the work you do if you didn't come from a place like Kingsbridge. How else would you know how the real people think?'

Louise turned to Sam and frowned.

'I may know about the real people,' she said, 'but I'm not one of them. Not any more. I've come a long way since those days.'

There was something about the way she said it that bothered Sam. It was too passionate. Too bitter.

He broke his brisk stride and took her arm.

'You worry too much about what other people think of you,' he said seriously. 'It doesn't matter a damn what suburb you grew up in or who your parents are. What matters is the way you are right now. The way you think. The things you care about. What kind of person you are. All the rest is so much garbage.'

Louise thought of Frances with her cut-glass accent and grand parentage. Try telling that to your wife, she thought.

27

Frances had thrown herself into New York the same way she had gone about her baby plans. She saw all the shows on Broadway. She went to every cocktail party Sam was invited to – some she went to even without Sam when he was working late. And she learned the names and the layouts of all the chic restaurants in town.

She didn't know them at first hand since Sam only visited that kind of expense-account joint during the day when he was with clients. With his wife, he preferred little neighbourhood places where they could talk and enjoy the food. That didn't stop Frances reading the listings in *New York* magazine and imagining how they might be. In her mind she lunched at Maxim's and Orsini's and Le Cirque. On very special occasions she was invited to intimate little parties in their private rooms.

One of her private fantasies was to belong to the society of ladies who lunch. She could afford to dress the part and she certainly had the right shape for expensive designer clothes, but there was one problem. She didn't know anybody who lunched. She knew women who ate between the hours of twelve and two-thirty. That was different. The women who Sam introduced her to ate at midday because they were hungry and that wasn't the kind of woman she wanted to know. The kind of woman she wanted to know lunched in order to be seen lunching. It was a kind of hobby. A frivolous, decadent pursuit – almost an art form.

For weeks on end Frances combed New York searching for this elusive creature.

Once, when she was really desperate, she made Sam take

her to Le Cirque in the middle of the day so that she could see them in action. It was then that her husband solved her problem.

When he had finally got her to explain why he had been dragged away from his office to a restaurant he despised, he roared with laughter.

'You can't really want to waste your time with a crowd of middle-aged air-heads.'

Frances's eyes took in the room. In every direction, everywhere she looked, the place was swarming with them. They were lifted and manicured, coiffed within an inch of their lives and the ones who hadn't been to the hairdresser that day were wearing hats.

This was the society she wanted to get into. Sam had called them air-heads. Well maybe they were but Frances had nothing to do, nothing to occupy her mind until her baby came along and to her these women looked like the good time she was in search of.

Frances turned to her husband.

'Sam,' she said in a small voice, 'would you really mind if I ran with that crowd for a bit. They're not doing any harm to anybody and they do seem to have a lot of fun.'

He looked hard at the slender blonde he had married. There was something very determined about her but it was a determination tinged with naivety. They'll eat her for breakfast, he thought. Then he started to smile. So what if they do, he reasoned. She might learn something and it will take her mind off the empty nursery.

'Of course I don't mind you having some fun,' he told Frances. 'I want you to get around a bit. So I'm going to arrange for you and Clay's wife to spend some time together.'

Frances hesitated, confused.

'You're talking about Tiffany,' she said. 'I thought she spent all her time in Westchester.'

Now Sam really did smile.

'Are you insane?' he said. 'The only time Tiffany sees the suburbs is on Sunday afternoon and not even then if she can wangle an invitation to the city.'

He took hold of Frances's hand.

'Listen, I'll have a word with Tiffany and maybe you two girls can get together for lunch. I know she'd love it.'

Tiffany did love it, though not for the reasons Sam imagined. She had little interest in the English girl, except as a means of getting to him – which is how Frances found herself with a new best friend.

The first time they met, Tiffany arranged a rendezvous at the Russian Tea Room. This is more like it, Frances thought. With any luck I'll get to grips with Manhattan after all.

She dressed herself up in a suede trouser suit Sam had bought her for her birthday, then she took an extra half an hour with her make-up. When she was completely satisfied with the result, she took a taxi to the restaurant on West 57th.

It was everything she imagined it would be, only better. The food magazines had told her the place was lined with banquettes. What they didn't say was that they were in bright red leather, or that the rest of the place was decorated in pine green so that the moment you walked in, you felt you were in the middle of a Christmas celebration. They didn't tell you anything about the buzz the place had either. Everywhere Frances looked there were movie moguls sitting talking money, famous actresses blowing kisses to the passing crowd and women in hats. For a moment she was completely overawed. Then she got a hold on herself. She was the wife of a well-known advertising genius, wasn't she? Not some out-of-work shopgirl. She caught her reflection in the plate-glass doors that framed the entrance where she was standing and she saw standing in front of her a skinny, leggy girl in an expensive suede suit. Frances didn't often spend much time looking at herself and, as always when she did, she was surprised. The girl she saw in the plate glass door was prettier than she thought and much younger. I look like a schoolgirl out for a special treat, she thought. Damn it, I wish I'd worn the Chanel suit.

A waiter decked out in a red tunic and shiny black boots showed her over to a banquette. Then he asked her what she would like to drink. Once more she felt like a schoolgirl.

'I'll just have a Perrier,' she stammered, 'I'm waiting for a friend.'

The waiter raised an eyebrow and looked questioningly at her.

'Are you sure you won't have a little Russian vodka?' She blushed to the roots. Of course, how silly she was.

She spent all her time reading *Gourmet* magazine and she'd completely forgotten that everybody who patronised this place came here for the vodka. It was practically the house speciality.

'I'll have a Stolychnia,' she said quickly, and when it came she downed it in one. She was damned if a waiter was going to patronise her.

Three vodkas later Frances started to get worried. There was no sign whatever of her lunch companion. She thought about calling Tiffany's home, then she remembered she didn't have her diary. You don't go to meet a social-ite in a fashionable watering hole clutching your life's filing system. After the fourth vodka, she decided to throw caution to the winds. She would consult the waiter. Trying to look unconcerned, she signalled him to come over.

'I'm meeting somebody called Mrs Greene,' she told him, 'and I can't seem to find her. Did she make a booking here by any chance?'

The waiter who had very black hair slicked down behind his ears made a note of the name and went to look at his list of reservations. Two minutes later he came back shaking his head.

'We have no Mrs Greene anywhere in the book,' he told her.

'But you must have,' Frances insisted. 'I remember her telling me she had her own special table here.'

Still the waiter shook his head. 'Maybe she uses another name,' he said.

Frances began to get hysterical.

'She hasn't got another name,' Frances protested. 'Her name is Greene. Tiffany Greene.'

The waiter's face suddenly cleared.

'Why didn't you tell me that in the first place?' he said. 'Of course there is a booking for Tiffany. I took it myself early this morning. Only here she is never Mrs Greene, she is only Tiffany. If you are her friend, she should have told you that.'

He regarded the woman sitting alone on the banquette. 'There's something else she should have told you. Tiffany never lunches upstairs. Upstairs at lunchtime is for the out crowd. I've heard her call it Siberia.'

'If this is Siberia,' Frances said, 'how do you talk about downstairs? I mean what do you call it?'

'The Tea Room, of course.'

Frances got to her feet. 'You'd better show me down there.'

The Tea Room was even more impressive than the room where she had been sitting. The whole place was hung with old-fashioned chandeliers and just in case their glitter wasn't enough the management had draped them in tinsel and Christmas-tree balls. Frances suppressed a giggle. The mad Russian tea-party, she thought. I knew this was going to be fun.

She saw Tiffany sitting at the far end of the restaurant, looking impatient and elegant at the same time. The reason she was able to maintain the pose was her hat. It was a big squashy affair in red fox. The kind of fox that put you in mind of fairy princesses. The glossy red fur feathering round her face accentuated the delicate high cheekbones and the red slash of her mouth.

'You're looking glamorous today,' said Frances arriving at the table. 'Sorry I'm late, there was a slight misunderstanding with the waiter. He didn't think to tell me you always came downstairs.'

Tiffany looked pained, but only for a second. If Frances had been a friend of hers, she might have given her a hard time for keeping her waiting, but she wasn't a friend, she was a business opportunity. So she smiled nicely and told Frances not to give it a thought.

They ordered lunch. This took Tiffany exactly five seconds.

'My usual,' she said to the waiter, 'and make it snappy, I'm starving.'

Frances struggled with the menu. Everything was so unfamiliar. Borscht, zakuska, karsky shashlik, cranberry kissel. She had visions of ordering a whole sheep's head, or some kind of exotic intestine and not being able to eat it. Finally she gave up and looked across to her companion.

'I've never been here before,' she admitted. 'What do you recommend?'

She thought Tiffany might look down on her for her lack of sophistication but she didn't. She was surprisingly cosy about the daunting menu, dismissing the whole thing with a wave of her shiny red nails.

'The food here is prepared specially for fat Russian peasants,' she told Frances. 'Half the showbusiness crowd who come here had a grandmother or an uncle from middle Europe. I wouldn't let it bother you. Do what I do. Have the blinis with caviar. You can't go wrong with caviar.'

If there was one thing that would stick in Frances's mind about that lunch, it was when Tiffany said, 'You can't go wrong with caviar.'

There was something about the phrase that perfectly summed her up. Extravagant, devil-may-care, accustomed to luxury. Tiffany never walked when she could take a limousine, never made dinner when she could make reservations at a restaurant and was never ever caught dead in last season's designer clothes.

'What do you do with them?' Frances asked, who was accustomed to taking up the hems and changing buttons.

Tiffany looked at her in astonishment.

'What do you think I do? I let my cleaning woman have the stuff I don't care about. The rest – the St Laurent and the Ralph Lauren – I take to a little thrift shop on Second Avenue. The woman there pays in cash if the things are in good condition.'

Talking to this woman was an eye view of a different world. A cruel, bitchy world populated by hucksters and poseurs. Frances knew she shouldn't be fascinated by it, for in its way it was as shallow as the world she had had with Richard Gregory. She wasn't with Richard Gregory now, though. She was on her own and she trusted her experience and her good sense to protect her.

It was nearly three when they finished lunch and when Frances made to get up she felt slightly dizzy. I shouldn't have drunk all that vodka, she thought. Next time I'll be more careful.

There was a next time. Tiffany had made sure of that. The English girl, who she imagined was going to be dull and stand-offish was anything but. She'd been around. That was apparent from the names she dropped and the places she had been, and she was lonely. Since she'd been in New York, she'd found no soulmates amongst the wives of her husband's friends and in a way Tiffany wasn't surprised. All Sam's friends were hardworking advertising men with homes and families in the suburbs. Frances, with her model girl looks and that curiosity of hers, wasn't going to be content with coffee mornings. She was looking for excitement, Tiffany was sure of that, but she wanted safe little thrills. Nothing that would rock her marriage. No, she thought, Frances Kurnitz would get all the excitement she needed from spending money in the stores and she couldn't have chosen a better instructor.

Tiffany worked out her plan of campaign. She would give Frances a taste of the good life. Whet her appetite for excess. Then once she was hooked, she would work out what to do with her next. It was going to be an interesting exercise.

During the following six months, Frances became a patron of the arts. Not in the literal sense; she didn't take part in the reconstruction of the Met, or pass the hat around for a starving artist. What she did do though, was to go to a lot of charity events. Tiffany was always coming up with tickets for a ball or an opening. It was always in a good cause and it always cost money.

In the beginning, Frances didn't think she could keep up. There were so many clothes to buy and everything she did required that she changed. You couldn't lunch in the same dress that you wore to an art appreciation class. You couldn't go to early evening drinks at the Plaza in the smart little suit you'd had lunch in. The opera required a whole different style of presenting yourself and embassy parties were a rule unto themselves.

'I've been overspent on my account for nearly four months now,' Frances protested to her new friend. 'Sam will never put up with it.'

Tiffany was unmoved.

'Stop being silly,' she said briskly. 'Sam isn't a pauper, you know. If he wants a well-dressed wife – and what successful advertising man doesn't – he'll come up with the cash. Clay does all the time. If Clay can find it, so can Sam.'

Frances wasn't sure of that and she wasn't even sure she wanted to bleed her husband dry in order to dress in the latest fashion. She repeated the conversation she had had with Tiffany to Sam, expecting him to be furious. He wasn't.

'If you like, I'll increase your allowance,' he said.

Frances was amazed.

'Are you sure?' she gasped. 'I seem to be wasting an awful lot of your money.'

Sam laughed.

'I know,' he said, 'but it's not going to last for ever. One day soon you'll start having babies, and when that happens we'll have to think about moving out of town.'

He paused.

'Think about what's happening now as a kind of holiday, a very exotic foreign holiday. You're indulging in all sorts of treats you'd never dream of having in real life and believe me, the life you're living now is nothing to do with reality. Reality is working hard and staying up nights when the baby is fretful. It's mowing the lawn and preparing dinner and listening to me bitch about the office when I come home at the end of the day. Once the babies start coming that will be your future. So do me a favour, darling, spend my money now will you? You'll never get another chance.'

Frances did what she was told. For the first two weeks she spent every night in an agony of guilt. Bergdorfs, Bendels and all the smart boutiques charged five times as much as the stores she was used to patronising. It didn't seem decent somehow to part with two hundred dollars for a pair of shoes, five hundred dollars for a silk T-shirt and a couple of thousand dollars for a suit to wear during the day. Frances made a note of everything she spent and once a day she would take out all the notes and total them all up. The exercise never failed to bring her out in a cold sweat but she made herself do it. If she got into a proper routine she reasoned, if she kept track of everything she was doing, she wouldn't do anything too foolish.

Then after two weeks, something extraordinary happened. Frances stopped being shocked at what she was doing every day. Worse, what she was doing began to seem perfectly natural and she realised that before she met Tiffany her senses had somehow been out of tune. The dresses she used to wear didn't come near to fitting her, let along flattering her. How could she have done without three pairs of boots for the winter and half a dozen cashmere sweaters, and scarves and handbags and silk shirts? The list was endless, yet to Frances it made perfect sense. She had been gauche when she first came to the city, gauche and badly groomed. Now she could go anywhere and feel confident she would never look out of place.

Her life started to take on a new rhythm. She would open her eyes around ten every morning to find Sam long gone and an empty coffee cup in the sink. She'd scramble out of bed, brew up some more coffee, then still in her dressing-gown she'd start on her calls. There were a whole lot of new people in her orbit now. People who came to life at night and spent their mornings on the telephone talking about it. She was one of them now. Part of the moving light show, and like all the other transients she lived off the gossip they generated. Candice had had another lift. Fay a new toy boy. And did you hear about Fay's husband? He's suing her for divorce. It seems he's discovered toy boys too.

They were silly conversations. Vapid and meaningless. The sane part of Frances shuddered and wondered what the hell she was doing, but there was another part of her, a part that was greedy and bored and living for kicks – and that part was growing stronger every day.

She was seeing Tiffany regularly now. They would meet for lunch two or three times a week and most evenings they would bump into each other at parties. Their main activity together was shopping. Clothes were becoming an obsession with Frances, a narcotic almost. Like a drug runner and a junkie, the two women lived off each other. One pandering and nurturing the other's addiction, until the right moment came for the sting.

They had known each other for one designer season now and Tiffany decided the time had come to introduce Frances to fur. Fur was the big one. The large investment. When Frances committed herself to a mink or a lynx or a sable, she was well on the way to total dependency.

They had arranged to meet at an address on Seventh Avenue where an auction of coats was being held. Tiffany was already there when Frances arrived, deep in conversation with a tall balding man.

'This is Al,' said Tiffany shortly. 'He's worth getting to know. He runs the sale room.'

'Tell him not to waste his time talking to me,' said Frances a little too quickly, 'I'm not in the market for fur. Not this season.'

Tiffany smiled, full of understanding. 'Of course, I should have known. You brought your furs with you from England. Listen, maybe I should introduce you to someone else in the business. Whatever you've got will need restyling. Or maybe you could do a part exchange . . .'

Frances cut in on her.

'Look,' she said urgently, 'I don't wear fur. I don't even like it all that much.'

'So why did you come?'

Tiffany looked angry now. And Frances was sorry she had been so candid. She didn't want to upset her friend. It was the last thing she had in mind. Which is why she'd agreed to come along in the first place.

She took her friend's arm and led her over to a chair.

'I've got some explaining to do,' she said. 'Sam and I have been going over my accounts.' She screwed up her face. 'Even by my standards, I'm way over the top. I'm not saying Sam can't afford it. Of course he can. But all this spending's stretching him. We're having to put off buying a second car this year because of the bills. And I promised I'd call a halt. To be honest, Tiffany, I can't buy a fur coat, even if I wanted one. I only came along today, if you must know, so as not to offend you. But I seem to have done that anyway.'

Tiffany laughed. 'This is New York you're living in, not London. You'll never get through the winter without one.'

'I'm going to try,' Frances said. 'For Sam's sake. Our budget just won't stretch to it.'

Her companion was silent for a moment. As if she was considering something. Finally she said,

'Why don't you just see the show. Get some idea of the prices and what's on offer. Then we'll talk about it some more.'

The English girl allowed herself to be guided to her seat. I'll sit through this, she decided, it's only polite. But nobody and nothing is going to convince me to blow money I haven't got.

An hour later she wasn't so sure, for she was dazzled to the point of temporary blindness. Never in her life had she seen so many red foxes, so many silver foxes, so many shades of mink. So much opulence under one roof. She knew she shouldn't want a fur coat. All her upbringing told her that flashy displays of animal pelts were for tarts or old women. Yet her eyes had told her otherwise. She knew that a soft, slinky mink or a long bushy fox would make her look a million dollars.

Al, the guy who ran the sale room, came across to her. 'I realise you're not interested in buying anything today,' he said, 'but perhaps you'd like to slip something on. Just to see how they fit.'

It was a blatant come-on. If I had an ounce of sense, Frances told herself, I'd walk out of the door, but her reason seemed to have deserted her. All she wanted to do was to bury herself up to her ears in glossy, silky, sinful fur.

Like a sleepwalker she followed the salesman across to a rack of coats. There were beavers and ermines and snow leopards. With a pang Frances realised that a lot of the fur was from protected species and should never have been on sale, yet she had to have it round her shoulders, on her back.

Frances tried the first coat, a ranch mink in swirling shades of pale toffee. Opposite her was a full-length mirror. She turned and pirouetted in front of it, watching the coat fly out around her. It was a long garment, reaching from around her ears to half way down her calves, yet it didn't swamp her. It fitted itself subtly to the lines of her body. Elongating her, making her look svelte and expensive.

As she stood there looking at herself, Frances realised she could never take this coat off. She had to possess it, to own it, to make it hers.

Tiffany came over to where she stood.

'You look wonderful,' she said. 'You've got to have it.'

Frances felt as if she was drowning.

'I can't,' she said desperately. 'I haven't got the money.'

The thoughtful, considering look that Tiffany had worn earlier came back.

'I've got a suggestion to make,' she said. 'Why don't you let me lend you the money? Just for now. So you can have the coat.'

Frances had never borrowed money before in her life and the idea of being in someone's debt made her feel uneasy.

'It will take me ages to pay you back,' she said.

The older woman smiled and put an arm round her. 'You're such a goose,' Tiffany said. 'Stop looking so agonised. The coat's lovely. You look like a million in it – I bet you the moment Sam sees you, he'll demand to pay for it. In full.'

Frances shook her head.

'I don't think so,' she said. 'Sam isn't all that keen on fur.'

Tiffany laughed and ran her hand down the length of the toffee-coloured mink, fussing it and fluffing it out as if it was some pampered pet.

'Do yourself a favour,' she said, 'and take my offer. Believe me, you won't regret it.'

Slowly Frances allowed herself to be persuaded. She suspected she was being coerced, but for the life of her she couldn't imagine what Tiffany had to gain by lending her money. Twenty thousand dollars seemed a fortune to her, but maybe Tiffany had a fortune stashed away, an inheritance possibly.

Frances left the sale room with the mink over her arm, yet the soft sinuous feel of the fur against her skin didn't excite her the way she thought it would. She was too worried about where she was going to find the money to pay for it.

28

Tiffany left the sale room ten minutes after Frances had, hailed a cab and rode down to Le Perigord on East 52nd. As soon as she walked into the restaurant she realised why he had chosen it. This man is an old hand at wooing, she thought. I must be on my guard.

Le Perigord had a kind of old-world charm that had nothing to do with the cut and thrust lunchtime crowd that she was used to. Rich people came here. The kind of rich people who had time for leisure as well as money to spend. Tiffany could tell just by looking at the extravagant arrangements of flowers and the well-spaced tables, that lunch here took a long time and nobody complained about the service.

He had got there first, and from the way he was occupying the best table in the genteel dining-room, Tiffany could tell he was a regular. She took a long time getting out of her mink for she needed a breathing space to collect her wits and to study this new conquest.

He was wearing a dark suit with a Savile Row cut and a Harvard tie, yet it was his tan that impressed Tiffany most. It wasn't the sort of colour you get from two weeks in Mexico on vacation. This man's tan came from a lifetime of yachting on the Sound, racing in Monte Carlo, partying in Rio. It gave him a jet-set look. An international look. She was glad she had agreed to have lunch with him.

Tiffany had met Abner Morris three weeks previously at a charity benefit. Clay knew him slightly and wanted to know him a great deal better because of General Tobacco. The guy ran it, her husband told her. He controlled hundreds of millions of dollars' worth of advertising money.

Tiffany looked at him as if he had lost his mind.

'So what,' she said. 'You know as well as I do that Sam won't work on tobacco. So why waste time shaking the guy's hand? Even if he liked you, it wouldn't do any good.'

Clay shook his head sadly.

'Stop being so negative,' he told her. 'Sam doesn't run the company. I do. If that guy over there gave the sign he was interested, I'd go to work on Sam so fast, he wouldn't know what hit him.'

Tiffany was unconvinced. Cigarettes were a hobby-horse of Sam's, almost an obsession. It would take someone with more clout than Clay to talk him out of it. Nevertheless she had let herself be led over to the tobacco tycoon and she did her best to be charming. It wasn't difficult. Abner Morris was witty and polished and to her surprise he seemed interested in what she was saying. Tiffany was holding forth about the stock market. One of the few subjects, apart from clothes and gossip, that genuinely intrigued her. When out of the corner of her eye she saw Clay. He was standing slightly to one side of her and the look on his face told her everything she wanted to know. He was proud of her, but it was more than that. He was impressed out of his mind that she had managed to nobble the most powerful man in the room. Go for it, he seemed to be saying. Get out there and grab.

She put on her most seductive smile. If Clay wanted tobacco billing, then tobacco billing is what she would get him. The complications she'd sort out later.

The band on the edge of the dance floor started to play and as Tiffany expected, the tall expensive-looking tycoon asked her to take a turn with him. She floated into his arms. Relaxed and provocative, as if she spent all her life dancing with influential strangers. Five minutes later, almost on cue, he asked if he could take her to lunch.

Tiffany was used to this kind of approach. It was what

had built her husband's business up in the first place, but it made her weary and she wondered if there would ever come a day when she could stop hustling and just enjoy her life. Enjoy her husband. Start a family, maybe. Then she pulled herself together. If she gave in to that sort of yearning, the agency would never be big and she would never be rich.

She tilted her head up at Abner Morris.

'I'd love to have lunch with you,' she said enthusiastically.

Now, three weeks later, she still felt good about her decision, though in her heart of hearts she wondered how she was going to talk the tough businessman into handing over a major cigarette brand. In the past her female wiles had done the trick, but she had been playing for low stakes then with dull dogs from out of town. This man was a different story.

Like everyone else, Tiffany had heard of Abner Morris's involvement with Macho. She knew about the girls, the parties, the mansion where he lived, and she was daunted.

I'm just an *hors d'oeuvre* for this man, she thought. A tasty titbit on the side. If I'm not careful he'll use me and discard me like all the other bimbos.

Across the restaurant, Abner Morris was thinking roughly along the same lines. He was studying Tiffany as she approached the table now. Approving the black Dior suit, the single string of pearls, the high crocodile shoes. She's an expensive piece of goods, he thought. I wonder how long it's going to take me to get her into bed.

Tiffany sat down at the table and accepted a glass of vintage champagne, then she settled back in her seat and let her host make the running. He had just come back from a shooting weekend in Scotland and he entertained her with tales of the stuffy English with their social rituals and their snobbery. By the time the waiter arrived to take their orders, Tiffany had started to relax. The menu was stunning: there were over two dozen choices of appetizer and most of them were displayed on a cold buffet table. There was only one problem: she wasn't very hungry. Abner sensed how she was feeling and took over the situation. 'Try the cold vegetable pâté,' he told her. 'It's good, and it won't fill you up.'

He ordered pâté for both of them, then, without consulting her, told the waiter to bring them fillets of sole with truffles to follow. Normally Tiffany didn't welcome anyone making decisions for her but in her present mood she let it go. There were more important things to concentrate her mind on.

When the food arrived she turned the conversation around to business. She wanted to know about Abner's company and what he did in it. Abner Morris was both surprised and flattered. He wasn't used to this kind of enquiry from a pretty woman. The girls he knew talked about the latest show in town or the latest 'in' place. Then he remembered the first time he had met Tiffany and the way she had gone on about the stock market. She had been talking nonsense of course, but what she had to say had nothing to do with it. It was the energy she used to say it that intrigued him.

He started to talk about General Tobacco and before he knew it he was telling her the story of his life.

He went right back to the early days when he was still married and working for his father, but he skipped the bit about the air hostess and his liking for bimbos and concentrated on his achievements – his rise up the ladder of General Tobacco, the way he set up the Macho organisation. This was the substance of his life. This was what made him a force to be reckoned with. As he expounded on his twin empires, he relaxed and felt at peace with the world.

If Abner was smiling inside, so was Tiffany. She had

expected to meet a middle-aged lecher over the *petits fours*. A fat cat on the hunt for a bunk-up in the afternoon. She had come face to face with a tiger.

Every woman has her fantasies, and Tiffany's favourite, her perennial favourite, was to meet her opposite number. Someone who could be a match for her. Clay had her heart-felt respect as a businessman, but as a man, he was only firing on three cylinders. Abner was the whole caboodle. A powerful tycoon but a man as well. His lifestyle was legendary and now Tiffany understood why. There would be few women, she thought, who could resist Abner's charm. She wondered if she could. Then she pulled herself together. She was here on a mission: to talk this lunch-date of hers into handing some of his business over to Clay. Pleasure was one thing, but with Tiffany, business always came first.

She started to talk about her husband's agency, con-centrating on Sam's creative prowess and staying away from anything that might suggest that he wouldn't touch cigarettes.

Abner was interested but then he seemed to like almost everything Tiffany had to say and she wondered if she was getting through to him at all.

They were onto the coffee stage of lunch and Abner asked her if she wanted a *digestif*. The waiter wheeled a trolley towards them and the bottles told their own story. There was kirsch, sloe gin, kummel, malt whiskey, apricot brandy, cherry brandy and every variety of bourbon she had ever forgotten. Abner indicated a squat bottle con-taining a pale gold liquid.

'It's Armagnac,' he told her. 'Very old. Very rare. I like it after this kind of lunch. Will you join me?'

Tiffany stiffened. What kind of lunch did he mean? A seduction lunch? A business lunch? A meeting of the minds? Before she could say yes or no to the drink, Abner motioned to the waiter to serve both of them, then after a few minutes he asked about Clay's agency some more.

'Does Kurnitz and Greene have a cigarette account at the moment?' he quizzed her.

Tiffany's heart rose. So he was paying attention after all. She explained that the agency was short on tobacco, then she waited for him to make his move. He didn't.

Instead he called for the bill and made to leave.

'It was fun having lunch today,' he said, 'we'll have to do it again sometime.'

Before she could draw breath, Tiffany found herself being hustled out of the restaurant. That can't be all there is to it, she thought. He had to want something from me. But he didn't appear to.

The moment they hit the sidewalk, a sleek black Mercedes purred up to where they stood and Abner's chauffeur jumped out.

'Can I give you a lift anywhere?' he asked.

Tiffany shook her head.

'I guess I'll walk for a while.'

Abner nodded briefly and jumped into the back seat. Then he waved as the car drew away.

Tiffany looked after it in a kind of daze. He hadn't even bothered to kiss her goodbye.

He called a week later and invited her to the opera. No reference was made to their last meeting. Or to the fact that she had a husband and Tiffany was astounded by his arrogance. He thinks he can pick me up at a moment's notice, she thought, like some bimbo, or one of those centre-spreads in *Macho* magazine.

She toyed with the idea of telling him to go to hell but she stopped herself. She had entered into this game with Abner because she had designs on his tobacco business and if he wanted to make a pitch for her body while they were watching 'Don Giovanni' at the Met, that was fair enough. She was quite capable of looking after herself.

She accepted Abner's invitation, then she did some hard thinking. There was no point in telling Clay about her date. He can know all about my friendship with Abner, she decided, when I've got the business. He'd understand then. Her conscience out of the way, Tiffany focused her mind on Sam. He was the one obstacle standing between her and what she wanted. Tobacco was anathema to him. She'd heard him say he'd rather starve than have it anywhere near the agency. Well, the time had come to put that to the test. His dear little wife was twenty thousand dollars in hock to her. The time had come to call in the money.

She dialled Frances's number and after five rings the maid answered.

'Mrs Kurnitz has gone out,' she informed her. 'She'll be back later this afternoon.'

Tiffany was irritated. She had made her mind up to tackle Frances and once the decision was taken, there was no time to waste.

'Where is she?' she demanded.

The maid responded to the authority in Tiffany's voice. She had never met her, but whoever this woman was, she was used to giving orders.

'Mrs Kurnitz has gone to Arden's to have her hair dyed,' she told her. 'She left half an hour ago, so she should be there by now.'

'Thank you,' said Tiffany abruptly and put the phone down. Then she picked up her bag, grabbed a jacket and made for the door. If she hurried she could be at the beauty parlour in time to catch her friend at her most vulnerable.

Arden's had been Tiffany's idea.

'If you're going to start wearing this season's collections,' she pointed out, 'you've got to have this season's look.'

This season's look, according to Tiffany and the people she partied with, was tough and aggressive. The 1980s girl was just beginning to hold her own in a man's world. Feminism had made its thumb print on her and she walked taller. Better, she walked with a swagger.

The natural look Frances had was just a little old-fashioned. It was pretty enough if you lived in some backwater but in trendy New York it was passé.

'What do I have to do to get today's look?' Frances demanded.

'Relax and leave it to me,' said Tiffany, and she took her to the tall, thin, red-painted building on Fifth Avenue, across the road from the Plaza Hotel. Elizabeth Arden's occupied the entire building. From the glossy reception on the ground floor right up to the top, there was a skilled team whose sole occupation was to paint, perm, primp and manicure the rich women of Manhattan.

Frances was fed into the system on the ground floor where she was cross-questioned and a number of appointments were made for her. Her day started on the second floor. Here she was relieved of her top clothes and draped in a pale pink dressing-gown, then she was put under the spotlight. Her transformation was to be given over to José, one of the salon's top stylists.

The moment she saw him, Frances took an immediate dislike to the man. There was something arrogant about him, as if he despised the way she was put together. José knew what was best, and he never stopped telling her so.

'It is best,' said José, 'to cut your hair off.' He twisted her pale blonde tresses viciously back from her face.

'See how your face looks without all that drapery. I can see your bones now and the shape of your eyes.'

He fiddled with the light above the dressing-table where she was sitting. Now Frances was in full glare and for a moment she was temporarily blinded.

'We'll have to change a few things,' José went on, half

to himself. 'Those eyebrows will never do. Nor will the hair colour.'

'You leave my eyebrows alone,' Frances said. 'And my hair. I'm perfectly happy with them the way they are.'

But José would not be deflected.

'You may be happy,' he said, 'but how do your friends feel? How does New York feel?'

Frances gave him a scornful look.

'I don't give a hoot how New York feels. That's New York's affair. What exactly are you getting at anyway?'

José stepped back from her, letting go of the long blonde hair bunched up in his hand. It was a dismissive gesture and despite herself, Frances felt small.

'If you don't care about how you look in society,' he told her, 'then go home. You're wasting my time. I've got a queue of women fighting for five minutes with me and none of them will give me an argument.'

Frances thought about the new Calvin Klein pantsuit she had bought that week and the Ralph Lauren cowgirl skirt. They were such tough clothes, so American, she almost felt like an imposter in them. She regarded her pale reflection in the mirror. I came here to buy myself a look, she thought, a look to go with this season and this decade. She sighed and mentally kissed herself goodbye.

'Calm down,' she said to the sulky stylist. 'I'm paying you good money to make me over, so do it. I promise I won't say anything else if you promise to stop frowning like that.'

He pirouetted round to face her then he lifted her hand and kissed the ends of her fingertips.

'At last,' he said, 'the lady sees sense. You won't regret it, I promise you.'

José kept Frances all day in Arden's. She was waxed and de-fuzzed all over. She was put to lie in a seaweed bath, then hosed down with ice-cold water. Her face was steamed, and covered in what felt like quick-setting concrete, and when that came off her eyebrows were plucked.

Then she was sent up to the hairdressing salon. As José predicted, her hair colour was changed. Frances had been a natural blonde all her life but by Arden's standards she wasn't blonde at all. She was mouse. They righted that by taking her up three shades until she could have passed for Bo Derek. Then José was summoned for his opinion and he gave it the thumbs down.

'She still looks too English,' he told the hairdresser. 'I want something sharper, something sassier.'

The stylist looked up.

'How do you feel about curls?' he asked.

José pulled a face. 'Too romantic,' he said. 'Right now all I can see is Mrs Kurnitz walking across a new-mown meadow. What I want to see is my client swinging her way into Studio 54.'

The hairdresser giggled.

'I don't mean ringlets, silly. I mean short curls, almost a bubble-cut. Like a young Monroe.'

There was a silence while both men regarded Frances. José made a frame of his hands and peered through it at her face, then he walked all the way round her, examining her from all angles. Finally he voiced his professional opinion.

'It's perfect,' he said. 'Exactly what I'm looking for.'

He turned to the hair man,

'Go on ahead and do it, darling. Create a young Monroe out of this milkmaid. Then buzz me when you're through. She'll need a few finishing touches.'

Frances had worn her hair touching her shoulderblades since she was ten years' old and normally she protested if anyone had taken so much as an inch off, but this thick yellow mane she seemed to have sprouted didn't seem to be part of her any more. When the stylist buried his scissors in it, she said not a word. She supposed it was all for the best.

Frances closed her eyes when the stinging perm lotion was applied to her scalp and she kept them closed until the whole performance was finally over. Then she allowed José to lead her down to the cubicle on the second floor where he was going to do her final make-up.

The head stylist noticed almost immediately she wasn't looking at her reflection in the mirrors round the room.

'Clever girl,' he observed. 'Nobody should watch themselves being transformed. The surprise is so much better when it's all over.'

It was certainly a surprise. What confronted Frances when she finally opened her eyes was a complete stranger. She viewed her objectively. She was attractive, this girl, in a go-getting, New Yorky sort of way. Her features were sculpted and her face was foxy-looking. Frances had lived a rackety kind of life, but whatever she had done, nothing had left its mark on her. Not Richard Gregory, not waitressing in the Macho Club, not taking her clothes off for the cameras. Even the things she got up to in bed hadn't hardened her expression. Until now. Now all her experiences were written across her face and for a moment she felt ashamed.

How can I go out like this, she thought.

How can I reveal myself this way? Sam will divorce me. But there was no going back. Frances had turned herself over to José and Elizabeth Arden who had re-made her in the image of the city.

Silently she turned to José and handed him his ten per cent. Then still without saying anything she walked down to the ground floor and paid her bill. After that, she took a taxi to Kurnitz and Greene and demanded to see her husband. If he was going to throw her out, she wanted to know right now.

Sam was surprisingly gentle. He knew she was going to the beauty parlour that day, so he was prepared to see changes in her, but when he saw what changes it took all

232

his self-control not to register his horror. They've made her look like a chippy, he thought, a cheap little hooker from the lower East Side, but I can't tell her that – it would break her heart. So he smiled and put his arms round Frances.

'You sure look different,' he told her, 'but I think it's kinda fun.'

Frances pulled away from her husband and looked at him hard.

'Don't lie to me,' she said. 'I look a fright. I've got eyes, you know.'

Sam wracked his brains for something to say, something that wouldn't sound phoney. Then he had it.

'It's not as bad as you think. Not when you've scraped some of that paint off.'

He was right. Without the glossy red lips and the arched brows a lot of the brassiness disappeared. Frances cleaned her face as soon as she got home and started to feel human again. Her eyebrows would grow back, she knew that, but there was one thing she couldn't change. The new blonde hairdo. She was stuck with it, and its upkeep. If she tried to grow it out, she faced six months of rats' tails. Twin-coloured rats' tails as her natural colour came through and she couldn't cope with that. Not when she'd invested so much of Sam's money in a designer wardrobe. Not when a whole season of social events stretched in front of her. So she lived with it and in time she got used to it, as she grew accustomed to visiting Arden's once every ten days to have her roots touched up.

Which is what she was having done when Tiffany came to talk to her. The stylist had put Frances in a private cubicle while the chemicals on her scalp did their work and she was sitting trying to concentrate on a copy of *Vogue* when the curtains in front of her parted to admit her friend.

'What on earth are you doing in here?' she asked.

'You've got to be at a loose end to come and see me here.'

Tiffany smiled furtively, then searched her mind for an excuse for her sudden appearance.

'I was passing the door,' she said, 'on my way to meet someone at the Plaza. I thought I'd come in and have a quick word.'

Frances put down her *Vogue*.

'Why, have you got something on your mind?'

'Yes, actually.'

She might as well give it to her straight and get it over with, thought Tiffany. There was no point in beating around the bush.

'It's the coat,' she said. 'The one we bought together. I need the money I lent you.'

Frances looked at her sharply.

'All twenty thousand dollars of it?'

Tiffany nodded. 'I'm sorry,' she said, 'but that's the way it is.'

For a moment Frances felt intensely annoyed. She was sitting here having God-knows-what put on her head all because her friend wanted her to have a new look. Now she was suddenly in debt as well, because her friend wanted her to drape herself in fur.

'I don't know what goes through your head half the time,' she said, 'but if you didn't have the money, why on earth did you offer me a loan? I could have lived without the coat.'

Tiffany looked uncomfortable.

'I know, I know,' she said. 'But I so wanted you to have it. I thought you deserved it. Anyway you look a knockout in it.'

'That's not the point,' said Frances. 'I'll look a bankrupt in it if I'm not careful. You shouldn't have pushed me into it, particularly when you knew you couldn't cover the loan.'

234

'I could cover it, at least I thought I could, till Clay told me otherwise.' Tiffany moaned softly and covered her eyes.

'It's all Sam's fault,' she said.

'What's Sam got to do with it?' Frances asked.

Tiffany went back to looking uncomfortable.

'I don't think I want to talk about this,' she said.

Frances was worried. 'I think you have to tell me what this is all about,' she said. 'We are friends after all, and if it's something to do with Sam, maybe I can sort it out.'

'I wonder if you could,' said Tiffany. 'After all, he does listen to you, which is more than he does to Clay.'

Frances thought about the mink coat she had bought a week ago. There was no way she could find the money to pay for it now. In six months' time she might have saved up half of it, but that wasn't good enough. She fought down a feeling of panic.

'Why don't you start by telling me how Sam's to blame for you not having any money?'

Tiffany started to relax, Frances had taken the bait. Now all she had to do was reel her in.

'It's to do with Sam not wanting to work on cigarette business,' she said.

Frances looked confused.

'He's never talked about that to me.'

'Why should he?' Tiffany said. 'It's a business matter. Clay probably wouldn't have even discussed it if I hadn't wanted to get my hands on twenty thousand dollars in a hurry.'

Now Frances was really puzzled.

'How does Sam not liking cigarettes make any difference?'

Tiffany leaned forward.

'I'll tell you how,' she said. 'A while ago the agency was offered a big pipe tobacco account and Clay did all the costings on the basis that we had the business. Then at the last moment, Sam vetoed it. Can you believe it, the guy actually said no to four million dollars' worth of billing. He told my husband it was something to do with his conscience. He didn't approve of people smoking and he didn't want to do anything to encourage the habit.

'At the time, Clay didn't put up an argument. If Sam felt that strongly, then he was prepared to go along with it. He only started to regret his decision when the end-of-year figures came in, because what showed up was a huge cash flow problem. The tobacco account would have solved it. Now it's too late, the business has gone somewhere else and we're all stuck with an embarrassing financial problem.'

Frances swallowed hard. It was worse than she thought. Far worse. If Kurnitz and Greene couldn't afford to pay its bills, then Sam couldn't afford to pay for a mink coat.

'If the problem's gone this far,' she said, 'how can anything I say make a difference?'

Tiffany looked shifty.

'Look,' she said. 'I'm going to tell you something, but you've got to promise me it won't go any further.'

Frances nodded, and Tiffany went on. 'Okay. There's a huge cigarette account coming up for grabs. Clay doesn't know this and neither does Sam, but I have a friend who could put the business our way. If we get it, it could add another sixty million dollars to our billing.'

Tiffany looked steadily at Frances.

'Sixty million could solve all our problems. More than that, it could start to make us rich.'

Understanding started to dawn.

'You want me to talk Sam into working on tobacco business,' Frances said, 'don't you?'

Tiffany nodded. It had taken nearly half an hour to feed the idea into the dumb broad, but she finally seemed to be getting the message.

Frances looked nervous.

236

'What if Sam won't listen to me?' she asked. 'What if he tells me to mind my own business?'

Tiffany leaned back in her chair.

'Has Sam ever not listened to you?' she said. 'Was there ever a time he didn't give you exactly what you wanted?'

Frances shook her head.

'Not that I can remember,' she muttered. 'But I've never asked him for anything important before. Not really important.'

Tiffany chuckled and lit a cigarette.

'Well, here's your chance to put a little pressure on that husband of yours. Don't tell me you don't know how to get what you want, because I won't believe you. Every woman can pull something out of the hat.'

Frances hesitated. She loved Sam and she didn't want to push him into something that went against his beliefs. Then she thought about the toffee-coloured mink and the money she owed.

'I can't promise anything,' she said, 'but I will talk to Sam.'

Tiffany took her friend's hand and gave it a squeeze.

'If you do that, I'll have a word with Clay,' she said. 'I'm sure I can get a bit more time on that loan.'

29

Sam had never told Frances he didn't like working on cigarettes. He'd told her almost everything else about his business. She knew for instance that Sam was the one who wrote the ads and Clay was the one who designed them. She also knew that underneath his tough salesman's front, her husband had a love affair going with the creation of his messages. The words, the ideas at the core of the commercials he produced seemed to possess him while he was working on them. Some nights she'd leave him still wrestling with a problem on his lay-out pad while she went to bed.

Right from the start, Frances realised there was a special magic about the world of advertising. The only other world she had been near was Richard Gregory's. The world of Macho. Night clubs and porn magazines. It had held no interest for her. Advertising was different because it was about dreams.

Where Macho presented reality in all its tacky glory, Sam created fantasy. In his world the Princess went to the ball in her Maidenform bra, a canned broccoli spear turned into a Jolly Green Giant and data systems circled the globe like Peter Pan and Wendy. Frances didn't pretend to understand it all and when Sam came home with his office problems a lot of what he told her went right over her head. She picked up on the main points, though. She knew when Sam was pitching for an important slice of business, and hoped she could tell the difference between a good ad and a bad one. She was damn sure if Sam had told her he had turned down four million dollars' worth of pipe tobacco business, she would have remembered it.

Frances decided to bring up the subject one night after supper. If she got to the bottom of why her husband could do without a big cigarette account, maybe she could swing the conversation round to the mink coat. She didn't want to talk about it. She knew there would be a monumental row when she confessed she had blown twenty thousand dollars, but there was no way out of it. Since she had last seen Tiffany, the woman had been on the phone twice asking about it. If she didn't sort it out soon, Tiffany would be contacting Sam direct. Because she felt nervous, she poured herself a drink after supper. A glass of wine always seemed to calm her down and after a sip or two Frances found herself saying quite naturally, 'Tiffany told me the other day you refused to work on cigarette business. Why is that?'

Sam looked irritated.

'What's Tiffany doing poking her nose into my business?' he demanded.

'It's her business too,' Frances pointed out. 'After all, she is married to your partner.'

Sam looked sour.

'The way I understood it,' he said, 'Clay earned the money and Tiffany spent it. It's always been their arrangement in the past, so I don't get this sudden interest in the workings of Kurnitz and Greene.'

Frances remembered Tiffany telling her about the friend of hers who was going to enrich the agency with sixty million dollars of billing.

'I think you've got Tiffany wrong,' she said. 'She does care what goes on at the agency. More than you know.'

Sam sighed. 'If you say so, darling. Now can we talk about something else?'

But Frances refused to be deflected. Not this time.

'First,' she said, 'tell me why you hate working on cigarettes.' Sam stood up and walked over to the window.

'What the hell is it to you, whether or not I work

on cigarettes? It's not going to alter our lives in any way is it?'

Frances thought for a moment.

'It might mean we have less money to spend,' she ventured.

Sam turned round to face her.

'How come?' he asked.

Frances was getting in deep and she knew it, but there was no turning back.

'Tiffany told me,' she said, 'that the agency had a cash flow problem. Something to do with a tobacco account you turned down.'

The moment the words were out of her mouth, she wished she hadn't said them. The expression on her husband's face told her she had gone too far.

'What the fuck does Tiffany know about the figures?' he snapped. 'For your information the tobacco business I was meant to turn down was a development project. We would have seen zilch out of it for at least two years, so how could it affect our cash flow?'

Sam looked at Frances thoughtfully. 'This discussion has nothing to do with cigarettes has it?' he asked.

Frances went pale.

'What do you mean?'

'Exactly what I say. You're not really interested in how I feel about smoking. You've got something else on your mind. Something to do with money.'

Frances hesitated.

If she continued the cigarette discussion, sooner or later she would have to tell Sam about the business Tiffany was going to bring in and she had promised not to do that. So she did the unavoidable. She came clean.

'I bought a coat,' she said, wincing. 'It cost rather a lot.'

Sam looked at her in dead silence and Frances felt her heart jump, yet she had to go on, to get the whole thing out.

'Actually,' she said, 'it cost twenty thousand dollars.'

Now it was Sam's turn to go pale.

'But you haven't got twenty thousand dollars,' he said, staggered. He paused. 'You didn't charge it, did you?'

'Don't be silly,' Frances said. 'My credit card wouldn't cover it.'

Sam was staring at her intently now.

'How did you get the money?' he asked.

'I borrowed it from Tiffany.'

There, it was out now. Frances waited for the world to fall apart.

'Have you lost your mind?' Sam asked her. 'That's the dumbest, stupidest, craziest thing I ever heard. You walked into a store and you borrowed twenty thousand dollars from Tiffany Greene.'

He was shouting now.

'Do you realise what you've done? You put yourself in hock to my partner's wife. What if Clay and I weren't getting on right now? What if we had troubles in the business? How do you think it would affect me?'

Frances felt the tears gather behind her eyes.

'I suppose I didn't think about that. Tiffany made it sound so simple, as if the money didn't matter at all.'

'Until she wanted it back,' Sam finished for her.

Frances looked up at him and at the fury on his face. The sheer malevolence made her recoil.

'How did you know that?' she asked.

Sam sighed.

'It's my fault,' he said. 'I should have told you about your friend before now. Only I thought you'd have the sense to see through her. Listen,' he said, 'Tiffany isn't like you. She doesn't have your loyalty, or your innocence. She only cares about one person in the world. Tiffany Greene. Anyone who gets in her way she treads on. My guess is she lent the money to you on a whim and the following day she found a better use for it.

There's only one thing I don't understand about this whole business.'

'What's that?' asked Frances faintly.

'Why should Tiffany tell you about the tobacco business I threw out?'

Frances thought hard. Whatever Sam said about her, she couldn't betray her friend, not totally. So she decided to tell half the story.

'She was concerned that you wouldn't handle that kind of business,' she said. 'Your agency is one of the few in the city without cigarettes. Tiffany said if you were prepared to take it on we could all be much richer.'

His voice was disturbingly quiet.

'Am I to understand,' he said, 'that if you were able to talk me into working on tobacco then Tiffany wouldn't press for the money you owe her.'

Frances's eyes were like saucers.

'Yes,' she said.

Sam took her by the shoulders and marched her into the bedroom.

'The coat,' he said. 'Where is it? I want to see it.'

Frances went over to the tallest of her closets and rummaged about inside. She found the coat right at the back where she had hidden it. She drew it out and the toffee-coloured fur shimmered and crackled with static.

Sam's face was grim.

'Put it on,' he ordered.

Frances draped the mink round her shoulders and felt ridiculous. She was wearing jeans and a sweatshirt and the coat made her look like a little girl dressing up in somebody else's clothes.

'Wear it properly,' he told her. 'Put your arms through the sleeves, then come into the other room. I want to explain something to you.'

Miserably Frances trailed after him. The fur made her

242

feel hot and bundled up. She wondered how she could have ever put her life on the line for it.

They both sat down, Sam on the sofa, Frances perched on the edge of a chair. Then Sam began to tell her about his father. He had died eight years before they met when Sam had just got back from Israel.

'Alex was only in his sixties when he died,' explained Sam. 'He had survived the war, he had even survived leaving Hungary, but there was one thing even he wasn't tough enough to survive. That was smoking. He had a weakness for Turkish cigarettes, the flat scented ones with no tips. They used to make him cough in the morning, but none of us took too much notice. It was normal to cough with cigarettes, wasn't it? The Turkish ones were so strong. No wonder they made him catch his breath.

'In the end, father's chest got so bad, he had to see the doctor, and that's when they told him. His smoking habit had done for him. He had cancer all through his lungs. He was condemned to die, Frances. Not in any clean way, not with dignity, but by slow suffocation.

'It took Alex six months until the end and we watched as he died. It was a bad time – worse than when Leah died. At least she didn't suffer. It was then that I made up my mind: I would never, as long as I lived, smoke another cigarette. I wouldn't stop anyone else from smoking but I wouldn't encourage it either. That meant I couldn't condone selling the habit.

'If I took on a cigarette account, I would be encouraging other people to die like my father died, and I couldn't do that, not after what I saw.'

Slowly Frances stood up and took off the mink coat.

'I think you've made your point,' she said.

He took it from her and threw it on the floor.

'Not quite,' he said. 'If I didn't have any money saved up, that piece of extravagance could have made me go back

243

on my decision. Clay wants cigarettes, he always has done. They bring in a fortune for very little effort on our part, and for a lousy twenty thousand dollars I would have been forced to go along with him.'

Frances looked at her husband.

'What are you going to do?' she asked faintly.

'Tomorrow,' he said, 'I'm going to ring up my banker and get him to release twenty thousand dollars. Then I'm going to pay the money into Tiffany's account.'

He stood up and headed for the door.

'But right now,' he said, 'I'm going to take a walk. On my own. Don't bother waiting up for me, I could be a long time, and when I get back I'll sleep in the spare room.'

A couple of minutes later Frances heard the front door crash behind him. Instinctively she knelt down and picked the coat up off the floor, spreading it carefully over the back of the sofa. As she did she noticed the intricately worked pelts, the softness of the fur, the way it glowed even under artificial light. As she stared at her new coat, her eyes took in the rest of the room. It had changed considerably since they had been married. When she first came to live there it had been an anonymous penthouse but piece by piece she had added things. A button back sofa she had found in an auction at Christie's. The soft velvet curtains that took up an entire wall. A painting she had snapped up at a private view. They weren't huge items on their own but together they added up to a sizeable sum of money.

I didn't know when to stop, Frances berated herself, I was in too much of a hurry. She ran her hand over the smooth surface of the fur lying in front of her. I should have bought it next season, she thought. If I'd waited till then, we wouldn't have had this row.

In her mind's eye she saw her husband pounding the pavements in the street outside. He'll get over it, she reasoned. By tomorrow the whole thing will have blown over. All the same, she found it hard getting to sleep that night, and it wasn't until she heard Sam slamming the front door behind him that she finally let go and dozed off.

30

Sam was so angry he'd forgotten what day it was. Only when he got to the office did his secretary remind him. He was pitching for the Kitten Catfood business. In San Francisco.

'What time are we on,' he asked desperately, 'and where the hell is Louise?'

Sarah, a large competent woman who had been looking after Sam for five years, sat him down with a cup of coffee.

'Everything's under control,' she told him. 'A car's coming in twenty minutes to take you to the airport. 'You're both booked on the ten-thirty which means you'll be at the Mark Hopkins in time for lunch. Oh, and remember to adjust your watch when you get there. There's a three-hour time difference.'

Sam gulped his coffee.

'I haven't packed,' he said anxiously.

'Then you'll have to pick up a change of shirt when we get there,' said Louise who had just walked in the door. She was carrying an enormous cardboard envelope which contained most of that afternoon's presentation. The remainder of it sat on Sarah's desk ready to go in Sam's briefcase.

Louise, he noticed, knew exactly what day it was. She had taken a certain amount of trouble with herself. Her long black hair was brushed back into a shining knot which she wore in the nape of her neck. She was wearing a short black leather skirt, black stockings and a long tweed jacket.

She looks like a mixture of a New York career woman

and an Etruscan vase, Sam thought. If I didn't have Frances, I'd count myself lucky to be travelling to the coast with her.

Then he remembered his wife's disloyalty. The way she had tried to push him into betraying his principles and he wondered, did he have Frances? How sure could he be of her now?

He sighed. It was going to take him a day or two to calm down. Maybe getting out of town was the best thing.

The flight was early and they made it into the hotel by quarter to one, just in time to grab a quick drink while they thought about lunch.

Sam ambled into the bar while Louise went to check her bags. They weren't due at the catfood offices until four-thirty, so there was time for lunch and time over to go into town and grab a razor and a change of underwear. Sam relaxed and ordered a bottle of Californian Chardonnay, then he leaned against the bar and looked around him.

There was a spic and span look about San Francisco that he loved. In a New York hotel bar the ashtrays would have been full and a light layer of city grime would have settled over the upholstery and all the wooden surfaces. Here everything sparkled. Sam always had the feeling that this town was inhabited by invisible old women. The ghosts of people's mothers and grandmothers who washed and cleaned and tidied after everyone who lived here.

Even though it was nearly one, the bar was deserted that day, except for a group of well-dressed housewives out for a girls' lunch, and a fat bearded man sitting by himself two tables away. There was something about the man that rang a bell. Then he remembered. It was Marty Stein, an old colleague from his Doyle Dane days. He remembered something else. Marty was working for the local agency who were also pitching for Kitten Catfood.

Marty saw Sam at the bar and came over.

'What are you doing in town,' he asked, 'as if I didn't know.'

Sam grinned and signalled the bartender.

'Let me get you something,' he said warmly, 'then we'll compare notes. As far as we can.'

Marty took hold of the glass of Chardonnay that was intended for Louise then turned to Sam.

'What do you want to know about Kitten?' he asked. 'We showed our stuff to them a couple of days ago, so I'm not giving away any trade secrets.'

Sam took a sip of the white wine.

'Tell me about Jim Parker,' he said.

Marty whistled. 'Are you in for a surprise. You see Jim isn't making the decision on the business any more.'

Sam looked startled.

'Are you sure?' he questioned. 'As of this morning, Jim was Kitten's marketing chief. If he isn't taking decisions, who is?'

Marty settled back against the bar and drew deeply on his drink.

'Prepare yourself for this,' he said. 'The guy who picks the agency for Kitten, the big honcho, isn't a guy at all. He's a cat, or rather it's a cat. I heard from Jim he had his balls taken away a couple of years ago. Not that it affects his judgement.'

Sam aimed a punch at his friend.

'Quit horsing around,' he said. 'We're on in just over three hours.'

'I'm not horsing around,' protested Marty. 'I'm telling the truth. Jim's neutered Tom, name of Henry, makes the final decision on who gets the brand.'

Sam grabbed the bottle and poured them both another drink.

'If what you say is true,' he said, 'who do we present to? Jim Parker and his team or the cat?'

Marty considered. Finally he said, 'You show your work

to all of them. The first bit of the pitch is the usual thing, you put your work on the boardroom table. Then you talk it up to Jim and his boys. If you've got slides they provide a screen and projector so you can show them. Next the cat comes in and takes a look at the work.'

'That's crazy,' Sam said. 'How can it do that?'

Marty looked around him, embarrassed in case they were overheard.

'What happens,' he said in an undertone, 'is a door opens and Jim calls "kitty, kitty, kitty" or whatever it is you say to cats. Then this big son-of-a-bitch walks into the room and looks around him. Then Jim says, wait for this, "Hi, boss. We've seen all the work today. Now tell how you feel about it."'

Sam shook his head.

'Then what happens?'

Marty moved in closer.

'Jim reaches down, picks up the cat and puts it on the table. Just a couple of yards from the paste-ups of your ads. After that it's up to the cat.'

Sam started to laugh.

'How did the boss-cat feel about your ads? If it's not a state secret.'

Marty shrugged and looked mournful.

'We got the thumbs-down, or should I say, the paws-down. Henry stalked around the table with his tail on high. Then his eyes lit on our campaign and he gave a great yowl, like someone had stuck a poker up his arse. Then he went for it. The stupid animal went crashing into the artwork and more or less ripped it to pieces with its claws. After that it was all downhill. The art director, the guy I had with me, nearly burst into tears. I made a grab for Henry to stop him doing any more damage but it was too late. As far as we were concerned it was all over. We just didn't make the grade.'

Sam was awestruck.

'Who else are Kitten putting through this ordeal or are we the only other agency?'

Marty grimaced.

'You're the last agency. Doyle Dane did their stuff the week before last, and PKL went on yesterday. From what I heard Henry, the son-of-a-bitch, wasn't impressed with either of them. Maybe he's allergic to the glue we use on paste-ups.'

Sam started to chuckle again.

'Nothing would surprise me,' he said. Then he saw Louise had come down and was making her way towards them. He signalled for another glass, then he held out his hand to her.

'Come and meet my old friend, Marty Stein. Has he got a story to tell you . . . '

Sam and Louise arrived in the offices of Kitten Catfood at four-fifteen. By four-thirty they were sitting at the head of a long polished wood table in the presence of Jim Parker and his four deputies.

Parker's sidekicks were dressed the way all marketing men dressed at the end of the Seventies. Three-piece dark suits, white shirts, golf club ties and polished brogues. Parker was the exception. For Parker dressed like an advertising man, or the way he imagined admen dressed. He was wearing faded denim jeans and a grubby T-shirt. Sam let Louise take the floor.

'My colleague will take you through the work,' he said. 'She will be showing you a poster campaign, press ads and a television storyboard.'

Louise arranged the work on the table. Why am I doing this, she thought. Whatever I say about these ads is completely futile. If the goddamned cat takes against it, we're canned anyway. She caught Sam looking at her. It was a look of such encouragement, such faith, that she forgot her reservations. The hell with it, she thought. I've worked my butt off on this for the past six weeks. We both have.

I might as well give the campaign a decent send-off.

She started presenting the ads. Sam had dreamed up the slogan, 'Brings out the kitten in your cat'. It was a straightforward line, a selling line. The way Louise had visualised it gave heart to the concept. The press ads and the posters showed the outline of a cat in silhouette. Then curled right in the centre of the cat was a tiny, fluffy kitten. As she talked about the way the campaign worked, Louise felt hollow inside. What if Henry, Jim's cat, didn't like silhouettes? What if he had a thing against kittens?

She came to the end of her pitch, wound up the campaign in a few more words and sat down. Now for the acid test. Both Sam and Louise looked at Jim Parker who looked towards the door. On cue, it swung open.

'Puss, puss, puss,' called Jim, and Henry stalked into the room. He was the biggest cat Louise had ever seen, and he was young, maybe four or five. But it was his coat and his colour that had her mesmerised, for Henry had dense powder grey fur culminating in a great ruff round his neck. She was put in mind not of a city cat, but of a puma or a tiger. She studied the creature standing in front of them. This character means business, she thought.

Jim Parker got to his feet and went over to the cat. Then he did exactly what Marty Stein had told them he would. He lifted the huge animal into his arms, and set him down in the middle of the boardroom table.

Everyone held their breath. Except for Henry, who pricked up his ears. He made for the ads standing on display. Louise groaned inwardly. Here it comes, she thought, he's going to dive in and rip the lot to pieces, the way he did the last time. But she was wrong. Instead of attacking the posters, Henry started to sniff them. Then he sniffed some more. Finally he went into a rubbing routine.

The great grey cat arched his back and pushed himself up against the ads.

Does this mean he likes them, wondered Louise, who had little understanding of felines. Then Henry let out a huge contented purr and started to roll on his back, and she knew they were home and dry. She glanced at Sam.

'I think it's okay,' she whispered. Then she noticed something. Sam was having a tough time keeping a straight face.

'It's not funny,' she hissed. 'What if it had gone the other way?'

'Do something for me,' murmured Sam. 'Get me out of here before I crack up.'

Louise stood up and turned to Jim.

'What do you think?' she asked.

The marketing supremo leaned over and tickled the animal's tummy.

'It's not what I think,' he said, 'it's what Henry thinks. This is the first batch of ads he's actually liked.'

Sam was making gurgling noises into his handkerchief, but Louise pressed on.

'Well,' she said, 'he is, after all, the consumer. So I guess he's worth paying attention to.'

The catfood supremo nodded.

'That's just what I think,' he said. 'So as far as the Kitten company is concerned, the business is yours. I'll put a letter of confirmation in the next post.'

Overcome with relief, Louise reached down and stroked Henry on his soft, fluffy tummy, the way she had seen Jim Parker do it. The cat sank his claws in and bit her savagely and Louise snatched her hand back.

'I guess he's tired after all the excitement,' she said quickly.

Then she wrapped a handkerchief around her wound, packed up the presentation and got herself and Sam out of the room before anyone could change their minds.

Ten minutes later when they were clear of the Kitten Company, Louise turned to Sam.

'What was that all about?' she said.

Sam was wide-eyed.

'I don't know what you mean.'

'You know damn well,' she snapped. 'That number you did when the cat decided he liked the ads. I thought you were going to fall apart in front of everybody. What was going on?'

They were sitting in the back of a taxi going back to the Mark Hopkins and the early evening traffic was already slowing their journey. Sam leaned against the seat.

'We're going to be stuck here for at least half an hour, so I guess I'd better explain it to you now. But first let me ask you a question. Did you ever keep a cat?'

Louise shook her head.

'My mother was allergic to them. She thought they brought bad luck, so we never had them around as kids.'

'So you don't know about catnip then?'

Louise looked blank.

'What's catnip?' she asked. 'It sounds like a kind of drink.'

Sam laughed.

'It's not a drink, it's a herb, and for some unknown reason, it has a magical effect on cats. It's like a drug to them. One sniff and they go completely crazy.'

The truth began to dawn, and as it did, Louise's face broke into a smile.

'So that's what you did, you madman. You got hold of some of the catnip stuff and you stuck it on the ads.'

Now it was Sam's turn to smile.

'Actually you can get it in a spray so it wasn't very difficult. I'm just astounded none of the other agencies did the same.'

'How could they?' Louise scoffed. 'None of them knew

253

about the cat. Competing agencies don't fall over themselves to discuss a pitch. If you'd hadn't run into Marty, you wouldn't have known either.'

Sam put his arm round her.

'But I did know. And we got the business. So how about hitting the town tonight?'

Now it's come, Louise thought. The moment I've been waiting for for six months. The moment I thought would never happen. She looked at Sam, relaxed and radiating victory.

At a time like this a man goes home to his wife, she thought. The little wife by the hearth who waits. Only tonight he's a long way from home.

Before he got into the shower Sam decided to call home. By now Sarah would have spoken to Frances and told her he was in San Francisco. Now it was his turn to pick up the phone. Explain about today, make amends for yesterday.

It was the first time they had quarrelled. There had been the odd squabble, a word or two spoken in anger, but in nearly two years of marriage there had never been a bad fight – until now. Already Sam was regretting it. He picked up the phone and dialled New York. It was seven o'clock on the Coast, so it would be ten her time. At least she wouldn't go to bed angry two nights running. He pressed the headset closer to his ear. Then he growled with irritation as he heard the engaged signal coming down the line. Frances must be talking to one of her air-head friends. What on earth did she see in these people? He slammed the receiver down and went to take his shower.

Half an hour later, he tried again. Still the engaged signal.

The woman does nothing but talk, he thought. Endlessly yak, yak, yak. Burning up the airwaves, clogging up the connections, wasting his time. He looked at his watch again. It was half seven. He said he'd meet Louise in the bar in fifteen minutes. Okay, he thought, tearing the wrappings off the new shirt he had bought that afternoon. I'll give Frances till seven forty-five to get off the line.

The line was still busy when he tried again and he gave up. If I get in before eleven, he decided, I'll call her again. It'll probably wake her up, but it can't be helped. At least we'll have the chance to make it up.

He strode down to the hotel bar, tall and impressive in his grey flannel suit. Three women on their way out to dinner looked round and wished they were meeting him, rather than the men who were waiting for them. Louise sat up as she approached and felt a flicker of anticipation. He was ten minutes late, but what did she care? Tonight they had more than enough time.

He took her down to Fisherman's Wharf. The whole of the harbourside was lit up with little restaurants and bars and Sam had booked them a table at Jerome's, the prettiest of them all. It was built along the lines of a cruise liner – all stripped pine and hanging ships' lanterns. In one corner there was a tiny bar with portholes for windows and Sam led Louise into it and ordered a bottle of champagne for them both.

'We earned it,' he said. 'It's not every day we present to a cat. And such a difficult cat.'

Louise laughed as the wine waiter popped the cork.

'To the cat,' she said lifting her glass, 'for being such a fine judge of advertising.'

They finished the bottle of champagne and as the waiter came and led them through to dinner, Sam began to be uncomfortably aware of Louise. He had acknowledged she was beautiful a long time ago, almost the first time he met her. Then Frances had come along and he had filed the memory of Louise's beauty away under the heading of missed opportunities. After that she had become merely another employee. A talented art director. Until, surprisingly, she had become a friend. Over the last six weeks while they had been working together, he had discovered another Louise. Not the New York career girl that she presented to the world but a foreigner. An immigrant like himself, with all the hang-ups and insecurities that come with that particular territory.

He knew the territory well. It had been his, until his stint in Israel, where he had found himself.

Because he knew what it was like to have doubts, he understood Louise better than she understood herself. Tonight though, she foxed him. Tonight she had changed from his workmate, his friend, to another creature entirely.

He wondered if it was the dress that had done it. It was an off-duty dress. A dress that showed she had a cleavage and the kind of waist a man could get his hands around.

Sam censored the thought as it came into his mind.

He had no business putting his hands around Louise's waist.

The wine waiter came to their table with the Zinfandel they had ordered. Sam waited while their glasses were filled, then he raised his in a salute.

'To the most beautiful woman here tonight,' he said. 'And the most talented.'

Louise looked at him steadily.

'I'll settle for being beautiful,' she said. 'Talent belongs in the office.'

There was something glowing about her and it bothered Sam. She shouldn't be this radiant. Not for a friend, or a workmate, or a man who was spoken for.

He looked at her with the beginnings of understanding. I'm getting in way beyond my depth, he thought.

Louise smiled at him softly.

'You're very quiet,' she said. 'Is something bothering you?'

Irrationally, Sam was annoyed.

256

'Don't play the vamp with me,' he said tightly, 'you know damn well what's bothering me.'

There was silence.

'Then why don't we do something about it?' Louise said.

He had the insane desire to take hold of her, to undo the clinging, provocative dress. With an effort he reined himself in.

'We can't,' he said harshly. 'I'm married . . . or have you forgotten?'

Louise arched her brows.

'Of course I haven't forgotten. I just didn't think that was terribly important right now. We're not discussing commitment. Or love. Or anything. Are we?'

With another girl, at another time Sam wouldn't have hesitated. But something told him Louise was dangerous. That he would look back on this night and regret it.

He regarded her steadily.

'You make it sound so effortless,' he said. 'A quick bunk-up after a hard day's work. Then back to New York in the morning with no regrets.'

Without meaning to he scowled.

'It wouldn't work that way for me, Louise. Not with you.'

She swirled the wine round in her glass, pretending to be flip and unconcerned.

'You mean with me you'd have regrets.'

'Of course I'd have regrets,' he said harshly. 'You're not just some willing bimbo I happened to pick up on a dark night. I know you now. We laugh at the same things. I listen to your opinions. If we went to bed tonight, we'd lose all that.'

She leaned forward slightly and the thin fabric of her dress lifted from her skin. It was nothing vulgar. She didn't show her cleavage or thrust her breasts towards him. She just rearranged her body underneath her dress. Yet this small subtle movement told him she was available to him.

'I'll take my chances with our friendship,' she said softly.

He knew this was the moment to tell her no. What did he want with a casual night? All his nights were spoken for now. Reserved for Frances.

He glanced up and saw she was studying him.

'You look furious,' she said. 'Is it me you're angry with?'

Sam thought about his wife, and the mink, and the fight they'd had.

'I'm not angry with you,' he said. 'I'm angry with myself.'

She leaned across the table and put her hand over his. 'I didn't mean to do this to you. I guess I misjudged the situation.' She took her hand away. 'I'm sorry.'

If she hadn't touched him, his whole life might have been different. As it was, the contact of her skin woke up something inside him. And he was filled with a need for her so urgent, so demanding that all his fine moral judgements disappeared.

'You don't have to apologise,' he told her. 'I'm the one who should be saying sorry. I behaved like an oaf.'

He stared at her with candour. And this time he didn't bother to disguise his desire.

'Did you mean what you said just now? The bit about taking your chances with our friendship.'

She nodded, her eyes wide.

'Good,' he said shortly, signalling the waiter for the bill. 'You just talked me into it.'

They left the restaurant in silence. And when they got into the street, he put his arm around her waist and she moved closer to him. There was about him an extraordinary lightness. Almost a feeling of relief. As if he had been running away from something for a very long time, and now there was no need any more.

It was dark outside the restaurant and he was tempted to take her in his arms and kiss her. But he delayed the moment. I have time with this woman, he thought. There is the whole night ahead. And the feeling she had woken up in him stirred beneath his skin, shortening his breath and heating his blood.

They got to the hotel just before midnight and the bar was still open.

'Do you want a drink before we go up?' he asked her.

Louise gave him the same wide-eyed stare she had in the restaurant.

'Not particularly,' she said, 'but if you need one to give you courage, I'll understand.'

She was playing with him. Treating him like a little boy nerving himself up to do something dangerous and difficult. His anger returned. I've known harder women than you, he thought. Women with more mileage under their belts than you'll ever know.

He walked across to the desk and picked up his keys. Then before she could do the same, he took her hand and led her towards the bank of elevators.

'We'll use my room,' he said shortly, 'it has a bar.'

When they got inside he didn't make the mistake of offering her a drink again. Instead he put his hands on her shoulders and pulled her towards him. She was taller than he first thought. And bigger. And when he kissed her she didn't open her mouth passively the way Frances did. She kissed him back, pushing her tongue between his teeth, pressing herself against him. They stayed kissing for a long time in the doorway. Until once more Sam took control and led her over to the sofa.

'Sit down,' he told her, 'I want to undress you.'

He took his time. First removing her shoes, then sliding his hands around her waist until he found the zipper on her dress. It came off easily. Too easily. And he wondered if she had put it on tonight with the express intention of sliding out of it at the first available moment.

Then he saw what happened underneath her coverings and he stopped wondering. For Louise was naked except for her stockings which were held up by the tiniest wisp of lace.

'You came prepared,' he said, 'didn't you. You knew in advance what was going to happen.'

She smiled.

'Why don't you stop being angry and start enjoying the situation.'

He didn't answer her. Instead he turned his back and started taking his clothes off.

When he was done he came round and looked her over slowly. Her body was superb. Full and fleshy with breasts the size of melons. He judged her to be somewhere in her twenties. But this was no girl stretched out underneath him. This was a woman who revelled in being a woman. And he wondered how he had resisted her for so long.

He started to touch her. Stroking the side of her face and running his hand down the long line of her neck. Even before he got to her breasts, her nipples came erect and he bent down and kissed them while his hand travelled downwards. She was moist between her legs. Moist and more than ready for him and he knew the time for subtlety was over.

He jammed himself into her. Abruptly, and without warning. It was a crude act of possession and he expected her to protest. Or to cry out, but she smiled.

'So Sam Kurnitz is a man after all,' she said. Then the hunger took over. He had no memory of what he did, how many times he made love to her. All he did know was that sometime during that long, long night Louise became his creature.

It was like breaking a wild young colt. And when the struggle was over and the fight was finally out of her, he knew she would do whatever he wanted.

31

Frances emptied the last of the Moët into her glass, then she went into the kitchen and fetched another bottle. It was eleven o'clock at night. She hadn't seen or heard from her husband for twenty-four hours.

The anxieties that had been hovering on the edge of her mind began to take shape.

Her marriage was in trouble and she didn't know it.

That can't be true, said the voice of her sanity. Sam and I are happy and have been for two years now. If there was anything wrong we would have discussed it. We don't keep secrets from each other.

What about the mink coat? That was a secret, wasn't it?

Only a temporary secret, her good sense answered back. Sooner or later we would have had it out.

And his father dying from cancer. Would he have told you about that if you hadn't prompted him?

Of course he would. We trust each other.

Now all the secrets are out. Do you trust him to come home?

It was the last of her doubts, and any sanity she might have hung onto disappeared in a puff of smoke, for Frances had no answer to it.

Sam had left early in the morning, before she was properly awake, and she waited around and drank coffee waiting for his call. They had never quarrelled like this before.

They had had their spats – brief shouting matches over a new dress or a painting he didn't like – but they were soon repaired. Sam had never walked out on her, or spent the night in the spare room.

Why did I listen to Tiffany, Frances thought bitterly. I could have lived without a mink. As she questioned her friendship Sam's words came back to her. 'Tiffany only cares about one person in the world, Tiffany Greene. Anyone who gets in her way she treads on.'

Sam was right about that, Frances thought ruefully. Sam got in her way by refusing to work on a tobacco account. Only she didn't tread on him. She trod on me instead. So that I could get to Sam.

Despite herself Frances smiled. I wonder what dear Tiffany will do when she finds her plan didn't work out. She glanced at the mantelpiece, checking the date on the gold-rimmed invitation. I'll be seeing her in a couple of hours, she thought. Maybe I'll break the news to her then.

They had both been invited to an exhibition at one of the smart galleries on the upper East side. The artist was one of the darlings of the smart set. *New York* magazine had done a profile of him recently and already some of the bigger collectors were buying him as an investment.

Normally Frances would have looked forward to an event like this. It was a chance to dress up, to drink champagne. To widen her circle of acquaintances. Today, though, she wasn't in the mood for any of that. All she wanted to do was sit in and wait for Sam to call.

She glanced at the clock on the mantel. It was coming on for twelve and she still hadn't heard from him. She thought of ringing his office but her pride wouldn't let her. He'd walked out on her hadn't he? It was up to him to say sorry. She decided to take a shower and get ready. It would pass the time and if Sam called in the meantime, she could always change her plans.

An hour later Frances was spraying herself with Chanel Number 19. She still hadn't heard a word from Sam and she needed to do something. Damn and blast, she thought, I'll go to the gallery. She walked over to her closet and pulled out the black leather St Laurent suit. The short, tight skirt ended just above her knees and the jacket belted into a figure-hugging tunic. When she was finally ready, she gave a last lingering look at the clock, then she fluffed out her bright blonde curls and ran her tongue across her newly rouged mouth.

I'm off, she decided. If Sam calls now the answering machine will have to pick it up.

When Frances arrived at the Santini Gallery the party was in full swing, and she noticed with approval that the beautiful people had turned out in force. Limp young men from Sotheby's jostled up against Broadway actresses and Wall Street bankers. It was the middle of the day, yet everyone had dressed as if they were going to a cocktail party. Frances had been in New York for just over two years yet the city never failed to amaze her. In England nobody dressed up to view a few abstract pictures, yet here, the slightest excuse for a celebration sent everyone scuttling for their designer glitz. She picked out three Chanel suits, a gold lamé dress and a suede trouser suit that could only be Calvin Klein.

That takes care of the people, Frances thought. Time I had a look at the paintings. She grabbed a glass of free champagne from a waiter bearing a silver tray and pushed her way through the crowd.

Close to, the pictures made her eyes smart. The painter expressed himself in bright primary colours, splashing them onto the canvasses in the manner of a child. The result was crude and earthy. Frances knew she should have felt exhilarated by them. The instructor on her interior design course had told her those were the emotions splashy abstracts produced, but they didn't excite her at all. The prices excited her, but the pictures left her cold.

'Dreadful aren't they,' said a voice behind her. 'I should say they were specially done for the sucker market. The rich sucker market.'

Frances turned round to see who was speaking and

encountered a small chubby man in a black velvet suit. He had fair, thinning hair and his features were set in a permanent twinkle, as if he had just heard a very good joke and was aching to share it.

'I don't think we've met,' Frances said.

The plump man extended a hand and introduced himself.

'Bernard Glenn,' he said, 'art critic of the *Daily News*.'

Frances knew the name. She read it on many occasions, but never on the arts pages, and never in the *Daily News*.

He caught her expression and laughed.

'Let me jolt your memory. The political column. *Daily Post*. I was there until last week.'

'Of course,' she said. 'I was a fan of yours. What on earth made you want to write about this kind of thing?'

He caught the eye of one of the waiters and held out his glass to be refilled. Then he said,

'I was getting bored with the *Post* and there was this job going on the *News*. So I grabbed it. For heaven's sake stop looking so surprised. The art world isn't that different from Washington. When it boils down to it, it's all about power and money. An artist or a gallery becomes popular because of the patrons. In the end, they are the people who determine our taste.'

He gestured at the canvas in front of them.

'Take this load of rubbish. Some Mr Moneybags in Texas or London decided this artist was worth watching, so he blew a few hundred thousand dollars in his direction. That excited all the other Moneybags in the art world and they jumped on the bandwagon behind him. It's got nothing to do with how pretty the picture is, or how talented the artist. Most people in the world don't give a damn about that.'

Frances smiled.

'I can't wait to read you in the *News*,' she said.

Out of the corner of her eye she saw Tiffany come into

the gallery. She waved and the dark woman came hurrying over to where she stood.

'Tiffany,' she said, 'meet Bernard Glenn, the new art critic on the *News*.'

They shook hands, then Bernard turned to her.

'You didn't tell me your name,' he said.

'Sorry,' she replied, 'I'm Frances Kurnitz.'

The little man brightened.

'You're not anything to do with Sam Kurnitz?' he asked.

'Actually I'm his wife. Why do you ask?'

'Because Sam and I used to belong to the same poker school. He's a great character, your husband. A great talent too. Though how he gets away with half the stunts he pulls, I'll never know. I've never known such a man for temperament.'

Tiffany looked irritated.

'You can say that again.' She turned to Frances. 'I've just had Clay on the phone telling me about Sam's latest brain-storm. It seems first thing this morning, he came roaring into the office yelling about some cigarette account.'

Frances was instantly apologetic.

'I didn't tell Sam about the business you were chatting up,' she said. 'I just said the agency could be richer if he agreed to work cigarettes.'

'You also told him about me making you buy a mink and lending you the money to do it.'

Her voice had an edge to it and Frances felt herself getting angry. Tiffany was trying to push her into a corner and this time she wasn't going to get away with it.

'Sam is my husband,' she said evenly. 'He pays the bills and I guess that entitles him to know how I spend his money. By the way, he's paying back your loan, so you don't have to worry about that any more.'

Frances glanced at the chubby journalist beside them.

She wasn't keen on discussing her private business in front of strangers but he seemed riveted, and there was no way she could shut Tiffany up.

'I have bigger worries than the few bucks Sam's handing over,' Tiffany continued. 'If he won't change his attitudes about tobacco business, we'll all starve. Do you realise the account I'm holding in my hand could turn the agency round? You've got to lean on him some more, Frances. You owe it to all of us.'

The conversation had gone on long enough. Frances decided to put an end to it.

'Tiffany,' she said, 'as of this morning, I don't owe you or anyone else a damn thing. Sam's paid back the money and I think that just about settles the account between you and me.'

Tiffany's chin came up.

'We'll talk about this later,' she said sharply. 'When you've come back to your senses.'

Then she turned on her heel and disappeared into the crowd. Bernard looked at Frances.

'What was all that about?' he asked. 'That was one furious lady.'

Frances sighed deeply.

'I don't want to talk about it,' she said. 'I came here to drink champagne and have some fun. I didn't expect a hassle.'

Her companion grabbed a bottle of Moët from a table nearby.

'Get stuck into this,' he instructed. 'I'll go look for some party people.'

An hour later, Frances looked into the street and saw it had grown dark. She had no idea of how much champagne she had consumed.

'I've got to be getting home,' she said. 'I'm expecting my husband to call. He'll miss me if I'm late.'

Bernard giggled.

'Let him miss you. It'll do him good. There's no need to break up the party.'

But she wouldn't be persuaded. It was nearly five. Sam would be home in an hour, and if the mid-town traffic was bad he would be home before she was. She said her goodbyes, promised to have lunch with Bernard the following week, then she beat it.

She had been right about the traffic. It took forty minutes in a taxi to get home and when she finally arrived she realised she was more than a little drunk. It took a good five minutes to get the door to the apartment open and she managed to drop the key three times.

As soon as she got in she made straight for the answering machine then stopped dead in surprise. There was nothing on it. She shook her head. It can't be true, she thought. Somebody always calls. She fiddled and clicked around with the machine to see if there was something wrong but she could find nothing.

In despair Frances took her coat off and flung it across the sofa. Then she looked at her watch. It had just gone five. Sam would be home in an hour or so and she realised what had happened. He had decided not to call because the things he had to say couldn't be said down the wire. How silly of me, she thought. I should have known all along.

Frances caught sight of herself in the mirror over the mantle and caught her breath. The girl that stared back at her was someone she hardly knew. Her make-up had smudged under her eyes, her skin was puffy and pink and it must have been raining while she was looking for a taxi, for her sleek curls were a mass of frizz.

'Yuk,' she said out loud. 'This is no way to look.'

She stomped off to the bathroom and started to fill the tub.

By dinner time she was more like herself. She had removed the heavy make-up, washed and blow-dried her

268

fine blonde hair and thrown on a pair of jeans and a cash-mere sweater. She was ready for Sam now, and whatever it was he had to say to her.

An hour later she was still ready but there was no sign of her husband. At half past seven Frances started to worry. He was never home this late. Where could he have got to?

She decided to call the agency. Maybe he had been caught up in a meeting? The unobtainable signal came down the line, so she hung up and called the operator. Five minutes later she got her first clue to what had gone wrong that day. Her phone was out of order.

That doesn't explain why Sam isn't here, she thought, but at least I know why I haven't heard from him. She decided to open a bottle of champagne. She was sober now. Too sober. What I need, she thought, is a helping of the courage I had at lunchtime. It will calm me and give me the patience to wait for Sam.

She had remained calm until eleven o'clock. Then she opened a second bottle of champagne and gave in to her fears. By midnight she had drunk herself into a stupor and as she drifted into blackness all she could remember was Sam's face when he told her he was going to sleep in the spare room. Will I ever see you again, she wondered.

The first thing Sam saw when he woke up was Louise. In sleep there was something mysterious about her. It was as if she locked her soul away when she closed her eyes and he wondered if he would ever really know her.

Sam sat up in the narrow hotel bed and studied the woman beside him, and as he did he was struck by the difference between her and his wife. Frances slept curled on her side like a kitten. Unconscious she was soft, open, accessible. He could scoop her up in his arms and shake her gently awake and she would snuggle close to him, with a tiny ladylike sigh.

Louise was no lady. Sam had learned that last night from her love-making. Now, even with her eyes closed, she was exciting. Her thick black hair curled and snaked around her as if it had some other life, some vitality of its own.

Sam could have gathered her in his arms the way he did his wife, yet he felt not the slightest inclination to do so. He might have broken down her defences last night, but come the morning this woman had a will of her own. She would waken from her slumber in her own time, and in her own way. To disturb her would be an imposition.

Sam got up and wandered into the bathroom. He would take a shower, he decided. Then he would organise some coffee. Then he would call his wife.

He felt no guilt about the night he had spent with Louise. She had made it clear from the start, it meant nothing to her and he had gone along with the spirit of the seduction.

They were two colleagues a long way from home. Friends who had shared each other's bodies. Each other's hungers. Last night he had needed to get the fight with Frances out of his system, to bury the sour taste it had left. Louise had helped him do that. He wondered about her ghosts. What memories, what experiences had he helped Louise bury during the long dark night?

As he came out of the shower, Sam sensed Louise had finally woken, for he heard her moving about the room. Then he saw her coming towards him, and all the lusts of the night before came back to him.

She had put on his shirt, only she hadn't remembered to do up all the buttons and it parted tantalisingly down the front giving him a view of heavy breasts tipped with dark brown nipples. He reached for her, slipping the shirt off her shoulders. Feeling the ripeness of her body against him, and he forgot all the plans he had made for the day. The coffee, the call to the office, the call to his wife. All he wanted was to push himself into that warm yielding flesh, to feel her life, her energy surround him. Sam took

Louise where she stood. Up against the bathroom wall. She responded with such passion that at the end of it neither of them remembered who they were or where they were, and a memory of the night before came back to Sam.

They were finishing dinner and Louise was playing the vamp. 'I know what's bothering you,' she had said. 'Why don't we do something about it.' He had had a foreboding about taking the conversation further and now the same feeling haunted him.

They dressed in a hurry, neither of them wanting to talk about what had gone before. It was only on the way to the airport that Sam remembered that he still hadn't spoken to Frances. She knows I'm out of town, he consoled himself. Sarah would have called and told her that yesterday. She would have probably told her what plane he was coming back on as well. He did a swift calculation. With any luck they'd be landing at seven. Traffic permitting, he'd be home before eight.

He decided to take his wife out to dinner that night. Normally after a trip like this he liked to put his feet up and relax but things were different now. They'd quarrelled, and he'd run away from the situation. Tonight he had to mend his bridges and the neutral atmosphere of a restaurant would make things easier.

He glanced across at Louise, sleek and self-contained. The independent career woman who seduced on a whim and forgot about it the next day. Sam felt challenged.

I'm more than just another scalp he thought.

The moment Sam came through the door, he knew something was wrong. She wasn't waiting for him. Every night, after the office, Frances would greet him with a freshly made martini. There would be music on the stereo and she would be sitting curled up in front of the fire.

This evening the drawing-room was empty and the whole place had a look of neglect about it, as if he lived there alone. He had a moment of panic. Frances had left him. She had moved out lock, stock and barrel and gone home to England. Then he heard her voice and the tension started to leave him.

She was in the kitchen making supper, and he called out to tell her not to bother.

'We'll get something out,' he explained. 'It will be easier.'

Frances turned around, and when Sam saw her face he realised she had been crying and he felt like a heel. What in God's name did I think I was playing at, he thought. First I shout at her. Then I don't call. And then ... he remembered Louise, and the guilt he had been suppressing all day threatened to overwhelm him.

He took hold of Frances like a drowning man and pulled her into his arms. She came to him slowly, almost fearfully.

'Don't worry,' he said quietly, 'I won't hurt you again.'

Sam felt Frances relax against him and in that moment he swore the thing with Louise was over.

They stayed holding each other for a long time and when they finally parted all the explanations, all the carefully rehearsed apologies seemed like so much garbage. All that mattered was that they had come back to each other.

'Don't ever do that to me again,' Frances said.

Sam went to the fridge and took out a bottle of Chablis.

Carefully he poured the cold white wine into two glasses. Then he handed her one.

'I have a feeling that if I did,' he said slowly, 'you might not be here for me when I got home.'

Frances smiled wearily.

'I'd be here,' she said. 'You can count on that. But I can't guarantee what kind of shape I'd be in.'

He took a sip of the Chablis, and looked worried. 'Sarah told you where I was, I hope.'

'When she finally got through,' Frances said. 'There was a fault on the line, but I don't expect you knew that.'

Now it all made sense. That was why he couldn't get through from San Francisco. Sam wondered, if he had, whether it would have made any difference to his evening.

'Actually I didn't know,' he told her. 'But I don't think that really matters now. What's important is that this doesn't happen to us again.'

Frances looked at him.

'How do we stop it?'

'We set up a few ground rules. If I promise never to walk out on you again, then you must promise me something. You must tell me what's going on. If you've spent too much money on a coat, or a dress or a piece of furniture, then for Christ's sake talk to me about it. It's not my money you're spending, it's our money. If we're going to share our lives, then we have to tell each other the truth. It can't work any other way.'

Frances nodded.

'I've learned my lesson,' she said. 'From now on there'll be no more secrets. For either of us.'

For an instant the image of Louise, hungry abandoned Louise, flashed across the retina of Sam's mind. He forced a smile.

'That sounds like a good plan,' he said. And he wondered why the words sounded so hollow.

He avoided Louise. They ran into each other at meetings, but the things they usually did – the lunches, the gallery visits, the picnics in the Park – were things of the past. Sam no longer wanted to be alone with her, because if he was they would talk about what had happened between them, and that would somehow make it real.

Louise sensed his feelings and kept her distance. The encounter had confused her. More than that. It had upset her. All her life love had been a game. A game where you were either the predator. Or the victim. But with Sam the game hadn't played out according to these rules. Sure, she had started out as the predator, but something strange happened after that. They had become friends, and that altered things since it involved her emotions. Sam had been right about seduction changing things. When Louise had gone to bed with him she had felt more than lust, and when he satisfied her, her heart responded as well as her body. She knew she was done for.

Sam had made her feel the way no other man had, and because she knew no other word for her condition, Louise suspected she was in love.

She felt better as soon as she recognised the fact. She knew it was hopeless. She knew the man she loved belonged to another woman. She knew the man she loved didn't love her. Yet she loved . . . Nobody could take that away from her, and it gave her a kind of strength.

Two months later Louise needed all the strength she could get, for it was then she heard that Frances was pregnant. Mike Calder, who she still saw from time to time, told her. And when she heard how far along the baby was, she was astonished. Sam had made his wife pregnant almost as soon as he had come back from San Francisco. It was as if what had happened between them counted for nothing, and it hurt Louise. She might be struck by love but the man who created the emotion didn't give a damn. All he cared about was his little wife. Little blonde, ineffectual Frances. The girl who had stolen Sam from under her nose two years ago.

Louise felt an unreasoning hatred for her. You don't deserve him, she thought. What did you ever do in your life to merit a man like that? I bet you don't even understand what he's saying half the time. She recalled the endless conversations she had had with Sam when they were friends, before sex had taken all the words away, and she missed them. She missed the arguments, the ideas sessions, the reminiscences about the Bronx.

Whatever happened between us, she thought, at least we can be friends. Not Frances, not even love, can take that away from me.

She picked up the phone on her desk and dialled Sam's office.

'I want to talk to you,' she said. 'When are you free?'

They had lunch the next day at Reuben's deli on Second Avenue. It was a cosy, bustling place with leather booths for the customers, and old-style waitresses. The kind of watering hole you took your mother to, or your best friend.

And that's why Louise chose it. She knew Sam was frightened of reviving the feeling between them and though she wanted to bring it back, she knew she would lose if she tried. So she didn't try. She relaxed and came on like an old pal.

She didn't fool anyone.

The moment they sat down, Sam came straight to the point.

'What do you want to talk about?' he asked.

Louise was thrown. Most lunch tables, most bars, demand a measure of small talk. She had expected that, counted on it. Instead she was confronted by this glowering, chilly stranger. She decided to be honest.

'There was nothing particular I wanted to discuss, if that's what you mean. I just wanted to talk. The way we used to talk before . . .' her voice trailed off.

'Before San Francisco,' Sam said harshly. 'Before we went to bed together.'

There was something crude about the way he said it.

'It wasn't so terrible,' Louise said, 'was it?'

She looked at him, and through the blackness of his fury, she saw something else. She saw he was frightened.

He cast his eyes down to the plastic surface of the table.

275

'It wasn't terrible,' Sam said softly, 'that's the problem.' He was silent for a moment. Then he went on.

'Look, I don't expect you to understand. How could you, you never committed yourself to anyone else. But I did. Two years ago, I told a girl I loved her and I would be true to her for the rest of my life. She believed me. Damn it, *I* believed me. Then you came along and all my promises were blown away.'

A waiter came over to take their orders and Louise asked him to bring the salt beef with coleslaw on the side. It was a meal she and Sam had shared half a dozen times before and Louise allowed herself a wry smile. I know what he wants to eat without having to ask, she thought. I wish I knew what he wanted to do with the rest of his life. 'You make it sound like it was all my fault,' she said gently. 'One minute you fell in love with Frances, the next I was there. It wasn't like that. We knew each other long before Frances even came into the picture.'

Now it was Sam's turn to smile. 'I suppose you want to know why I didn't take things further at the time.'

Louise was curious.

'Yes, actually.'

The waiter came with knives and forks and dishes of pickles, and Sam ordered martinis for them both. The presence of alcohol, he felt, would ease the conversation, or at least take some of the sting out of it.

'You had a lover,' he said without preamble. 'I found out about it before I hired you. I was asking around about your work, how you were in meetings, that sort of thing and Brian Elder's name came up. From what I could make of it, he was the reason you succeeded as quickly as you did, and it made a lot of sense. Girls in their twenties don't have your kind of track record. Nobody trusts them to work on the really big accounts, unless their uncle is the chairman of the board, or they have a friend in court.'

'And you didn't want to know me,' Louise said, 'because of Brian. Is that it?'

Sam nodded.

'I don't poach on other people's territory. There are enough girls available without that.'

The waiter arrived with the martinis and Sam took a swallow of the chilled liquid before he went on.

'There was something else I didn't like. The way you and Brian were set up . . . He was married and powerful, and you were beautiful and ambitious. The whole thing sounded more like a negotiation than an affair, and I didn't want to be caught up in something like that. I like my sex private, and nothing to do with business.'

Louise looked at him, her drink untouched. Sam saw the beginnings of anger on her face.

'What the hell do you know about it?' she demanded. 'You were one of the lucky ones with education and choices. Well, I didn't have your start in life – and I wasn't a man either, so I didn't get to call the shots. When I started work I was the lowest of the low. A slum bunny from Kingsbridge. Even the secretaries had more clout than I did. If I didn't toe the line and I mean toe the line, then I was out. No questions asked. And no references.'

She sighed.

'You had me typecast as a ruthless ambitious woman, when all I was was a scared little girl trying to hold onto her job.'

'That's not the way I heard it,' Sam said softly. 'The way the story was told to me you had half the guys in the account group running scared, and you knew how to call the shots all right.'

Louise looked at Sam steadily, the anger still bright in her eyes.

'It didn't start out that way,' she said bitterly. 'In the beginning I played the game Brian Elder's way, and when

277

he clicked his fingers, I jumped, turned somersaults, lay on my back – or anything else he wanted me to do. Then after a while I learned I didn't have to take it all the time. I might not be able to tell Brian Elder what to do, but there were other people who would listen to me. People who would jump when I clicked my fingers.

'Listen, what I did wasn't very moral or very praiseworthy, but at least when Brian kicked me, I knew I didn't have to absorb all the pain myself. I could pass it down the line. And every time I did, every time I threw my weight about, it made me feel a bit better about what I was doing.'

Sam was reminded of a soldier he knew back in Israel. He was a brave man – more of an agent than a soldier – and because of it he spent a lot of time behind enemy lines. He never spoke of his experiences, but Sam knew he had suffered. His suffering, like Louise's, showed in his attitude to the men under him.

Sam understood the soldier. He was a patriot who martyred himself for his country, but Louise was a different story. What, he wondered, made a girl like her take on all that grief?

'Surely the job wasn't that important,' he said.

Louise took hold of her martini now, swallowing it quickly and the strong drink revived memories of the past.

'It may not have been important to a lot of girls,' she told him, 'but for me, it was everything. It was my one means of staying in the city. Without that job, without that salary I would have had to go home again. I couldn't do that. I couldn't go back to the Bronx.

'Look, I don't hate my parents. I love them, and I'm not ashamed of being Greek. But I am ashamed of being a poor Greek. A greaseball. I was damned if I was going to live with the icons and the Orthodox Church and all the baby greaseballs clinging to my skirts. I'd seen my sisters and my girlfriends settle for that. I wanted better.'

Sam looked at her, finally understanding.

'And Brian Elder was better than going home.'

Louise pulled a wry face.

'I guess you could say that.'

With a suddenness Sam remembered his own childhood. His father the threadbare intellectual. His mother with her Hungarian rituals. Both of them clinging to the old ways. The foreign ways. He'd escaped from them by going to Israel. Louise had opted for the woman's choice. She'd taken a lover.

And now as he looked at her, he realised why he had been fascinated. Why he had betrayed his wife. For he and this woman were one and the same person. If he had had a sister or a twin she would have been just like Louise. Only I don't have a sister, he reflected ruefully. I have a lover.

He reached across the table and took her hand.

'I think it's time we stopped pretending,' he said. She looked at him then, her eyes searching his face. 'I never pretended,' she replied. 'I always loved you.'

'Enough for a hole-in-the-corner romance? Enough to deny me to your friends? Enough to be alone at weekends and Christmas? Surely you want better than that.'

She didn't drop her gaze.

'Are you asking me or telling me?'

For a moment Sam thought of Frances waiting for him at home. Frances who trusted him. Frances who needed him. Then Sam thought of his own need. And the moment passed.

'It's not going to be easy,' he told this new woman in his life, 'we'll both have to tell lies. And there'll be compromises. But if you can live with that, I can too. I can't deny you any more.'

32

In the spring Abner Morris took Tiffany to see 'Rigoletto', 'The Marriage of Figaro' and 'Tosca'. Now he was proposing to escort her to 'Don Giovanni', and she was in a quandary. As much as she enjoyed doing the town with the tobacco baron, it couldn't go on like this.

Clay condoned her friendship with Abner for one reason and one reason only. He had come up with a big slug of business for the agency. The cigarette account he had hinted at had become a reality. The Frisco brand was Tiffany's for the taking. All sixty million dollars' worth of it. Only she couldn't take it, because Sam wouldn't hear of it.

Tiffany knew she was going to have to tell Abner the news and it frustrated her. Sixty million bucks' worth of billing didn't come along every day of the week. Nor did men like Abner Morris.

In the past she had traded her body for business favours and it had been a duty, a chore almost. Abner Morris was in a different class altogether. Right from the start she had found him attractive and the attraction had been mutual. Tiffany, whose knowledge of music began and ended with the Beatles, suddenly found she had a taste for Verdi and Mozart. Abner liked that kind of thing, therefore so did she. She bought herself a copy of *Kobbe's Opera Guide* and read it from cover to cover. She bought old recordings of Callas and Mario Lanza and played them while she was in the bath. When Clay remarked on her sudden interest in classical music she reacted sharply. Too sharply.

'Do you want Abner Morris to think I'm a half wit?' she demanded.

'I didn't say that,' Clay said patiently. 'All I wondered

was why you became so interested in these operas he keeps taking you to. I thought it was the guy's business you were after. That's what you should get serious about. The rest is a waste of time.'

Tiffany kept quiet. There was no point in telling her husband that everything about Abner – his business, his intellect, his body – completely fascinated her. She'd been around long enough to know that devoted breadwinners didn't grow on trees. No, she decided, she'd have her fling with Abner and keep quiet about it. As long as she brought in the business nobody was going to look at her too closely.

Only she wasn't bringing in the business. Damn you, Sam, she thought. There has to be a way of convincing you to take Frisco. And if Clay can't talk you into it, and Frances can't move you, then it's high time I tried my luck.

Which is how Clay, Sam, Tiffany and Louise came to be sitting in the bar of the Four Seasons early one Thursday evening. Louise was present at the meeting due to her recent promotion to junior partner and Tiffany was pleased to see her there. She had recognised Louise's ambition right from the first time they had met, and she suspected that any scheme which meant profits for the agency would meet with her support.

Her suspicions proved right. As soon as she brought up the subject of the meeting, the Greek girl was full of enthusiasm.

'This is the break we've been looking for,' she said eagerly. 'A chunk of business this size could turn us into quite a different sort of agency.'

'You bet your life it will,' interrupted Sam. 'For a start I won't have anything to do with it.'

Tiffany expected Louise to back down but she did nothing of the sort.

'Look,' she said, 'I know how you feel about working on cigarettes, but you don't have to handle the business yourself. Clay and I will work on it, then your hands will be clean.'

Sam was unconvinced.

'As long as my name is on the door, I'm involved. Anyway it's difficult to turn a blind eye to any slug of business that size.'

Tiffany interrupted them.

'I've been sitting listening to you refuse tobacco accounts for nearly ten years now and I'm getting bored with it. For Christ's sake, you must have some kind of responsibility to your partner. If you were in business for yourself, I could understand your attitude, but you aren't. You've got two partners with bank loans and bills to pay. Try considering them for a change.'

Sam looked around the large wood-panelled room. All around them were men in business suits doing multi-million dollar deals. The women who accompanied them were dressed in fur coats and real diamonds. Everyone present was paying over the odds to drink in comfort.

'If we were all up against it,' he said evenly, 'I might listen to what you're saying, but we aren't. You and Clay live high on the hog and you can well afford to do it. Louise started dressing at Ralph Lauren a couple of months ago, and thanks to you Frances spent twenty thousand dollars on a mink only the other week. To put it mildly, we're hardly in danger of starving.'

'That's not the point,' said Tiffany. 'We live well enough now, I can't argue with that, but what this new piece of business will do is put us in the big league. Kurnitz and Greene will be seen to be a serious agency and more serious slugs of business will come our way.'

Sam looked at Tiffany in despair.

'And what will you do when you're in the big league?' he asked her. 'Buy more designer tat? Eat two lunches instead of one? Join another golf club? Surely there has to come a time when more money is superfluous. Even for you.'

To Tiffany's surprise it was Louise who came to her rescue.

'I think you're going off at a tangent,' she told Sam. 'Ambition isn't just about money. It's about building. When I work on a tiny account, I break my back to turn it into a medium-sized account. Yes, it makes everybody richer, but that's not all of it. If my expertise can grow a business – be it an advertising account, or an advertising agency – then it's a measure of how good I am. Right now I'm a partner in a medium-sized agency, but I'm working like crazy for it to be a big agency. I know Clay is doing the same thing, and so are you. So why not take on American Tobacco? It will get us to where we want to go. And it will get us there fast.'

Sam rounded on her.

'Did you ever think of the consequences of this great ambition of yours? Did any of you? Or are you all so hell bent on success that you don't care a damn about who you might kill on the way.'

He put his drink down and stood up.

'Tobacco is a killer you know. It rots the lungs. It gives you cancer. Or did that escape your notice?'

Before anyone could say anything, he was on his way out of the bar.

A week later, Tiffany was reliving the scene with Abner.

They were at the Met during the first interval of 'Don Giovanni', and they had decided to drink their champagne at the base of the grand staircase.

For Abner, one of the treats of visiting the opera house was to gaze up at the Chagall murals. He particularly enjoyed seeing Sir Rudolph Bing, who ran the Met, all dressed up as a gypsy. He liked Sir Rudolph even more than the depictions of Verdi and Wagner floating down the Hudson River. Though it was a close-run thing.

Abner's fascination was starting to irritate Tiffany. She was half way through telling him how Sam walked out on everyone at the Four Seasons when she realised he wasn't taking a blind bit of notice. She decided to give him a jolt.

'So you see,' she said, 'we just can't go on meeting each other any more.'

Abner refocused his attention. Fast.

'What was that?' he asked. 'I'm sorry, I'm not hearing you very clearly.'

Tiffany raised her voice.

'Our friendship,' she said. 'It's finished. Over.'

Abner noticed for the first time that Tiffany was wearing a Paris original. It had to be a Dior or a Balmain for it was cut on classical lines. Severe and simple. But what drew his eyes was her décolleté. The dress plunged halfway to her navel and despite himself, he felt a sense of outrage. How dare she tell him that this courtship would not end up in bed, when that's what she was dressed for?

'Do you mean to tell me,' he demanded, 'that just because your husband can't take my business, I don't get to see you any more?'

Tiffany nodded.

'Without an above-board reason like an advertising account, how can we? And incidentally it's not my husband who won't take your business. It's Sam Kurnitz.'

'And who the fuck is Sam Kurnitz?' Abner was shouting now and a group of blue-rinsed matrons in full evening dress turned to stare. He opened his programme and attempted to hide behind it. Tiffany gently disentangled him. Then she explained about Sam. He could hardly believe her.

'What makes this guy so independent that he can afford to turn away sixty million bucks' worth of billing?' Abner said, amazed.

Tiffany shrugged and her cleavage moved disturbingly.

'Don't think we haven't all asked that question,' she said, 'because we have. But every time we try to make him see sense, it's the same old story. "Tobacco kills. Tobacco's immoral." There seems to be no way round it.'

With an effort Abner dragged his eyes away from Tiffany's breasts. He had set his heart on possessing her and he had been willing to pay the price. So what was Sam Kurnitz doing standing on his wallet?

'There's a way round everything,' he said finally. 'There's even a way round Sam Kurnitz.'

The bell for the second act sounded in their ears and Abner offered his arm to the vibrantly lovely woman he was escorting. Tiffany took it and they made their way to the auditorium. As they took their seats in the front circle, Abner leaned across and whispered in her ear.

'The next time we meet,' he informed her, 'I'll tell you exactly how we're going to make Sam Kurnitz work on a tobacco account.'

The following day Abner Morris got to work. His personnel consisted of one personal assistant, two junior executives and a battery of secretaries. He set them all on finding out about Sam Kurnitz. He wanted to know the man's parentage, the kind of education he had, his business history from the moment he earned his first dollar.

In the first few days he had all the details in his hands and they told him nothing. Sam was the son of an immigrant. So were most of the citizens of New York. Sam won a scholarship to Columbia, he got good grades, he had a brief career as a novelist before serving in the Israeli Army. He was a good adman. Interesting information in itself, but it still didn't give Abner a handle on the man. What Abner was looking for was a weakness. A vice. A shameful secret. Something that could be used against him.

Find out more about Kurnitz, he instructed his staff.

285

What does he drink and how much? Does he have a temper? What are his loves, his hates, his fears?

Two weeks later a full report was on his desk.

Sam Kurnitz had had two great loves in his life. His first wife, the girl he married in Israel, and his present wife, the girl he married in New York. They were called Leah and Frances respectively. Nothing interesting there. Abner turned the page.

Over the next half hour Abner learned that Sam liked small casual restaurants, was a moderate drinker, had no homosexual tendencies and apart from smoking a little pot, had no discernible vices.

It was a good report, there was no getting away from that. His staff had visited the man's tailor, his barber, even the local delicatessen he patronised. They could come up with no flaw.

Abner pulled two top marketing men away from his tobacco business and let them loose on Sam. They had instructions to infiltrate the advertising business. Speak to friends and contacts they were told, start drinking around the industry bars, cultivate Sam Kurnitz's former rivals, his present rivals, the mistresses he left behind.

The next report was a little more forthcoming and what it revealed to Abner was that Sam was an emotional man. A passionate man. The girls who had loved him spoke of crazy weekends on the West Coast, picnics in the park, sex that set them alight. Sam Kurnitz, it appeared, was an energetic and skilful lover. Abner sighed in disappointment. If he had been a kinky lover, that would have been different. If he had liked dressing up or being beaten Abner could have used the information against his quarry. But apart from a few unusual positions, the report revealed nothing out of the ordinary. Sam was a hard living, well endowed all-American stud.

The remainder of the report dealt with Sam's temperament. Abner scrutinised it closely. Here, he thought, could be the weakness he was looking for. Sam, it seemed, didn't suffer fools gladly. He was given to having furious arguments with executives who didn't agree with what he was doing. The man didn't just scream and shout either. There had been occasions when he threw things. Once he had even punched an agency vice president who had gone against him.

Abner read on. Sam cared about his work with the same passion that he cared about his women and he put everything he had into it. There were details of brilliant campaigns, Clio awards, huge profits for his clients. As a potential client it should have pleased Abner to know about Sam's skills, but the information frustrated him. If the guy was that good, that talented, then he could yell at whom he pleased and it would make no difference. He skimmed over accounts of Sam's legendary fights with clients. So what, he thought, Kurnitz may be a rude bastard but the punters kept coming back for more.

He threw the dossier down in disgust. He had wasted weeks on what seemed like a fruitless quest. His best men and women spending all the money in the world could turn up nothing incriminating on Sam Kurnitz. It was then he made his final decision. He would put a private detective on the case. If he put a permanent tail on the man, then something was bound to turn up. In Abner's experience, there was no human being invented who could stand that kind of scrutiny.

He took a leather-bound address book out of one of his desk drawers and turned the pages until he got to Ken Baker. The man was a snoop he used for very special occasions. If he wanted to nail somebody or bury somebody, Ken could provide the ammunition. And if there was no ammunition, then Ken could plant it. But maybe he wouldn't have to, Abner mused. Who knows what adventures Sam Kurnitz got up to when his wife wasn't looking?

Abner dialled the number he found in the address book, then he put the phone down in disgust. There was no reply. Never mind, he thought, Ken will surface sooner or later, and when he does I have a very special, very secret assignment for him.

He took hold of the dossier he had been reading and made to throw it in the wastepaper basket. As he did, an envelope that was clipped to the back page fell onto his desk. He picked it up in curiosity and emptied out the contents. They were a set of photographs of Sam and a tall fair girl who was probably his wife.

There was something about the girl that arrested Abner's attention. He recognised her, though for the life of him he didn't know from where. In his working day Abner supervised the lives of a hundred Macho girls and a hundred more potential Macho girls. In the end tall, sexy looking blondes all blurred into one.

He took hold of the picture again and tried to identify the girl. Then he glanced at the caption at the bottom. Her name was Frances. Frances Buckingham. Suddenly it all clicked into place, and Abner knew exactly who she was. More importantly he knew who she had been. The girl in the picture was the former mistress of his English partner, Richard Gregory.

He remembered the disdainful way she had looked at him when they first met, and the way he had won her round when they got to know each other better. He had earmarked her then for his own personal pleasure, and when she and Richard started to drift apart he had moved in. Only things hadn't worked out the way he'd planned.

Abner shook his head regretfully. He had been so sure Frances would see things his way. All Richard's other girls had believed him when he told them his partner had lost interest. Anyway, who could say it was an out-and-out lie? Frances wasn't the only girl sharing Richard's bed. He was bound to throw her out one day. All Abner had been doing was hastening the moment.

Damn, he thought. How could she have been such a fool?

Abner could still see the pale, delicate-looking girl sitting behind the dinner table he had prepared for her. She had been wearing a black lace cocktail gown and he had calculated to the second exactly how long it was going to take him to get her out of it. I should have waited until dinner was over, he berated himself. Maybe she would have been more amenable then.

In his heart, he knew he was kidding himself. The blonde had wanted nothing to do with him. She made that clear when he tried to take her in his arms. He winced at the memory now, for she had taken hold of the table arrangement and cracked him over the head with it. When he came to after the event, the girl had gone.

He had put the whole business down to experience. Women were unpredictable. The coldest ones were attainable. The ones you thought were a pushover turned out to have hearts of steel. The Frances Buckingham fiasco was regrettable but it was par for the course.

He looked down at the picture in front of him. And now she shows up again, he thought. Well, what do you know.

Abner picked up the buzzer on his desk and signalled through to his secretary. When she answered he gave her the following instructions.

'Go down to the Macho file for three years ago and find me all the photographs taken around 1975. What I'm looking for are pictures of potential centrespreads. Girls we were considering for the magazine, but who we didn't use. Get together everything you can find and bring it up to me as soon as you can.'

Then he sat back in his chair and gazed at the view from his window. From the 89th floor he could see the Chrysler building, the Empire State and shimmering in the distance the Hudson River.

No matter how many times he looked at the vista, it never failed to give him pleasure. Abner felt in a strange way that he owned it, that the town was his, and he was lord of everything in creation.

It was a power complex and he knew it, yet it didn't bother him. He had earned his power just as he had earned his millions. He was entitled to call the shots.

Abner's secretary came into his office bearing a mound of paperwork. There were colour transparencies, black and white negatives, glossy prints. Somewhere in that lot was the solution to his problems. The girl deposited the pile on his desk and he started to rummage through it.

The girls who had posed for *Macho* magazine were no innocents. They displayed their flesh without the slightest shame or the slightest embarrassment. There were hungry looking brunettes and raunchy blondes. Even Abner, who had seen it all before, was stirred beyond the call of duty. But he wasn't looking to be stirred. He was looking to get even.

For the next hour he gave himself a headache squinting at transparencies and finally, when he was beginning to despair of finding anything, he saw them. Right at the bottom of the pile. They were glossy prints, black and white, seven by five and slightly fuzzy round the edges. The quality of the pictures didn't bother Abner, though.

What concerned him, what riveted him, was the content. For there in front of him was the evidence he had been looking for. Frances Buckingham, naked as nature made her, sprawled on a rumpled bed. It was evident from the look in her eye that she and some unseen man had coupled on that bed and the afterglow of sex permeated the glossy prints.

I wonder what Sam Kurnitz would think if he saw these, Abner wondered. He can't have any idea that the girl he

290

married, that uptight, snotty English rose would stoop to posing like this for a men's magazine. For a second he put himself into the other man's shoes. If it was me, he thought, I'd kill her for this. Or I'd divorce her. Or both.

Abner considered sending them to Sam. Then he thought again. What would that achieve? A break-up with his wife. He smiled. That would even the score with Frances but would it further Abner's cause? Would it make Sam take on his cigarette account? He decided it wouldn't. No, there had to be a better way.

He turned his attention to Frances. According to the dossier she and Sam had been married for nearly three years. That made them virtually newly-weds. He probably still paid attention to what she was saying over the breakfast toast. Then he knew what he had to do. It wasn't Sam he was going to send the pictures to. It was Frances. If she knew that he had evidence that could bury her and her marriage, then she would move heaven and earth to keep that evidence quiet. She might even lean on her husband hard enough to make him work on a cigarette account.

33

Frances woke up starving hungry. She yawned and turned on the bedside lamp. It was three o'clock in the morning and everything was quiet and still. Stealthily, taking care not to disturb Sam, she crept out of bed and shrugged on a dressing gown, then she made her way down the hall and into the kitchen.

Frances knew what she was looking for. It was on the top shelf of her food cupboard, nestling between a pack of spaghetti and an instant cake mix. She opened the cupboard and squinted upwards, then she cursed under her breath. It was just out of her reach.

Frances grabbed hold of the kitchen stool and was about to clamber on top of it when Sam came through the door.

'How many times do I have to tell you to wake me when you get one of your cravings,' he said. He rubbed his eyes and grinned.

'What is it now?' he asked.

She looked shamefaced.

'Pickled gherkins. I did my best to resist, but in the end it was too much for me.'

Sam put his arms round her and gave her a hug.

'You don't have to apologise. You're nearly six months' pregnant. The pickles fixation is perfectly normal at your stage. Just don't get a yen for coal, I've no idea where I could come by it in New York City.'

The cravings had started two months previously and coincided with the change in Frances's shape. One moment she was carrying a few pounds too many. The next she had a tummy the size of a barrage balloon. The rest of her quickly expanded to match.

Some women carry their babies discreetly, needing maternity clothes only in the last month or so of their pregnancy. Frances was the opposite. As soon as she knew she was going to have a baby she started to bloom. Her hair shone. Her teeth sparkled. She gained in confidence. The change came over her the day the doctor told her the news.

Until that moment she had been marking time. Other women might have envied her her designer dresses and party invitations. Frances saw them now for what they were. Ephemeral, passing, infinitely fragile. The dresses would go out of fashion the next season. The party people would desert her the moment somebody more interesting came along. But nobody could take a baby away. Her baby was for ever.

She knew it would be a he. A little boy with black curly hair and a dimple in his chin like his father. Frances spent her days dreaming of what she would teach him and where she would take him when he was finally born into the world.

When she wasn't dreaming, she was preparing. She redecorated the nursery she had painted yellow, papering it pale blue and covering the floor with soft squashy carpet.

Tiffany was initially amused, but after a few weeks of pre-natal classes and proud X-ray photographs of the foetus, boredom set in. To her the baby was an intrusion into their friendship. The mink coat fiasco, she could forgive.

It was a major difference. A bad row. But in the end, they'd patched it up and put the incident behind them. The baby couldn't be disposed of so easily. He influenced everything Frances did. They couldn't order their usual bottle of champagne with lunch because alcohol was bad for the baby. Their prowling round the shops was severely curtailed because the baby made Frances tired and she had to go and lie down most afternoons. Gallery openings always seemed to clash with pre-natal classes and her interests began to change.

In the old days they would gossip endlessly about the love affairs of their friends, who was wearing what and where the next party was being held. Now all Frances's attention was concentrated on her womb. She struck up friendships with one or two of the other young mothers who went to the same classes as she did and Tiffany began to feel like an outsider.

So far she had avoided pregnancy because she feared a baby might interfere with her social whirl. Now she knew for certain it would and the baby fantasy receded even further from her consciousness. Her friendship with Frances suffered much the same fate.

She'll be different when she's had the brat, Tiffany decided. Once she's got rid of her bump and fixed herself up with a decent nanny she'll be part of the human race again.

Frances didn't miss her friend, for now she had company of a different kind. Before her pregnancy she had been alone in the world. Of course, she loved her husband, but he wasn't part of her, not like the life growing in her body. The baby completed her.

Frances took to wandering the streets of New York, sightseeing like a tourist. She haunted the galleries of her previous life, but now she went to look at the pictures rather than the people. On a number of occasions she would stop off and have a long solitary lunch and she chose places where a woman on her own would melt into the background. Irish bars with a changing lunchtime crowd. Chintzy little cafés frequented by shoppers. Her favourite was Serendipity just behind Bloomingdales. It was a dark cavernous place hung about with coloured glass lanterns of the art deco style. You could eat a steak sandwich there, or a pile of chopped liver and gherkins or a huge extravagant salad full of avocado and fruits out of season.

When Frances went to Serendipity she liked to sit at a table in the back. There she could be on her own for hours watching the passing parade of slim-hipped young men and trendy girls dressed in the latest street fashions.

She was sitting there on Tuesday afternoon when she was joined by a stranger. He was tall with the sort of clean cut features she associated with someone who lived in the Hamptons, yet there was a sharpness about him that spoke of the city. She supposed he was a rising executive in one of the banks and she was surprised: that kind of slicker didn't come to Serendipity. They didn't have the time or the leisure. She looked around her. At three o'clock in the afternoon, the restaurant wasn't full. Why is he sitting with me, she wondered.

There are at least two or three other tables free. Why doesn't he drink his cup of coffee at one of those?

She wondered if he was trying to pick her up. Then she looked down at herself and smiled inwardly. No man in his right mind would be interested in a plump matron like her. Not in her condition.

A couple of brightly coloured boys in psychedelic shirts wandered past them and the man sitting beside her chuckled.

'I bet they don't work in a bank,' he observed.

He had a nice voice, well modulated and cultured and Frances was drawn into conversation. He can't rape me, she told herself, not in broad daylight, and he doesn't look like a mugger.

His name was Brian Elder and Frances discovered he worked for McCann Erickson, one of the biggest advertising agencies in the city.

'What a coincidence,' she said. 'My husband works in advertising too. He's got his own agency, Kurnitz and Greene.'

Her companion smiled.

'I know,' he said.

Frances was pulled up sharp.

'How do you know?' she said. 'You've never met me before in your life.'

Brian Elder turned round in his seat blocking off the main restaurant from her view and it was then that she knew that the stranger sitting beside her wasn't there by coincidence. This man wanted to see her. He probably engineered the whole meeting.

Frightened, she started to get up from where she was sitting but the man put a hand on her arm and pushed her back.

'I'm not some kind of lunatic,' Brian Elder said softly. 'And I haven't come here to hurt you.'

'Then why are you here? And how do you know my husband?'

He looked sad.

'It's a long story,' he said. 'I won't bore you with the details. But if you let me buy you another cup of coffee I'll try to explain a few things to you.'

Frances knew she should tell him to go to hell. Sam had told her over and over not to talk to strangers in the City, yet she was intrigued. This nice looking, well spoken man in his Ivy League suit had sought her out to tell her something. Something maybe to do with her husband. Curiosity got the better of her. She had to have another cup of coffee and hear him out.

It turned out that Brian Elder didn't know Sam after all. He knew who Sam was, and he had tried to get a job in Kurnitz and Greene through a friend of his. A woman called Louise Tragos.

'I know Louise Tragos,' said Frances. 'I can't say I know her all that well, but I've met her once or twice – the last time over dinner at the Greenes'.'

Brian looked tense.

'Did you notice anything unusual about her?'

Frances considered.

'Not really. She seemed a bit intense. A bit hung up about

her work, but then Louise Tragos is one of those New York career women who make a religion out of what they do. Whenever I see her she always manages to make me feel small. Like some kind of appendage or something.'

The coffee arrived together with a dish of chocolate chip cookies. Brian offered Frances one and watched her bite into it.

'You don't like her, do you?'

She looked up.

'Who, Louise Tragos? No I suppose I don't, but then she and I are worlds apart.'

'You're not as far apart as you think.'

Frances took a sip of her coffee.

'How do you mean?'

There was a silence and Brian looked worried. He clearly had something on his mind. Something he wanted to impart, yet he seemed reluctant to come clean. Finally he said,

'Do you have any idea how close Louise is to your husband?'

'I don't know about close,' Frances said guardedly. 'They work together quite a lot. Is that what you mean?'

He looked at her.

'No, Frances, it isn't what I mean.'

Frances felt as if she was playing a scene from a movie. She was in Manhattan, sitting in a fashionable café, and a well-dressed stranger was telling her a woman she loathed was getting close to her husband.

'This is silly,' she said. 'Sam isn't like that. He's not some kind of playboy. He doesn't look at other women.'

'Then what was he doing in Chinatown last Tuesday night?'

Frances sighed with relief. She knew Brian had to be making it up and here at last was the proof.

'Sam wasn't in Chinatown last Tuesday,' she told him.

'He was in San Francisco, talking to some people about a catfood. I know, he called me from there.'

Her companion shook his head.

'You're either very naive, or very stupid. How do you know your husband called you from San Francisco? Was the long distance operator on the line, or did he tell you he was calling from there?'

Frances felt annoyed.

'He told me of course. And I didn't see any reason not to believe him. Why should he lie to me?'

'Because he was spending the night with Louise Tragos and he didn't want you to know.'

Frances began to feel dizzy and faintly nauseous, then she took a hold of herself. If she threw up in Serendipity she could never come back.

'What proof have you got?' she asked the well-tailored man sitting beside her. 'How do you know my husband spent Tuesday night with this Tragos woman? How do you know they are as close as you say they are? And what is it to you?'

Brian didn't miss a beat.

'Because I've made it my business to know. One of the things I was going to explain to you was that Louise Tragos used to be my mistress. I'm married, have been for a long time, but it didn't seem to put her off. She likes married men. Eats them for breakfast. That's how she came to get her hooks into your husband.'

Frances looked around the restaurant, desperately seeking a means of escape, yet something in her refused to get up from her seat. She had to hear Brian Elder out, however far-fetched it was, however unbelievable.

'Do you still see her?' Frances demanded. 'Or do you just follow her around at night?'

He took it on the chin.

'I don't see Louise any more,' Elder said. 'She dropped me the moment I stopped being useful to her.'

'Is that why you're running around telling lies about her and my husband. Are you trying to get some kind of revenge?'

Brian smiled without humour and for the first time since they met, Frances saw the shadows on his face.

'Am I trying to get revenge, she asks me. Sure I'm looking for revenge. But I'm not telling lies. Louise and your old man have been an item for the last two months. Maybe longer. And I'm not the only one who's saying it. Everyone at Kurnitz and Greene knows. Which means that by now most people in Manhattan advertising know. This business is like a village. You can't have a fight with a client without half a dozen agencies pitching for his business the next day.

'Listen, lady, you don't have to take my word for what's going on with your husband and Louise. Ask somebody at the agency. Ask Clay Greene. He's covered up for them often enough.'

Frances got up abruptly, fighting down bile.

'I've heard enough,' she said. 'I'm getting out of here.'

Suddenly it was important to her to disprove what this stranger had just told her. It was a vile story. A vindictive piece of gossip from a man who had been spurned. It needed to be squashed, and she had to find someone who could do just that. Tiffany. If anything was going on, Tiffany would know about it. She was the gossip queen of New York.

Frances made the call from a booth off Fifth, and it was her lucky day. Tiffany was home that afternoon. What Tiffany said wasn't very forthcoming. When Frances asked if she'd heard about Sam having an affair, there was a curious silence. For a moment she wondered if there was something wrong with the phone she was calling from, but there were no problems with the line. The problem lay with Tiffany. She didn't want to talk.

Frances tried threatening her with a visit to Clay. 'Go

ahead,' said Tiffany, 'maybe he'll tell you what you want to know.'

She tried pleading. That was no dice either. Finally she burst into tears.

'You have to help me, Tiffany,' Frances begged. 'I've got no-one else to turn to.'

In the end Tiffany softened, though she wasn't prepared to do any explaining over the phone. Instead she instructed Frances to make her way to the Palm Court at the Plaza.

'It's getting on for five,' she told her friend. 'If I hurry I can be there before six. Why don't you take a walk around Bloomingdales. By the time you're through you'll be in good time to meet me.'

Frances agreed to the plan. If Tiffany had suggested they met in the Men's room, she would have said yes, for her whole life depended on knowing one simple truth. Was her husband cheating on her? The question haunted her as she pushed her way through Bloomingdales. Everything she looked at – the career girl handbags, the junk costume jewellery, the designer jeans – all reminded her of Louise. In her mind's eye she could see her, tall, black haired, somehow foreign-looking. The very opposite of Frances. And it confused her. In her wildest nightmares she could never imagine Sam giving Louise a second glance. But then she didn't think her husband gave anyone a second glance.

Am I blind, Frances wondered, or just stupid. She felt a headache coming on and decided she'd had enough of Bloomingdales. The best plan was to grab a cab and make straight for the Plaza. At least if she was early, she could sit down and gather her wits.

She arrived at the Plaza with half an hour to spare and immediately ordered herself a drink. She knew she shouldn't, not with the baby coming in three months, but after Brian Elder's little bombshell nothing seemed to matter much any more. The baby, her marriage, her future had all started to evaporate in front of her. There was nothing to hold onto any more. Nothing to believe in.

The drink arrived. A whisky sour, milky and somehow innocent looking. Frances gulped it back in one and warmth started to spread through her. Warmth and a curious lightheadedness, as if all the edges were blurring into one. She suspected she was getting drunk but any state of mind was better than the one she had now, so she ordered another glass.

She was half way through it when Tiffany arrived.

'I see you've made a start on the cocktail hour,' Tiffany observed. 'Well, go easy. You're not used to it.'

Frances wasn't paying any attention. 'Don't you think I need this,' she muttered, 'with what we've got to talk about?'

Tiffany grimaced and put in her own order to the waiter. This wasn't going to be an easy couple of hours.

It was Frances who opened the conversation. She told Tiffany about her meeting with Brian Elder whom she had never seen before in her life.

'I shouldn't have bothered with him. I never speak to strangers but he seemed so civilized and kind of friendly.'

She finished the rest of her glass.

'I must have been out of my mind.'

The waiter arrived with two more drinks. A Gibson for Tiffany and another whisky sour for Frances. Tiffany looked worried.

'Do you think you should be having any more of that?'

Then she saw her friend's face and backed off.

'Look,' she said, 'before you get completely pie-eyed, I'd better tell you what's going on with your husband.'

Frances looked wretched.

'I know what's going on with my husband. He's having an affair with Louise Tragos. Apparently it's common knowledge. The whole of Manhattan knows and now I know.'

A tear rolled down her cheek and she wiped it away with the back of her hand. Tiffany sighed and took a pull on her drink.

'It's not the end of the world you know. A lot of men have flings when their wives get pregnant. It's an occupational hazard but they never last. The moment you have the baby and get back to yourself, the other woman disappears in a puff of smoke. She was only there in the first place because you weren't firing on all cylinders.'

Frances was confused.

'What do you mean, I wasn't firing on all cylinders?'

'I'm talking about bed,' said Tiffany briskly. 'Everyone knows once you get pregnant you lose all interest in sex and looking at you, I'm not surprised. If I was carrying that lot on board I wouldn't exactly be in the mood for love.'

There was a silence, during which Frances struggled to her feet.

'There's nothing wrong with Sam in that department,' she said shakily. 'There's nothing wrong with me either. If anything, being pregnant makes things better.'

She started to move away from their table and Tiffany put out a hand to stop her.

'Where do you think you're going?' she asked.

Frances smiled wanly.

'Don't look so worried,' she said, 'I'm only paying a visit to the ladies. I'll be back in a tick.'

Frances made her way across the carpet on shaking legs. During the past few months those same legs had carried her firmly across the City. Now she wondered if she would make it to the hotel lobby. For a moment she regretted the whisky she had consumed. But only for a moment. Her chief concern was locating the cloakroom.

In the end she found it at the far end of the lobby. Down a flight of stairs. With a sigh of relief she grabbed the handrail and started to make her way down. Frances had no idea how she lost her footing, but one moment both her feet were stepping in front of each other, the next she had somehow tripped and her legs were going in all directions. She struggled to keep hold of the rail, but somehow she lost it. And then she fell, bumping her knees, her hips, her back against the twisting staircase. The last thing she thought of before she lost consciousness was her baby. But by then it was too late.

She woke up in a white room with the taste of disinfectant in her mouth. She was lying on a narrow bed and there was a bright light shining in her eyes.

I'm in hospital, she thought. How the hell did I get here? Then she remembered the Plaza Hotel, the drinks she had with Tiffany. The long fall down the twisting, spiralling staircase.

Somebody must have found me and called an ambulance, she decided. As the notion occurred her hands went involuntarily to her stomach.

Only she found she couldn't move them. They were attached on either side to rubber tubes that seemed to come from somewhere above her.

'What am I doing here?' she called out in panic. A nurse in a starched white overall came hurrying through the door.

'Shush,' she soothed, 'you've been very ill. I'll get the doctor to take a look at you now you're with us again.'

She brushed the nurse aside.

'What about my baby?' she asked. 'Is my baby alright?'

The nurse looked worried and fussed with her pillows.

'I'll get the doctor,' she said.

Ten minutes later a small plump man came waddling through the door. He had an air of money about him, as if he would be more comfortable dealing from a private consulting room, rather than a hospital. Frances's heart sank. Men like him never got to the point. They dealt

303

in euphemisms and half truths. Right now she needed to know everything.

She had judged accurately. The little doctor talked at length about what a lucky escape she had had, how her friend Tiffany got her to hospital in the nick of time, how her husband had pulled out all the stops to get her the best private care. Twice Frances asked about her baby and twice the doctor didn't seem to hear her. Instead he hovered around her bed, taking her pulse. Frances waited till he had finished all his tasks, then she waited another five minutes until he had stopped talking. Finally she turned to him.

'It's no good you know,' she said. 'You're going to have to tell me about my baby sooner or later.'

The doctor fidgeted and looked down at his hands.

'What do you want to know?'

Frances nearly cried with frustration. With an effort she said, 'Before I fell down the stairs at the Plaza I was six months' pregnant. Am I still pregnant, or have I lost my baby?'

A pained expression came over the chubby face.

'I put it so bluntly,' the doctor said. 'I don't like to think of it as losing your baby. I prefer to say we saved you.'

Frances looked him in the eye and there was murder in her face.

'I lost my baby,' she said. 'That's all I wanted to know. You can leave me now.'

Then she turned on her side, away from him. The doctor stared at her for a minute or two. Then he shook his head sadly.

'You'll get over it,' he said. 'Try talking about it to your husband. It will help, you know.'

The tears poured silently down her cheeks and into the pillow.

'My husband,' she said bitterly, 'is the last person I want to talk to.'

Later on a nurse came in and gave her a sleeping pill

to get her through the night, but she refused to take it. Instead she left it by her bedside table, promising to swallow it when she needed it. Then she started to think about her life.

When she had heard about Sam and Louise, she had been wounded. Mortally wounded, but not destroyed.

She had had one consolation, however, she had her baby. Her husband could betray her. He could even leave her, and she would go on living because in her body, living alongside her, was the sum total of her and Sam. One day that life she was nurturing would come into the world and after that she wouldn't be alone.

Only it hadn't happened that way. She had got drunk and had a silly accident. Then all her hopes, all her dreams, all her future had died. In one afternoon she had lost first her husband. Then her baby. What next, she wondered.

She knew she couldn't stay in New York. Not now. Not with everything she cared about dead and gone. She sighed wearily. She supposed she could go home. Her family would always have her back now she had done the respectable thing and got married.

Dispassionately she weighed up her advantages. She was twenty-eight, still young enough to find another husband, have another baby. Thanks to Tiffany she had a million-dollar wardrobe and a mink coat. She supposed in time she would get her figure back.

There's only one problem, she thought. When everything has healed and mended and they patch me up and send me home, I wonder if they'll issue me with a new heart. If I'm to fall in love again and make a fresh start, I'll need a heart to do it with.

Unbidden into her mind came the image of Sam. The man she had loved. The man who had betrayed her. Reluctantly she reached for the sleeping pill on her bed-side table.

She could be rational about anything. Her fall. The loss

305

of her baby. The destruction of her future. But she couldn't think about Sam. Not yet. Maybe not ever.

Sam had been in a meeting when he heard about Frances. His secretary had handed him a hurriedly scrawled note.

'Your wife has had a fall. She's in the Mount Sinai.'

The girl had put urgent in capital letters across the top of the piece of paper, but Sam didn't need to be told. He stood up, excused himself and came rushing through to his office.

'What happened?' he demanded. 'Is the baby all right?'

Nobody knew anything beyond the message. The casualty department at the Mount Sinai would say nothing except that Frances Kurnitz was in the accident ward. Shouting at them got Sam nowhere. The switchboard operator seemed indifferent to the fact that Sam was Mr Kurnitz. All he could extract from them was that when he turned up, a doctor would be available to talk to him.

He grabbed his coat and ran out into the street. The sooner he got there the better. It took him fifteen minutes, pushing and shoving his way up Madison Avenue to reach the hospital, another ten to find the right ward. After that the waiting started.

Nobody would let him see his wife. The nurse on duty told him she was not allowed visitors, and when he demanded to see a doctor, he had to stand outside in a corridor for an hour before anyone appeared. Just as he was starting to lose patience, a small plump man in a city suit came towards him through the swing doors.

He introduced himself as Dr Graham and told him that Frances's condition was stable.

'You'll be able to see your wife tomorrow morning,' the doctor said. 'After she's had a night's sleep.'

But Sam had had enough. He grabbed the little doctor by the lapels.

'Listen,' he said, 'just over an hour ago somebody tells

me my wife – my very pregnant wife – has met with an accident. So I come rushing over here like a lunatic. And what happens? Zilch happens. Nobody wants to talk to me. Nobody lets me see my wife. She could be dead for all I know.'

The doctor, who was stronger than he looked, took a step backwards and disentangled himself.

'Your wife isn't dead,' he said. 'At least she wasn't half an hour ago when I looked in on her, but she's full of dope and I'd rather you didn't see her till the morning.'

Sam fought for control.

'Would you mind telling me what's going on. What happened to my wife that you had to fill her with dope?' Then he saw the expression on the doctor's face, and the fight went out of him.

'It's not the baby is it?' he asked.

The fat man nodded.

'We did what we could, but it was already too late by the time she came in. It seems she'd taken a tumble down some stairs. From the sound of it, she's lucky she didn't break her neck.'

Once more Sam rounded on the doctor.

'Damn the dope,' he yelled. 'And damn your petty bureaucratic rules. If you don't let me see my wife – and right now – I'll tear the place apart.'

Dr Graham put an arm out and steered him down the corridor. Then he said,

'I didn't want to tell you this, but I'm not the one who's keeping you from seeing your wife.'

Sam ran a hand through the black wiry hair until it stood on end.

'Then who the hell is?' he demanded.

There was a silence.

'Your wife herself,' explained the doctor. 'She left strict instructions she didn't want to see anyone. Not even you. Look, I wouldn't get too upset about it. She's had a terrible shock. That baby was very important to her, and she needs to come to terms with her loss. Mourn for it if you like. When she's through she'll see you. I can promise you that.'

Sam sat down on the hard wooden bench.

'I don't understand,' he said. 'She needs me. Now more than ever. It's not like her to turn her back.'

The doctor rummaged in his jacket pocket and produced a small box of Nembutal.

'Go home and take one of these,' he instructed, 'then come back in the morning. She'll be back in the land of the living by then.'

He took hold of the pills distractedly. Then he said,

'Look, is there anything I can do for her now? I hate to go home and just leave her like this.'

Dr Graham looked thoughtful.

'There is one thing,' he said. 'You might have your wife transferred to private care. In the state she's in, it will do her a world of good.'

Sam made the necessary arrangements on the way out, then he grabbed a taxi on the sidewalk and went home. He thought of calling Louise. He needed to confide, to give voice to his fears about Frances. Then he canned the idea. He and Louise never talked about his wife. It was one of the first rules of their relationship.

He looked back over the past two months and wondered, as he often wondered, just what it was he had got himself into. It hadn't been easy loving Louise. He'd had to do a lot of lying. A lot of pretending to be in places he'd never seen. A lot of play-acting. Every time he betrayed himself he felt a little grubby, a little ashamed. He promised himself time and time again that it had to stop.

Then he would see her and he realised it could never stop. It was as if both of them were on a giant breaker that swept aside everything in its path, and when they were together they consumed each other.

With Frances it had been different. She had pleased Sam,

delighted him even, but she had never possessed him. He could leave her in the morning and be at peace with himself. She didn't stay on his conscience, she didn't haunt him. With Frances love had been a liberating experience. With Louise it was the opposite. He felt bound to her.

He had to be near her all the time and some days when she was too busy to come to his office, he would go to wherever she was and see her, touch her, inhale her perfume. He would walk out of meetings to consult her on the smallest point. He would break lunch dates if she was free to see him and from time to time he would break dinner dates as well.

He hated himself for lying to Frances. He hadn't stopped loving her, he had simply grafted another love on top of the feeling he had for his wife. Both of his loves tore him apart. When he was with Louise he felt guilty about Frances, and when he was with Frances he worried about Louise.

He knew he couldn't continue to live like this. In the end he would have to make a choice. Now the choice had been taken out of his hands. Frances losing the baby had made up his mind. His wife would need him now. All of him. He could no longer jog along in their marriage the way he had been, with only half an eye on his wife, and half a heart. She deserved all his attention, and from now on in, she was going to get it.

When Sam arrived at the Mount Sinai the next morning he was optimistic. It was going to be tough forgetting Louise but he had only really known her for two months. They would both recover from it.

He made his way up to the private wards on the tenth floor and after asking directions three times, finally found his wife's room. He banged on the door three times and called out her name. There was no response. She's probably in the bathroom, he thought. I'll go in.

Frances was sitting up in bed as he came through the

door and he was shocked at how pale she was and how black under the eyes.

Sam went to her and took her in his arms. She didn't resist him, yet he could feel no response from her. It was like holding a china doll, or a dead person. He let her go, then he sat on the bed and looked at her.

'What is it?' he asked gently. 'What's the matter?'

Frances started to cry. Silent bitter tears that she made no attempt to hide. From deep inside Sam came a compassion he never knew he had.

'I'm sorry,' he said. 'I loved him too, but there'll be more babies. Lots more babies.'

Frances shook her head, scrubbing her cheeks with the back of her hand.

'There won't be,' she said, 'not for us.'

Sam was stunned.

'The doctor didn't tell me you couldn't have any more children. Tell me it's not true.'

Frances smiled sadly.

'If it was true, it would be so much easier, but having children isn't my problem. My problem is you. You and Louise.'

Suddenly Sam understood everything. Her refusal to see him last night, when she most needed him. The dead weight of her in his arms. Her tears. He put his head in his hands, covering his face.

'I'm sorry, my darling,' he whispered. 'I'm so sorry.'

'There's no need.' Her voice was brisk. Businesslike. 'I don't want your apologies, or your explanations. It's too late for that.'

Sam looked at Frances, pale and wretched in the hospital bed and he had an overwhelming urge to gather her in his arms and take her home. She didn't belong in this antiseptic room – it made her antiseptic, too.

'You'll feel different when I get you out of here,' he said reassuringly.

Frances shook her head.

'I won't feel different. Being home won't alter what's happened, or what's going to happen.'

There was a silence, and for the first time since he had known her, Sam felt scared at what she might do. He took hold of her hands.

'Don't leave me,' he begged. 'I can't go on without you.'

Frances twisted her mouth.

'Spare me the crocodile tears,' she said curtly. 'You'll survive. And survive very nicely with Louise by your side.'

'I don't want to survive with Louise,' Sam said. 'She's not my wife. You're my wife. You're the one I want to be with.'

Frances laughed.

'It's a pity you didn't think of that when you climbed into bed with her. Or maybe you did. Maybe you thought you could have a wife and a mistress. A bit like running a second car.'

She paused, letting the anger gather inside her. 'I'm sorry, Sam,' she said, 'but that kind of set-up just isn't my style.'

Sam let go of her hands, got up and walked over to the window. Below him the city hummed and throbbed in the morning rush. Somewhere in the Eighties, Louise would be getting ready to go to the office. She would be applying her scarlet lipstick, the way she always did with a tiny brush. Outlining her mouth sharply, precisely. Painting in the main colour. Then blotting. Then painting.

Sam realised that he'd never see Louise do that again, just as he would never kiss her again or hold her in his arms. The pain of that realisation knocked the breath out of him. Yet there was a greater pain. That of losing his wife.

He turned round and faced her.

'The Louise thing is finished.' The words came out

harshly. With effort. 'It was over when I knew about the baby. I won't see her again.'

Frances looked cynical.

'How can I believe that?'

'Because I'm going to send her away.'

It was a promise he didn't know he'd make until he made it and now it was out the decision was taken.

Frances started to smile, a watery sun breaking through the clouds.

'You don't mean that,' she said. 'Do you?'

Sam hardened his heart.

'Sure I mean it. You're worth more to me than some Greek bit of skirt. What do I want with a girl from the slums?'

34

Every Tuesday evening after work, Clay Greene visited Zilli's Turkish baths in the Bowery. Like many fat men, he believed in the therapeutic qualities of massage and steam baths. He could have achieved better results by simply eating less, but cutting down was boring. Besides, a long, hot session in Zilli's relaxed him. He could think better after spending an hour or so in jungle conditions and it was here he came to grips with some of the tougher problems facing Kurnitz and Greene.

When Sam asked him if he could come with him to Zilli's on Tuesday, he didn't sense anything out of the ordinary. The two of them hammered out some of their best campaigns in the steam room, and Clay reasoned Sam wanted to talk about some ad that was going in the wrong direction. Maybe he wanted to discuss the cigarette business some more. Clay still had hopes of changing Sam's mind on that front. Sixty million bucks was not something a man turned his back on without a struggle.

Sam did not want to talk tobacco. In fact he didn't want to talk about business at all. He wanted to pour his heart out about Louise. The bloodletting didn't surprise Clay. Sam hadn't been exactly discreet about his liaison with the Greek girl. Whenever he looked they always seemed to be touching each other. Her hand would connect with Sam's hair. He'd take her elbow crossing the street. It was nothing obvious. They weren't holding hands and whispering endearments, but people who worked together didn't behave like that unless they were having an affair.

Clay hadn't asked any questions. He knew better than

that. When Sam was ready to talk, he'd come and find him. And he had. In Zilli's Turkish baths.

Clay leaned back against the pine-slatted bench and let the hot steam sink into his pores. I'll give myself two more hours of this, he thought. That should be good for at least five pounds. Then I'll stop off at the deli on the way home and pick up some chopped liver.

The liver and the weight loss generally cancelled each other out. Not that Clay cared, he had no serious intention of ever being any thinner. Only tonight, without meaning to, he strongly suspected he would lose weight for what Sam was telling him was crippling his appetite.

'You can't mean you want to fire Louise,' he said. 'She's just about the best thing we've got. Our three strongest accounts are business she's pulled in, and they could well walk out the door if she does.'

Sam looked agonised.

'Don't think I don't know it,' he said. 'I've been up the last few nights thinking about it, but I can't see any other way. I can't go on working with her in the same office, not after the way it's been between us.'

Clay lumbered to his feet, tucking his towel more securely round him.

'Let's move into the next room,' he suggested. 'A bit more heat will help me think better.'

Sam scowled. A bit more heat will probably finish me off, he thought. Nevertheless he fell in line behind his partner. He needed him now to come up with some answers and if he had to sit and cook while he waited for those answers, then cook he would.

Zilli's was constructed along the lines of an old Roman spa. Each room was connected to the next by a series of grand marble arches and the rooms themselves were divided into cubicles big enough for two acquaintances, or four close friends. Clay made his way into the first vacant space he saw and lay his towel along the pine bench, spreading himself out full length on top of it. Half an hour later he sat up and stared at his partner.

'I think I'm starting to get somewhere,' he said. 'Let's go into the next room and I'll tell you about it.'

Wearily, Sam picked up his towel. At this rate, he decided, Clay will dispose of Louise, my marriage will be saved and I will dissolve into a puddle.

The fourth room reminded Sam of Hades. In here the steam was so thick you couldn't see a hand in front of you. With difficulty he managed to make out Clay's face. He was smiling.

'Tell me about the plan for the London office,' the fat man asked, changing the subject. 'How far is it developed?'

Sam was confused.

'You know how far we've got. You wrote the report yourself only last week.'

Clay smiled some more.

'I want to hear it from you,' he said. 'In case I missed something out.'

Sam recited Clay's expansion plans. Their biggest client, Californian Mills, wanted to extend their business into Europe. The spend across the whole territory would amount to well over one hundred million dollars. With that kind of budget, Kurnitz and Greene could afford the luxury of a London office.

Clay had sounded out their other clients about the project and one or two of them had agreed to let them handle their European business. All the agency needed now was someone to set up the office and run the show.

During the past three months Clay and Sam had interviewed most of Madison Avenue's top managers and they had come up with a blank. The good ones wanted too much money, and the rest couldn't run a bath, let alone an agency.

Then Californian Mills got in touch again. They wanted

to know how the London office plans were going. Their first few brands were scheduled to launch in the autumn and they wanted action. If Kurnitz and Greene couldn't get their plans off the ground, it was tough, but they couldn't wait. The business would have to go to another shop.

Clay turned to Sam.

'How much time have we got left?' he asked.

Sam made a face.

'I'd say just under two weeks. Chet Davis at Californian rang me three days ago to tell me they'd more or less decided to give everything to PKL if we couldn't get our act together.'

Clay started rubbing himself with a loofah, working it down from his shoulders to his arms.

'I think I've got the answer we're looking for,' he said slowly.

Sam looked up.

'Am I to understand you've found someone to run London?'

Clay looked pleased with himself.

'You are. Do you want to know who it is? It's that girlfriend of yours. The fiery Greek. Louise Tragos.'

'You've got to be joking!' Sam threw his towel down in disgust. 'Louise is no manager. She's a brilliant art director, I'll give you that, but she wouldn't have the first clue about running an office.'

Clay didn't change his expression. He took to his feet again and led the way through to the fifth and final room. This was built around a deep marble plunge pool. Clay contemplated it for five seconds, then changed his mind and sat down on the edge. The cool down could wait till later, when he'd managed to talk Sam into the idea of Louise going to London.

He turned to his partner.

'What makes you say Louise couldn't run a business? Is it because she's a woman?'

'It's because she's an art director,' said Sam, deeply irritated. 'I've just told you that. She's just not that interested in business.'

But his voice lacked conviction and he knew it. Clay decided it was time to present a few facts.

'If your girl isn't interested in business,' he said, 'how come she managed to pull in five million dollars' worth of billing? The way I hear it, she gets on better with her clients than the account men do. For Christ's sake, Sam, we both decided to make her a partner because she's such a hot item. So why are you trying to hold her back? Anyone would think you didn't want to send her away after all.'

Sam had suffered long enough. The heat was starting to boil his brains and the cool, blue pool beckoned.

'Maybe I was wrong,' he said. 'Louise could probably run London standing on her head, and if she can't, at least it gives us a breathing space to find somebody who can.'

Clay started to smile.

'So we're agreed then. Louise goes to set up our European branch.'

Sam was poised now at the edge of the pool. Any minute now he would hit the surface. He looked back over his shoulder.

'It's fine by me,' he said. 'But on one condition. You tell her about her new job. It's easier if I don't see her.'

His feet left the tiles as he launched himself into the water and suddenly he was human again. All around him, in the crevices between his toes, in his hair, on every surface of his skin it was deliciously cool. As his sanity returned he wondered if he had done the right thing by Louise. Maybe she didn't want to go and work in Europe? Even if she did, shouldn't he have told her about the move himself?

How could I, Sam thought. I found it tough sending her to work in the next office, let alone sending her to work in the next continent. He had a vision of himself on his knees begging her to stay. 'Don't go to London.

317

Don't leave me.' He could almost hear his voice saying the words.

He frowned and shook the water out of his hair. I was right the first time, he thought. Clay will say goodbye much better than I can.

35

With an effort Louise fixed her mind on the lay-out pad in front of her. It was a simple job. A lettering job, really. She could do it with her hands tied behind her back. So why was she making such heavy weather of it?

Louise took hold of the magic marker and drew it across the page but the deft touch she had always relied on deserted her. The crayon slid out of control and before she could stop it, the whole design was ruined.

What am I doing? Louise asked herself. What has got into me? She knew the answers to both those questions, she just didn't want to think about them – not yet. Not until she got out of the office. Not until she was alone.

She glanced at her watch. It was five-thirty. The happy hour had started at Charlie O's. The hell with it, she thought, I'm not doing any good here and I could use a stiff drink. She stood up and grabbed hold of the suede poncho Calvin Klein was selling that year, then flinging it over her shoulders she made her way out of the door.

She got to the Irish bar on the corner of the Rockefeller Plaza just before six. With some surprise she looked around her. The place was deserted. All she had for company were the blown-up portraits of famous boozers that decorated the bar. Above her Errol Flynn looked down, while the caption underneath him pronounced 'Any guy who has more than ten grand left when he's dead is a failure'. In an alcove another reprobate declared, 'I'll keep drinking it as long as they keep making it.'

But nobody was drinking anything in Charlie O's except for Louise and a couple of copywriters. Then she realised what day it was and she knew why.

It was Friday evening and everyone was rushing away for the weekend. Everyone who was married. Everyone who had someone. She turned to the barman and ordered a Gibson straight up. Every evening Monday to Thursday it's the happy hour in here, she reflected bitterly. It's just my luck to go and choose Friday, the lonely hour.

The drink arrived and Louise sipped it slowly. She was tempted to knock it back, but that wasn't going to solve anything. She needed all her strength, all her resources to face the truth of her situation. For the truth was that Sam no longer loved her.

Louise had known something was wrong the moment she started the day. Sam wasn't in his office. She asked his secretary where she could find him, but she didn't seem to know. Then she asked Clay. The agency chief looked embarrassed. 'Sam's gone away for a few days,' he said. 'It's something to do with his family. I don't know any of the details.'

Louise couldn't draw him any further. Clay wouldn't say when he had left, or where he was going. He didn't have an address where he could be contacted. Or a phone number.

When Louise tried to question him more closely, he retired into his office and shut the door.

Louise was thoroughly perplexed. As long as she'd known him Sam had never gone away without telling her where he was going. Even before they were lovers she always knew where she could find him, and now when they were closer than they had ever been, he went and disappeared into thin air. She remembered they had a lunch date that day. Sam wanted to investigate a new sushi bar on Seventh Avenue and he had booked a table there for twelve-thirty.

I'll go on my own, Louise decided. He hasn't left a message saying he can't make it. She arrived at the sushi bar at twelve-thirty prompt and the waiter showed her to the table. Sam hadn't got there yet. Louise decided to order for both of them and get it out of the way. Looking at the menu, she selected two seaweed starters, the special platter of raw fish and a salad for two.

An hour later Louise was still sitting there alone. Spread around her on all sides was the food. It was arranged in the way that only the Japanese know how. Delicate, like a work of art. On any other day Louise would have devoured it, but today she seemed to have lost her appetite. Something was wrong. Terribly wrong. She realised that now.

At two-thirty she paid the bill and headed back for the agency. She decided to give Clay till four o'clock to come clean and if he continued to hide from her, she would go to him and demand the truth. All the way back to the office, she was assailed by terrible fears. Sam had met with an accident, he was lying in hospital terribly injured and Clay didn't want her to know. An awful premonition hit her. Maybe Sam wasn't injured. Maybe he was dead.

Louise took hold of herself. If Sam was dead, she thought, we'd all know it. We'd have to. There'd be no point in hiding it. No, it was something else. Clay had said something about a family problem. It could be his mother, or even his wife. The thought of Frances terribly injured, perhaps dying, restored her confidence. I shouldn't think like this, she chided herself. It will bring me bad luck.

Louise sat in her office for over an hour waiting for news of Sam. None came. Finally at four, she walked down the corridor to Clay's office. He was sitting at his desk when she came in and he didn't seem very busy. Louise had a feeling he had been waiting for her, for the moment she sat down, he asked her if he could get her a drink.

'It's a bit early for that isn't it?' she said. 'Or am I going to need it?'

Clay said nothing. Instead he started talking about the agency's plans to open a European headquarters. Louise let him ramble on. She had sat in countless meetings going

321

over the project. She knew what the problems were and she mentally tuned out. When Clay got to the point, she'd listen harder.

She was jolted to attention by the mention of Sam's name.

'Sam thought, we both did, you'd be perfect for the job.'

Louise was disoriented.

'What job would I be perfect for?' she asked, puzzled. 'Sorry, I wasn't clear on what you said just now.'

Clay looked impatient.

'I know occasionally I bore you,' he said, 'but I do wish you'd listen when I offer you your own set-up. Other girls would kill for this chance.'

Now Louise was floundering. Clay was giving her something to kill for, something worth having. She searched her mind. What was he getting at? Then the light began to dawn.

'You're not talking about letting me take over the London operation, are you?'

Now the fat man started to relax. She'd taken the bait.

'Well, what do you think?' he asked.

'It's what I've always wanted,' she said. 'What I've dreamed about since I left art college.' But it wasn't that simple, and she knew it. Nobody threw a plum like that into her lap without there being strings.

'Why me?' she asked. 'What's the catch?'

'Why should there be a catch?' Clay said. 'You know the business inside out. You're a junior partner, the only partner besides ourselves without a better half. I would have thought you were the obvious choice.'

Then Louise knew what it was all about. It was so blindingly obvious, she wondered why she hadn't spotted it when he first mentioned the job. This plum wasn't in New York, or even in Chicago. This plum was half way across the world in London.

'Whose idea was it to send me away?' she demanded. 'Was it you, or is this something Sam wanted?'

The question hung between them, like a weapon. A weapon that needed to be defused. Clay levelled with her.

'It's something we both wanted. Face it, Louise. You and Sam couldn't go on the way you were going. Sooner or later something had to give and it did, twenty-four hours ago.'

'What happened?' Louise was worried now. She suspected that whatever had taken place had something to do with Sam's disappearance.

Clay looked at her steadily.

'Frances found out what was going on. The shock of it made her lose the baby.'

Disbelief washed over Louise, mingled with a sense of outrage.

'Why didn't Sam tell me what had happened? We had no secrets from each other.'

'Maybe he couldn't tell you.'

For the first time since Louise had known him, Clay looked serious.

'I don't think you understand,' he said. 'Sam's obsessed with you. Crazy for you. How could any guy in that state find the words to tell you he's going back to his wife?'

Louise sighed.

'So he got you to do his dirty work, and in case I cut up rough, you awarded me a consolation prize. You didn't choose me because of any talent I might have, or because you thought I could run a business. I'm simply a mistress who has become surplus to requirements. So you're sending me far far away where I can't be an embarrassment.'

Clay sat up straighter in his chair, then he selected a cigar from the humidor in front of him. Slowly he held it under his nose and inhaled its fragrance. He took his time cutting the end and lighting it, then turned to Louise.

'I can do without the self-pity,' he said sharply. 'Either you want the job in London, or you don't. Which is it to be?'

I should walk out, Louise thought savagely. I should tell him to stuff his job where the monkey keeps his nuts. She put on her best smile.

'I'll take the London posting,' she said. 'On condition you make me a full partner.'

Clay puffed on his cigar.

'You're in no position to negotiate,' he said. 'As you pointed out yourself, you wouldn't have been offered the job in the first place if it hadn't been for the business with Sam. If I were you I'd take the job and be grateful for it.'

Louise hung on in. Her personal life had just gone down in flames. Her professional one was all she had left.

'I want the partnership,' she persisted. 'I won't take no for an answer.'

Clay considered.

'I'll do a deal with you,' he said. 'If you can set the London business up and run it at a profit, I'll give you what you ask. If you can't, you're out on your ass. You've got nine months to prove yourself.'

Louise held out her hand.

'When do I leave?' she asked.

Louise ordered another vodka and looked around the bar. Over an hour had gone by and the place was still empty. The writers she had spotted previously had ambled off into the sunset. And the evening crowd had yet to arrive. She thought of going home. There was a lot to organise. Furniture had to be put in store. Books had to be set aside or thrown away. Clothes had to be cleaned. She searched around for her purse to pay the bill when she saw him.

He was tall and blond and reminded her of a lion out on the prowl. This guy was looking for a pick-up. It was written all over him. He swung over to the bar and ordered himself a beer. Then he leaned back against the long brass rail and took stock of the place.

Louise studied him with a certain curiosity. He was a beautiful animal, that was for sure. His shoulders were the shoulders of a baseball player and there was an arrogance about him. This guy loved himself to death, and any woman who found herself in his bed tonight would be certain to know it.

Louise straightened up and flipped her hair back over her shoulders. She might be down, but she wasn't completely finished. So this guy was looking for a pick-up was he? Well, she was just about ready for that. It might even restore her perspective on life.

She noticed the blond had seen her and was making his way across the bar. As he did, she saw the hardness in his face. So he's mean as well as beautiful, she thought. Louise felt the stirrings of an old familiar excitement. The same excitement she had felt with Brian Elder.

The big guy was going to hurt her. She knew that, knew it for certain. Just as she knew she was going to enjoy it. Yet she felt sour inside. My lover has just left me, she reflected. I should be home now, weeping and repairing my wounds.

She sighed. Why do I do it? she asked herself. Why do I go out looking for punishment?

36

Before she left for London, Louise touched base with two people, both of them from her past. Her first call was to Mike Calder, the copywriter she had worked with at Acker and Stein. She would need a writer to give flesh to her ideas. A top writer. A writer who understood her. Mike Calder would fit the bill. Right from the start, Mike went for the idea. He needed a change of scene and the money Louise was offering finally made his mind up. The following morning he quit his job and put his apartment on the market.

Louise's next call was to her old boss, Joe Rivers. When she saw Joe she wasn't looking for know-how or even guidance, she was looking for a contact. Acker and Stein had a large European office in London's Berkeley Square. Somewhere in that office was a man who knew the ropes, a man who could tell her how the hell she set about opening up shop in London.

All Louise had to do was find him and she hoped Joe would do that for her.

The creative chief came through for her, the way Mike Calder did. Within half an hour of seeing him, Joe was on the phone to his opposite number in London. Two hours after that a date had been arranged for Louise to meet with the agency's London manager. She was on her way.

On her last day in New York, Louise gave a final polish to her image. Until this moment she had been an artist, a creator of images. Now she was going into business and she had to look like she meant it.

The first thing that had to go was her hair. It was fine for a crazy art director to have a head of curls like Medusa but they didn't belong on a managing director. She checked into Lily Dache early in the morning and had Kenneth redesign her. She emerged just before lunch with her hair swept back into a heavy knot. It was a style that was going to take her half an hour every morning to achieve and she knew she would make the effort, for Kenneth had turned her into a formidable woman. With this look she could hire staff and win business. She could launch an agency. She could finally be taken seriously.

The rest of the day Louise spent shopping for tailored suits and dark leather accessories. She bought shoes from Gucci and Maud Frizon. Instead of a briefcase, she spent her dollars on a vast crocodile handbag. It was the kind of bag Jackie Onassis or Mary Wells would carry. It spoke of money and power and the kind of glamour that Hollywood had before the talkies.

When she got home she took out all her suede pants, her fringed jackets, her cowboy boots and packed them away.

They belonged to her past, just as Sam did. From now on she would show a different face to the world. She wondered how the world would like it.

She arrived in London in the middle of an August heatwave and checked into a suite in the Mayfair Hotel. Mike had got there a day before her and was waiting to see her. In his hand was a telex from Californian Mills. They wanted a new campaign drafted and ready to go inside the month. Louise was staggered.

'We haven't got premises or even a proper staff. We aren't allowed to operate in the territory yet. Are they crazy or something?'

Mike smiled sadly.

'They're crazy alright,' he said, 'but they also intend to spend two million dollars this year, and that gives them the right to be crazy. If we can't get it together in time, there are plenty of other agencies who can.'

Louise collapsed into the nearest chair.

'Terrific,' she said. 'This is all I need. Our biggest customer pushing me into the middle of next week.' She sighed. 'Are there any other messages?'

Mike wandered over to the desk by the window and rummaged through a pile of papers.

'A few good luck telegrams,' he reported. 'There's one from Clay and Sam. Our second client, Kitten Catfood, wishes us well, and so does Acker and Stein. By the way their managing director, Colin Brooke, confirmed that you're meeting him for lunch tomorrow. It's at Mark's Club just around the corner from the hotel.'

Louise nodded wearily. Right now all she wanted was a shower and to get out of her travelling clothes.

The following day she showed up at Mark's at twelve-thirty sharp and from the moment she walked into the club she got a taste of the world she was about to enter. It was exactly how she imagined it would be. Everything was grand and formal. The smartly painted townhouse door just off Berkeley Square gave off the message that you had to be rich to belong here. Rich and well connected.

The door was opened by a liveried servant who ushered Louise through a carpeted vestibule arched with mirrors. Out of the corner of her eye Louise glimpsed polished wood furniture and oil paintings in dark colours. It was the atmosphere, though, that got to her. In New York even the grandest places she knew had a noise and bustle about them. Here there was just silence. It was as if the grandeur around her had somehow absorbed the energy of the people who had come to lunch, so all they could do was whisper to each other.

Louise was shown into a low-lit room full of comfortable arm chairs and tiny round tables. A tall lean man in his mid-thirties rose to greet her.

'You must be Louise Tragos,' he said. 'Welcome to London.'

So this is the guy who runs Acker and Stein's London operation, Louise thought. He doesn't look tough enough. It was his languid air that foxed her, for Colin Brooke affected the manners of a gentleman. He was concerned about every aspect of her well-being, from the comfort of the hotel bed to what she wanted to eat for lunch.

He even fussed over the strength of her drink. What finally set her teeth on edge was that he wouldn't talk business. She had agreed to have lunch with the man because she wanted to know how to organise her London operation, yet all he wanted to do was make small talk.

When they were shown into the dining-room, Louise realised all the exaggerated courtliness was an English ritual. A dance before getting down to cases. When Colin started to talk about the agency game, she realised the effete-looking man knew exactly what he was talking about, and he was tougher than most New Yorkers. In just under an hour he had wised her up about lawyers, accountants and the London property market. She made a mental note to set about finding premises. What was simple and quick in New York was time consuming and expensive in this town. Her real nightmare was yet to come. Colin started telling her about recognition and the word literally meant what it said. Louise couldn't set up in business unless she was officially recognised by the newspaper industry. She could place her clients' ads in newspapers. That wasn't against the law, but the media wouldn't give her the agency's fifteen per cent commission. Without that there was no business.

'How do I set about getting this precious recognition?' she demanded. 'There must be some body of officials I can apply to.'

Colin Brooke took a sip of his club claret and nodded. 'There is. It's called the "Newspaper Proprietors' Association". But I wouldn't bother until you've prepared your ground.'

He stared intently at the dark, glossy-looking American girl.

'At the moment you wouldn't stand a chance.'

Louise started to get angry.

'Why the hell not? I've got two clients billing roughly two and a half million dollars. That's business in anybody's language.'

'Not in the language of this town,' said her companion. 'Look, before you lose your temper let me explain the ground rules for getting recognition. First of all, you're not going to get it on your own. The NPA won't recognise an American.'

Louise started to interrupt, but he waved her down.

'I know what you're going to tell me, you're a force to be reckoned with on Madison Avenue. That counts for nothing over here. PKL is a bigger force than you are, but they still had to hire an Englishman as their managing director before they could do business over here. My advice to you is to go out and find yourself a top British adman with a track record. Make him chairman if you still insist on running the show, but give him some responsibilities or the NPA will see right through you.'

Louise looked down at the plate in front of her. Her kidneys and bacon were done to perfection and she hadn't eaten a proper meal for the last twenty-four hours, yet her appetite failed her. She signalled to the waiter to clear her lunch away. Then she turned to her companion.

'Do I really have to take on an English partner?' she asked.

Brooke nodded.

'And not just a partner either. You've got to hire a media expert that everyone's heard of. You'll need a full staff. And two accounts aren't going to be enough. No matter what they're billing. You need a minimum of three for recognition.'

Louise put her head in her hands.

330

'Then I'm finished,' she said. 'I don't know anyone in London apart from the girls in Judy Wald's office and it's going to take more than a headhunter to find me the kind of chairman I'm looking for.'

Colin leaned over and filled up Louise's wine glass, then ordered coffee and brandy.

'What kind of chairman are you looking for?' he asked.

Louise made a face. 'Someone with clout. I need to lay hands on a third client fast, but the guy I hire has got to have more than influence. He's got to know his way around too. For my kind of agency I'm going to need some top talent, so this man has got to know where the bodies are buried. On top of all that he has to be looking for a job. Listen, there must be a handful of men in London who fit my description, but do any of them need me, an unknown American?'

Colin Brooke smiled. 'I can think of one man who does. His name is Nigel Farquharson. He's somewhere in his late fifties and just after the war he and a media man set up Farquharson and Milne, currently number three in the league tables.'

Louise interrupted him.

'Why would he want a job if he's got his own business?'

'I'm coming to that. Five years ago, Nigel got outmanoeuvred in the boardroom. The upshot of it was that he sold out his stake in the agency and retired to his country house. Only he got bored. Hunting wasn't as much fun as advertising.'

Louise warmed the brandy balloon in the palms of her hands and inhaled the heady, intoxicating perfume.

'What is Nigel Farquharson doing at the moment?' she asked.

Colin Brooke shrugged.

'Ticking over. He runs a small consultancy from his grand house in West Halkin Street but he's looking for something bigger. Kurnitz and Greene have a pretty hot reputation in New York. Repeating that kind of success in London could just amuse him.'

Suddenly Louise couldn't wait to get started. The mannered grey city that had looked so austere, so off-putting when she arrived was approachable after all. All you needed was to know the right people.

'How do I go about getting hold of him?' she asked eagerly.

'Leave that to me. I'll drop by and see him in the next day or so and tell him about you. If he's interested I'll set up a meeting. Then you can both take it from there.'

As Louise finished the last of her brandy, the jet lag finally caught up with her. She didn't bother to resist it. There was nothing she could do until she saw Nigel Farquharson. She might as well lie back and enjoy it.

Nigel Farquharson's house was in a Georgian terrace just behind the Carlton Tower. His dining-room on the ground floor afforded him a view of the Knightsbridge shoppers with their Harrods bags and mink coats. From his drawing-room on the first floor, the whole of Hyde Park Corner was on display. And it was here that Louise was invited to take tea.

The room reminded her of houses she had been in in New York. There was nothing personal about it, no wife had matched the carpet to the wall covering and no woman's hand had arranged the photographs in their Gucci frames. The entire interior was a testament to the skills of Farquharson's interior decorator who had succeeded in creating an expensive backdrop for entertaining business contacts.

Louise felt immediately at ease. This was a world she understood. You didn't need class to belong here, just money and power. Her new position with Kurnitz and Greene had equipped her with both.

She patted the gilt buttons on her navy Chanel suit and waited for Nigel Farquharson to put in an appearance. Five minutes later he came through the door and she was immediately impressed. He was a tall man with a florid complexion and a waistline that spoke of too many expense account lunches. Yet there was nothing sloppy about him. Farquharson carried himself like a leader. There was a sureness about him, a confidence that told her he was in the habit of getting what he wanted.

He took Louise by the hand, smiled pleasantly and sat down in an armchair opposite, then he asked her about herself. Normally Louise resented being quizzed, it reminded her of being back at school and having to make excuses for whatever it was she lacked, but Farquharson didn't push her. He coaxed her life story from her and at the end of the afternoon she discovered that not only did this man know all about Kurnitz and Greene, he also knew far too much about Louise Tragos.

However it didn't bother her. Somewhere on the journey between Manhattan and London Louise had stopped being ashamed of her background. Now she had finally made it, where she came from no longer mattered. She was what she was right now: a confident career woman in a two thousand dollar suit and she realised that it didn't matter what this man thought of her. What counted was what she thought of him. It was her judgement that was going to hire him.

She began to ask Nigel about his life and he was as forthcoming as she had been. He had started out selling car accessories to the motor trade, from there he climbed up the ladder to sales director and finally became the marketing director in charge of the company's advertising budget. It was this job that changed his life, for he came into contact with J. Walter Thompson, the agency that handled his car accessories and from that moment he fell out of love with the motor business and began a lifelong affair with advertising.

Within six months JWT had offered him a job on their account handling team and he gave in his notice and joined the agency almost immediately. Nigel Farquharson discovered he was brilliant at handling advertising business. He became all things to all men and in his new career it worked like a charm. Very soon he was running his own section of the agency and within the space of five years he had made it to deputy managing director.

Then he got itchy feet, for he realised just how much business he was holding down. He decided his efforts could be better spent on his own behalf. A drinking friend of his in the media department felt exactly the same way and the two decided to break away and set up on their own.

It was naturally against all the rules to poach clients away from their employers, but Nigel never worried too much about the rules. Before he left, he extracted promises from half a dozen of the agency's top spenders and within three months they had joined the newly formed Farquharson and Milne. Right from the start the agency made money. In the early Fifties consumer goods were beginning to come back into the shops and the public wanted to know what was on offer.

Nigel and Bobby his new partner worked all the hours God gave supplying that information. By the middle of the Sixties they were a force to be reckoned with. Then Bobby died suddenly and unexpectedly of a heart attack. His fifty-one per cent stake in the agency passed to his two sons. They were already working at Farquharson and Milne, one of them in the media department and one of them as an account director. Almost immediately they became joint managing directors and Nigel's days were numbered. If the two boys voted together they could over-rule him, and they did vote together: on every issue that was raised.

It took them five years to get rid of Nigel Farquharson

and he didn't go without a fight, but in the end the struggle sapped his energy and his will. Nigel got his revenge by selling his equity at a vastly inflated rate to the Milne boys.

Now he was rich and bored and looking for something to get his teeth into. He liked the notion of Kurnitz and Greene right from the start. Creative agencies had been making a lot of money in the Seventies because they thumbed their noses at the rules. It was an activity Nigel had virtually invented and he wanted to find out if he still knew how.

It took Louise two days to draw up an agreement with him and by the end of the week they were working together.

The first thing Nigel did was to arrange a date with the Recognition Committee.

'But we don't have a staff. We don't have enough business. We don't even have any premises,' protested Louise.

'Calm yourself,' instructed her new chairman. 'When we see them in two and a half weeks' time we'll have all those things. Or the promise of them.'

He was as good as his word. People started joining them from all over town. They got account men from Hobson Bates and J. Walter Thompson, a crack media man came over from Thames Television and PKL's best copywriter arrived on their doorstep during Louise's second week in London.

'How do you do it?' she asked Nigel.

All he said was, 'Hold tight. The best is yet to come.'

Three days before the meeting with the Recognition Committee Nigel produced a handful of small accounts. Cyprus Oranges, Herbal Bath salts, a gourmet tea, a top fashion lipstick. They had belonged to his consultancy. And now he was chairman of an agency, they followed him.

The Committee had demanded a minimum of three accounts. With Nigel's contribution they had seven. They looked like standing a fighting chance of getting recognition. The only thing Nigel couldn't come up with was premises. They had all worn out their shoe leather tramping round offices in Knightsbridge and Chelsea. They found nothing. Either there was too much space, or too little, or the landlords wanted too much money. In the end they decided to operate out of hotel suites until something came up.

'We can always tell the Committee we've got something,' Nigel informed her.

So in the meantime Kurnitz and Greene worked from a suite in Mayfair, the smoking-room of the Basil Street Hotel, Nigel's house in West Halkin Street and a black taxi.

The production staff lived in the taxi, ferrying half finished ads between the fragmented departments of the new agency. All they needed now was recognition and they could start taking commission for the ads they were creating.

The meeting with the Committee was scheduled for eleven o'clock on Monday morning. Louise and Nigel arrived together at the NPA's offices in Fleet Street, then for half an hour they sat waiting in an anteroom. At the end of the room were two vast wooden doors that led into the main chamber and Louise sat and stared at them, shivering slightly. It was the end of summer but inside the cavernous grey stone building the temperature hovered at a permanent fifty degrees Fahrenheit.

'This place reminds me of a morgue,' she complained.

Nigel smiled wanly.

'I'm not surprised,' he said. 'Enough people died here.'

Suddenly it was time to go in. The double doors opened majestically to reveal a vast polished mahogany table, but it wasn't the table that held their attention. It was the men sitting round it. There were around fifteen of them. All top men with powerful Fleet Street papers.

The chairman invited them to sit down at the far end of the table, then the questions started. The Committee wanted to know about Kurnitz and Greene. Who were they? How did they come to set up in business? How did they qualify to be in advertising?

They were tough questions, intrusive to the point of rudeness. The name Kurnitz came in for comment. Was Sam Kurnitz a naturalised American?

Louise answered everything as honestly as she could. In other circumstances she would have lost her temper, but here there was no point. These men determined whether or not she was going to do business in this country. So she told them about Sam's Hungarian ancestry and for good measure she talked about her own Greek roots.

Nigel nudged her in the ribs.

'You don't have to tell them everything,' he whispered.

Then it was his turn. The Committee made him describe in detail how he was qualified to set up an agency. Then the questions moved on to clients. They wanted to know everything about Kurnitz and Greene's American list. They needed to know billings, projections over the next five years, agency profitability. Nigel and Louise handled that part of the presentation together.

They all seemed to be impressed with their biggest London client, Californian Mills. The company specialised in cereal products, focusing in on the new mueslis and breakfast brans. The man from the *Guardian* felt this was a huge growth area and could see years of profits for his paper. Louise began to feel more positive. She should have put a block on her feelings until the end of the meeting, for the Committee came down hard on Nigel's accounts. They were too small and too dependent on the whims of fashion. At least two of the men there doubted whether they would see any of them advertising longer than two or three years.

Nigel rose to the challenge.

'I agree with the Committee that fashion changes,' he said, 'but in three years Kurnitz and Greene will have made itself a reputation as a stylish shop. Other fashion accounts will come in because of this, replacing the business that dies off naturally.'

They all seemed satisfied with that. After two gruelling hours, the meeting wound to an end. They were told they would hear the verdict in a day or so, then they were shown out through the great carved wooden doors.

In the street, Louise turned to Nigel.

'How did it go?' she asked. 'Do you think we'll get past them?'

Nigel looked impassive.

'I'm not going to count my chickens,' he said.

Louise didn't sleep that night. She was haunted by the spectre of failure. She knew if she didn't get recognition for Kurnitz and Greene in London, she was all washed up. She couldn't get her old job back in New York because of Sam, and what other agency would want her? She would be known forever as the girl who went to England and bombed out. Yesterday's news. A new body for the scrap heap.

She walked around in a daze for the next twenty-four hours. Every time Mike Calder asked her a question, he was met with a blank stare. Only Nigel didn't bother to talk to her. He had been through the same agony nearly twenty years ago and he knew there was nothing he could do to help her now.

Towards the end of the second day, she wandered into Mike's office and asked if he had a drink. By way of reply the copywriter produced a bottle of champagne.

'You don't have to go over the top,' she said crossly. 'All I wanted was some alcohol.'

Mike ignored her and popped the cork. Then he splashed it into half a dozen glasses.

'What the hell's going on?' Louise demanded.

Then the penny dropped. For in the doorway Nigel appeared with the media director and one of the account handlers. They were all smiling broadly.

'We made it,' he said simply. 'I got the call five minutes ago. But we had to send somebody out to get the champagne before we could tell you.'

Louise grabbed a glass and felt the bubbles tickle her nose. Then she took a gulp and realised she was drinking something special. A glance at the bottle told her how special.

When Nigel sent out for champagne, he didn't order any old brand. He went the whole hog and bought Louis Roederer Crystale.

It's a great send-off, Louise thought. I just hope we can live up to it.

37

For the hundredth time Abner Morris riffled through the stack of photographs on his desk. They were a great set, there was no denying that. Frances would freak out when she saw them. Only she hadn't seen them. Not yet. Abner wanted to handle this situation with the utmost care. He had to be quite certain how Frances would react when she saw them and to know that, he had to know the woman better.

He thought about the problem. He hadn't seen Frances in nearly four years. When he had known her she was a bimbo, a classy piece of goods, there was no doubt about that, but a bimbo nonetheless. Now events had moved on. The broad had gone respectable and got married. For all he knew she might have a couple of children in tow by now. There were any number of unknown factors to consider before he dropped his bombshell. He needed to update himself on Frances and Tiffany could supply all the information he was looking for. She was married to Sam Kurnitz's partner wasn't she? She and Frances had probably been swapping recipes for years.

Abner picked up the phone and dialled Tiffany's home. She answered on the second ring.

'Abner here,' he said without preamble. 'I want to see you.'

There was a small gasp, then silence. Abner could almost see Tiffany hesitate.

'We've been through that,' she said finally. 'I can't see you, not now. It's too risky.'

Abner smiled.

'It's not risky any more,' he told her. 'I've got something

on my desk that's going to silence Sam Kurnitz. More than silence him. Knock him for six. He'll be putty in my hands.'

Tiffany couldn't keep the excitement out of her voice.

'What is it?' she demanded.

She heard him laugh.

'To know that you'll have to come over and see for yourself. I've got an office here as well as a bedroom. Don't tell me you don't trust yourself to be alone with me.'

Again Abner heard the small intake of breath. It was incredibly sexy. Almost Victorian. He promised himself if everything went according to plan he'd lay Tiffany that afternoon. He'd waited far too long already.

'Of course I trust myself,' he heard her say. 'What time shall I come by?'

Abner looked at his watch. It was two-thirty. It would take Tiffany half an hour to get here, an hour to discuss Frances and the pictures. That brought it up to tea time. Too early for a drink. No, he thought. I need her nice and relaxed for what I have in mind.

'Be here by five,' he instructed. 'Can you make it by then? I thought I might open a bottle of champagne when we've finished talking business.'

'Terrific,' said Tiffany.

She put down the phone and started to smile. So Abner finally has the evidence to nail Sam to the cross. That could only mean one thing. Kurnitz and Greene would be billing another sixty million bucks any minute now. With something like triumph, she took out a pack of cigarettes, selected a filter and lit it. Tobacco, she thought. My passport to riches.

She arrived at Abner's just as the sun was going down and from his window he could see the red reflections of the dying day all around him. It was his favourite time. Soon the laughter and the frenzy of the night would be with him and he would start to live.

341

Tiffany came into the room, dark and sultry and smelling of overblown roses. He felt his blood quicken. During his working day he had flirted with a hundred pretty girls, but none of them stirred him the way this woman did. He leaned across and kissed her on the cheek.

'I told you I had something to show you,' he said. 'Take a look at these.'

He handed her the set of photographs in a buff-coloured envelope. Then he studied Tiffany's face as she got them out and went through them.

At first she didn't show any reaction. Then as she started to recognise the girl in the pictures, her mouth dropped.

'It can't be Frances,' she gasped. 'It's someone who looks like her.'

Abner shook his head.

'No way, José. That's the real thing. Before she married and went straight, your friend Frances was a wild girl with a very interesting past.'

Tiffany was riveted.

'Were these pictures ever printed anywhere?'

Once more the tycoon shook his head.

'The pictures were only a test session. She was going to do the real thing in New York. That's why she came over here. Only she couldn't go through with it. It happens to girls from time to time. One minute it's gung ho and bare everything, the next they come over all modest.'

Tiffany looked at Abner.

'I hope you told her she was being silly. London to New York seems an awfully long way to travel just to change your mind.'

Abner was tempted to tell her the whole story, then he reconsidered. I want to impress Tiffany, he thought. Coming on like a loser only makes me look like a wimp.

He smiled.

'I did what I could with Frances, but the poor girl was terrified. In the end I let her go on her way. I assumed she

342

scuttled back to London on the next plane. Now it seems I was wrong.'

Tiffany lit a cigarette.

'How long ago did all this happen?'

'About three or four years ago, why?'

She inhaled deeply on her filter tip. Considering. Remembering.

'Because it's about then that Sam first got together with Frances. It's funny, at the time we all thought it was a bit sudden. He runs into a girl, shacks up with her and the next thing everyone knows, he's getting married.'

Tiffany wrinkled her brow.

'I asked Clay at the time whether he knew anything about Frances, but he didn't – apart from the fact she was English and came from a grand family. Her father's some kind of lord. Anyway after that it seemed kind of tacky to ask any more questions.'

Abner laughed.

'Don't you wish now you had?'

'Not really,' said Tiffany. 'What good would it have done? Sam was in love with the girl. He was married to her. Why should I want to rake up her past?'

Abner reached across and took the pictures away from her.

'Do you still feel like that?' he asked.

'What are you trying to say?'

'Just this. Frances Kurnitz, or Frances Buckingham as I knew her, has a history she'd rather keep quiet about. My guess is her husband knows nothing about it and I bet she'll go to the ends of the earth to keep it that way.'

There was silence and Tiffany started to look worried.

'What are you going to do to Frances?' she said.

'Nothing,' Abner told her, 'as long as she goes along with what I suggest. Look, Sam Kurnitz is not going to take on Frisco cigarettes unless he really has to. The fact that it will make his agency rich doesn't seem to affect him. So I have to persuade him another way. Or rather his wife does.'

Tiffany sighed.

'I tried that once, but she wasn't playing. She owed me money, quite a lot of money, and I said I would press for it if she talked to Sam about Frisco. The whole thing backfired dreadfully. Frances ran to Sam and told him all about the money. Then they both turned on me.'

Abner weighed the pictures in his hands.

'This time it won't backfire. I'll see Frances myself and when I've finished with her I can guarantee that the cigarette business will be in place.'

Tiffany regarded the tall saturnine man sitting opposite her and her heart lifted. He was going to an awful lot of trouble to make sure her husband's agency was going to get his business. He wasn't doing it out of love for Clay or admiration for Sam either. He was giving it to Kurnitz and Greene for one reason only, because he found her attractive. Now, Tiffany decided, was the time to show her appreciation.

Although it was early in the autumn, the weather was surprisingly cold that year and to warm her that evening Tiffany was swathed in a silver fox. It was a dramatic coat, something a Russian princess would wear and the long shimmering fur accented the darkness of her hair.

There's something mysterious about her tonight, Abner thought, looking at her. Something exciting. He walked across the room to the bureau where he kept his drinks. And from a small fridge he extracted a bottle of champagne.

'Why don't you get rid of that coat,' he suggested. 'Then you can make yourself comfortable and we'll have that drink I promised.'

'How comfortable do you want me to get?' Tiffany asked.

Abner was standing with his back to her opening the

champagne, and when he turned round he saw she was shrugging off her silver fox. He drew in his breath, for he saw she was wearing nothing underneath her coat except for the garter belt holding up her stockings.

Without flinching, Abner poured the wine into two crystal glasses and brought them across to the sofa. Tiffany had thrown her fur coat carelessly across the cushions and now she was poised in front of it, figuring out her next move.

Abner took a decision. Rather than show Tiffany the next room where he had a large water bed, he was going to follow his impulses.

'Let's sit down,' he said, motioning towards the sofa. He handed Tiffany the crystal glass and made a toast.

'To success,' he said. 'For both of us.'

He sipped the champagne, never taking his eyes from her body and she wondered what he was going to do next. He did nothing, except go on talking to her. Tiffany began to feel excited. Another man would have grabbed her. Taken her on the spot.

But this man was savouring the experience. The way he was savouring his champagne. She leaned back against the fur coat. Then she giggled.

'I must look like a dirty postcard,' she said. Abner dipped his finger in his glass and dripped champagne onto one rosy nipple.

'You do,' he replied.

Then he leaned forward and tasted the wine he had spilt. He anointed both her breasts and sucked them clean. Then he explored the rest of her. With practised hands he unhooked her garter belt, rolled her stockings down, and when she was completely naked he undid the top of his trousers and parted her legs. Then he kissed her and Tiffany felt his tongue, hard and insistent in her mouth. And she felt something else. His penis. He had somehow managed to get astride her and before she

345

38

Frances had been completely ruthless and it was starting to pay off, for she no longer dreaded getting on the scales in the morning. When they let her out of hospital, three weeks ago, she had been one hundred and fifty pounds and climbing. Her short blonde cap of hair was showing dark roots and there were circles under her eyes.

Frances's immediate reaction on seeing her reflection in the mirror was to take to her bed again and burst into tears. After that she pulled herself together. A regime was what she needed. She went out and bought a stack of reading – *Health and Fitness*, *The Vogue Beauty Book*, *Slimming Magazine* and *Your Diet*. *Your Diet* seemed to have what she was looking for, for that month they featured a complete makeover plan. The emphasis was on health. Spartan health. Health that made you hurt.

Every morning Frances started with a glass of lemon juice and seltzer, then she pulled on her tracksuit and went jogging for an hour. When she arrived home, she was allowed a piece of melba toast with a scraping of butter and a cup of black coffee. Lunch was two hard-boiled eggs and more black coffee. Then she went to the gym.

To get herself back into shape Frances had been set a tough programme. On two hard-boiled eggs and a cup of coffee, the programme was more than tough. It was punishing.

Her first half-hour was spent on the exercise bicycle, then when she was completely wrung out she dragged herself over to the Nautilus machines. Each machine was designed to exercise a different part of her body. On one she sat and pulled down on levers attached to weights. That toned her

347

upper body. There was a different machine for her thighs, one for her back and yet another for her bottom. It took her an hour to get round all the Nautilus equipment.

Then came the worst part: the exercises on the mat. An instructor took her through these and as the days wore on she decided he must be some kind of sadist, for everything he asked her to do was either totally impossible or it hurt like hell.

By the time Frances got home every evening, she was starving hungry. Her regime allowed her four ounces of lean meat and a plain boiled vegetable. Frances looked forward to it all day.

Sometimes Sam would ask her if she wasn't going at things too hard.

'I love you just as much a little heavier,' he would tell her, but Frances didn't believe him. Louise had been reed thin with a flat stomach and a taut, tight bottom. Frances would be thinner, tauter, tighter too.

Sam's affair had left its mark on Frances. She had forgiven him for it because she loved him, but afterwards when she settled back into her life, she found she believed in herself less. Before, she had thought she was attractive. Now she wondered. If the man she married had found Louise desirable, how could he desire her too?

She started to wonder if she was bright enough, or if she bored Sam, and she worried about her lack of achievements. Louise might have left New York, but she didn't leave Frances. Her image stayed behind. The mocking, self-confident image of the successful career woman, and it challenged Frances to measure up. It made her stick to her diet. It drove her through the gym, and when she climbed on the scales in the morning and discovered she was down on her weight, she felt reprieved. I might have failed once, she told herself, but I'm not falling down this time.

She was tempted to celebrate. There was champagne in the fridge. Sam always kept it there for special clients or just to drink because he knew she enjoyed it but she hadn't touched liquor for nearly a month now. Her regime forbade it and so she went to the fridge and got out a bottle of diet cola instead. She was drinking the diet cola and thinking about lunch when the phone rang. It must be Sam, she thought, telling me about tonight's plan for the theatre. She grabbed it, expecting to hear the hurried instructions Sam always gave her on the phone. Only Sam wasn't on the phone. It was someone else.

'Who is it?' Frances asked, momentarily confused.

'Surely you know,' said the voice. 'You always used to.'

It was a man speaking. An American. She judged from the accent that he came from the top end of the social scale and there was an arrogance that she felt, rather than heard. She racked her brains trying to work out who it might be. A friend of Sam's perhaps, someone she had met at a party, but nobody came to mind.

'I'm sorry,' she said, 'I've no idea who you are.'

Then the man on the end of the phone chuckled.

'I could play cat and mouse with you all day,' he said, 'but why waste time. The name's Abner Morris. We had dinner one night, four years ago.'

There was a sofa behind Frances and she sat down on it, hard. It can't be, she thought. Abner doesn't know anything about me now, I've even got a different name. How on earth did he find me?

Nervously she spoke into the receiver.

'It's not the same Abner Morris who runs the Macho Club?'

Again the man laughed. He was thoroughly enjoying this conversation.

'So she finally remembers,' he said. 'I would have thought any man you knocked out cold would spring to mind instantly, but maybe you do that all the time to your admirers.'

349

'I don't have admirers,' Frances said quickly, too quickly. 'I'm married now. My life's different.'

There was a short silence. Then Abner said, 'I know that, Frances. I even know who your husband is, and that's why I'm calling you. There's a little business matter involving Sam I want to talk to you about.'

Now Frances was really rattled. More than rattled. She was terrified. Abner Morris, Richard Gregory, the sleazy sordid Macho Clubs belonged to a life she had put far behind her. The whole episode had been a mistake. A juvenile error of judgement when she knew no better. It had nothing to do with her now and she wanted nothing of it.

'If it's business,' she said, 'why don't you talk to Sam about it. Why involve me?'

The voice was teasing now.

'Because I want to see you,' Abner said. 'I've been looking forward to it.'

Frances started to feel hot and breathless.

'Why can't you just leave me alone?' she shouted. 'I don't want to see you. Any of you. I don't want anything to do with the damn Macho Clubs ever again.'

She felt like slamming the phone down, but she knew it was pointless. Abner would only ring back and next time he called, Sam might be in. She didn't want to risk that.

'What can I do for you now?' she enquired. 'I'm nearly thirty. I don't look the part any more. You wouldn't even want me to pose for you.'

'I suggest you let me be the judge of that,' said Abner. 'I've got a set of pictures here that amply demonstrate your charms. You can't have changed that much in four years.'

Now Frances was really worried. So the bastard had kept the pictures Richard had taken of her, and now he wanted to trade them for something. Some favour. Otherwise why would he waste his time calling her?

'What is it you're after?' she asked. 'There must be lots of girls you can frighten. So why pick on me?'

Abner went silent again. Then finally when she had decided to put down the phone, he started to speak.

'You're right,' he said. 'I do want something from you, but it's not anything I'm prepared to discuss over the phone. This little matter is something we talk about face to face. So you tell me a place that's good for you and I'll be there.'

There was no getting out of it. Frances had to see him. It was either that or risk exposing her past. She thought of the pictures she had posed for. The shots of her with nothing on.

She would rather die than have anyone she knew see them. She set her jaw. She wouldn't meet Abner Morris in a restaurant or a bar. People went to those places to have fun and this wasn't going to be fun. She knew that already. No, she would see him somewhere formal and austere. Grand Central Station crossed her mind, then she rejected it. There would be too many people around. She thought about an art gallery. No, that would be too intimate. Then she had it. She would meet Abner Morris in a museum. Somewhere opulent and chilly. Somewhere where they could sit down, yet where they could walk as well if they needed to.

'Abner,' she said into the phone, 'you know the Frick, don't you? I'll meet you there this afternoon.'

'Terrific,' came the reply. 'I'll see you in the South Hall by the Boucher. Make it around four.'

He rang off leaving Frances wondering. What did Abner know about pictures? His appreciation of art as far as she knew was limited to the centrespreads in his girlie magazine.

She got to the Frick early and headed past the Hogarths and the Fragonards towards the South Hall. As she came into the room her eye was taken by a picture of a soldier

351

with his arm round a lusty wench. From the look of them the couple were about to tumble into bed. Then she saw the Boucher. This was where Abner had told Frances to meet him and now she knew why.

The painting was a picture of Boucher's wife without any clothes on. It wasn't a spiritual nude, or even a modest one. Like the Vermeer with the soldier and the girl it was intimate and loaded with meaning.

Frances shivered slightly. The man she was meeting could turn any situation – even the Frick Collection – to his own advantage. I have no defences against him, she thought. He even pokes fun at my intellect.

Frances saw Abner coming towards her down the long hall and noticed he hadn't changed. He still wore his hair slightly too long and the hard face still wore a permanent grin, as if life was something trivial, something to be laughed at.

The grin intensified when he saw her and he took her hand and gave her a peck on the cheek.

'Do you like my taste in pictures?' he asked. 'I chose the Boucher because it reminded me of you.'

'That's a cheap joke,' she said. 'Even now I'm thinner than that.'

Abner looked at her. It was the same appraisement she remembered him giving her when they first met in London, objective and somehow brutal. As if she was so much flesh.

'You were right when you told me you'd changed. If I wasn't looking for you, I wouldn't have known it was the same girl.' He nodded sadly. 'You were a foxy little thing when I first met you. All skinny hips and great girlish eyes. Now you look like somebody's wife.'

'I am somebody's wife,' Frances said, 'that's why I'm here. You wanted to talk about my husband.'

Abner took her arm and led her down the room.

'Come outside into the gardens,' he said. 'I can see the

352

pictures disturb you. We can talk there – where you'll be calmer.'

Frances allowed herself to be taken into the closed court-yard at the centre of the museum. Damn you, she thought, you've got me on the defensive from the word go.

Abner selected a bench underneath a marble fountain. If she had been on her own, Frances would have felt at peace here for there was a serenity in these classical gardens that she couldn't find anywhere else in the city. But she wasn't on her own. She was with Abner Morris and the peace she sought failed to touch her.

She turned to him.

'You wanted something from me,' she said. 'What is it?'

'To know what it is,' he told her, 'you have to know more about my business life. When we first met I think I told you my empire was founded on tobacco.'

Frances nodded.

'I remember,' she said. 'What about it?'

Abner leaned against the back of the bench and put his hands behind his neck.

'My company distributes a number of cigarette brands. One of them is called Frisco. I wanted your husband's agency to handle it.'

Suddenly Frances knew what this meeting was all about. The wretched cigarette account.

Frances remembered it with distaste. Her first major row with her husband had been over that damned brand and she had since sworn she wouldn't poke her nose into his business ever again. She sighed. The promise she made to Sam had been in vain, for she knew now what Abner wanted from her.

'What makes you think,' she asked him, 'that I could change Sam's mind about Frisco? You know he doesn't want to work on it, and you also know why. So how could I make any difference?'

353

'A woman can be very persuasive,' Abner said. 'I know that from my own experience. And Sam loves you, so you start out with a full deck of cards.'

Frances looked desperate.

'Look, I tried to talk Sam round once and it didn't work. So what do you want me to do now? Nag him, threaten him, say I'll commit suicide if he doesn't take on the brand?'

Abner took her hands in his and she thought she saw compassion in his eyes.

'Calm down,' he said. 'There are better ways to work on your husband. Easier ways.'

He had her attention now and he smiled.

'How do you rate yourself as a hostess?' he asked. 'Do you go in for big bashes, or intimate little dinners. What are you best at?'

Frances thought for a moment.

'I guess dinner parties are where I shine. The conversation's better when there are fewer people, also they get to know each other properly.'

Abner nodded.

'Good,' he said. 'I hoped you'd say that. Now I can tell you how you start softening up Sam.'

He let go of her hands. Then he got to his feet.

'Let's walk a little,' he said.

Frances followed him through the trailing greenery. Everywhere she looked there were marble columns, showy displays of plant life, classical fountains. Abner had brought her to a wonderland, a garden of Eden, and soon, like all serpents, he was going to destroy it for her.

She turned to him.

'How can I talk my husband round by giving a dinner?' she asked.

Abner grinned.

'You invite me to your table. I'll work on him.'

Frances drew in her breath. So that's what he had in mind. A rearguard action. An invasion of her territory.

'It's not that simple,' she said. 'You're not part of our group. None of my friends knows you.'

The friendly air Abner assumed earlier started to fade.

'If your friends come from the world of advertising, and I assume they do, they will want to know me. I don't think you realise, Frances, just what an important man I am. I get hundreds of letters every day from men like your husband begging for my business. And you're wrong,' he said. 'I do know your friends. I ran into Tiffany and Clay Greene a few months ago. I'm sure they'd be delighted to see me again at this dinner you're planning.'

Frances felt she was caught in the slipstream of this man's will. She put up one last struggle.

'You told me there were all sorts of ways, easy ways to get round my husband. If I can't invite you to dinner, what are my other choices?'

Abner enumerated them on his fingers.

'The big drinks party I was talking about. Tennis week-ends. You and Sam can come as guests on my yacht . . .'

He took a look at her face and stopped talking.

'You hate the idea, don't you?'

'Are you surprised?' Frances burst out. 'You tried to rape me, remember. You thought I was some kind of tart to be used and discarded. Why should I want you in my house? Why should I want you anywhere near me?'

Abner broke his stride and turned round to face her.

'I'll tell you why you want me in your life. It's very simple. If you turn me down, if you refuse to go along with my plan, then I send Sam the pictures. After that he'll come to me for the rest of the story.'

Frances looked at the tall, impeccably suited man in front of her and knew she was beaten. Running a hand through her short blonde curls she turned around and headed back to the museum.

'I'll get cooking,' she shouted back over her shoulder. 'Tell your secretary to call me and we'll fix a date.'

Dinner was arranged for the following week, and as she was instructed, Frances invited Tiffany and Clay. She didn't for a moment think they would be free, but to her surprise Tiffany found a space in her crowded diary.

'How lucky,' said her friend, 'we had a cancellation.'

The second couple she invited was Bernard Glenn and his wife. During the last months of her pregnancy she had struck up a surprising friendship with the foppish little art critic. They both discovered a similar taste in pictures and Bernard frequently took Frances to galleries to look at new artists and dish the dirt on old ones.

Bernard was one of the few people in New York Frances had met on her own account. He wasn't a friend of Tiffany's, and he didn't work with Sam, and it gave her confidence to know there was someone who liked her for herself.

I'm going to need all the confidence I can get for this party, she told herself grimly. And she meant it. Since her meeting with Abner, her regime had gone to pot. She was eating for comfort now and drinking for reassurance.

The pounds she had lost started to pile on again. She couldn't pass a mirror now without feeling depressed. All the new things she had bought fitted too tightly. When she looked at herself she saw the outline of her thighs pushing out the shape of her skirts. She saw a bosom with too much cleavage. She hated herself.

What's happening to me, she wondered. Then she thought about Abner Morris. She remembered the pictures taken of her undressed and she poured herself another glass of champagne. I'll diet tomorrow, she promised herself. When I get this dinner out of the way.

Frances had invited everyone for drinks at seven-thirty and Tiffany and Clay turned up on the dot. Tiffany was looking stunning that night. She was wearing an Oscar de la Renta Frances had never seen before. Black taffeta. Sculpted to her body, showing every curve. For a moment she felt envious. You lead a charmed life, she thought. I know how much you spend on clothes and I've seen you flirt when Clay's not looking, yet you always get away with it.

She went over to the pitcher of martini she had made and poured one out for Tiffany. Then she poured a large one for herself.

'That's a lovely diamond brooch,' Frances said, looking at the blazing cluster decorating her friend's dress. 'Is it new?'

To her surprise Tiffany blushed and looked down.

'No,' she said, 'I've had it for ages. My mother gave it to me.'

Now Frances was thoroughly confused.

Tiffany's mother lived in the Bronx on the tiny pension her late husband had left her. If she had ever possessed a diamond brooch she would have sold it to pay the rent.

'I didn't know your mother had that kind of jewellery,' Frances said. 'Where did she get it?'

But Tiffany had suddenly remembered something she wanted to say to Sam and didn't seem to have heard.

Frances was distracted by the doorbell. Bernard Glenn and his wife were the next to arrive and she welcomed them like long-lost family. They were so pleased to see her, so warm and she wondered how Abner would greet her.

She had told Sam he was someone she had met in London, someone she didn't know very well who she had run into again at a party. It was an approximation of the truth and she felt honour bound to stay as close to reality as she could. That way she had some control over the situation.

She glanced at her watch. It was eight o'clock and Abner and his date still hadn't arrived. A crazy thought struck her. Maybe he had decided not to come after all. Maybe he decided Sam was a lost cause. Someone not worth wasting time on.

The doorbell went for the third time and she knew she had been fooling herself. She squared her shoulders and was about to go to the door when she remembered something. Her drink. She must have put it down somewhere and forgotten it. She made herself another. I won't go over the top, she promised herself, but tonight I need some kind of help.

Abner arrived with a girl from the Macho Club, or at least that's what Frances assumed, for she had all the hallmarks of a woman who came to life after dark.

Frances caught Tiffany looking at the girl in disbelief and she suppressed a smile. Abner was so confident he would fit in here. He even claimed friendship with Tiffany. With this kind of bimbo on his arm, there was no way the Greenes would give him the time of day.

Frances was wrong. Abner fitted in perfectly to her dinner. More than that. He was a hit. Tiffany seemed genuinely interested in the man. He and Bernard Glenn turned out to have friends in common. But it was Sam who was the surprise. For Sam was overwhelmed by him. The reason was Israel. Abner was involved in some government committee over there and when he discovered that Sam had fought in the six-day war, they had plenty to say to each other.

Frances sat watching them both exchanging names, laughing over shared experiences, reaching out the tentacles of friendship and she wanted to scream: don't you know you're being taken? This man doesn't want to know you. He doesn't even like you. All he wants is to soften you up.

She said nothing. Instead she picked up the tiny bell on the table in front of her and summoned the maid to serve the next course.

The cook came in, staggering under the weight of a Boeuf en Croûte. She put it down and returned seconds later with round beans, glazed carrots and tiny new potatoes.

As Frances arranged the plates, Sam caught her eye.

'How clever of you to invite Abner here tonight,' he said. 'How did you two meet?'

Frances felt her heart begin to thump in her ears. What do I tell him, she thought. I met him at the Macho Club while I was working there as a waitress. My lover of the time, a playboy called Richard Gregory, introduced us.

She looked at Abner and saw him smile. Then she took hold of her wine-glass and drank half the contents.

'I knew Frances's father,' she heard Abner say. 'He and I had business dealings together.'

Frances felt her heart rate go back to normal, then she heard Sam ask Abner what his business was. The waitress came round and refilled her glass and Frances didn't stop her.

The moment she had been dreading had finally arrived. Abner was going to declare himself and there was nothing she could do about it.

'I'm chairman of American Tobacco,' said Abner, 'the company that makes Frisco. I understand you turned us down a couple of weeks ago.'

Frances took a gulp of her wine and looked at her husband. Apart from the fact that he was slightly out of focus he was doing fine.

'So you're the man who wants to give away sixty million bucks,' he said pleasantly. 'It's a pity we can't take the business. I might have enjoyed working with you.'

Abner smiled and clapped Sam on the back.

'I can see you and I are going to have to have a long talk about the tobacco game,' he said. 'It's not the horror you think it is.'

'Wanna bet?' said Sam.

359

Abner went on smiling, and Frances hated the smooth-talking tycoon. He'd conned his way into her home, and now he'd persuaded her husband to listen to him.

She tuned back into the conversation and heard Sam accepting an invitation to spend the weekend in the Hamptons. Abner had a house there – a big house on the beach.

'We could do a little sailing if it's fine,' he said. 'And if it's not, maybe we could get in some golf.'

For the first time since she'd agreed to put on this ludicrous dinner, Frances felt trapped. She had imagined the evening might have been dull. At its worst it could have been embarrassing. Not in her wildest dreams did she think Abner would get through to her husband.

For a moment she thought about the story he had told her about his father who had smoked, and died from it. Sam had been very moral about cigarettes then. Very outraged. Frances wondered how long his outrage would last. In the face of Abner Morris's charm.

39

Frances knew she was drinking too much. There were dark circles under her eyes and she found it difficult to get up in the morning, but she didn't think she had a problem. I can always give it up she told herself, when Abner Morris gets off my back.

Alcohol was Frances's way of coping with the situation. Since Sam discovered Abner and vice versa, her life had become a nightmare. She knew she was sitting on an unexploded time-bomb. One day, Abner would ask her to do something against her wishes, something she didn't want to do, and if she didn't deliver, he would ruin her.

She lived with her nerves exposed, looking permanently over one shoulder. When things got bad she drank. It started slowly. Sam liked to play tennis at the weekends and Abner's weekend spread in the Hamptons had its own courts, indoor and outdoor. In the beginning they would drive down on Saturday, stay for lunch and come back in the evening. But Abner always pressed them to stay over and after a while it seemed pointless not to. There was always something going on over Sunday: a lunch party to which they would be invited, sailing if the weather was fine or more tennis.

Sam loved these weekends. The atmosphere was so far removed from the pressures and the hustle of the agency that it gave him a chance to relax. For Frances the whole thing operated in reverse. Where most people wound down towards Friday night, she wound up, starting on Thursday. It was then the tension started to build. To take her mind off it she would go out to lunch, usually with Bernard Glenn.

Bernard liked to drink, his years in journalism had turned him into something of a boozer and he thought nothing of killing two pitchers of martini over lunch.

When she was with Bernard, Frances abandoned the Perrier water and spritzers she had with Tiffany and her usual lunching crowd and went for the hard stuff. Almost immediately she found it didn't suit her. Martini straight up made her pink in the face and gave her a crashing hangover. So she switched her drinks until she found something that suited her better.

Champagne seemed to do the trick. It was less alcoholic, so she could drink more of it and it didn't give the impression that she was hitting the bottle. She could start sipping the fizzy wine as early as noon and look like a lady. Occasionally, after a long lunch, she would have to take a nap in the afternoon but that wasn't a problem. She didn't have an office to go to and as long as she was reasonably sober when Sam came home, what harm was she doing?

Two months after Abner came back into her life, Frances started to drink at home. Tiffany, noticing her latest preference, bought her a champagne stopper. This meant she could open a bottle at eleven in the morning and take just one glass out of it to keep her going. The stopper would ensure the wine didn't lose its fizz for at least three days. Frances never really put this to the test. A bottle of champagne rarely lasted beyond the early evening.

Sam didn't comment at the change in Frances. He knew she was drinking but he decided to live with it for the time being, anyway.

The crisis in their marriage was too recent to start making waves, and the wounds were too fresh. They still couldn't talk about the baby they'd lost. They couldn't talk about Louise either and in a way he was glad about that. The Greek girl and the way he felt about her was something he wanted to bury. Maybe forever.

Sam retreated into his work. Most evenings he didn't make it back to the apartment until seven, sometimes eight at night. When he did get home, he always brought an unfinished campaign or an urgent report with him in his briefcase.

He took to meeting clients over the weekends that they weren't visiting Abner, and the space between him and his wife started to widen.

Some days when he was on his own waiting for a meeting to begin, or sitting in the office after one had ended, he thought about Louise. He tried not to. Every time the image of her swam into his mind, he tried to blank it out but it was no good. And with the memory of Louise came regret.

If San Francisco had never happened he and Frances would be happy today. There would be a baby and plans for another. They would both be looking around for a family house somewhere out of the city, and the nights would be different. Neither of them slept very much these days. Frances would drink herself to sleep and wake up three hours later thirsty and restless. Sam always woke too when that happened and they would lie side by side in the big double bed, both of them pretending to be asleep. Neither of them daring to touch.

At times like this, Sam longed to take Frances in his arms and make love to her the way he used to when she had a bad dream. But there were too many unspoken words between them now. So they remained isolated from each other, wrapped in their own private torment.

The days were better. When Sam wasn't working, they rarely stayed in, and in the company of other people, they relaxed. Frances paraded her expensive designer clothes and talked to the other wives and Sam talked business and baseball to his cronies. When a group of them were together Frances always seemed to be babbling about the

363

latest painter on the circuit, a new show in town, a juicy scandal passed on to her by Tiffany.

I can take my wife anywhere, he thought. We may have our problems, but nothing anyone else would notice. Then one night Frances got drunk, and Sam realised that all along he had been fooling himself.

There were four of them dining when it happened – Sam, Abner, Frances and Tiffany. It was a Friday night and Clay was working late and driving down the following morning. Nobody was very hungry, so Abner had decided to take them all out to the country club for an extravagant snack. The speciality that week was Russian caviar. They all had it with lemon vodka, another speciality. It was a jolly end-of-week kind of gathering. Christmas was behind them, the frost was melting, the nights were beginning to draw out and already the promise of spring was just around the corner.

Sam was the brightest among them that evening. The paper mill tycoon Abner had introduced had decided to spend another half million with the agency and he was in the mood for celebration.

'What does everyone say to a little more caviar?' he asked. 'Kurnitz and Greene can pick up the cheque. With the profits we're making, we can afford it.'

Everyone laughed and agreed, and when the waiter appeared with the distinctive blue and black tin on its bed of crushed ice, Abner extended the party and ordered another bottle of vodka. Tiffany's eyes sparkled.

'Are you planning on leading me astray?' she asked. 'This much liquor could make me do something I'd regret.'

She was looking very beautiful that night. In blue jeans with hardly a trace of make-up. There was a glow about her that Frances would have given her eyes for. How long is it, she asked herself, since I was that radiant? She turned to her friend.

'What could it make you do?' she teased.

Tiffany rolled her eyes.

'Tear off my clothes and run into the sea.'

'Not bad,' said Frances. She looked at Abner.

'How about you? If you drank too much what would you do?'

Abner grinned.

'Maybe I'd try to talk Sam into taking on one of my accounts. After all he works for a couple of my friends now. So why not me?'

Frances looked across at Sam expecting to see the familiar glower that came over him when anybody touched on the taboo subject of Abner's business. But for once Sam was untroubled.

'You can always ask,' he said.

'And would you always say no?' Abner asked curiously.

Sam hesitated, considering.

'Almost always,' he said.

The waiter arrived with the fresh bottle of lemon vodka and Abner filled up everyone's glass again.

'If it's almost always,' he said, 'what would be the exception to the rule? What would make you say yes?'

Frances threw back her drink. In the past there had been banter about Abner's business. The two men had joked about Sam's principles but Abner had never pushed it. Now, for the first time, he was asking the question: what would make you take my business? A small silence fell over the four of them and all eyes were on Sam.

'I wouldn't work on cigarettes for myself,' he said slowly. 'I can dig myself out of whatever hole I find myself in without resorting to compromises. No, if I sold myself down the river it would be to save somebody else.'

Tiffany leaned forward, an intense expression in her eyes.

'Like who?' she asked.

Sam put his arm round Frances.

'Like my wife,' he replied. 'Or any child we might have together.'

Frances started to feel frightened. Without knowing it, Sam was playing right into the tobacco baron's hands. She dreaded what would come next, but nothing did. Abner started telling funny stories and flirting with Tiffany and Sam began to start planning the next day's tennis. But Frances couldn't leave the subject of cigarettes alone. She worried it like a child with a sore patch and the more she fussed and fretted, the more she drank.

Abner tried to shut her up.

'Enough about my business,' he told her, 'the subject is closed.'

Frances narrowed her eyes at him.

'For how long?' she asked.

'Until I get back to my office,' said Abner firmly. 'This is a friendly weekend. We're here to relax, not talk turkey.'

Frances started to laugh. Wild hysterical laughter that bubbled up in the back of her throat and escaped from her lips in gasps. Sam looked concerned.

'What's so funny?' he asked. 'Did I miss some kind of joke?'

Now Frances turned to him and he saw there were tears in her eyes.

'You missed the joke,' she said, slurring slightly, 'because you *are* the joke. Can't you see Abner laughing behind his hand every time he talks about his goddamned business? Can't you see he's setting you up? Can't you see you'll end up doing exactly what he wants you to do in the end?'

The colour drained out of Sam's face.

'Stop it,' he said harshly. 'You're spoiling the party.'

'The party,' Frances said, mimicking his voice. 'That's all you care about isn't it. The goddamned party.' She looked around her. 'When I met you you didn't go to fancy places like this and you didn't hang about with the likes of Abner Morris either.'

Sam put his hand under her arm and jerked her to her feet.

'We're going,' he said. 'My wife's had too much to drink.'

But Frances had no intention of leaving. She struggled out of his grasp and walked unsteadily round the table. Before anyone could stop her, she helped herself to more vodka, swallowing the glass in one.

'Do you feel uncomfortable hearing the truth?' she asked thickly. 'Or are you embarrassed because it's me that's speaking out? Women like me don't speak out, do we? We keep our mouths shut and look grateful for all the treats.' She waved her hands round the table.

'Thank you for the caviar, Abner. Thank you for the country club. Thank you for nothing.'

She reached forward to pour herself another drink. But Abner took the bottle out of her hands.

'Get out of here,' he said quietly, 'before you make a complete fool of yourself. If you want to get smashed tonight, I've got plenty of vodka back at the house.'

She started to say something, but Sam was right behind her. Putting a firm arm round her waist, he wheeled her round and marched her towards the door. When they got into the street, Frances realised she could hardly stand up. Through a haze she saw a taxi pull up to the kerb and somehow, she didn't know how, she managed to get inside it. After that she remembered nothing at all.

Tiffany leaned back against the padded banquette and caught the waiter's eye.

'After that little performance,' she said, 'I think I'll have a cup of coffee.'

Abner grinned and looked up. 'Make it two,' he said, agreeing. 'Any more vodka could spoil what I have in mind for later.'

Tiffany moved closer to him on the long velvet seat and

ran her hand across his thigh. It was an intimate gesture, a lover's gesture and Abner was relieved the table prevented anyone else in the Club from seeing it.

'What if Clay gets through early,' Tiffany asked, 'and drives down tonight? He could, you know.'

Abner frowned.

'I'll tell him you got drunk and I was putting you to bed. He'll swallow that – he's swallowed everything else so far.'

It was not the reply she wanted and Tiffany looked irritated.

'I'm not some bimbo like Frances Kurnitz,' she snapped. 'I don't get smashed at dinner parties and I don't speak out of turn. My husband knows that.'

Abner changed the subject.

'What about Frances?' he said. 'I've never seen her like that before.'

'You're not around her as much as I am,' said Tiffany. 'She's been hitting the bottle for a few months now. Ever since you came back into her life.'

She looked worried.

'Are you sure you're not being too tough with her? After all she's had a hard time lately.'

Abner reached inside his pocket and produced a cigar which he proceeded to clamp between his teeth.

'Why this sudden concern?' he asked. 'I thought you wanted this business for your old man's firm. If that means turning Frances into a lush, it's unfortunate but it can't be helped.'

Tiffany straightened up and moved away from him. 'You're a cold bastard aren't you,' she said harshly. 'Don't you care about anything or anyone?'

Abner lit the end of his Havana, considering.

'I care about myself,' he replied. 'And getting what I want. Right now I want you in my bed and Sam Kurnitz working on my business.'

Tiffany looked at him.

'This is getting silly,' she said. 'The reason you wanted Sam to work on your business was because of me. Well, you've got me. I won't stop going to bed with you if you give the brand to somebody else. In a way it might be the best thing.'

It was as if the temperature had gone down in the restaurant. Abner seemed to withdraw into himself and Tiffany noticed how hard his eyes looked.

'You don't understand me at all,' he said softly. 'The reasons why I want my business to go to Sam no longer matter. What matters is I took a decision to put it there. It's the only thing that's important now.'

'Why?' Tiffany asked him.

'Because I don't like being crossed.' The words sounded tough as he said them. Threatening almost. 'A long time ago,' he went on, 'my father crossed me. I'd left my wife for somebody else, and he said if I didn't go back to her, he'd cut me off. I didn't have any money in those days and I worked for my old man. So he had me by the short and curlies. Except he didn't. You see, there was no way I was going to let him push me around. I was prepared to starve rather than let him do that. And I did starve for a bit. But I came through in the end. I made money. More money than father ever had. It taught me something. Once I'd made up my mind to do a thing, whatever it was, I had to see it through to the end. I owed it to myself.'

'But this thing with Sam,' Tiffany persisted, 'it's irrational. You're trying to force the guy into handling business he doesn't want. For what? You don't gain anything by it.'

Abner signalled the waiter for the bill. Impatiently. Tiffany was becoming tiresome and he wanted to get out of the club.

'I'm not looking to gain anything,' he said crossly. 'I told you before, all I want is my own way. And I'll get it. Whatever Frances says when she's stoned.'

But Tiffany wouldn't let it go.

'What makes you so sure?' she asked. 'She sailed pretty close to the wind tonight. All that stuff about you setting him up sounded like a warning to me. If Sam takes notice he could just be packing his bags right now and heading back to New York.'

The waiter arrived with the coffee, leaving the pot on the table between them.

'Sam won't take any notice,' Abner said. 'Can't you understand, men don't listen to air-heads like Frances. That's why he reacted the way he did when she tried to talk him into working on cigarettes the first time round. He's not interested in what she wants or what she hopes for. Frances is there to warm his bed, cook his meals and have his babies. And furthermore she knows it.'

'So how are you going to use Frances to push Sam into taking your business?'

Abner picked up the coffee pot and filled both their cups.

'Well I'm not going to use her influence and powers of persuasion – and that's for sure. What I'm going to do is put her in a risky situation, threaten her life in some way. Sam gave me the clue when he said he'd take on the business to get her out of trouble.'

'What kind of trouble?'

Abner stirred his coffee.

'I haven't worked that one out yet. But I'll get to it.'

On the way back in the car Tiffany put Frances out of her mind. She'd tried to help her and failed. Now it was time to think of herself and her next move. Should she go to bed with Abner, she wondered, or should she be cautious in case Clay turned up unexpectedly early? She'd been seeing Abner twice a week for the past three months now and he'd come to expect it. Depend on it almost.

It was that fact that never failed to amaze her. Here was a man who lived in a place where he had sex on tap. An endless supply of centrefolds willing and eager whenever he wanted them. But he didn't want them. Or at least he wanted them less. For now he had her, he seemed insatiable. Tiffany knew that if she were available every night, Abner would see her every night.

She sometimes put it to the test, cancelling their dates and remaking them at times when she knew he was doing something else, and he always came through for her. Whatever and whoever he was seeing got pushed to one side when she was around.

Her power over him gave her confidence. It also gave her ideas. As the weeks grew into months she began to wonder about the future of this affair.

In her twelve-year marriage she had always had affairs. Sometimes for business, sometimes for pleasure, but never for both. No lover had ever had her whole attention. And when she got bored – as she always did – she moved on to the next. Her life was her husband and her family. Her lovers were icing on the cake.

If she hadn't got involved with Abner, the situation would have remained that way. For Abner was different. He was rich. Richer than anyone she had known in her life. But it wasn't just his money that fascinated her. It was the way he spent it.

Abner had made an art, a science almost, out of enjoying himself. He could ski and play tennis to championship standard. He sailed only the fastest boats. He was a connoisseur of all the Arts, and he didn't just lavish money on his houses willy-nilly. He supervised their decoration, often personally. The result was that everywhere he inhabited had a certain class, an unmistakable style. A style Tiffany began to want for herself.

Her months with Abner made her realise she was outgrowing her marriage. Until she knew the tobacco magnate, Clay had given her everything she had wanted. Companionship, money to spend, freedom to find the

371

passion he could no longer supply. Now she wanted more than that. She wanted a man who could cater for all her needs, and Abner fitted the bill.

Now all she had to do was convince Abner it was time to settle down. She wasn't finding it easy. Sex, her most powerful weapon, persuaded him not at all. She tried all the variations. She dressed like a tart, she whipped and was beaten in return, she explored the rubber fetish, and on one occasion she experimented with a threesome.

Abner enjoyed all of it, then he asked her what she wanted. He posed the question after a hectic session under an ice-cold shower had nearly succeeded in drowning them both.

'What is it with you?' he enquired. 'Every time I want to screw you, you turn it into a Cecil B. de Mille production.'

Tiffany looked pained. 'I thought you enjoyed this kind of thing,' she said, towelling her hair.

'I do enjoy it,' he told her. 'I've been exploring the variations most of my adult life. I just don't need to explore them with you. At least not all the time. You turn me on enough without the exotic trimmings. Don't you understand, you silly woman, I only go in for the fetishes when I'm bored with someone. They help concentrate the mind.'

Tiffany started to lose her temper. 'Are you telling me I've been wasting my time?'

'Not if you enjoy dressing up in rubber.'

'I hate dressing up in rubber,' she screamed. 'I loathe being beaten. And this number under the shower will probably give me a cold.'

Abner took her in his arms. 'Then why did you bother?'

She sneezed.

'I thought you'd get more interested in me.'

'What do you mean, more interested? I'm crazy about you already.'

'I don't want crazy. I want serious.'

Abner looked at Tiffany, comprehension dawning. 'Serious as in commitment? Settling down?' he asked.

She nodded.

He walked away from her and started to get dressed.

'I'm not very good at that kind of thing,' he said. 'I was married once. To a very nice girl. The best. But it didn't work out. I can't be permanently joined to one woman. Not in the formal sense. It makes me nervous.'

He took a look at her face and changed tack.

'Look,' he said, 'I *am* capable of an exclusive relationship. In a way I have that with you right now. Since we got together I haven't been interested in any of the other girls. But that's because I chose the situation. If it had been chosen for me by a priest or a lawyer I'd have been screwing the first piece of tail that said "Yes".'

'We don't have to get married,' Tiffany said. 'We could live together.'

Abner finished dressing and started to rake a comb through his springy black hair.

'You'd leave Clay?' he said.

'Yes, if you were serious.'

He looked at her speculatively. She had to be thirty-five – give or take a year, and everything he could see was in working order. She hadn't got round to putting on her bra yet and her breasts were firm and round and rosy tipped. Out of curiosity he went over and took one in his hand.

'Lovely,' he murmured half to himself. 'But how long can it last?'

Tiffany drew closer and started to kiss him. Open mouthed kisses. Kisses using her tongue. Abner felt his desire return and he pulled back from her.

'I've got a meeting in five minutes,' he said.

But it was too late. His flies were undone and Tiffany's panties were half way down to her knees. He took hold of the wisp of lace between them and tore it off her, then

373

he pushed her down to the floor and parted her legs. She smiled as he ground into her.

'It looks like the meeting will be starting late,' she said.

Sex, Tiffany discovered, could make Abner scramble up his business life. It could wreak complete havoc with his social plans. But what it couldn't do was make him commit himself.

Every time they talked about the possibility of her leaving Clay, Abner deflected her.

'I want to know you better', he would say, or 'I need to be convinced', or 'the responsibility frightens me'.

Every time it was a 'maybe', never a 'yes'. Tiffany was undeterred. All her life she had always got everything she had wanted. Sometimes she had to compromise, other times she'd had to cheat. But in the end things she'd set her mind on fell into her hands. Abner would be the same sooner or later.

The car pulled into the drive of Abner's spread in the Hamptons and Tiffany waited for him to come round and let her out.

She could have opened the door herself and jumped out but that would have been too easy. This man she had set her sights on had to work to stay in her favour. He had to open doors and cancel meetings.

They were little gestures, she knew that, but if she was going to get him to make the big gesture then he had to be in the habit of obliging her.

They went into the house and Tiffany headed for the lounge.

'I don't feel sleepy yet,' she said. 'Let's have a night-cap.'

Abner shrugged and followed her. 'I think I've something that will make you feel like going straight to bed,' he said.

She went over to the bar and poured herself an Armagnac.

'I wouldn't bank on it,' Tiffany smiled. Abner didn't reply. Instead he reached inside his breast pocket and drew out a small flat package. Then he took the brandy balloon out of her hands and gave her the parcel.

'Open it,' he instructed. She saw the wrapping paper was Cartier's and Tiffany started to smile.

Her pleasure intensified as she opened the box, for inside was a circle of diamonds, eight flawless stones that just fitted round her second finger.

Abner looked at her face, her glowing excitement.

'It's not an engagement ring,' he said. 'It's an eternity ring. A piece of decoration.'

'But what does it mean?' she asked, her eyes misting over.

Abner drew in his breath. 'It means,' he said, 'that unless you walk down the hall and into my bedroom fast, I'll have it back, straight away.'

40

The taxi pulled up outside Lennard's boutique in Sloane Street and Louise stepped out. As always these days she was in a hurry and although the meter told her she owed three pounds thirty, she slapped four pound notes into the driver's hand and was on her way. There was no time to wait around for change. Not today. Not now their new office was ready.

An estate agent had come up with the goods two weeks after Kurnitz and Greene won their recognition. An office on the second floor of a new block in Sloane Street. Down the street was Allen and Frazer, the London equivalent of Bloomingdales. Around the block was Harrods, and underneath there were some of the most expensive fashion boutiques in the city.

If Louise had dreamed up the location herself it couldn't have been more perfect. The moment they had the lease she went to work. At the beginning all they had was a huge space like a warehouse with a single large office at one end.

Louise remembered the hours she had laboured over the drawing-board. Hours of discussion and rejection until she had the blueprint she was looking for. Now, this morning, Kurnitz and Greene officially opened its doors for business.

She held her breath as she sped up the short concrete staircase. Will it look like the blueprint, she wondered?

Will it look like the picture I've been carrying around in my head these past two months?

She pushed her way through the double doors until she

stood in the reception area. Then she breathed out. It was better than she had dared hope.

In front of her was the huge teak desk she had ordered from a catalogue. In reality it was bigger than she'd anticipated, and she was pleased. It had an air of grandeur, a mark of authority. She nodded, the clients would be impressed when they walked in. Louise started to prowl around the space she had designed. On each side of the reception desk were two long corridors lined with glass offices. The account directors and creative people were starting to gather and again Louise nodded her satisfaction. Every time she walked through the office she could see at a glance who was there and what they were doing. These people she employed were crack troops. Her own private army poised and ready to conquer London for her.

She had pinned up her American ads so they covered the cork walls. Soon, she told herself, I'll be tearing them down, for any time now the English work will start appearing and then I'll know I'm in business.

She waved at a copywriter/art director team she had just stolen away from another agency. Together they had cost sixty thousand pounds a year. A fortune. Far more than she could justify, let alone afford. Yet despite Nigel's misgivings and Clay's protests Louise had stood her ground. 'Our only value as an agency,' she had insisted, 'is the talent we hire. For they create the ads. And with good ads I can destroy the competition.'

What fighting words they were, she reflected as she made her way to her office at the end of the corridor, yet as she threw open the tall black painted door that led to her inner sanctum she had misgivings. Despite the skills she had to offer, she hadn't convinced anyone to give the agency any new accounts.

For three months she and Nigel had knocked on doors and given presentations. Some of the country's biggest manufacturers had seen the ads she and her American colleagues had created and they had nodded their heads and said 'Very nice. Very effective for the USA but England is a different market. What have you done here?'

There was nothing she could say. None of the agency's work would be appearing until later in the year. She could only tell people about past successes, and the past was of little interest to the hard men she was facing now. She sat down at her desk and ran through the list of figures her accountant had given her. The rent and salaries she was paying out far exceeded the money she was getting in from her existing business.

Soon, she knew, she would have to start laying people off. There was a knock on the door and she looked up as Nigel came through the door.

'Sorry to disturb you,' he apologised, 'but I've got a delegation outside. It seems your top creative talent wants to see you.'

Her heart sank. How do they know what trouble we're in, she thought. I've only just seen the figures myself. She tried to look happy as she called for them to come in. They're probably going to call it quits, she told herself. Rats deserting a sinking ship.

Four men and one woman came through the door. Most of them were in jeans and one or two were sporting the thonged leather jackets and hippy beads that were fashionable that season. There appeared to be no particular leader. Instead they all lined up in front of her and linked arms. Then at some hidden signal a tape deck began playing and she heard the strains of the Cole Porter classic 'There's no business like show business'.

The five of them started jigging to the music, kicking their legs up like a chorus line in a variety show. Then they sang in unison to the music.

'There's no business . . .'

Louise started to smile and then she chuckled softly until finally she could no longer contain herself and the laughter

378

burst out of her. The makeshift chorus line joined in. Even Nigel let go.

For five minutes the entire office was in pandemonium until she reluctantly called a halt.

'You're lovely,' she spluttered. 'Just looking at you makes me feel better. But you said it. There's no business. Nothing new anyway. Honestly I won't hold it against you if you start looking around.'

The tallest and youngest of them, a copywriter with a beaky nose called Owl spoke for all of them.

'How long can you go on paying us?' he asked.

Louise considered. 'If I push it, I can go to the end of the month.'

The five looked at each other and nodded agreement.

'We won't start looking,' said Owl, 'until the very last moment. And you're going to have to tell us when that is.'

Louise leaned back in her chair and regarded them with wonder.

'I must have done something very good in my life to deserve you,' she told them.

Hannah, the art director in hippy beads came forward and pointed at the walls bearing the ads Louise had designed in Manhattan.

'You did,' was all she said.

Ten days after Louise arrived in her new offices, the work she and Clay did for Californian Mills started to appear. Up and down the country posters appeared showing ears of corn and bearing the legend 'The Yellow King'. At first people stared in astonishment. Then they laughed. Finally they walked into the shops and asked for 'The Yellow King'.

Several days later a tiny press campaign for an alcoholic hangover cure started to run in evening papers. The headline said, 'How I cured my hangover by turning to drink'.

Two weeks after that Louise's first new client walked through the door. His name was David Hepton. He was small and bald and his suit was so shabby the receptionist thought he was the man from the window cleaning agency. Then the stranger announced himself and she jumped to attention and picked up the internal phone.

'Louise,' she squeaked over the wires, 'the marketing director of Allen and Frazer – the shop down the road – has just walked in to see you.'

When the call came through Louise was doing nothing. Her first reaction was to get Nigel into the office and convene a meeting. Then she stopped herself. I'm the London office of a fashionable Madison Avenue agency, she told herself. My new campaigns are breaking all over this little country, so I should look busy. If I see David Hepton now he'll think I'm desperate, and that's no way to start a relationship.

She called back her receptionist. 'Tell Mr Hepton I'd be delighted to see him, but I'm in the middle of a meeting with Californian Mills,' she said. 'Then give him a selection of dates starting with tomorrow morning.'

'Are you sure?' stammered the girl. 'Damn right I'm sure,' said Louise crisply. 'Stop asking silly questions.' Then she broke the connection. Five minutes later the receptionist knocked on Louise's door.

'David Hepton's coming to see us at nine o'clock tomorrow morning,' she said.

Allen and Frazer marked the turning point for the agency. The shop was only prepared to give them a small slice of their business, a billing of £250,000 a year – barely enough to support one top art director. But Allen and Frazer had something better than billing going for it. It had prestige.

The Knightsbridge department store stood for everything that was trendy in the early Eighties. Where they went, others followed. Their latest venture was a new boutique on the top floor to compete with the small fashionable shops in Sloane Street. It was going to be expensive, more so than any other area of the store and it planned to stock two exclusive Paris labels and one top designer from Milan.

Louise put her best creative team on the business. Now she had her chance, she took a decision. She would go on paying her top creative people and stop drawing her own salary. If her gamble paid off, their work would attract more business and she could pay herself again. She refused to consider what would happen if it didn't.

Retailing is a fast business and that was what saved her. For Allen and Frazer needed the ads to run the second they opened their boutique, so there were none of the usual client committee meetings. Nobody slept on anything because there simply wasn't time. If Kurnitz and Greene's work was going to help their business the shop would know virtually within days of the ads appearing.

Louise kept her expensive team working round the clock and when she wasn't running the agency, she kept an eye on what they were doing. She was a hard task master, ruthlessly rejecting everything but the best ideas. Even the great work was cut and honed and beaten into shape.

The ads that finally appeared were designed to attract attention. They did more than that.

The phones started ringing at Kurnitz and Greene the following morning. In the space of a month three large manufacturers fixed meetings for that week. Their name started to be whispered around town. *Campaign*, the media magazine, ran a profile on Nigel Farquharson – the fallen tycoon who rose again.

Louise felt a twinge of outraged pride and suppressed it. It didn't matter that Nigel, not her, was attracting attention. What mattered was that clients were suddenly interested in Kurnitz and Greene. In the next three months the agency added twenty new accounts to their roster and every time the agency put on another piece of business, *Campaign* ran a story about them on their front page. Louise heaved a sigh of relief and started paying herself again.

Then she checked the date in her diary. It was the third of May. Six months almost to the day she had left New York. She decided to write a letter to Clay in New York.

'You gave me nine months,' she wrote, 'to make the London agency work. I know everyone involved is convinced that it does.' Then she neatly typed out a list of her newly won clients. By the side of each of them she filled in the projected billing or the fees. She was surprised how little some of them paid. Then she looked at the length of the list and was reassured. It all adds up, she thought. We really are the fastest growing shop in the UK. She felt a glow of achievement. Now I can ask, she decided. It's the right moment.

She went back to her letter. 'You told me,' she went on writing, 'that if I didn't make a go of things, I was out on my ass. Well I did make it work. Kurnitz and Greene in London is a thriving concern and because of that I'm asking you to fulfil your side of the bargain. You promised me a full partnership, Clay. I know it's only been six months, but I'm calling in that promise. I've worked too hard and worried too much to wait any longer.'

She finished the letter by sending her regards to Sam. Then she wished Tiffany well, just for good measure.

Clay's letter reached her by return post.

'Over here,' he wrote, 'we're all over the moon about your success in England. Your growth is phenomenal, the work is superb and even Tiffany has caught your publicity in the trades. You're kicking up a storm and we're proud of you. But it's no dice on the partnership.'

As she read the last sentence, Louise went cold. Bastard, she thought. He can't get away with it. But Clay could, the rest of his letter explained why. Despite the welter of new business, there were no true profits. They could pay the rent and all the overheads – including the high-flying creative men and women. Yet at the end of the day, they just broke even. The terms of their agreement, Clay reminded her, was a full partnership when Kurnitz and Greene turned in a profit. He ended his letter by noting the dates. 'I gave you nine months to come good,' he wrote. 'By my reckoning you've got another three months to prove yourself.'

He signed off by wishing her luck. Sam sent regards.

She flung the letter down in disgust. Then she asked Nigel to come and see her. Louise wasted no time telling him about her correspondence with Clay. He sighed and sat down in a chair.

'Why didn't you discuss it with me before you wrote to him?' he asked.

Louise was irritated.

'Why should I?' she said. 'I was asking for a promotion. It's got nothing to do with you.'

The Englishman sighed heavily. 'It's got everything to do with me,' he told her, 'unless you've forgotten I keep an eye on the running of the business. I've known for some time about the profits – or rather the lack of them. I was going to come and talk to you about it, but you've been so busy recently, I thought I'd wait till we could give it a decent block of time.'

Louise got up and paced around the office. All her old American ads had been taken down now and it was her new product, her British ads that gazed down at her from the walls.

'I thought I was doing so well,' she raged. 'And now everyone tells me it's not good enough.'

She looked at Nigel in his striped Savile Row suit.

'How did I get into this mess?' she asked. 'How did *you* let me get in this mess?'

Nigel got up and walked over to where she was standing,

then he put his arm round her and led her over to the Conran sofa at the far end of her office.

'Sit down,' he instructed. 'We've got some talking to do and when I'm finished you're going to have to take a decision.'

Nigel started by giving her a breakdown of their business. The way he told it, it sounded good – Louise expected that. They had thirty accounts now, covering everything from breakfast food to a building society. What she didn't expect was the way many of their clients conducted their business. There was a handbag client who took up weeks of time in meetings and still couldn't make a firm decision on the advertising, a package tour company who commissioned expensive print work and took months settling their bills. The list was endless. All the non-profitable accounts had one thing in common. They were small time. At a casual glance Louise could see they had over a dozen bits of business spending around £150,000 a year that weren't doing anything for the bottom line.

'Why on earth did we take them on?' Louise asked.

Nigel smiled.

'At the time the agency needed them, or thought it did. We were going through a crisis of confidence. The creative staff had time on their hands and our public profile was at an all-time low. If we hadn't taken on the business we could easily have gone under.'

She made a face. 'We're going to go under anyway at this rate. We can't go on treading water indefinitely.'

Nigel got up and went over to the window.

Below him the Knightsbridge shoppers were out in force and he could see there was money on the streets. The Conservatives had been in power for a year or so now and the effects of the new Government were starting to show. Nigel swung round and looked at Louise.

'I've got a hunch that now's the time to take our biggest gamble to date.'

'What do you have in mind?' Louise asked.

The Englishman took a deep breath. 'I think we should get rid of half our business. The fifty per cent that isn't making any money.'

Louise looked at him. 'But that means laying off staff.'

He nodded.

'So we lay off people. Agencies do it, you know. In my opinion we've got too many juniors and secretaries cluttering up the place.'

'Okay,' Louise agreed. 'So we cut the agency in two in one fell swoop. What's that going to do to us as far as the outside world is concerned? We'll look like losers, that I can guarantee. None of the clients will admit to being fired and our competitors will put it around that there's been a run on the agency. I don't know if we can afford that.'

Nigel looked smug. 'We don't have to afford it. Not if I take the editor of *Campaign* out to lunch and give him the story first. It's a sure thing he'll splash it on the front page. It's not every day an agency fires nearly two million pounds' worth of business and you'll cause a sensation. The publicity value alone makes it worthwhile.'

Louise thought about the Allen and Frazer marketing director and how she had made him wait for a meeting. She had done it at a time when she could least afford it but he didn't know that. As far as he was concerned she didn't need him and that made him even keener to do business. So what would the world think if she showed them she didn't need two million pounds' worth of advertising spend? The thought made her smile.

'Do we tell *Campaign* the truth?' she asked. 'Do we say we couldn't make money on the business we fired?'

Nigel thought for a moment. 'No we don't,' he said. 'What we tell them is we want to keep our agency small and tight-knit. We want to limit the staff to seniors only. That takes care of the bad smell when we get rid of the second division.'

'I don't see how that justifies ditching all those accounts.'

Nigel smiled. 'I'm coming to that. Look, a small account takes just as much time as a big account so the quality senior staff we employ only has time to work on big business. What we're aiming for is a small number of accounts spending a lot of money. What we're offering is a Rolls-Royce service.'

What he was saying made perfect sense and Louise wondered why she hadn't planned her business along those lines in the first place. Then she remembered the chaos of her first weeks in London. I can't order my life the way I order a meal in a restaurant, she reflected. I can only work with what there is.

'Do you think we'll get away with it?' she asked.

Her companion ran his hand through thinning hair.

'Your guess is as good as mine.'

The story broke in the trade press the following Thursday and almost immediately there was an uproar in the business. Clay called her from New York and demanded to know what she was playing at. Three agency heads made representations to the NPA, asking for her recognition to be withdrawn and the agency's remaining clients started to feel insecure.

Through all the fuss and the shouting Louise sat tight. She had been taking gambles all her life. The affair with Brian Elder right at the beginning had been a risk and she had weathered it and made it work for her. Since she had come to London she had put herself out on a limb and she was still alive to tell the tale. She would survive this fight as well.

Within seven weeks she was proved right. She replaced the twelve unprofitable accounts with two bits of business that made her money. A motor oil firm that spent one and a half million and a retail chain billing £600,000. In just under eight months of running her own agency, Louise was in the black. This time when she wrote to Clay she didn't ask for a full partnership. She demanded one.

41

Clay called an emergency meeting of the board at the Reform Health Club on Second Avenue. He had recently become bored with the Turkish baths, they seemed too passive a way of punishing his system. What he wanted was something that made his flesh wobble and his muscles ache, and the Reform with its air-conditioned gym fitted the bill.

Sam groaned when his secretary told him about the meeting with his partner. They talked seriously about the agency once every ten days and the gym was getting him down. It wasn't as if he could get away with just ten minutes on the exercise bicycle either. Clay insisted on two circuits of the gym and stood over him while he pushed and pulled his way round the Nautilus machines. Sam was no weakling. He would have happily stayed on a squash court all afternoon or run five miles round the park, but organised exercise in air conditioning bored him rigid.

As he made his way to Second Avenue he wondered for the thousandth time why he put up with Clay's whims. Any other partner would thrash things out over a drink in the 21 Club. Then he mentally shrugged his shoulders. He and Clay had been in business for nearly ten years. They liked working together, they were making money and apart from a minor disagreement over taking on cigarettes, the partnership had been a success. So he makes me schlep around a few weights, thought Sam. It's not going to kill me.

He got to the Reform around six and found Clay had already checked in. He hurried his way through the changing-room and made it to the gym as Clay was starting a session on the running machine. The moving belt next to him was vacant and Sam jumped on. The meeting was in session.

It lasted all of three minutes. At the mention of Louise's name, Sam fell out of step, the belt developed a fault and they both came screeching to a halt. Clay regarded his partner.

'I'm going to break the habits of a lifetime,' he announced. 'I'm going to can the gym and buy you a drink. You look like you could do with one.'

Half an hour later, showered and changed they were sitting in the Irish bar down the street. Over a freshly made pitcher of martini, Clay was going into detail about Louise's success in London.

'I would have put money on it that she was going to fall flat on her face. I had it all worked out. In nine months I'd planned to quietly pay her off and neither of us would have heard another word from her. Instead she goes and does the impossible and makes a go of the business.'

Sam laughed.

'That shows how well you knew her. I expected she'd pull it off. She's tougher than she looks. Had to be where she's come from. Are we going to give her the partnership?'

Clay poured himself another drink. 'We don't have any other option. I'm not happy splitting the agency three ways, but I did promise Louise a full partnership and I put it in writing. She made me do it.'

The news came as a surprise to Sam. There had been talk of her promotion. He and Clay never kept anything from each other. But putting it in writing. Promising a third of the equity. What could his partner have been thinking of?

'Why the hell didn't you consult me before you committed yourself?' he demanded.

The fat man shrugged. 'You weren't around to be consulted. If you remember you ran away and hid while I did your dirty work. When Louise was telling me what it was going to cost to make her disappear you were sunning yourself in Palm Springs with your lawful wedded wife.'

Sam winced. Palm Springs had been a disaster. Frances was still grieving after the baby she had lost. He was racked with guilt over the whole business. And part of him, the part that mattered, was still missing Louise.

I should have stayed and faced the music, he thought. I've never run away from things. Never in my life – until now. He turned to his partner.

'There's no way we can get out of this, is there?'

Clay shook his head.

'Then give her the partnership,' said Sam finally. 'She's worked for it.'

Sam decided to walk home. He was in no hurry tonight, they weren't going anywhere. Nowadays he and Frances didn't go out too much in the evenings.

He had been aware of her drinking since the night at Abner's, when she had made a fool of herself. The next day he had tried to talk to her about it, but she wasn't having any. As far as she was concerned, she didn't have a problem. She liked a glass of wine every so often, it helped relax her, it got her through tricky social situations.

'We don't have any tricky social situations,' exploded Sam. 'All the people we see are friends. I do my best to keep away from clients out of the office.'

'What about Abner Morris?' Frances asked.

Sam sighed and looked at his wife in despair.

'Abner is different,' he told her. 'Number one, he's not a client and he's never going to be. Number two, I like the guy.'

Frances went quiet after that. To be fair to her she didn't get bombed any more, not in public at any rate. But Sam was aware she was never sober either. Most evenings when he got home she was glassy-eyed and clutching a glass of champagne in her hand. By the time the late-night news came on television, she was nearly asleep. Once or twice he'd had to put her to bed.

He sighed as he approached 72nd Street. He was going to have to do something about Frances before it was too late; she was slipping away from him, slipping away from their marriage. There were days when he hardly recognised the girl he had met four years ago. The girl who was a ringer for his dead first wife, Leah. The girl he fell in love with on sight.

He wondered if he ran into her today whether he'd feel the same emotion. Frances was so different now. The long silky hair he used to run his fingers through was short now and so bleached, so lacquered, it didn't feel like hair at all. Maybe the hair is the reason she doesn't look the same any more, he thought. But he knew he was lying to himself. The reason Frances looked ten years older was the booze.

It had made her stout and somehow blowsy. She had to be carrying an extra fifteen pounds, minimum. The flab had changed her. Before there was an elfin quality to her face. It was something to do with the combination of huge clear eyes and delicate cheekbones. Now her eyes were small and piggy and he couldn't see her cheekbones any more.

He felt a stab of disloyalty and suppressed it. I'm going to have to do something about Frances, he decided. Tonight.

When he got in, she was chatting to the maid who almost always prepared dinner nowadays. I paid a fortune for her fancy cookery lessons, he thought, and she lets the maid do the work. He blamed that bit on Tiffany. Ever since she and Frances got friendly things had changed.

Sam was tempted to sound off about it, but he stopped

himself. One thing at a time, he decided. First I have to put a stop to the drinking.

As usual Frances was half way through a bottle of champagne. He wondered if it was her first bottle or her fifth. He went to the fridge and got himself a beer, then he changed his mind, put it back, and settled for a glass of Perrier. He waved the tall green bottle at Frances.

'Why don't you join me?' he suggested.

She shook her head and held on to her drink.

'I'm fine with this,' she said, following him through to the lounge. In summer the glass wall at the end of the room slid back to reveal a roof terrace. During the years he had lived there Sam had trained vines up an overhead trellis, and now they formed a green canopy giving the appearance of a greenhouse. Frances had added terracotta pots full of orange trees and sweet-smelling flowers. Now it was warm they spent most of their evenings out there.

Frances settled herself into a wide wicker chair and asked Sam about his day. He looked at her.

'I'm not interested in discussing my day,' he said, 'and you're not really interested in what I do at the office either. So I've got an idea. Why don't we talk about your day.'

There was something about the question Frances didn't like. Maybe it was the way he was looking at her. She stiffened.

'I didn't do anything worth talking about,' she replied.

'I don't care,' Sam persisted. 'I still want to hear about it. Start with this morning when you got up. What did you do then?'

She groaned. 'What I always do. I struggled to the kitchen and brewed up some strong coffee.'

'Why the struggle?'

She made a face. 'You know why. I don't feel so good in the mornings. It's something to do with my metabolism or my circulation. I'm not sure which.'

He hesitated, then went on. 'What did you do next, after the coffee?'

Frances began to get irritated. 'Why all this sudden curiosity about my boring life? Surely we've got better things to talk about?'

Sam set his face. The next hour or so was going to be tough, but he had to have it out, for both their sakes. He ignored her question.

'Go on with your day,' he said.

She drew in her breath. 'Okay,' she said. 'After coffee I took a shower, washed my hair, did my face. Then I had a lunch with Bernard and some people.'

'What time were you ready?'

'Around eleven, why?'

'I'm coming to that. What did you do while you were waiting to go out. When you were all done up and ready?'

She thought for a moment and shook her head.

'I can't think of anything.'

'Try harder,' Sam pressed. 'You didn't just sit there and count your fingers.'

Frances looked around the terrace, trying to bring back the morning.

'I poured out another glass of champagne,' she said flatly.

There was a silence. 'You didn't tell me about the first glass,' Sam said. 'Or was it the first two glasses.'

Frances put down her drink on the glass table at her side.

'What is this?' she demanded. 'Since when did you start counting how many glasses of champagne I drink before lunch?'

'Since now,' Sam said quietly. 'It's got to stop.'

So this was what he was getting at. He thought she was turning into a lush.

'You're worrying about nothing,' Frances told him. 'If I

was working in an office, I'd probably have a drink before lunch. You do. Clay does. Just because I'm your wife does that disqualify me?'

He shook his head. 'People who work for a living,' he said, 'have one drink before lunch. Then we switch to iced water. From what I know of your habits, you have three drinks before lunch and you go on drinking.'

Frances looked injured. 'What does that matter,' she said. 'I don't have to do anything in the afternoon, and if we're going out in the evening I make sure I'm sober.'

Sam got out of his chair and went over to where she sat.

'Did you hear what you just said? You make sure you're sober if you have to go out. What does that make you the rest of the time? Bombed?'

Frances began to get out of her chair, but Sam pushed her back.

'I haven't finished yet, Frances. Listen to me. For the last six months I've seen you change. When we met you hardly drank at all, maybe you had a glass of wine with dinner but that was it. Now you never seem to be without a glass of wine and I'm not just imagining it. Every evening when I get in you're drinking. You smell of booze. Even in the morning when you wake up you stink of the stuff.'

Frances had gone very pale. 'You're exaggerating,' she said. 'Okay, recently I've gone over my limit, but I've had a couple of things on my mind. I'll slow up a bit.'

'You won't slow up,' Sam told her. 'You'll cut it out if you know what's good for you.'

Frances went on protesting. There were a thousand reasons, a thousand excuses why she should go on drinking. Finally Sam decided he had heard enough.

'Have you taken a good look at yourself lately?' he asked.

Frances looked curious.

'Why do you ask?'

Sam paused for a second. This was the tough part. The make or break part.

'Because you've changed,' he said frankly.

Now Frances was worried. 'What do you mean I've changed? Nobody said anything about it to me.'

Sam sighed. 'Maybe they didn't like to. Maybe your chums were embarrassed to tell you you've turned into a butterball. When I met you you were skinny, I could get my hands round your waist – even your face was skinny. And you had this thick blonde hair nearly to your waist. You reminded me of a fairy princess.'

Frances laughed without mirth. 'And now I remind you of a fairy elephant.' The tears started to gather in the corners of her eyes.

'Since when did I stop being attractive to you?' she asked.

Then she grimaced. 'No don't answer that. I can answer it for you. You stopped wanting me months ago. After that business with the girl in your office.'

Sam started to feel ashamed. 'It's not true,' he said. 'I love you, Frances, and I'll go on loving you no matter what you look like.'

Now the tears started in earnest, spilling down her cheeks, leaving ugly black runways where they passed.

'Love,' she said bitterly. 'What's that got to do with anything. It doesn't make you reach for me in the night. It doesn't make you desire me. When was the last time you felt anything at all, when you took me to bed?'

She emptied her glass and reached for the bottle.

'No, don't stop me,' she said. 'The feeling I get from this might not be as good as sex, but it's better than nothing at all.'

Sam bent down and took the glass out of her hand.

'Come here,' he said softly. 'You silly woman.'

He lifted her into his arms and kissed the places where the tears had been. Then he kissed her throat and her lips.

'Come to bed,' he whispered.

Frances let him lead her through the apartment and as they went he gently unbuttoned her, separating the too tight clothing from her too full body. When they were in the bedroom, he undressed himself, then he lay down beside her on the bed.

Frances felt his hands on her, gently exploring her outline and all her secret places. For the first time since she had known Sam she felt ashamed, for now she knew she was ugly in his eyes his skilful, probing fingers no longer roused her.

Before, when she had lain with him they had somehow fused, their hearts and their souls melting into one. Now the warmth had gone and they were just two bodies coupling. She wondered how it had been with Louise. Was he tender and patient the way he was now? The way he was with her? Or did he have more urgency with the other girl?

Sam moved above her, his face tender and serious, yet in her mind's eye she had another vision of him. She had kept this vision with her, like a love letter. It was a picture of her husband the way he looked on the first night they had gone to bed. His eyes blazed then with hunger and with fire, and she had been frightened he would consume her.

Once more she looked into the patient face of the man making love to her and she longed to see the other face he wore. The face he kept for passion.

42

It was decided that Clay should deal with Louise. Two sets of lawyers had taken the best part of eight weeks to finalise her partnership. Under the new terms the agency was to be re-named Kurnitz Tragos and Greene. Louise was allocated ten per cent of the equity which she bought with a generous loan from the bank, and in exchange she was given a seat on the board with full voting rights. Everything was in place for her signature – except that there were loose ends.

In every negotiation between consenting adults there were always loose ends. How much holiday was Louise allowed to take, could she sell back her shares at the price she bought them at or would she have to accept the value the market put on them? The lawyers did what they could to settle every question but in the end it was up to the partners to come to a final agreement face to face. And that was where Clay came in.

With Sam's agreement, he was to fly to London and finalise the partnership with Louise. When the two of them had hammered it out, he would return to New York with her signature. Ideally both men should have gone to London. The agency was entering a new era, expanding into Europe, changing its name. All three partners should have discussed the changes and started to plan for the future. Only the situation wasn't ideal.

In time Sam knew he would have to make his peace with Louise. They couldn't go on ignoring each other. Not if they were going to do business. But for Sam the time was still too soon.

'I don't know how she'll behave when she sees me again,'

he told Clay. 'She's a woman, she's Greek, she could go right over the top if we're not very careful. To be honest I wouldn't blame her if she did. I didn't behave all that well towards her.'

Clay gave his partner an old-fashioned look. He's not frightened of Louise, he thought, he's frightened of himself. The guy's still in love with her. It's written all over him. He knows he'll tumble into bed with her the moment he sets eyes on her again. He knows it and I know it. He just doesn't want to face it.

Aloud he said, 'Leave Louise to me. There's nothing in the contract we can't sort out quickly. If there is a problem, I can always call you in New York.'

So that was how they left it, until Tiffany delivered her bombshell and changed the whole ball game.

Shortly before Clay was due to fly out to London, Tiffany called him at the office. Was he free to have lunch, she asked? Clay's antennae sounded a warning signal. Why was his wife wasting her time having lunch with him? She saw him every evening didn't she? What was the rush?

'Is there a problem?' he asked her.

There was a long nervous silence.

'Yes,' she said, her voice unnaturally shrill. 'I need to see you.'

Clay paused for a second. She's overspent on her allowance, he thought. She's been wearing some pretty fancy jewellery lately. He remembered the diamond eternity ring that suddenly appeared a couple of months ago and the emerald spray that came after it. What's got into her, he wondered. I'm doing well, but I'm not doing that well.

He sighed heavily. She'd take him to one of the chic restaurants she went to, then she'd tell him a long story about having to keep up appearances. They'd eat a list of expensive food, drink too much expensive booze and he'd be lumbered with the bill as well as the crushing expense for the jewellery.

'No,' he said forcibly. 'I'm not free to have lunch. I've got an important client coming in. Whatever it is will have to wait till this evening.'

He put the phone down quickly before she could argue with him. Tiffany, he cursed under his breath. Sometimes she's more trouble than she's worth.

She was waiting for him in the bar when he got home and the first thing that struck him was she hadn't tried with herself. Usually when she wanted something Tiffany put on the ritz – the full make-up, the perfume from Paris.

Tonight was different. She was wearing a tracksuit and she'd pulled her hair back into a bunch. If he hadn't known better he would have thought she was deliberately making herself unattractive to him.

'What's the matter,' Clay asked. 'Did somebody die?'

Tiffany made a face and handed him a drink.

'Not exactly,' she said.

It's the jewellery, he thought. It's got to be. He sat down heavily and took a strong pull on his martini.

'Okay, so let's talk about your allowance. That's what's bothering you isn't it?'

Again she pulled a face. Mournful and worried. 'Not exactly,' she said. 'It's not about money.'

Clay started to lose patience.

'It's not about money, nobody died. So what the fuck is it about? And why are you looking like a wet weekend all of a sudden? You usually get changed when I come home.'

She got up and started pacing the floor in front of the bar. There was something furtive about her, something uncomfortable and Clay was reminded of circus animals he had seen behind bars. All strung out with nowhere to go.

He came up behind her and circled her with his arms.

'Stop this,' he said softly, 'you'll drive us both mad. Whatever it is you have to tell me I can handle. Believe me. I've known you long enough.'

The tension seemed to go out of her and she let him

help her back to her chair. Then she swallowed the rest of her drink and set her chin.

'I want out of our marriage,' she said. 'I met someone else. I'm sorry.'

So that's what the fancy jewellery was about. She hadn't been bleeding him dry after all. She'd been robbing some other poor sucker blind.

'Do I know this ... someone else?' Clay asked cautiously.

Tiffany started to cry, genuine tears and Clay marvelled at them. In all the years he had known Tiffany she had only wept crocodile tears to get what she wanted. She's serious, he thought with something like alarm. This time she really means it.

She wiped her face with the back of her hand.

'Of course you know him,' she said. 'It's Abner Morris. I'm surprised you hadn't found out by now.'

Clay had known it all along of course. Right from the start when she started going to the opera with Abner, he had smelt a rat, but he let her get on with it. In the years they had been married Clay had got used to his wife having affairs. She liked to pretend she was helping the agency get business but he knew better. Tiffany wasn't after business, she was after sex and he accepted it. He didn't like it, but the alternative – divorcing her – he liked even less. For all her faults Clay loved his wife and if she needed more sex than he could provide at home, then she was welcome to go shopping for it.

'Why do you want to leave me?' he enquired gently. 'You didn't want out of the marriage all the other times.'

She regarded him warily.

'What do you mean, all the other times?'

Clay started to get angry. Tiffany was entitled to try his patience, but not his intelligence.

'Grow up,' he told her. 'Do you really think after all these years I didn't know you've been playing around. Of

400

course I knew. I'd have to be blind, deaf and dumb not to know. But I live with it, like I live with indigestion after too much *gefilte* fish.'

Tiffany laughed bitterly.

'So that's how you see our break-up. Like a bad case of wind.'

'How do you want me to see it? Like an outrage? A crime against the nation? The next thing I know you'll want me to fight a duel with Abner. Well I won't do it. My health won't stand it – and neither will my bank balance. Under the right circumstances the guy could be our biggest client.'

Tiffany looked at him in frank surprise.

'Don't you care about me at all?' she asked. 'Any other man would be worried sick about his wife leaving him.'

Clay stood up and took hold of the martini pitcher. Then with great deliberation he refilled his glass. He did not offer Tiffany a drink.

'You're not leaving me,' he said. It was a statement of fact, so terse and tough that it made her sit up straighter.

'Why do you say that?'

'Because I know you.'

Tiffany didn't miss a beat.

'What exactly do you mean by that?'

He thought for a moment, taking his time collecting his facts. Finally he turned to her.

'When I say I know you,' he said, 'I wasn't talking about your temperament or the way you spend my money. I was talking about cases. To my knowledge you've had three abortions – one from a man who was working here looking after the pool. You've had your face lifted once, and about two years ago you acquired a very expensive cocaine habit.'

Tiffany sucked her breath in.

'Are you threatening me?' she asked.

Clay smiled the genial fat man's smile he used with particularly difficult clients.

'To use your own words, not exactly. But if your new love should find out one or two of your little secrets, I don't think he'd be impressed.'

Tiffany reacted like an outraged kitten. Jumping out of her chair and hurling herself at her husband, claws unsheathed, spitting with rage. Clay caught her neatly round the waist and before she knew it she was off her feet and facing down across his knees. Still she went on struggling and yelling for blood, so Clay brought his hand down across her buttocks. He didn't mean to hit her hard, but he figured he must have done because she stopped everything she was doing and went quiet. So he hit her again. Out of curiosity to see what she would do and because he felt like it.

She started calling him names using language from the gutter he had never heard on her lips before, and for some reason it excited him.

'You asked for this,' he said. Then he pulled down her pants and really laid into her. He had never touched her or any other woman this way before, and he should have felt ashamed. Except he didn't. He felt justified. For over ten years he had kept his mouth shut while Tiffany made a fool of him with every pretty boy that took her fancy. And had he suffered. Well now that was finished with. Now it was his turn to dish out the punishment.

After a few moments he stopped what he was doing and stood up. Tiffany fell off his lap and landed in a heap on the floor. Her hair had come loose from the rubber band that was holding it back and her face was flushed. Clay thought she looked very sexy.

'Do you plan to go on lying there all night,' he asked. 'Or are you going to get up and finish your drink?'

With an effort she pulled up her tracksuit and struggled

to her feet. Then she looked at the man she had married with the beginnings of respect.

'What do you want to do?' she asked quietly. 'About Abner, I mean.'

'That depends on your plans.'

Tiffany swore silently to herself. Her husband had her on the run and she knew it. When she left Abner after lunch she thought she had it all worked out. She had finally persuaded him to set up home with her and he had agreed to move into a brownstone she had chosen near the Park. Now all those plans would have to go on ice. What Clay knew about her was far too dangerous to risk anyone knowing, least of all Abner Morris. No, she would have to tell him her husband begged for a second chance and for the sake of all their years together she couldn't deny him that. She knew Abner would buy a story like that. Particularly if she told it right.

In the meantime there was Clay to deal with. She gave him her best smile.

'My plans,' she told him demurely, 'have taken a sudden change of direction. You were very masculine back there.' She lowered her eyes. 'When you were hitting me. I didn't know you could get so physical.'

Clay knew her well enough to know she was playing with him. Then he thought, what the hell. What's wrong with a few games between couples. He started undoing the buttons in the front of her tracksuit and Tiffany didn't stop him.

'I could get more physical,' he told her.

She shrugged off the top of her suit, and he saw she wasn't wearing a bra. Then she did something with her tongue and her nipples that made him gasp.

'Show me,' she said.

For the first time since the early days of their marriage, Clay started to take an interest in what his wife was doing. If she

403

bought a new dress he wanted to know how much it cost and where she got it. If she went out for dinner without him, he insisted on knowing who she was spending her evening with.

In spite of Tiffany's protests, Clay stood firm. He had signed a contract ten years previously promising to cherish and care for her and now he was standing by his vows.

When Clay started dating Tiffany he had no illusions about her. He knew from the word go she was the office bicycle, but as he got to know her, he forgave her for it, for she had other qualities. She was bright, brighter than most of the guys he knew, and she needed to succeed in the world. It was this unquenchable desire to win that made Clay fall in love with her.

He realised early on that she wanted to get married and he was firmly in her sights. So he did a little hard thinking. He was getting a bargain, he knew that. He was too homely for a girl like Tiffany. But Tiffany was shop soiled. Used goods. So she had to take second best. Looked at unemotionally the marriage was a compromise and Clay should never have settled for it. Except Clay didn't look at it unemotionally. He was crazy about the girl and couldn't wait to spend the rest of his life with her, so he went through with the wedding and made allowances.

He made allowances for Tiffany's extravagance, her vanity, her lovers because she had so many other things going for her. Then the Abner Morris business happened and he realised he had been too patient. He didn't blame Abner at all. How could any man resist a woman like Tiffany? And he wasn't really angry with his wife either. The person responsible for the whole mess, the person he was really furious with was himself.

He should have kept a closer eye on her. He knew her faults, her fatal flaw and because he understood her so well, he knew that this side of her had to be kept firmly under control. If the business wasn't so demanding, he berated himself, I would have seen she was going off the rails. I could have stopped it from happening. At least he could console himself things hadn't got completely out of hand. He'd stopped her from walking out on him. He'd had to threaten her of course. But in time she would realise it was for her own good.

Tiffany's view of the situation was less rational for she was in love with Abner and if she could have strangled her husband and got away with it, she would have done so, cheerfully. As it was, she played for time.

Abner had been very understanding when she told him how Clay had broken down and begged her not to leave.

'Poor sap,' he said. 'I can guess what he's going through. He needs a chance to get used to the idea.'

He needs a hole in the head raged Tiffany, but she kept this opinion to herself. Instead she deceived her husband with greater skill than she had done previously. She took to meeting Abner at eccentric hours.

Some days she would wander into his office before lunch and seduce him while he sat at his desk. They would arrange to run into each other at gallery openings and cocktail parties and after a decent interval they would leave separately and head for a nearby hotel. The element of secrecy gave the affair a new lease of life for now their time together was limited, it became valuable. They would both spend days plotting and planning their meetings. They each told extravagant lies to their friends and acquaintances and when they did get together, it was nothing short of ecstatic.

One afternoon in the Pierre Hotel Tiffany had some news.

'Clay,' she announced, 'is going to London next week. He and Sam have decided to make Louise a partner and Clay has to see her over there to thrash out the deal.'

Abner opened the fridge by the bed and extracted a bottle of champagne.

'This calls for a celebration,' he said. 'How long is Clay going to be away?'

'About two or three days I should think. From what I know of Louise she'll argue over every clause.'

Abner opened the split with the ease of someone who had been doing it all his life. Then, careful not to spill any, he splashed it into two tooth mugs he had brought in from the bathroom.

'What shall we drink to?' he asked. 'Louise's partnership or the long weekend we're going to spend together in Paris?'

Tiffany never got to Paris.

For Clay decided he couldn't go away and leave her for three days. It wasn't right or responsible. Since he'd been keeping an eye on her, Tiffany was beginning to settle down at last. The Abner affair had fizzled out, as he knew it would and she didn't even seem interested in throwing away money every afternoon at Bergdorfs.

If he left her now, he reasoned, he would be throwing temptation in her path. And he would be undoing all his good work. No, he would just have to persuade Sam to go to London instead. Sam didn't have his problems, or his responsibilities. The worst his wife could do while he was away was get stoned on champagne – and she did that while he was there anyway.

43

The seatbelt sign clicked on as the plane started its descent into Heathrow Airport. Sam adjusted his watch forward four hours and prepared himself for the meeting ahead of him. He hadn't told Louise he was coming instead of Clay. Part of him was worried she'd refuse to see him. And the other part? The other part he didn't think about.

He had spent the best part of a year trying to forget her, trying to pretend they had never met, never loved, never even known each other. He had failed miserably. At moments when he least expected it – driving to the office, standing under the shower – she came back to him. It was like carrying around his own personal video.

Sam would recall whole conversations with her. Clear in every detail as if they had happened only a couple of hours ago. But what he had going around in his head was worse than any video, for not only did he carry a record of the curve of her mouth, the exact shade of her hair, but he also remembered how she tasted, and how it felt to hold her in his arms.

How did she do it, he asked himself. How did she manage to print herself so indelibly on me? For a moment he thought about Frances and in that instant he managed to feel guilty. He hadn't told her he was going to London. He hadn't told her because he didn't think she'd be strong enough to handle it. With an effort he made himself think about his wife in New York. She was falling apart, he recognised that. There was nothing he could do to stop her. For the thousandth time he wondered where they had gone wrong. Was it Louise that had pushed them away from each other? Was it losing the baby? Or was it something that had happened a long time ago, before he had even met her?

They were coming in to land now and deliberately he rid his mind of both his problems. Louise and Frances. Frances and Louise. He had agonised over them for too many months and he could come up with no solutions. I'm in London, he thought. A new city with no past for me. No memories to haunt me. He sighed. It seemed he had taken responsibility for everything that had happened to him up till now. Suddenly, he yearned to be free.

Sam arrived at his hotel around lunchtime, took a shower and ordered room service. In any other place in town, he thought, I could have wandered down to the restaurant and grabbed a snack. But the Connaught, he reflected, didn't favour the casual approach. When he called to reserve a table, the manager informed him they were booked three months ahead. He would have to make other arrangements.

The hotel hadn't been his idea. Clay had done all the bookings after consulting with Tiffany.

The moment Sam had walked into the lobby of the Connaught he felt as if he was entering a different world. The hotels he had been used to were vast cavernous affairs full of noise and bustle. There were always rows of receptionists to answer the jangling phones and the business of the day seemed to be conducted at the top of everyone's voice.

The Connaught belonged to a different century. Here the furniture was neither functional nor modern. Everything he laid eyes on seemed to be antique and made of dark-stained mahogany. Bevelled mirrors gleamed out of carved surrounds, huge displays of fresh-cut flowers stood on every surface and there were no receptionists, no bellhops. There were servants dressed in immaculate livery, ready to do your bidding in hushed whispers.

Sam looked up as one of their number tapped discreetly at the door of his suite. The room service had arrived. He glanced at his watch and smiled. It had taken precisely ten minutes. The Waldorf or the Plaza would have made him wait at least half an hour, maybe longer. Perhaps there were consolations in not going to the restaurant.

Sam had ordered a steak sandwich and a beer. The Connaught had fancied it up with a bowl of salad and a bottle of mineral water.

'I didn't order the extras,' he told the waiter who was busily setting it out on a linen-covered table in the window.

'It's all part of the service,' he explained.

Sam handed him a ten-dollar note as he left the room. How much, he wondered, would this immaculate service load on to his bill? He put the question out of his mind. He had more important things to worry about on this trip than the size of his expenses.

He started to think about calling Louise. There was no point in seeing her today even if she was free. Sam made a point of never doing business while he was jet lagged. Whatever they had been to each other, the reason for this trip was to iron out her contract. For that he needed a clear head. No, he decided, he would call Louise's secretary, tell her where he was staying and make a date for the following day.

Once he'd taken his decision, he took a walk and bought the London evening paper. He had always heard the theatre in this town was a match for Broadway and he decided to put it to the test. He shortlisted three plays: a new production of 'Hamlet' at the Old Vic, an Ayckbourn piece that had been a smash for the past six months, and a Noel Coward revival.

When he got back to the Connaught, he discovered the only tickets available were for 'Hamlet'. He sighed and told the desk clerk to reserve him a seat in the stalls.

Shakespeare was a little heavy after a long journey, but he had no alternative.

He glanced at his watch and discovered there was only half an hour left to contact Louise's secretary. Swiftly he put in the call and when the girl came on the line he was surprised to discover she had been expecting him. New York must have been in touch, he thought. Top marks to Clay.

'Do you want to speak to Miss Tragos?' the secretary asked him. 'She's in her office right now.'

Sam told her he didn't. 'I've only just arrived,' he explained, 'and I'm bushed. Tell her I'll make contact with her first thing in the morning. Oh, and tell her to pencil out most of her day. We're going to need that kind of time to get everything done.'

He gave the girl his extension and wound up the conversation, then he went through into the bedroom and started to change his suit.

What's the matter with me, he wondered, as he started to prepare himself for the theatre. I picked up the phone to my lover after a year's silence and I don't even have the balls to talk to her in person. He shrugged. Tomorrow is another day, he decided. Maybe I'll feel stronger after a night's sleep.

'Hamlet' was longer than he remembered, and more difficult to follow, yet in a way he welcomed the effort of having to concentrate. It took his mind off his office, his problems and his wife. It also took his mind off Louise. There was some kind of salvation in that.

He had a late dinner after the theatre and it was past twelve when he finally got back to the hotel.

The night desk clerk handed him his messages. Clay had called and would try again the next day, his secretary had been in touch twice and the booking agency had contacted him to say there had been a last minute cancellation and there were tickets available for the Ayckbourn play tomorrow. He made a mental note to call them in the morning.

Automatically he turned back to the desk clerk.

'There was nothing else was there?' he asked.

The man thought for a moment, then he said,

'There was something, but it's not important. A woman turned up and asked for you but you had gone out and she said not to worry, she'd talk to you the next day.'

Sam frowned.

'The woman,' he said. 'What did she look like?'

'I don't remember clearly, Sir. She didn't stay long.'

'Think,' Sam told the clerk harshly. 'Concentrate your mind.'

The man passed his hand over his bald patch. Then he broke into a grin.

'She was very pretty, Sir. In a foreign sort of way. Lots of dark hair. She might have been Spanish, or maybe Italian.'

Sam nodded, ending the conversation. He had heard all he needed. Louise had been to the hotel looking for him. He cursed himself for a fool. What the hell was he doing making theatre bookings on his first night in town? Her town. Anyone would think he was trying to run away.

He picked up his key and made his way towards the lifts. It was too late to do anything about the situation now. Whatever Louise wanted he'd deal with in the morning.

When he let himself into his suite, he noticed he had left a light on in the bedroom.

Wearily he pushed his way into the next room, then he stopped in his tracks. Lying in the middle of his bed with the covers drawn up to her chin was the one person he had been avoiding from the moment he had arrived. Louise.

She sat up as he came through the door, and the coverlet fell away from her shoulders and told the rest of the story. She had taken her things off before she had climbed into his bed. There was no mistaking her intention. Sam fought

411

down his excitement. It's been a year, he told himself. You're married to Frances. Where's your loyalty? Then Louise smiled and he forgot every promise he had ever made. Sam walked towards where she was sitting half hidden in the shadows and as he did the familiar scent of her seemed to be everywhere.

'Why?' he asked. 'What made you come?'

She brushed dark curls out of her eyes.

Then she looked at him candidly and without shame.

'I couldn't stay away,' she said.

Sam reached out for her. It was a blind instinctive gesture, the gesture of a man who had been adrift for a long time and who had finally come home and she did not deny him.

Sam had always prided himself he could recall every inch of her yet as he touched her, he realised there had been great blanks in his memory. How could he have forgotten her skin? Taut and smooth and smelling slightly of apricots. As his fingers probed her breasts, her ribcage and the warm, soft triangle between her legs, he marvelled at her. Other women wore their sexual identity in their hair or their breasts or their legs. Louise had it all over.

He moved closer to her now, inhaling her perfume, tasting the long forgotten, too familiar mouth. Under his touch she was coming alive, the way she always used to come alive; her nipples hardening, her hips quickening and he knew at that moment he could have taken her. Plundered soft flesh without ceremony, or politeness or asking the way. Only he wanted better than that.

He took his mouth from her and followed the line of her neck with his lips, pausing at the base of her throat until he found her breasts. From a long way off he heard her voice.

'Take me,' she beseeched him. 'Take me, do it to me. Now.'

But there was still more of her to know. Sam put his

hands between her thighs and parted her legs. Then, still close to her skin he made his way past the curve of her stomach until he found the entrance to her. At that instant he knew he could wait no longer.

He drew himself above her now, entering her with such hunger that she screamed with the pleasure and the pain of it. Then she arched beneath him, finding the rhythm they thought they had once lost.

He made love to her three times that night and each time he died a little and lived a little and died a little. Finally he slept, long and deep, and in the morning when he opened his eyes, he felt renewed.

He looked across to the pillow where she had been sleeping and saw it was empty. 'Louise,' he shouted out sleepily, expecting an answer from the bathroom. There was no answer. He sat up and stretched. Then he got out of bed and padded through to the drawing-room. There was no sign of her. He made his way through the suite, calling her name, but she had taken her leave. Neatly and silently. As if she had never been there in the first place. Sam passed a hand through his hair. This wasn't like Louise at all. She was always there in the morning, making coffee or at least causing it to appear. Coffee and breakfast and the morning papers. What on earth was the matter with her?

He walked into the shower and forty minutes later, bathed and shaved, he felt more in charge of the situation. She probably went home early to change, he thought. Then he smiled. What on earth was she changing from, he wondered. Last night hadn't exactly been a fashion parade.

Sam decided to have breakfast in the restaurant, to give her time to get herself together and make it to the office. Tonight of course they would have to come to a different arrangement. All this to-ing and fro-ing in the morning was a pain in the ass. Louise will have to move in here for a few days, Sam decided. At least we'll know where we are.

413

To his surprise the Connaught restaurant was nearly full. If he had left it any longer, he would have had a repetition of the day before. No room at the inn. What is it with this place, Sam wondered. You'd think it was the only place in town to break bread. All around him dark-suited men were in earnest discussion. They sat at the tables in groups of twos and threes. Some of them had the contents of their briefcases strewn across the cloth. All of them were more interested in their meetings than the croissants and coffee that were being served. At the far end of the room he recognised Maurice Saatchi with a small fat man who seemed to be giving him a hard time. He had read in the financial press the brothers were having take-over talks and he wondered if this was one of them.

Sam took his time and had the full English deal. Bacon, eggs, grilled tomato and mushrooms, fresh squeezed orange juice, brown toast, Oxford marmalade and coffee. By the time he signed the bill it was nearly ten o'clock. She'll be there by now, he thought. She'll have talked to her secretary. Gone through her post. She might have even had time to make a call or two. Time to get going.

Louise and I have got a lot of talking to do, and not all of it business. He wondered where she liked to go for lunch and whether he should book a restaurant. Then he remembered another lunch. He had arranged to meet her in some Japanese restaurant on Seventh Avenue, only he hadn't gone because Frances had lost their baby the night before. He wondered if the memory still hurt. Then he shrugged. He would make it up to her. He got the concierge to arrange a table at L'Etoile in Charlotte Street. Somebody in New York had told him it was the London equivalent of Le Circle. He hoped Louise would approve.

The firm's offices in Knightsbridge were smaller than he imagined, and busier. The girl behind the huge teak desk in the lobby had to deal with two people before she got to Sam and when she did the phone rang and delayed her another five minutes. I'll have to tell her to hire more staff, Sam thought. Kurnitz and Greene don't believe in skimping. With a pang he realised that after tomorrow the agency would no longer be Kurnitz and Greene. It would be Kurnitz Tragos and Greene. The business would probably abbreviate it to Kurnitz Tragos, and Sam wondered if he would be comfortable with it. Louise was his partner now and the world would know it. His partner as well as his mistress. His sleeping partner.

The girl behind the reception desk looked up at him.

'Sorry to keep you waiting, sir. Can I help you?'

Sam smiled.

'Sure. I'm come to see Miss Tragos. Can you show me where I can find her office?'

The girl looked confused.

'I'm sorry,' she said, 'I don't think Louise is in yet. Did you have an appointment to see her?'

Sam looked at his watch and he felt a flicker of annoyance. It was past ten-thirty. She was taking her time this morning.

'Can you try her at home?' he asked. Then he saw the expression on the receptionist's face and softened.

'We haven't met,' he said. 'My name's Sam Kurnitz – the American end of the agency. I flew in yesterday to see Louise on an important matter. Can you see what's happened to her.'

The girl grinned.

'Absolutely, Mr Kurnitz,' she said. Then she held out her hand. 'I'm Daisy Arden, and I'm really thrilled to meet you. Why don't you go and sit down by the coffee table over there in the window and I'll chase up Louise. She's probably been held up in the traffic and she'll come walking through the door the moment I dial her number.'

Ten minutes later Daisy put down the phone for a second time. Then she got up and went over to where Sam was sitting. She was frowning slightly.

'I can't get any answer from Louise's home number,' she told him. 'But I've just been talking to her secretary. Louise isn't in yet, but there seems to be a package for you in her office. If you go through, her secretary will give it to you.'

Sam didn't know what to make of it. Last night Louise was in his arms, passionate and pliable. Goddamn it, he had owned her.

And today, nothing. She disappears into thin air.

He strode past the rows of glass offices towards the imposing door at the end. The Managing Director's space. Outside a willowy blonde girl sat behind a typewriter. At his approach she looked up.

'Mr Kurnitz,' she said, 'I've been expecting you.'

She handed him a large brown envelope. Inside it was an airline ticket to Athens. Attached to it with a paperclip was a travel agent's booking form for a night at the Grande Bretagne. Sam looked at the blonde in frank bewilderment.

'What the fuck am I meant to do with this? I came to London for a business meeting, not a magical mystery tour.'

The girl smiled patiently. From her expression it was clear she wasn't used to being shouted at.

'Louise told me yesterday she was going to be away for a few days. I imagine if you want to see her, you'll make use of the ticket she left you.'

Sam was irritated beyond measure. He had travelled all the way from New York to give Louise a chunk of the agency. He had ended up giving her a chunk of himself as well and the bitch turned round and ran away to Athens. This was no way to run a business. Or a life. Or a love affair. What the fuck did she think she was playing at? And what the fuck was she doing in Greece?

Dimly Sam remembered her family had originally come from Athens, or somewhere outside it. Had she gone home to Mama? No, she was better than that. Louise wasn't the kind of girl to hide in anyone's skirts. So why had she disappeared? They hadn't quarrelled last night. Quite the contrary. What had happened between them was a confirmation of everything they were to each other. And had been.

Sam shook his head. Maybe she had a lover in Greece. Maybe she was married with a family he didn't know about. Nothing she could do now would surprise him. Then he thought back. Her secretary had said just now that Louise had planned to go away yesterday. At least Louise had told her about it yesterday, so she had intended to leave the country knowing he was coming to London with a contract for her to sign.

Now he was really in trouble. He could understand it if she'd wanted to avoid him. After the way he'd dumped her back in New York she was entitled to be mad at him. But what he couldn't figure out was why she would turn her back on the business. She had worked her tail off for this partnership. He'd seen the figures and the correspondence with Clay. Why would Louise run away from her one big chance to make something of herself?

Sam looked up and realised the blonde behind the type-writer was staring at him.

'Why don't you just go to Heathrow and use the ticket,' she said. 'You've come this far. What have you got to lose by making the rest of the journey?'

Sam was tempted to tell her that if he wanted her opinion he would ask for it. Who the hell did she think she was sending him on a wild goose chase? Then he thought better of it.

He had business to finish with Louise. Real business as well as personal business. It didn't do to antagonise the help.

44

Sam studied the menu in front of him. He was faced with a choice of taramasalata, a creamy fish paste; tsatsiki, cucumber in yoghurt; or melitzana, a mess of puréed aubergines. Underneath the list of starters was a selection of kebabs and lamb on the spit. Sam fought down a feeling of nausea. He had eaten his way through the tourist menu enough times to know he wouldn't be sorry if he never tasted Greek cuisine again in his life.

His seat in an open-air café on Plaka afforded him a view of the Acropolis. It was one view in this grimy, overheated, fly infested city that never failed to delight him, and he would sit drinking a glass of ouzo, watching it as the sun went down. The Greeks had rigged up some kind of moving light show so that when darkness fell, coloured floodlights played across its colonnades and ruined façades, giving the impression of a living history book.

Sam had been in Athens two days now and there had been no word from Louise. At first, not hearing from her didn't bother him. Athens reminded him of Israel and the Middle East. The smells, the look of the people, even the poverty and ugliness of the buildings filled him with nostalgia. He spent his first day there on foot, exploring. There were street markets cheek-by-jowl with shopping areas full of trendy boutiques, dark bars full of old men playing backgammon, and everywhere he went tourist shops selling tourist junk.

On the second day Sam began to feel antsy. Why hadn't Louise called him? She knew where he was staying. The booking had been done by her office. What was she playing at?

Sam decided to give her another day. If he hadn't heard from her by the evening, he would take the first flight back to New York. He didn't have all the time in the world to spend chasing after Louise, not when he promised his wife he would be back by the weekend. Now he was kicking his heels in Athens, he wished he hadn't lied to her. The seminar in Cincinnati had been a reasonable enough excuse at the time, but if Frances tried to call and check up on him, she would discover it had ended yesterday. Sam sighed. He supposed he could tell her he stopped off to visit a client en route for New York.

He got back to the Grande Bretagne and put in a call to Frances. It was eleven o'clock Athens time, New York was five hours behind – she wouldn't be sitting down to supper yet.

Frances picked up the phone almost immediately. She was glad to hear Sam's voice, though he could tell she was on edge.

'Where are you?' she asked. 'I thought you'd be on your way home by now.'

Sam wondered if she'd spoken to his secretary, but he decided not to ask. He'd left the girl strict instructions to tell all callers he was in Cincinnati. Even if Frances had contacted the office she wouldn't be any the wiser.

'I was on my way home,' he said, 'only I've been intercepted. A client in Ohio, a soft toy manufacturer, got wind I was down here and wants me to call in on my way back to New York. The detour should take me a day or so. I'll call you when I'm through.'

'So you won't be coming back the weekend.' It was a statement, not a question.

'No,' he said. 'I haven't messed up any plans, have I?'

'Nothing that wasn't messed up a long time ago.'

'Just what exactly do you mean by that?'

'Nothing,' Frances said flatly. 'I'll see you when you get back.'

She put down the phone before he could question her any further. What the hell could have upset her, he wondered. This isn't the first time I've been delayed on business. Then he got out his bags and started packing. I'll get the midday flight back to New York tomorrow he decided. I'll have it out with her then.

Half an hour after midnight the phone rang. He picked it up and found himself speaking to Louise. He felt disbelief, elation and another stronger emotion. Anger.

'What the hell happened to you?' he yelled. 'I've been hanging around this dirty stinking hole for two days now. I've got contracts for you to sign, a whole future to plan and suddenly you go missing.'

He heard her throaty chuckle on the other end of the line.

'You sound sore as hell.'

If Louise had been standing next to him, Sam would have hit her.

'Sure I'm sore,' he said tightly. 'I'm also mystified. One moment you're in love with me. The next, I don't see you for dust. How am I supposed to feel? How do you want me to feel?'

There was a silence, and when Louise spoke again she sounded as if she was a long way away.

'I'll tell you how I want you to feel,' she said. 'I want you to feel the way I did when you went out of my life. It wasn't all that nice being stood up in a sushi bar on Seventh Avenue. Finding out why was even worse – and from Clay, of all people. You didn't even have the balls to tell me yourself.'

Suddenly it all fell into place. The easy seduction in his room at the Connaught. Sam should have known her better than to believe she would fall into his arms without one single reproach. The whole thing had been a set-up. A night of phoney passion followed by a disappearing act.

'I suppose you feel very proud of yourself,' he told

her. 'And so you should. You came on like a regular Mata Hari.'

'Not really. Mata Hari was in the business of pretending.'

It was Sam's turn to laugh.

'You don't mean to tell me all that panting and screaming was for real, do you?'

He heard Louise catch her breath. He had hit her where it hurt and for some perverse reason he felt glad.

'I expected better from you than that,' she said quietly.

'Whereabouts in Athens are you calling from?' Sam asked.

'I'm not in Athens. I'm out on one of the islands. My family has a house here. They let me use it from time to time.'

His curiosity was aroused.

'Will I see you while I'm here? Or are you going to let me go back to New York with my tail between my legs.'

She paused and Sam was aware she was turning the idea over in her mind. Finally she said,

'I'm not coming back to Athens for another week. But if you like, you can come out here.'

'Where is "here"?'

'Hydra. It's an hour by hydrofoil from Piraeus. They run a regular service from there. Most taxi drivers know where it is.'

Sam had visions of himself trailing round the world after her, arriving God-knows-where, and every time he got there finding she was one step ahead of him.

'If I get on the hydrofoil will you be there, or is this just another one of your games?'

'I'll be there,' Louise said. 'If you take the midday flight tomorrow I'll be waiting for you on the harbour.'

A rational man would have told her to go to hell. With the contract he had in his briefcase, she should have come

421

to Athens. Then he thought about Clay and the row they'd have if he came back empty handed.

'I'll be there tomorrow,' he said.

The hydrofoil was hot and crowded. Two seats away a family of Greeks were transporting the family cat in his wicker basket. The animal clearly didn't like sea trips for it yowled and wailed all the way out to the islands. Once more Sam wondered what he was doing. Fierce cross winds had blown up and several of his fellow passengers had been sick. This is the last time, Sam vowed, I agree to any more of Louise's schemes. I'll stay the afternoon, talk about the contract and with any luck I'll be able to catch the evening boat back to Athens.

Through the window he could see they were approaching land, and as they drew closer the island of Hydra reared out of the ocean. Sam had island-hopped across the West Indies as a student, so he was familiar with holiday hideouts, but Hydra was different.

There was something primitive about it, something about the white stone houses and sheer cliffs that told him the place had been unchanged since medieval times. He came up on deck as they pulled into the harbour and his eye was struck by cobbled streets and groups of donkeys. All around the quay were the cafés, jumbles of bright awnings and tables scattered willy-nilly by the water's edge. There were no cars, no neon signs, not even a motor bike that he could make out.

Sam grabbed his suitcase and pushed his way through the jostle of new arrivals. Then he saw her.

Louise was wearing tiny white shorts that emphasised the curve of her bottom and her caramel-coloured suntan. The blue denim shirt she had on was knotted round her midriff and she had let her hair flow free. All at once Sam's anger with her evaporated. He wanted to take hold of her and put his lips against her skin and drown in the apricot smell of her.

Louise must have spotted him at the same moment for she rose from the table where she was sitting and came over to him.

'You managed to find your way here then?'

Behind the dark glasses she looked strained and Sam realised he wasn't the only one who had been on the line. It must have been a hell of a gamble to do what she did. How did she know he wouldn't just turn round and go back to New York after she disappeared like that.

He put down his case.

'I could use a drink,' he said. 'It wasn't the easiest journey.'

Louise led him to one of the waterside cafés. All around them Greeks in their holiday clothes were eating ice-creams and the sticky pastries the country seemed to go in for.

Without consulting Sam, Louise ordered two ouzos and a bottle of mineral water. Then, as an afterthought, she asked the waiter for a plate of olives and some salted nuts.

'I thought we'd wait and have lunch up at the house,' she said. 'It will give you a chance to get out of some of those clothes.'

Uninvited a memory of her came back to Sam, like a snapshot from a trip he had taken long ago.

She was lying on her back with the bedclothes pulled down and she wasn't wearing anything. In the shadows he could make out the outlines of her breasts and the soft curve of her belly.

All at once he wanted to get away from the sunlight and the tourists in their loud T-shirts. He took hold of her hand and stood up.

'I can wait for the drink until we get back,' he said.

Louise didn't say anything. Instead she walked through the crowded tables until they were back on the harbour-front. Then she took him down a slanting sidestreet that led away from the town. Sam realised everything was built on a steep slope. The cobbled walkway led them up and through the town, past tiny bars with zinc counters, gold jewellery shops and tavernas with their tables on the sidewalk. As they climbed higher he was aware that the houses on either side of them belonged to the villagers, and through open doors he caught glimpses of covered courtyards and trailing vines.

The path in front of them was a series of long shallow steps leading upwards. Whoever had built them had done so a long time ago, for the cobbles were worn smooth from centuries of men and donkeys tramping homewards under the blazing sun. Sam was aware of the smell of jasmine and he saw that above the town there were any number of flowering Mediterranean plants and bushes. He spotted bougainvillea, jasmine, hibiscus.

Louise turned to him.

'I'm sorry about the climb. It's one of the hazards of living on an island without cars. Everything here is protected by a sort of Greek national trust. You can't even build a hotel here without asking permission of the Government.'

Sam smiled and for the first time he felt himself relax. 'I can stand getting away from the tourist facilities,' he told her. 'I had as much as I could take in Athens.'

They had turned into a dark winding avenue off the cobbled road and three houses along Louise stopped in front of a blue painted wooden door. She took a key out of her pocket and undid the lock, swinging the door inwards. Sam found himself in a low cool room done, he imagined, in the local style.

All the furniture was made of a dark wood, low and rough hewn. The floor was natural stone with kelims thrown over it and dominating the room was a wide wood-burning stove. Sam put his case down and followed

Louise as she led the way through the room and out onto a shaded terrace.

The vista in front of him made Sam draw in his breath. The whole house looked out over the harbour. Spread out below him was the smooth cobalt sea dotted with tiny sailing boats. To his left he saw the curve of the harbour with its cluster of yachts and rich men's gin palaces and arching out round the island were the cliff sides, sheer and jagged and fringed with olive trees and dark scrub.

Louise came up behind him carrying a bottle of white wine and two glasses.

'You've had a long hot climb,' she said. 'Come and sit down.'

She had set up a table under a trellis woven with vines. On it was a salad in a wooden bowl, a dish of black olives and the white feta cheese he had seen in Athens.

Louise poured the wine and pushed it towards him. Then she raised her own glass in a toast.

'To the future,' she said, 'whatever we decide to do with it.'

Sam had been at the villa two days before Louise brought up the subject of his wife, and it was at that moment he started to think about going home.

Until then he felt as if he was, in some way, suspended in time, as if the sun and Hydra had faded out reality and all that was left was him and Louise and the way they felt about each other.

When he had first arrived there had been a tension between them. Sam was still smarting from the events of the last few days and Louise was wary of being hurt again. So they quarrelled. All the way through the salad and the olives and the feta cheese, Louise poured bitter recriminations on Sam's head. He neither argued with her, nor did he defend himself.

They finished one bottle of white wine and started on

a second and still he had no answers for her. Then, as the sun was going down in the sky she turned to him.

'If you have so little to say for yourself,' she demanded, 'why the hell are you here?'

Sam looked at her in despair. He felt as if he had known her for ever. That they had a kinship that went beyond the demands of the flesh. Yet now, looking at this dark, bad-tempered woman sitting on her vine-covered terrace, he realised he knew her hardly at all.

'I'm here,' he said, 'because I love you. I don't think it's very clever of me to love you. You're far too tough for me and anyway I have a wife who needs me far more than you do.'

He sighed. 'But I do love you, Louise. For whatever it's worth.'

She stood up and came towards him.

'I know,' she said. 'It's the same for me.'

He took her in his arms then, bringing his mouth down on hers to silence all the unspoken questions and she returned his kiss with a passion he had never felt before. For a moment they pulled away from each other and Sam regarded Louise with a mixture of hunger and desire, drinking in the thick black hair, the golden skin, the wide peasant mouth.

'I want you,' he said, and he leaned forward and loosened the knot that held her shirt together around her ribcage. Her breasts spilled out and for a moment he thought she would abandon herself to him. Instead she turned and led him back into the house.

'There are better places for this than the terrace,' she said.

They went into a cool white bedroom and Louise closed the shutters against the evening sun. Then she sank down on her double bed and drew him to her.

They made love for hours. First with a kind of passionate desperation, as if they were trying to drive the world

426

and its problems away from them, and finally when they settled back into their own familiar rhythm, they loved with infinite tenderness.

They got up around ten and went to a waterfront bar where they ordered fried squid and *loup de mer* that the fishing boats had brought in that morning. Then they sat out in front of the sea where a waiter had put a table covered in oilcloth and waited for the patron to serve their dinner. While they were waiting they drank rough red wine and listened to the sounds of the ocean and to Sam, the agency and the demands of his wife seemed a million miles away.

Louise started to talk about Frances the following evening. They were sitting in the same café they had been to the night before. The shadows were drawing out across the sea and the water took on the look of molten black oil. High above the harbour on the surrounding cliffs, the lights of the houses started to wink on and all around the port, the shops selling gold jewellery illuminated their windows. Then the cats came out. Thin, starved toms out on the prowl. Tabby queens several weeks' pregnant. Kittens only weeks old begging for their supper. The Greeks who were used to them cuffed them affectionately and threw them scraps. These creatures were nobody's pets, but a communal responsibility.

One of the kittens, a tiny ginger tom, leapt into Louise's lap and she cuddled him briefly then returned him to the sidewalk. She had more important things on her mind than petting a tomcat.

'Clay told me about Frances losing the baby,' she said. 'It must have been a terrible shock for her. Is she over it yet?'

Sam felt himself being pulled back to the real world. A world with a partner who had an obsession about exercise and a wife who had an obsession about champagne. He was tempted to lie about Frances. Her problems were none of Louise's business. Then he reconsidered.

Why not tell her about what he had been going through the past year? Maybe it would help her understand the situation. One thing was for sure. He couldn't go on alone any longer. He had to share the burden with somebody. He emptied some more wine into his glass and stared out over the sea.

'With Frances,' he said, 'it wasn't just a simple matter of losing a baby. If it was it might have been easier to deal with.'

Louise looked at him.

'Explain,' she said.

So Sam told her about it from the beginning.

'As you probably realised, it was a dreadful business. If she'd just found out about you and made a fuss, I could have dealt with it. We'd hardly been married two years. If I'd walked out then and there, Frances would have been hurt, but she would have got over it. The baby fudged the issue. Right from the moment she got pregnant I was committed – to her and to the child. Just because she lost the baby I couldn't take back that commitment. In a way she needed me more then, so I did the right thing and stayed. At least I thought it was the right thing at the time.'

Louise pulled out a cigarette and lit it, squinting into the flame.

'You don't have to tell me all this,' she said.

Sam looked at the tension in her face. This confession was obviously hurting her but he felt no desire to protect her from it. Louise had been around a long time. She was a tough girl. She could take it.

'It's important that I tell you,' he said. 'I want you to know all of it.'

Louise nodded and inhaled smoke, blowing it out against the warm breeze the way he had seen Greta Garbo do in Hollywood movies.

'You said you thought you were doing the right thing,'

she murmured. 'Did you give me a passing thought or were you too wound up with your wife?'

He leaned towards her.

'Of course I thought about you. Most of the time I thought about nothing else, but I was so damn guilty about Frances. She was so young when I met her. She had so many dreams. Little girl fantasies really. And I was one of them, until I let her down.'

'You take too much on yourself,' said Louise, roughly. 'If you'd loved Frances so much, you wouldn't have looked at me. Look, I'm not knocking her, I'm sure your wife's a very nice girl but she isn't a saint. I bet she wasn't a virgin either when you met her.'

Sam didn't want to hear it, but Louise was right, of course. No girl, and certainly no girl as pretty as Frances, could have led a blameless life. Maybe he had put her on a pedestal, expected too much of her, and when everything went wrong and she fell apart, she acted the way any girl would have under that kind of pressure.

Sam saw Louise looking at him and adjusted his expression. But she'd seen the pain on his face, and she was curious.

'There's something else the matter, isn't there?' she asked.

Sam sighed and took another slug of his wine.

'Yes,' he said heavily. 'You were right about Frances. I found out she wasn't a saint when she started to drink.'

'Was it because of the baby or was it finding out about me that brought that on?'

He passed a hand over his eyes.

'Christ knows,' he said. 'When she came back from our trip to Palm Springs Frances seemed to be getting over things. She started to go on this incredible regime – dieting, visiting the gym every afternoon, and for a while she really looked as if she was getting back in shape. I was convinced we stood a chance – by that I mean the marriage. I was still dreaming about you. But I thought in time . . .' his voice trailed off.

'Go on,' she urged. 'When did the drinking start?'

'I'm not sure,' Sam said. 'We were having a pretty hectic social life at the time. Lots of parties, weekends away, that kind of thing and Frances was enjoying it. We all were. So when she started to put away one glass of wine too many, I guess I didn't notice. Then one weekend I did notice. We were staying with Abner Morris, the guy who runs American Tobacco, when it happened. We were all celebrating something, I can't remember exactly what it was, and right in the middle of the party, Frances got very drunk and started insulting the host. She'd always been very polite to Abner, only now she went on at him as if he was some kind of criminal plotting against me.'

Louise raised an eyebrow.

'And was he?'

'Of course he wasn't. Abner and I are buddies. We trust each other. I know he'd like me to take on his business but he understands the way I feel about handling cigarettes and he doesn't push it. The way Frances was talking, you'd think he was trying to slip his account into the agency behind my back.'

Louise scooped up one of the kittens who had managed to crawl up on to the table and put him firmly back where he belonged. Then she signalled the waiter for another bottle of wine.

'Tell me,' she said. 'How much would one of Abner's cigarette accounts pay the agency?'

Sam considered.

'About sixty million. Why do you ask?'

'Because it's probably high time you adjusted your attitudes about smoking. I know it's a killer and advertising only encourages it, but no advertising, however good it is, holds a gun to anyone's head. We're in the business of

430

persuasion, not coercion. Anyway sixty million is a lot of money to turn your nose up at.'

Sam was annoyed. One moment he was sitting on a magical island with the woman he loved, the next he was suddenly talking to an ambitious agency principal. The new partnership was beginning to go to her head.

'We'll talk about the business another time,' he said. 'Right now I'm baring my soul about my wife. Or aren't you interested?'

Louise smiled and lit another cigarette.

'Sorry,' she said.

'Frances passed out cold the moment I got her home,' Sam continued. 'The girl had drunk her way into oblivion and she went on doing it. Every time I got home, she had a glass in her hand. Most evenings she couldn't stand up to come to bed.'

As he said it, he remembered the last time he took his wife into the bedroom. She had been so desperate then, so unsure of herself. All at once he was overwhelmed with compassion. What was he doing, he wondered, sitting lotus-eating with Louise when he should be at home looking after Frances?

He felt her touch his hand and he came out of his reverie.

'Sorry,' he said. 'I was miles away.'

'I know. You're thinking of going back to New York, aren't you?'

Sam looked up at the lovely woman sitting opposite and his heart ached.

'I have to,' he said. 'I'm needed there.'

Louise didn't say anything. She got up from where she was sitting and walked over to the water's edge. A big cruise ship was coming in, dwarfing Louise and the tables around them. All of a sudden Sam had a feeling he was losing her, she was starting to slip through his fingers. He hurried across to her, grabbing her by the shoulders, pulling her towards him.

'I won't be in New York for long,' he told her. 'Not now. Not after this.'

She held herself apart from him.

'What will you do?' she asked, suspiciously.

'I'll come to London. Often. As often as I can until I've settled this business with Frances. The woman's in trouble right now. She needs help, not divorcing. I have to help her. At least you can understand that.'

'And what will you do when you've sorted out Frances's problems?' Louise asked.

Sam looked at her as if she'd gone completely crazy.

'I'll leave her and marry you of course. Isn't that what you want?'

45

Frances had known that her marriage was over for two days now and still she could feel no emotion. The truth of the situation had acted like a kind of anaesthetic. She went through the motions of her life, eating, sleeping, seeing her friends. Yet it was as if she was wrapped in a layer of cotton wool and nothing that was happening around her made any impression.

If I hadn't called the agency, she thought, I wouldn't have been going through any of this. Sam could have been in London with Louise and I wouldn't have known anything about it.

She knew he had been lying about Cincinnati the moment she got on to the office. Sam's secretary wasn't at her desk and to save time, Frances had the call transferred to Clay.

'Have you any idea when Sam's due in from Cincinnati?' she asked. 'I was thinking of going to an early movie but I won't if it clashes with him getting back.'

Clay sounded genuinely confused.

'Sam isn't in Cincinnati,' he told Frances. 'At least I don't think he is. When I waved him goodbye he was on his way to London.'

Frances drew in her breath.

'Why would he be going to London?' she asked.

There was an embarrassed silence on the other end of the line. At last Clay said, 'I think you should ask your husband that question. I don't want to get in between you two.'

Sam lied to me, Frances thought. He wasn't going to any seminar in Cincinnati – he was on his way to see that bitch Louise.

'How long has this been going on?' she asked tightly. 'When did he start seeing her again?'

'He isn't seeing her again,' Clay said quickly. 'Sam's gone over to give her a contract. I was going to do it, but I was held back in New York so your husband went instead. Listen Frances, I wouldn't get neurotic about this. We're making Louise a full partner in the business. That means we have to deal with her. Sam's not a child, and nor is Louise. Nor incidentally are you. What happened between them is in the past. It's dead and buried. All we have now, all three of us, is a business arrangement.'

Frances sighed in disbelief. This was Clay she was talking to, fat, clever Clay who'd known her from the first moment she set foot in this town. Who'd known her even before she and Sam were married. What kind of fool did he take her for?

'Pull the other one,' she told him sharply. 'It's got bells on it.'

Part of her wanted to believe Clay. All through the day she kept telling herself that perhaps Sam was really going to London to hand over a contract. But he didn't have to lie to me, she thought. He didn't have to insult my intelligence by saying he was going to some seminar.

Then Sam called at five to say he had been delayed over the weekend and she knew she had lost. Handing over a contract doesn't take longer than a few minutes. If they wanted to talk about it, maybe it could take a few hours, a day even, but it didn't take a weekend. Not by any stretch of the imagination. Frances wondered what she was going to do when he got back. He didn't want a divorce or why would he be keeping this whole trip a secret? Why not come straight out with it and say 'I'm going to London to see Louise. You know the girl I was having the big affair with.'

No, she thought. Sam wants to keep his options open. But can I live like that? She considered the alternative.

Walking out on her marriage, making her life on her own again, and she flinched. Not because she was scared of being alone, but because she loved. In spite of everything, losing the baby, the drinking problem, the Abner problem, she still needed Sam. He was the centre of her life. The reason she went on with it. She would still rather die than do without him.

The phone rang and interrupted her thoughts. It was Abner.

'Sam's not here,' Frances said. 'I'll get him to call you after the weekend when he's back.'

'I don't want to speak to Sam,' Abner told her. 'I want to speak to you.'

She sat down on the sofa.

'What do you want to talk to me about?'

'I'll tell you when I see you.'

Frances felt cornered. Why did this man always do this to her? She decided to stand up for herself.

'Can't we deal with whatever it is on the phone, I'm short of time at the moment.'

'Well make time.' The voice was curt and abrupt. Delivering an order.

Frances was tempted to argue, but her strength failed her. Everything and everyone was suddenly conspiring against her. Sam, Clay, Louise and now Abner.

'When do you want to see me?' she asked.

'Can you make it this evening for a drink?'

'If you want,' she replied. 'How does six-thirty at P. J. Clarke's suit you?'

Abner hesitated for a moment and Frances wondered if he would insist on dragging her up to the Macho Club. If he does, she decided, I'm not going. Whatever he threatens.

He came back on the line. 'Okay, fine,' he said. 'If you get there first, grab a table.'

Frances arrived in the Irish bar at six-fifteen and selected a table in the back room. She wanted a couple of glasses

435

of champagne inside her before she spoke to Abner again and she wanted to do her drinking in private.

Even though it was Friday, the place was crowded that night. Frances shrank deeper into the shadows. Tonight she wanted to be anonymous. She wasn't here for any social reason.

Abner was nearly ten minutes late and for a moment she thought he wasn't coming. Then she saw the tall spare man in the Savile Row suit and the yacht-club tie burst through the door, and she knew her luck was out.

'Hi,' she said, indicating a chair. 'Do you want a glass of this champagne or will you go for something stronger?'

Abner smiled and Frances caught just a hint of patronage.

'I'll settle for a tomato juice,' he told her. 'I wouldn't want to deprive you of your little satisfaction.'

It was the way he said the word 'satisfaction'. On his lips it sounded disgusting, as if she was indulging in some fetish and Frances felt ashamed. Normally she would have lifted the bottle and poured herself another glass, but something inside her rebelled.

'I'll join you in a tomato juice,' she said evenly. 'The change will be nice.'

Abner lifted an eyebrow and said nothing. He called over a waiter and placed the order, then he turned to her.

'Let's get down to business,' he said. 'I haven't come to talk about the weather.'

Frances felt her heart lurch. He was going to raise the subject of Sam and whether she'd talked him round to taking on his business. It had been months since they'd had this conversation. The last time had been at the Frick and then all he'd wanted was to be included in their social life. 'Leave your husband to me,' he had said.

Well she had and it hadn't worked out the way he thought it would. Whenever Abner brought up his account,

436

Sam told him the score. He wasn't interested whatever the price.

So now he was leaning on her again. She might have guessed it would come to that.

She looked down at the check tablecloth in front of her.

'I've done everything I can. Everything you asked me,' she said. 'I can't do more than that.'

Abner leaned forward, his face close to hers, and Frances fought down a feeling of panic.

'I think you can.'

Icy fingers of terror gripped her stomach. She had put her house, her friends, her husband at his disposal. What could he ask from her now? She was tempted to get up and run out of the door, but something stopped her. It was the same feeling, the same resolve that made her order tomato juice when everything in her craved the comfort of alcohol.

'Suppose you tell me what you want,' she said more calmly. 'Then I'll decide what I can and what I can't do.'

Abner sat back in his chair and looked at her.

'Don't try to be cute with me,' he said. 'I've got too much on you for that.'

Frances thought about the set of pictures he had of her and suddenly she didn't care any more. All he can do, she thought, is discredit me with Sam and the way things are with him, I can't get too worked up about that.

'Get on with it, will you,' she said irritably. 'And save the bullying tactics for your little girls.'

Abner regarded her with a kind of caution she hadn't seen before. It wasn't respect exactly but it was near enough.

'I've been cooking up a little plan,' he said slowly. 'It involves you and me and your husband but first cast your mind back a couple of months to a dinner we had down at the Hamptons. We were talking about the possibility of Sam taking on my business and he was

437

saying no as usual. Only this time I pushed him a bit further.'

Frances remembered the scene at the country club. Tiffany had been there that night. Tiffany and Sam and the vodka bottle.

'Wasn't that when you asked him if there was anything that would make him change his mind?'

Abner nodded approvingly.

'Good girl,' he said. 'Right on the button. Do you remember what Sam's reply was?'

Frances caught her breath.

'He said he would take on your business to save my life or something.' Once more the terror clawed at her stomach. 'You're not thinking of trying to kill me, are you?'

Abner put out a hand and stroked her hair soothingly, the way he would calm a frightened animal.

'Now would I do that?' he asked.

Frances's eyes burned brightly and even though she'd been sipping tomato juice, her cheeks started to feel hot.

'You would if it suited you,' she replied. Abner didn't flinch but, smiling broadly, he helped himself to a glass of her champagne. Anyone looking at us, Frances thought, would think we were old friends having a good time instead of old enemies.

'Why don't you tell me some more about your little plan,' she said. 'The one involving me and Sam. I'm dying to know what you have in store for me.'

Abner raised his champagne glass in a salute. 'There's my brave girl.'

He started to tell her in some detail what was on his mind. The key to Sam, he said, was the fact that he would move heaven and earth to protect her.

'I can't very well have you kidnapped and held to ransom,' Abner explained. 'That would put me in the role of blackmailer and I need your husband's goodwill if this plan is going to come off. No, what I had in mind for you was an accident.'

The man's completely mad, Frances thought. For some reason she felt like laughing out loud as she knew in a moment of blinding clarity that she didn't have to go along with anything Abner suggested. He could shout at her, he could threaten her, he could stand on his head, but if she didn't want to play she didn't have to.

She felt as if she had been swimming underwater for a long time, lost in the murky depths of some ocean, until suddenly she had come to the surface where the sun was shining and the air was clean. She was free. The feeling was so intoxicating that for a moment she felt like playing.

'Do I get hurt in this accident you have planned for me,' she asked, 'or does somebody come to my rescue?'

Abner smiled his approval.

'I come to your rescue,' he told her.

Frances struggled to contain her mirth. The thought of Abner playing the white knight was too ludicrous to contemplate.

'I see,' she said, keeping a straight face. 'And when you save me from whatever it is, Sam is forever in your debt.'

She put her tomato juice down on the counter and looked at Abner levelly.

'I won't do it. I know you think you can frighten me into anything but this time you don't hold all the cards. You see, those pictures you have of me won't work any more. If we had had this little chat a month ago, even a day ago, things might have been different but an hour or so back, the whole ball game changed. Whatever my husband thinks about me now, doesn't matter any more. Or it matters less.'

Frances got to her feet and held out her hand.

'I can't say it's been nice doing business with you, Abner, because it hasn't. You're a rotten negotiator. Your idea of involving me in a phoney accident stinks, and wouldn't have impressed Sam. But most of all, you have no timing. None at all.'

46

Frances would remember his face for ever. Open mouthed, slack jawed, Abner looked like a man who had seen the impossible and didn't believe it was happening. Somebody had had the temerity to stand up to him and say no, and that somebody was a woman. A woman he disregarded – despised almost.

Frances smiled on the subway all the way home. All the misery, all the sleepless nights had been somehow vindicated by that one moment of victory. For a few hours it blotted out Sam's defection and her own questions about the future.

She made herself a light supper, then curled up in front of the television set and watched an old movie. It occurred to her to have something to drink, but she really didn't feel like going to the trouble of opening a fresh bottle of champagne, so she settled for a glass of orange juice. By eleven-thirty she felt so sleepy she crawled into bed and dozed off the minute her head hit the pillow.

She woke up with a start and almost immediately she knew something was wrong. Reaching across, she turned on the bedside lamp and saw it was four o'clock in the morning. Monday morning. In a few hours Sam would be home. Then what would she do? She sat up in bed drawing the covers around her. It was an instinctive gesture and had nothing to do with the warmth of the apartment. She felt cold inside. In the marrow of her bones. Cold and alone.

Out of habit, she got up and went into the kitchen. When she couldn't sleep she would fix herself a drink. A brandy, or occasionally a Jack Daniels. She walked over to where she kept the booze and took down a bottle of Armagnac. It

441

was an old château-bottled liqueur. A costly item that Sam brought out for high days and celebrations. She pulled the cork out and was assailed by brandy fumes. Every drink had its scent. Bourbon smelt raw. Red wine, smooth and mysterious. Champagne reminded her of laughter. And brandy was intoxicating.

Yet tonight the smell didn't please her. Frances hadn't had a drink since early that evening and she thought that something had gone wrong with her ability to appreciate it. She poured out the Armagnac and took a sip. It tasted stronger than she remembered and it left an unpleasant tang at the back of her mouth.

What's wrong with me, she wondered. At times like this I love a brandy, it consoles me. She peered at the label on the bottle and she wondered if Armagnac had a sell-by date. Then she laughed at herself. Being aged is the whole point of it she thought. Nevertheless she decided to try something else. There was a half drunk bottle of Rioja left over from a dinner party. She splashed some of it into a glass, and sampled it. It was disgusting. Acrid and full of tannin. She poured the wine away. There was nothing for it. She would have to open a bottle of champagne.

She went to the fridge and lifted a bottle of her favourite Crystale off the shelf. For everyday drinking she made do with Moët. The Crystale was there for emergencies when she really needed a lift. After today, she thought, a lift is definitely called for. She took her time levering off the cork, savouring the moments before she rewarded herself with this special treat. Then the stopper popped with the familiar satisfying clunk and Frances wiped the foam from the neck of the bottle and carefully decanted the pale gold liquid into a teacup she had handy.

She took a sip and waited for the remembered pleasure to spread across her tongue. Only there was no pleasure. The taste in her mouth was bitter, rank almost. Frances walked across to the fridge and poured herself a glass of

442

orange juice, gulping it back to wash away the memory of the drink and she began to wonder what was happening to her. She couldn't have developed an aversion to alcohol, could she? She thought back to her last glass of champagne. Abner had been rude about it. What did he call it? 'Your little satisfaction.' As if there was nothing else in her life that mattered.

Frances smiled ruefully. He was nearer the mark than he knew. What else did she have of any importance? Her marriage? That had been a sham since she lost their baby. Her social life? Nowadays that meant lunches with Tiffany or Bernard Glenn when he wasn't busy. Dreary weekends in the country with Abner. So what was there left except a consoling glass of fizz? Only it didn't console her any more, because it didn't solve anything.

Frances wondered if there had been a moment in her life when alcohol gave her courage and she decided there hadn't. She always thought when she was drinking it was going to help her but the only thing that happened was the edges got blurred and she made no sense at all. Then she remembered something: a few hours ago she had faced one of the biggest scares of her life. The final confrontation with Abner Morris, and she had come through it with flying colours.

I didn't have a drink, she told herself happily. Well, maybe one beforehand, but while it was going on, while he was putting me on the spot, all I consumed was tomato juice. I wasn't blurred and in the end I wasn't even frightened. I felt terrific.

Frances had an idea, a wasteful extravagant idea and before she lost her nerve she acted on it. With great care, she collected together all the bottles of booze in the apartment: the vintage port she kept on the dresser in the dining-room, Sam's bourbon, her stock of champagne and half a case of red wine they kept for dinner parties.

For a moment she hesitated over the bourbon and the

dinner party wine. Then she thought, in a few hours my life with Sam is going to change and the question of whether or not we entertain our friends will be purely academic.

She assembled everything on the draining board. Then, one by one, she emptied each bottle down the sink. As she did so, she felt few regrets. Instead she experienced the same feeling of freedom she had when she finally turned her back on Abner. When it was over, she didn't go back to bed. She brewed up some coffee and took it into the main room, then she sat and thought about her marriage and the man she loved until the sun came up over the city.

Sam was home that evening, weary from travelling and crying out for a hot shower and a long nap. Normally Frances unpacked for him, stowing away his used underwear and dirty shirts, pressing the wrinkles out of his suits. This time she was damned if she was going to play the handmaiden.

Instead she went into the kitchen and threw together a cold supper. Chicken legs from the deli, cold ham, salad and a big bowl of fruit. It was a movable feast. Something they could eat, or pick at, while they talked about his trip. And there was a lot of talking to do.

Frances had set up a table in the conservatory and when Sam finally came through from the shower, he was both delighted and irritated.

'Where the hell have you put my bourbon?' he demanded.

Frances didn't move a muscle.

'Down the sink,' she informed Sam.

'What did you do that for?'

'If you sit down for a moment, I'll explain.'

And she did. She went all through her wakeful night with him, from the moment she walked into the kitchen, and poured herself an Armagnac, to the final decision when she poured away every drop of alcohol they owned.

Sam regarded Frances with a kind of wonder.

'What decided you to do it?' he asked. 'I mean apart from the fact that it tasted bad.'

'Maybe I decided I liked myself,' Frances said. 'I didn't want to punish myself any more. You see for a long time I believed I was responsible for all the bad things. Your affair with Louise. Losing the baby. Losing my looks. But none of that was my fault at all. They were just things that happened. Nobody could help them happening. All that could be done was to take stock of things when they were over and decide what to do then. My drinking just confused things.'

Sam shook his head.

'I never thought you'd do it,' he said.

Frances walked out on to the terrace and looked down on the city. The traffic was building up again with the theatre crowds and early dinner set and shiny black limousines and yellow cabs jostled bumper to bumper in the streets below her. There was an excitement in the air, a feeling of anticipation and Frances knew in one of the chic restaurants around her someone was bound to be falling in love tonight. The knowledge gave her courage to go on with what she had to do.

'It's not going to be easy, giving up,' she said. 'Oh, right now I've convinced myself that liquor tastes bad and I'm full of good intentions and self-righteousness. But there will be bad moments when I'm feeling below par, or I'm just sad, when I'm going to crave a drink. I've depended on it too long not to, and during the bad moments it's going to be tough.'

Sam came over and put his arm round her.

'Don't worry about it,' he said. 'I'll be there to help you.'

Frances moved away from him.

'No you won't.'

If she had turned round and hit him, Sam couldn't have been more surprised. This wasn't like Frances at all. He

445

was used to her leaning on him. Needing him. What could have got into her?

'You're being silly,' he said. 'You can't go through this on your own.'

She looked at him sharply.

'And what are you going to do? Play the model husband and come home early from the office every night? Give up jolly weekends with your friend Abner to stay by my side? I'm not convinced you'll do that, because I know that isn't what you want.'

Sam had a feeling that something had changed. Something was up. The conversation he had had with Frances in Athens had sounded warning bells, and now they were ringing again. This time, though, they were louder.

'Tell me,' Sam said. 'What do you think I want?'

She took a breath. Then she let him have it.

'Louise,' she said.

There was a moment of silence. So clear and so still that Frances imagined the traffic on the street below them had stopped turning and in that moment she allowed herself to feel regret. She'd burned her boats now, and taken the first step along the path she had set herself. She had no idea where it would lead her, or where it would end. She only knew one thing. She had to follow it or perish.

'You shouldn't have lied to me,' she said quietly. 'If you'd just been straight and told me you were going to London to give Louise a partnership, I'd have gone along with it. I wanted to trust you. I loved you enough for that.'

'You say you loved me,' Sam said harshly. 'Does that mean you don't love me any more?'

Frances smiled.

'No,' she said. 'I wish it did. It would make what I have to say to you so much easier. I'm going to go away for a while. I'm not leaving you. It's nothing as final as that but I've got a lot of thinking to do. A lot of growing up. For that I need to be on my own.'

446

'Where will you go?' Sam asked quietly.

'London, I think. If my old flatmate's got a spare bedroom, I'll stay there. If not I'll go home to my parents. I haven't seen much of them in the last few years and they'll be pleased to see me.'

Sam should have been overjoyed. Frances was solving all his problems. With her out of the way, he would be able to see Louise as often as he wanted. He could even part her from that precious London operation now it was running under its own steam and bring her back to New York.

That wasn't what he wanted, however. He wanted everything: his wife in New York, and Louise in London – until he decided how he felt about the situation.

'Have you definitely made up your mind,' he asked, 'or will you listen to reason? If you let me talk it through with you, I'm sure we could work out a better way.'

Frances shook her head.

'There's no better way. Anyway there's something else I haven't told you about and you can't help me with that.'

She went across to the table she had set so carefully, and sat behind it. Somehow with the supper between them, she felt more in control.

'You must have guessed by now I don't like Abner Morris. Actually it's stronger than dislike. I can't stand the man, and it's not because of the way he is towards me. You see him treating me like a fluffy little wife. I see him treating me like trash. Because when I knew him, that's what I was.'

Sam started to interrupt her, but she wouldn't let him.

'There's a whole lot I didn't tell you when we first ran into each other. In the beginning I didn't think it was any of your business and by the time you had every right to know, it was too late. By then I ran the risk of you not loving me because of what I'd done. So I kept quiet.'

Sam thought about Louise and the man she had walked over to get to where she was.

'You're being too hard on yourself,' Sam said. 'Love isn't about what people have done in the past before you knew them.'

Frances smiled.

'I know that now, but I might as well tell you about all the things I was hiding. I owe you that. For a while, before I came to New York, I lived with a very wicked man. He was the brains behind *Macho* magazine and all those sleazy clubs and while I was with him, I truly thought I loved him. If I hadn't I wouldn't have let him take pictures of me in bed without any clothes on.'

She poured herself a glass of orange juice and went on.

'Those pictures changed everything between us. You see he sent them to his partner in America – Abner Morris – and Abner liked what he saw and wanted to use them in his magazine. Only the quality wasn't right. So I was somehow persuaded to come across to New York and do a studio session. The whole thing was a mistake of course. I realised that when I got here. When I told Abner I couldn't go through with it, he cut up rough. The upshot was that I walked out on him. And the next day I walked into you.'

Sam looked at her with new understanding.

'No wonder you couldn't stand having the guy around. If you'd told me all this, instead of bottling it up, I would never have put you through it.'

'You still don't get it,' Frances insisted. 'Abner Morris has been blackmailing me. He threatened to use the nudes he had of me and if I didn't do what he asked, he was going to send you the pictures and supply a suitably juiced-up version of my past.'

Sam passed a hand across his eyes and Frances noticed for the first time how tired he was.

'What did Abner want you to do?'

Frances sighed.

'What do you think? He wanted me to talk you into

taking his business. He thought I could pressure you into it.'

Sam got up and prowled around the terrace and Frances saw he was distracted. More than distracted. He looked completely thrown.

'My anti-smoking attitude has caused you a lot of grief, hasn't it? First you get flak from Tiffany because I wouldn't go along with it. Then Abner tries his pitch.'

He turned to her.

'Look, I can understand how he pushed you into a corner. After losing the baby and all your other problems, you didn't need me to see a juicy set of pictures of you in the altogether, but there's one thing I can't figure out. Why didn't you put more pressure on me? At that moment in our marriage I would have done almost anything to make you happy. I virtually said as much in front of Abner himself. So why didn't you make more of a fuss? Why didn't you demand I took on American Tobacco? I would have done it, you know.'

Frances took a sip of her orange juice. This is a fine moment to tell me, she thought. She remembered the fight they had the first time round, when he'd told her about his father and how the old man died. In spite of everything she was glad she hadn't gone against him.

'I didn't want you to sell out,' she said firmly. 'You talked about loving people for what they are, not what they had been. And what you are is an impossible idealist. You remind me of one of those knights riding into battle. You're so gallant, such a dreamer, and you'd go to your death defending those dreams. If I didn't love you as much as I do, I might have tried to make you see reason. But I do love you. I love you much too much for my own good. So you see I couldn't have lived with myself if you'd taken on American Tobacco over a set of nude pictures.'

'So you risked everything you had,' Sam said softly. He looked at the plump blonde woman sitting in front of him. Her face was starting to show signs of the booze and the disappointment. There were dark roots that needed touching up, and the way she wore her hair was less than becoming. Yet he wished she wasn't going away.

There was something real about Frances, something brave and gutsy that went beyond manicures and size ten dresses.

'Don't go to London,' he begged her. 'You don't have to run away and hide just because you made a couple of mistakes when you were a little girl. You've grown since then. You've become important. More important than you know.'

Frances nodded sadly.

'It's too late to ask me that now,' she said. 'I've already made up my mind.'

Sam thought about Louise. Slim, black haired, confident Louise. If you stood her beside his wife, she would be the one most men would choose, but most men didn't know Frances. Couldn't see her for what she really was. And Sam realised with a pang, he was being forced to settle for second best. The woman he wanted, the real prize, was on her way out the door.

47

Sam didn't let Frances go empty-handed. At his insistence Frances was to draw on the joint bank account for all the big bills and for her everyday expenses he opened an account for her at the National Westminster Bank in London's Grosvenor Square.

Then he found her somewhere to live. She was still his wife. He wasn't having her sleeping in some ex-flatmate's spare room. So he called the porter at the Connaught. Apart from Louise, it was his only London contact. The Connaught didn't let him down. They were used to visiting Americans asking for the impossible and renting a decent apartment sight unseen was nearly impossible, unless you knew the right people. He was referred to a Mrs Meynell at Rudland and Stubbs. This particular lady had been finding places to live in the centre of London for a quarter of a century. She knew the standards required by the rich and because her clients were willing to pay top dollar, landlords favoured her.

When she arrived back in town, Frances discovered she was living in a mews house off Eaton Square, courtesy of her husband. The place consisted of a tiny cluttered drawing-room opening on to a perfect rose garden, a dining-room with a polished mahogany table and a huge antique dresser and a well-equipped kitchen.

The whole of the top floor was given over to a roomy bedroom and an en suite bathroom.

The first thing Frances did was call her parents. She hadn't told them of her troubles in New York and she wasn't going to go into detail on the telephone. All she said was she was in London for an extended visit.

She wasn't with her husband and she would explain the rest when she came down to see them.

She had forgotten how much she missed the English country. It was the skies that filled her with nostalgia. In America the horizon was huge and in a way uncompromising. Because of the suddenness of the seasons you were either surrounded by clear blue porcelain, or thick clouds. There were no in betweens. In England it was all in betweens. Little clouds scudded across pale blue that shaded off to soft grey. Sometimes when it was raining there was a translucent quality about the heavens, as if it could all change in the twinkling of an eye to black thunder or filtered sunlight. There was nothing expected about the English sky and this very unpredictability comforted Frances.

Her parents' house outside Oxford looked just the same as she remembered it. Originally it had been a Queen Anne farmhouse, but now it was a rambling red stone structure with stables in the back, and a sloping sweeping lawn at the front. The taxi from the station took Frances up the front drive and she noticed that the sheep grazing in the fields on either side of her were growing their winter coats. I wonder if I'll still be here in the lambing season, she thought.

Then she dismissed the future from her mind. The present was what she had in front of her. The present, and her parents to deal with. That was quite enough to be getting on with.

Her father greeted her with affection and restraint. He knew everything was not right with her but he was an English gentleman and he played the situation by the rules. First she had to hand over her suitcase to the maid, who would unpack for her, then she was settled into an armchair by the fire and offered a drink. The Buckinghams often had a sherry before lunch but they hadn't seen their daughter for over four years, so they bent the rules and opened a bottle of champagne.

Sir Gerald was astonished at the expression on Frances's face when he brought in the chilled bottle.

'I'm not having any,' she said quickly, refusing to pick up the tall crystal flute he offered her. 'I don't drink any more.'

'But this is a celebration, my dear,' protested her father. 'Go on, you know you enjoy a glass of fizz.'

Frances just shook her head and reached instead for a tumbler of orange juice. For the twenty minutes before lunch they talked about neutral subjects: the weather, the antics of the local hunt, the activities of the other members of the Buckingham family. Then just before they went into the dining-room, Frances's mother asked her about Sam.

'Will he be joining you in London?' she asked. 'Or is his work keeping him in New York?'

'Sam won't be joining me,' she said truthfully. 'Not because of the agency, but because I don't want him to. We're separating for a while.'

There was an uncomfortable silence while they all trooped into lunch and unfolded their napkins.

'What happened?' her mother suddenly asked.

Frances went into a well-rehearsed speech, omitting any mention of Abner. Instead she concentrated on her main reason for leaving New York. Louise Tragos.

Her mother was horrified.

'Poor baby,' she said, 'you didn't deserve that. Not after that other man. What was his name, Richard something?'

'Richard Gregory,' said Frances patiently, reflecting on her own stupidity. How could she imagine her mother would ever forget the *Macho* business, any more than she would forget the way she left poor Archie at the altar. It was Frances who wanted to forget, not Fiona. Before they could pursue the subject any further, her father cut in.

'Do you think it was wise to walk out like that? I mean shouldn't you have stayed and faced up to the situation.

With you out of the way this Louise woman could come right in and help herself to your husband.'

'I think she rather did that while I was living in New York.' Frances pulled a wry face. 'There comes a moment when it's pointless to go on fighting. If Sam really wants Louise Tragos then he can have her. There's nothing I can do, and there's nothing more I want to do. To be honest, I haven't really been the same since I lost the baby. I was tempted to come home the minute it happened but I stayed on and stuck it out. Now I've had enough of being brave to please other people. I want some time for myself.'

Her parents understood and didn't probe her any further and Frances realised she had underestimated them. Like many children she had spent her life fighting them, rebelling against them. When all the time she was really rebelling against herself. All they wanted was the best for her. They were on her side. They weren't enemies like Louise Tragos or Abner Morris.

After lunch Frances went out for a walk around her father's fields. Sir Gerald Buckingham owned all the land he could see from his front porch. Hundreds of acres of rich grass supporting cows and sheep. Some of his fields supported crops, wheat and barley and maize and all of it, Frances knew, would one day come to her. The thought gave her comfort. I'm conforming, she thought. At the grand old age of thirty, I'm finally growing into my family.

She stayed in the country for the next six weeks.

After a while she realised she was losing weight. She hadn't tried to do it and she only noticed because her jeans didn't fit her any more and she had to go into the local town and buy a smaller size. While she was there she had her hair cut. Her roots had grown out to such an extent that she was two colours now – dark blonde, the colour she was born with and bright blonde, the colour Elizabeth Arden in New York had given her. Arden's blonde belonged with the

454

bright lights and smoky rooms and cocktail party chatter. Here in the country it looked out of place. Frances told the girl in the local salon to cut it all away and when she emerged, her hair was short like a boy's. Her cheekbones were coming back and her chinline. Even the dark circles were disappearing in the fresh air.

I'm beginning to look the way I did before I went away, she thought. Except for my eyes. For the eyes that looked back at her from the mirror were no longer the eyes of a girl. They were a woman's eyes, full of experience and remembered pain. Frances knew no matter what she gave up, booze, fatty food, fast living, she would never get her innocence back.

It was that realisation that finally decided her to return to London. She had cleansed herself in the country with her parents, emptied out the poisons from her system. Now she had to face her life and her problems once more.

When Frances got back, she tried on everything she had and found nothing fitted any more or suited her either.

She was no longer a New York socialite and she wondered if she really ever had been. She returned to her old haunts: Joseph's, Kensington Market, Edina Ronay, and got together a collection of simple, unstructured clothes that fitted her body, yet made no demands on it.

She bought short leather skirts, flannel trousers and knitted dresses that looked like football jerseys. All her spike-heeled shoes she threw away. In their stead she wore soft, suede boots and flat leather pumps that looked like ballet shoes.

When she had finished readjusting herself, Frances felt ready to face the world and she picked up the phone to call Richard Gregory. She knew she was going to contact him from the moment she left New York. During that long night while she was waiting for Sam to come back from London, she had taken a fundamental decision: she wasn't going to run away any more. She had spent her life running away – from her parents, from the husband they had chosen for her and from the past that she had tried to bury. Now the running was over, and though she couldn't go back and find Archie, Richard Gregory, who cast a far longer shadow, was still around. Still there to be faced and dealt with.

Frances rang his house in the early evening when she knew he would be there and he sounded pleased to hear her voice. Pleased and surprised.

'What are you doing in London?' he enquired affably. 'I thought you were based in New York these days.'

'I'm over here on a visit,' Frances told him. 'I thought I might come by and say hello.'

Richard didn't hesitate.

'Are you on your own?' he asked.

'Yes. Why?'

'Because I thought we might have dinner. For old times' sake.'

So he was up to his old tricks, Frances thought. Sniffing around her, wanting to know if she was available. She smiled to herself. Abner couldn't have told him that she'd lost her looks.

'I'd love to have dinner,' she said. 'Only I'm married now. I expect Abner told you that.'

Richard didn't say anything for a moment and when he came back on the line he sounded fainter.

'Abner,' he said. 'I haven't spoken to him for nearly two years now, and the last time he didn't mention you at all.'

'Then how did you know I was in New York?' Frances asked.

He chuckled.

'I'll tell you all about it over dinner. Give me your address and I'll send a car for you. How does tomorrow night sound?'

Frances dressed carefully in a silk crêpe dress from Jean Muir. It was completely plain with long tight sleeves and a high round neck and she relieved its severity with a pair of dangly earrings she had bought that afternoon. Now she was thin again and her hair was cut short she liked to wear earrings. They made her look less like a boy.

When she saw Richard again, she knew she shouldn't have worried. He didn't think she looked like a boy and he made that clear from the first moment he took her hand.

The car had brought her to San Lorenzo, the Italian restaurant in Beauchamp Place. They used to have dinner there in the old days and the place hadn't changed. It was still a hang out for the music business and the glittering people, and Frances caught a glimpse of Bianca Jagger and Olivier de Montal in a tête-à-tête at the far end of the bar.

She was the first to arrive, and she decided to wait for Richard in the bar. It was the one bar, she reflected, that a girl could hang about on her own and not worry. It was like somebody's drawing-room with a long padded sofa and trailing green plants everywhere. She ordered herself a glass of fizzy water and wondered if the years between had changed Richard.

Five minutes later she discovered they hadn't. She was the one who had changed. It was as if he had stepped out of a photograph. His hair was still the colour of tow, still hung around his shoulders, and he still clung to his Sixties garb of faded jeans and leather jacket. Now, because she had changed, Frances failed to be impressed with it. She merely saw it as slightly ridiculous.

If Richard saw her reaction, he didn't register it. He looked her up and down with evident pleasure and remarked that America had made little impression on her.

'You should have seen me a couple of months ago,' Frances laughed. 'You wouldn't have said that.'

'Well I didn't see you then,' Richard said. 'I'm looking at you now, and apart from that funny haircut you could be the same girl.'

Frances followed him into the restaurant.

'But I'm not the same girl,' she said. 'I'm older and tougher and things don't frighten me any more.'

Richard turned round and grinned.

'I'd like to hear you say that if they gave us the wrong table here. I bet if they made us sit in the back room in one of those cramped little affairs for two you'd be terrified.'

'That's different,' Frances said, allowing the waiter to guide them into Richard's regular place at the foot of the staircase. 'I was talking about grown-up things. Like standing up to Abner Morris for instance.'

Richard looked interested.

'I'd like to have seen that. There are times when I miss the old rogue, but not often. I told you on the phone we'd parted company, didn't I?'

'Sort of,' she replied. 'You said you hadn't spoken to him in two years. So I assumed it was something like that. What happened?'

Richard waved the waiter over and called for a bottle of Frascati. The Italian boy saw Frances's expression and came over to her side of the table.

'You wanted something Signorina?'

'Water,' she said firmly. Then she turned her attention back to her companion.

'It started with that business over your pictures,' Richard said, studying her face for signs of a reaction. 'Abner told me you didn't want to do the session and I assumed you'd be on the next plane back to me. When you didn't turn up I waited around for a couple of days, then I caught a plane to New York. After a few hours with Mr Morris, I found out what had really happened.'

As if it was only the other day Frances remembered how Abner had broken the news to her that she had been passed on to him. 'Richard is bored with you,' he had said. 'It's my turn now.' The pain came flooding back to her.

'How could you have done that to me?' she asked Richard. 'I can understand if you wanted to call it quits, but handing me over to Abner, like a piece of goods. That was the worst part. I don't think I've ever really forgiven you for that.'

Richard looked at her.

'Then why are you here tonight?'

'Because I wanted to take a good look at you. You're like one of those phantoms in the night, Richard. You've haunted me for a long time now and I wanted to put an end to it. I wanted to find out who you really were, and I wanted to ask you what the hell you thought you were doing.'

He had the grace to look embarrassed.

'I might have known you didn't want to play a chorus of Auld Lang Syne. I suppose you expect me to apologise?'

For the first time Frances saw him with the eyes of her new maturity. Instead of seeing a lover, she saw a little boy. An ageing little boy dressing up in a young man's clothes. Wearing a young man's hairdo. She could only feel sorry. 'I don't expect anything,' she told him. 'I'm not here because I wanted you to grovel. All I'd like to know was why you did it. Why didn't you just throw me out and have done with it?'

Richard frowned and took a sip of his wine.

'It wasn't as simple as that. Look, way back when we were together, I sensed you were getting bored. I'm not the most faithful of men – never pretended I was – and I knew you weren't going to put up with me for long. So, if you like, I gave you the option to leave. Abner is attractive, or so women tell me. He's rich. He had the hots for you. I thought you might give it a whirl for a bit.'

How could I have loved this man? Frances thought. He's

459

without depth. Without perception. Without even common humanity.

'So that's what you told him,' she said. 'I was getting fed up and the time was ripe for Abner to step in and take over.'

'It wasn't like that. I didn't say a damn thing to Abner. If you must know that was part of the reason we fell out in the end. The guy always assumed he had some divine right over the Macho girls. They were working for Macho. He owned Macho. Ergo, he owned them. He never acknowledged the girls might have some say in it.'

Frances had promised herself she wouldn't lose her temper tonight but she felt it building up inside her.

'Don't lie to me,' she said quietly. 'I distinctly remember Abner telling me I had been passed on. You were finished with me and it was his turn.'

Richard sighed and pushed his hair back out of his face.

'Frances,' he said, 'this is not going to make you feel any better, but for what it's worth you were one of a long line of girls Abner came on to. And if they had any doubts, if they looked like they might change their minds or give him trouble, he always fed them the same story. I was finished with them. He was the only option they had left. I told you, the Macho girls weren't girls as far as he was concerned. They were possessions.'

'And how did you feel, when you found out Abner was lying?'

'How do you think I felt? Bloody furious. I'm not in the white slave trade. I don't pass my girlfriends out like a bag of sweeties. When the fourth girl it happened to came back and gave me hell, I decided to take some action.'

For the first time that evening Frances started to listen to what Richard was saying. He might be a shallow playboy, but he had a certain integrity. It was that integrity that she

460

had been drawn to. Perhaps he's telling the truth, after all, she thought.

'What did you do?' she asked.

'I took a plane to New York and had it out with him. I told him I didn't like my name taken in vain and the next time he wanted to take a girl to bed would he cut out the bullshit. Abner laughed of course. I knew he would. "They're only bimbos," he said. "Why hurt our relationship just because a couple of bimbos get upset?" I remember saying, "Frances isn't a bimbo. She was my girl-friend, she lived with me for over three years." And Abner said, "So what does that make her. A Madonna?" '

Frances could almost see the tall American saying it.

'Does Abner like any women at all?' she asked, curious. Richard smiled.

'Sure,' he said. 'Abner likes women like him. Hard cases. There's some married bitch he's involved with at the moment. Tiffany . . . Tiffany Greene. She's more than a match for him and I hear he enjoys every minute.'

Frances was dumbfounded. Abner involved with Tiffany? Her friend Tiffany?

'But Tiffany's married to my husband's partner. Are you sure? How long's it been going on?' she spluttered.

'I'm not sure,' Richard said, soothing her. 'I told you I don't see Abner any more, but my spies at Kurnitz and Greene tell me they've been an item for some little time.'

Frances was still taken aback. 'How come you have spies at the agency?' she asked.

'My agent gets me the odd photographic session with them,' Richard explained. 'Life didn't come to a standstill when Abner and I parted company. I still go out and click my camera now and then.'

Frances realised how small the world was. Richard, Abner, Tiffany, even Sam were all somehow connected to each other by the strands of business. It was as if there

461

was an invisible network cast across half the world. The half that worked in the communications business.

'Have you met my husband?' she asked curiously.

Richard nodded. 'Once. On a catfood shoot. How do you think I knew you lived in New York?'

Frances suddenly felt very foolish.

'I thought Abner must have told you all about me. I realise now he didn't tell you anything. Not even the way we parted company.'

Now it was Richard's turn to look curious.

'No. What happened?'

Frances looked embarrassed. 'He tried to rape me, actually. So I grabbed something heavy and knocked him cold.'

Richard leaned back in his chair and started to laugh. It was so infectious that several of the other diners turned round to see what had amused him.

'Good for you,' he said. 'I knew he'd get his come-uppance, tough bastard.'

Frances felt a moment of concern. When she had met him, Richard had been sitting on top of the world. He had magazines, clubs, a rich American partner. Now they had quarrelled and parted company, and she was part of that quarrel.

'What happened between you and Abner?'

'I wasn't left penniless, if that's what you're worried about,' Richard said. 'Nearly three years ago, Abner simply announced he was buying out my share of the equity. I didn't put up a fight. I was pretty well sick of him by then and he was offering a mountain of cash, so I took the money and ran. I still go on taking pictures, but it's really just to keep my hand in.'

The waiter came and cleared away their plates. Then he returned with the drinks trolley.

'Have an Armagnac,' said Richard. 'You always liked to finish dinner with a little something to keep you going.'

Frances shook her head.

'There are a lot of things I haven't told you. One of them is I don't drink any more. But I'd love a coffee, if that's okay.'

He turned around in his seat and looked at her.

'I've got a better idea. Why don't I take you home and make you a coffee there. I've got one of those flash bachelor penthouses in Green Street. I've been dying to show it to you.'

I bet you have, Frances thought. If I don't look out it will be once round the bedroom for old times' sake. Then she shrugged. What am I worrying about? I'm on the loose again now. Sam's probably moved Louise into the apartment. And the thought of the black-haired girl sitting at her table, lying in her bed made her catch her breath.

Richard looked concerned.

'Is something the matter?'

She shook her head.

'Just someone walking over my grave.'

48

It was just like old times. Richard had obviously cleared out his last abode, lock, stock and barrel and transported it to the luxury apartment in the West End. The books in the bookcase were in the places Frances remembered. A fire was lit, the way it had always been, and along with the furniture Richard had kidnapped the maid, for the same Asian woman she'd seen in Knightsbridge came to ask her how she wanted her coffee.

'She takes it white,' said Richard, 'with a lump of brown sugar.' He turned to her. 'See how I remember. Now come and curl up by the fire and tell me what's been happening to you. I won't pounce on you till later. I promise.'

Frances grinned.

'Don't push it,' she said, but she was glad to be there. Richard was shallow, she knew that, and nothing he did was for ever, but she wasn't in the mood for anything serious. Anyway, she was used to him.

She sat up half the night telling him her story. Every now and then he interrupted and asked for descriptions of people he didn't know, like Tiffany. Then he leaned back and gave her his verdict.

'You're still in love with Sam,' he said.

'What makes you say that?' Frances asked.

'Because you stuck it out and didn't lose your cool. Any other girl would have quit the moment Abner came on the scene. What was there to stay for? A husband who's there out of a sense of duty. A lost baby. Abner making life a misery. If I'd been in your shoes I'd have packed my bags and run.'

'But I couldn't just leave Sam for no reason.'

'Yes you could. But you didn't because you loved the guy. Frances,' Richard said cautiously, 'what are you going to do about him?'

Frances looked at him from under her eyelashes.

'Why don't you ask me that question in the morning?' she said.

He reached for her then and she came into his arms, searching for remembered warmth. When she found it, she finally relaxed.

It had been a long time since a man had made love to her and meant it. There was nothing tender about Richard. He didn't treat her with care and compassion, worrying about her feelings. As far as Richard was concerned, she was a grown woman and he was hungry for her. The rest could take care of itself. Frances let him carry her into the bedroom. Then without any modesty at all, she allowed him to undress her. She had blown over a hundred pounds on a lacy camisole by La Perla, and now she was glad of it because Richard was glad of it. He ran his hands over her, feeling her body through the lace. Then slowly he peeled it from her, kissing the newly naked flesh as he did so.

Frances gave herself up to sensation and Richard didn't disappoint her. Using first his fingers, then his mouth he aroused her to the point of screaming. Then, just as she was beginning to lose control, he buried himself in her. She came quickly, too quickly, but Richard didn't seem to notice. As he went on taking his pleasure, she opened her eyes and took a good look at him.

His face was blurred with desire and there was something lost about him, as if he was being propelled by an emotion stronger than survival. Frances felt both blessed and sad. She knew she had driven this man to fever pitch. She and she alone. Only the man with the fever, the man making love to her, was the wrong man. Why couldn't I do this to Sam, she asked herself?

In the morning Richard made love to her again, then

465

chased her into the kitchen and demanded she make breakfast. She did so, falling into a habit she thought she had forgotten years ago. First there was muesli, and she squeezed fresh oranges, knowing he preferred it to milk on his cereal. Then there were boiled eggs. Two of them. Done for three and a half minutes exactly. Finally she toasted rough brown bread and covered it with low-fat spread she found in the fridge.

She served the whole thing up on the scrubbed pine table and sat back, waiting for his appreciation. It didn't come. He sliced off the tops of his eggs and inspected them critically.

'How do you feel about working for a change?' he said.

'Charming,' Frances said. 'Next time get your own breakfast.'

Richard looked at her affronted face and laughed.

'I wasn't being rude about all this,' he said. 'Honestly Frances, you're an angel in the kitchen. You always were. I just thought you could do better than waiting on some man.'

She stared at him blankly.

'I'm not trained for anything except for looking after people. Even when I did work, I washed dishes and waited on tables. Frankly, if I'm going to do that, I'd rather do it for someone I know and like.'

Richard was exasperated.

'Where have you been living for the past few years? Turkey? The Middle East? Women do other things apart from serve you know, or hadn't they heard of liberation in your part of New York?'

Frances began to pour the coffee, a dreamy expression on her face.

'For heaven's sake, Frances, pay attention to what I'm saying, will you? You're not a coffee-making machine. Or a fucking machine either.'

'You've changed your tune since the old days,' she observed. 'What about all those Macho girls tramping in and out of your bedroom. Are you telling me you didn't appreciate them now?'

Richard took the jug out of her hands and set it down, pushed the plates to one side and took hold of her hands.

'My sexual preferences are nothing to do with it,' he told her. 'We're talking about you. I happen to think you're capable of being more than a housewife. You had the guts to pick yourself up and walk away from Abner when he got too much for you and you didn't do it once either. You told that bastard where to put it twice. Not many people can do that. Not many men can do that. You managed it all on your own.'

He looked at her, a smile forming on his lips.

'I've decided to put that pushy, ballsy thing you have to work.'

Frances let go of his hands.

'What kind of work?' she asked.

'Reporting work,' he told her, 'on an advertising magazine. After four years of being around Sam Kurnitz you must know something about the business.'

Frances shook her head.

'Not enough,' she said. 'I was good at listening when Sam brought his problems home and I can make passable small-talk at dinner parties, but that's it. I don't know enough about the business to work on a magazine.'

'Well it's time you learned.'

Richard saw the trepidation in her eyes.

'It's not that difficult you know. I'm not asking you to do anything beyond your intelligence. You can pick up all you need to know by simply reading, and all the material's available.'

Frances still didn't like it.

'Where is it available?' she demanded. 'In the archives of J. Walter Thompson?'

Richard tried his best to be patient. He wanted this girl he used to know to do something on her own account. She deserved better than the fate life had chosen for her.

'Look,' he said. 'Have you heard of a magazine called *Campaign*?'

Frances hesitated for a moment.

'Sam used to get it. I remember seeing it among his mail. Isn't it something like *Ad Age*?'

Richard nodded.

'It's the English version of *Ad Age*. It rounds up the ad business every week. Up-dates it. If you read it week by week you'd know about every account that was on the loose. Every top executive who was about to move agencies. They even do a critique of the best new campaigns. What I want you to do is settle down and study it. After you've digested the first three months, you'll begin to get some idea of how the business works.'

Frances put her coffee cup down and shook her head.

'You're serious about all this aren't you? You really think that with a bit of reading and a quick introduction or two, I'll make a crack reporter. It won't work you know. It can't work. I don't have that kind of mind. Or the drive something like that takes.'

Richard observed her closely.

'Will you do something for me?' he asked. 'Just a little something. If I send you some copies of the magazine I was just telling you about, will you read them? If they bore you to tears, it's okay by me. We'll drop the whole idea. But I'd like you to give it a whirl.'

Frances considered the alternatives. She could turn him down flat, then suggest she moved in with him. It would be easy to do. It wasn't as if she hadn't done it before. Then she remembered Richard's casual attitude to sex. No, she thought, I've come a long way since those days. I can't go back to the girl I used to be.

She thought about working on an advertising magazine again. If I could hack it, she thought, maybe it wouldn't be such a bad idea after all.

The following morning two years' issues of *Campaign* arrived at her house. There were three piles standing almost waist high and she let out a groan. It will take me weeks to get through this lot, she thought. Then she set her chin. So it takes me weeks, so it takes me months. I'm not doing anything else at the moment.

She decided to make her way through from where they started, two years ago to the present time. The first thing she noticed was that the magazine came out every Thursday. There seemed nothing remarkable about that, or about the front page of the edition she picked up. It told her that a major brand of fish fingers was looking for a new agency to handle its business. On that same page she saw one of the hot creative talents at J. Walter Thompson had been headhunted to join a consultancy she had never heard of. And the Electricity Board was looking for someone to handle a new washing-up machine. She sighed and turned the page. If she worked for an agency she might have been turned on, but she didn't, and the gossip meant nothing. The second, third, fourth and fifth pages contained more of the same. Business was moving. New products were coming on to the marketplace. People were being hired and fired. Frances flicked over three or four more pages and came to a double-page spread of ads. The one that caught her eye was of a pregnant man. He had a naked hairy chest and was definitely carrying a baby. The silliness of the notion made her smile. She glanced at the headline: 'Would you be more careful,' it said, 'if it was you that got pregnant?' The ad was for the Health Education Council and was pushing contraception. I like it, she thought. The guy who wrote that knew what he was doing. Quickly she scanned the copy and saw that someone by the name of Charles Saatchi was responsible for it. I'd like to meet him, she thought. He sounds interesting. A damn sight more interesting than washing-up machines and fish fingers.

Two pages on she found a profile of Charles Saatchi and because he had grabbed her attention, she read it.

It was a gossipy piece detailing how this son of an Iraqi Jewish immigrant had made his way. Saatchi was as irreverent as the ads he created: he was temperamental, original and reclusive and because of the latter, his story was told through the eyes of his colleagues and friends in the business. All of it fascinated Frances, for when everyone had had their say about this man he remained as much of an enigma as he had before.

There have to be more Charlie Saatchis, Frances thought, more characters that make this world come alive. She started to search for them in the feature pages and opinion columns and as the people in the business became visible to her, so did the business itself.

It took her nearly two weeks to get through the pile on her floor but she was never bored. Sometimes it was difficult to understand and there were times when she wished Sam was around to explain some of it to her, but never once was she tempted to give up reading. The advertising world reminded her of a kaleidoscope with all the pieces forming intricate patterns which moved and changed once a week to form an ever more delicate tracery.

Too late Frances realised why Sam was enthralled with it and how boring it must have been for him to come home to her and talk of little things. Then she put her regrets behind her. What's done is done, she thought. I have a whole new life to start.

She rang up Richard and told him she had finished the task he set her.

'How was it?' he asked, keeping his voice carefully neutral.

'I loved it,' she told him. 'What did you think I'd say?'

He laughed.

'The last time we talked you told me you weren't interested in anything apart from looking after a man. I'm glad you changed your mind.'

'Why,' she asked. 'Have you found another girl?'

'No,' Richard said, 'I've got something better than that.'

'What?'

'I've found you a job on *Campaign*.'

The editor of the advertising magazine, Bob Davidson, had once done a brief stint on *Macho* as a layout man. It hadn't suited him. He was a Scottish presbyterian and his puritan upbringing was at odds with a girlie magazine. At the end of six months he had handed in his notice. Richard talked him into staying on another three months at an inflated salary. Their arrangement was simple. He was free to look for another job and Richard was able to use the time to search for his replacement.

A replacement was found for Bob Davidson in two weeks but Richard kept to his side of the bargain. He went on paying Bob's salary right to the end of three months. The money kept him afloat until he found a job on *Campaign* as a sub editor – tidying up the reporters' copy and organising the feature pages.

That was five years ago and Bob Davidson had risen since then to the job of editor, but he hadn't forgotten Richard. Or his debt to him. So when Richard asked him to give Frances a chance, he agreed. With reservations.

'She'll have to start at the bottom,' he said. 'We do take on trainees now and then but we don't pay them enough to live on. How does your friend feel about that?'

Richard told him money wasn't a problem.

'She's married to Sam Kurnitz.'

'Of Kurnitz and Greene?'

471

'The same one.'

'So why does she need to come and work for me? The agency's hot, it's making money. Why doesn't she go back to New York and play the rich married lady?'

Richard paused, wondering how much to tell his friend. Finally he said, 'Frances and Sam haven't been seeing eye to eye recently and she decided to spend some time apart from him over here. Does that answer your question?'

The tall Scotsman nodded.

'It will do,' he said. 'Can she use a typewriter?'

'I don't think so, but she can learn.'

'Then send her on a course and while you're about it, get her to do shorthand as well. It will come in handy when she goes out on stories.'

Four weeks later, her crash-course diploma from secretarial college in her bag, Frances turned up for her first day of work on *Campaign*.

The offices were next door to the Café Royale at the bottom of Regent Street. From their windows on the second floor she could see Eros and the traffic going around Piccadilly Circus, the department store across the road and Veeraswami's Indian restaurant bang next door to it.

It was a vista of London at its fastest and most cosmopolitan. The view looking inside was less exciting. The room Frances worked in was open-plan – open-plan utility, rather than open-plan modern. There were rows of shabby metal desks lined up on a moth-eaten grey carpet and the other reporters showed their respect for the floor covering by tossing press releases and screwed up balls of discarded paper all over it.

On every desk was an old-fashioned manual typewriter – nothing like the smart electric model Frances had learned on in secretarial college. Frances was given a wire in-tray piled with press releases. They weren't stories but announcements of new appointments in various ad agencies. She had to arrange the hirings in the form of a list under several separate headings – depending on what the jobs involved. In some cases where the company had failed to include the person's age or previous job, she had to make a phone call and find out these details. As a job, it was small, but it was a start.

For the first three days Frances didn't meet the editor. Her focus and everybody else's was on the news editor who appeared to run the show.

A tall, skinny young man in jeans and a threadbare sweater, he sat in the middle of the room behind his desk and shouted orders in between taking phone calls. There were six other reporters apart from her. Between them they handled all the work of the magazine. From Monday to Wednesday they dug out news items by ringing round their contacts in the advertising agencies, and occasionally going out to lunch or drinks. Thursdays and Fridays, when the magazine had gone to bed, they wrote feature articles for next week's edition. Everyone there was younger than Frances and they were all overworked to the point of fatigue, but she had never in her life met a happier bunch of people.

Most lunchtimes they all grouped together in one of the pubs in nearby Soho and right from the start, she was included. Nobody remarked on her expensive clothes, but after a couple of days she took to coming into the office in jeans and a sweatshirt and she stopped bothering with lipstick. She had never gone to college but she imagined this was what it felt like to be a student.

On her third week, when one of the other reporters was off sick, she was sent out on her first story. She made a complete hash of it. The man she went to interview was rumoured to have lost a million pound account. Frances was instructed to verify the story one way or the other and come back to the office the moment she had her answer. She arrived back at the office two hours late, flushed from a heavy lunch.

'What kept you?' demanded the news editor. 'You know we go to press tonight and there's no time to spare.'

Frances shuffled her feet and looked embarrassed.

'The guy knew my husband back in New York. He wanted to talk about mutual friends over lunch and I thought it would be rude to say no.'

The news chief, Bill, sighed and tried to look patient.

'Did you find out about the million pounds he's meant to have lost?'

Again she looked worried.

'He didn't want to talk about it,' she said. 'And I felt because we were friends in a way, I shouldn't push it.'

Bill scowled and despite the fact that he was younger than her and considerably poorer, Frances began to get alarmed.

'Have I done something wrong?' she stammered. 'I thought we were meant to cultivate contacts and honestly because of my husband and everything, I thought he could be valuable to *Campaign*.'

'Explain to me how this guy could be valuable,' Bill asked her. 'He buys you lunch, wastes your time on press day and refuses to say a word. What's so precious about that? My cleaning woman could have told you more – and she wouldn't have taken so long about it either.'

Frances trailed back to her desk. She had got her chance to be a reporter and she'd muffed it. They'd probably keep her typing the appointments page for another nine months at this rate. She gazed hopelessly at the stiff old typewriter. She wasn't a rich man's slave any longer. She was a slave to this rickety old machine.

She brushed away the tears at the corners of her eyes and went on with her work.

At four-thirty, an hour before the magazine went to bed, she had an idea. Cautiously she got up and wandered over to the news desk.

'Bill,' she asked uncertainly, 'have you got a moment?'

He looked up distractedly.

'Whatever it is, make it fast. The front page is falling down round my ears and I've got to cobble up something, or get Charlie Saatchi to cobble up something if he's in a good mood.'

Frances screwed her courage up.

'You know I said earlier that Frank Thompson, the guy who lost a million, didn't want to talk. Well there's a reason for that. You see, he's setting up his own agency. And the million pounds is his first account.'

Bill took his glasses off and looked at her with something approaching wonder.

'Why didn't you tell me this before instead of snowing me with all that shit about him being a good friend of your husband?'

'Maybe I got my priorities wrong,' she said. 'I only started in the job a couple of weeks ago. I wasn't quite sure how it worked.'

The news editor ignored her excuses and got down to business.

'You say Thompson's setting up on his own? Has he registered the company yet? Does it have a name? How many partners has he got? And what about premises?'

Frances looked at her watch. It was getting on for five. In half an hour the edition would be away.

'Why don't you let me write what I've got?' she asked. 'You can knock it into shape afterwards. It could be quicker than talking about it.'

The news chief turned her round and pushed her towards her desk.

'Get a move on,' he said. 'We haven't got all day.'

The story ran on page one the next morning. It was the main item, and underneath the headline in small type was her name. Frances Buckingham. She didn't imagine for a moment that using her maiden name would fool Frank Thompson. It didn't. Two days later she got a letter from him. It was the sort of letter a headmaster would give to a naughty schoolgirl, listing a catalogue of her crimes ranging from betrayal to attempted seduction and it terrified her. When the editor sees this, she thought, I'll be for the sack. They won't want to employ anybody who offends an important man like Frank.

She showed it to Bill on the news desk and to her astonishment he roared with laughter.

'Miserable bastard,' he said. 'Anyone would think you'd stolen the crown jewels.'

'I did something nearly as bad – I got the man pushed out of his job. When Frank's agency heard he was setting up on his own, they turned him off the premises.'

Bill looked at Frances's ashen face and put an arm round her.

'Don't be a goose,' he said. 'Your precious Frank was going to leave anyway. You just hurried him up a bit. Anyway I don't see what he's got to gripe about. He's got his own consultancy, a million pounds' worth of business and a bloody great puff on page one of *Campaign* telling the world about it. I wouldn't be surprised if a lot of other accounts don't come his way as a result of it. If I were you I'd write back and ask him for a bottle of champagne. It's the least you can expect.'

Frances didn't do it, of course. She didn't have the nerve. But the experience did make her think. She'd got her name on page one of the magazine she worked for and she had made an enemy. She didn't know which mattered more.

After her first by-line things improved. She didn't have to type out all the job moves any more. Now they were shared round all the reporting staff and Frances was given a beat of her own.

Her job was to look after four small agencies. They were little more than consultancies but she made the most of them. Every time any of them won a new account she would write reams about it and see it reduced in the magazine to two small paragraphs on page ten. She knew she couldn't expect any better. The businesses she reported on were pinpricks compared to J. Walter Thompson or Young and Rubicam, but she kept at it.

'Rudd Brothers win gymshoes account,' she would write boldly, or 'The Joe Anderson Partnership shortlisted for dogfood.' Surprisingly, she cared if Joe Anderson picked up his fifty thousand pounds' worth of petfood for she liked Joe, and all the other small time admen whose fortunes she charted. They didn't patronise her the way the high flyers did. Frank Thompson might write pompous letters to her but the guys she knew bought her a drink in their locals after the office and thanked her nicely for the stories she wrote about them.

She started to learn from her new friends. When Sam talked to her about advertising she had tuned out because she was convinced what he was saying was beyond her grasp. Now she knew it wasn't, not if she concentrated and asked questions and she asked questions all the time. She didn't have to impress any of the men. She wasn't their wife or even their date. She was a junior reporter on a trade paper.

It was her job to understand what they were saying. Over pints of beer and sandwich lunches she got to know what made the business tick. She found out how agencies bought air time on television and she became quite fascinated when she discovered that people didn't just use their clients' money to buy up pages of magazines or miles of poster sites. This kind of space had to be haggled for. Other agencies with more clout wanted the same space and deals were struck under the table.

Of course Frances wanted to write about it all for *Campaign* and she encountered a curious silence. It was as if one day she had a group of new friends and the next she had been sent to Coventry. None of her phone calls was answered, and when she finally got hold of one of their secretaries, she discovered that everyone was out at a meeting.

She took her problem to the news editor. 'Nobody wants to talk to me any more,' she wailed. 'What have I done wrong?'

Bill looked at her sourly.

'Just about everything,' he told her.

Then he sat her down and explained.

'Look,' he said, 'there was nothing the matter with getting close to your agencies. That's what you were meant to do. What you weren't expected to do was to treat them like long-lost family.'

Frances shook her head.

'I'm not with you.'

Bill regarded the girl sitting in front of him closely and he felt despair settle over him. In the beginning he thought she had the makings of a reporter. The way she eventually got to grips with the Frank Thompson story showed promise, but he should have known better than to take her seriously. When you took away the gloss and the nice accent all she was was just another little girl. She'd be better off at home, he thought, cooking some man's dinner. Then he remembered what his chief had told him.

'Taking on Frances was payment for an old favour.' It must have been a bloody big favour, he thought. And it's landed me with a bloody big problem. What on earth do I do with this layabout?

Frances must have seen something in his expression, for she interrupted before he could reply to her.

'I know you're fed up with me,' she said in a small voice. 'And honestly I don't blame you. I don't think I'm really cut out for this.'

The news editor looked at her with the beginnings of sympathy. He had fallen on his face just like Frances five years before on a small local paper and like her he had apologised for it. It had gained him one final chance and he felt Frances deserved the same charity.

'I'm going to give you four more agencies to look after,' he told her, 'and another month to prove yourself. After that you're out. Do you understand?'

She nodded miserably and got up to go.

Bill pushed her back into her seat.

'I haven't finished with you yet,' he said. 'Before I let you loose on any more advertising contacts, there are a couple of things you ought to know. First, whatever you may think, none of these men who buy you drinks and sandwiches really trusts you. They may be charming to you. But that's because you're in a position to give them publicity. Wait until you write something bad about them, and then see how friendly they are.'

He paused.

'Now, if you bear in mind the fact that these men deep down don't like you, you might start to understand why four agencies suddenly went dead on you.'

Frances searched her mind for some of the conversations she had had with her erstwhile buddies. They had parted with a lot of trade secrets over the pints of beer, dirty secrets they didn't want to hear repeated and she had wanted to write about them.

'It still doesn't make sense,' she said. 'Why would these men who don't really trust me tell me all their dirt, and then go mad when I say I want to put it in the paper?'

Bill wondered why he had persevered with Frances.

'If you stay on this paper,' he told her, 'an awful lot of men are going to tell you things they could regret. You're pretty enough for Christ's sake, that's one of the reasons I took you on. But let me give you a tip. Next time somebody parts with a secret, don't look too impressed. Don't jump up and down and say you're going to use it in the paper. Just keep it under your hat and pretend it doesn't matter.

'It does matter, of course, and you're going to have to learn how to use some of the dirt you collect. But for the time being, remember everything your contacts tell you and tell me about it. Then we'll take it from there.'

The knowledge of what she had to do made Frances miserable for days. It was so cloak and dagger, like the old spy movies she used to watch on television. She was being paid to chat up a lot of businessmen and betray everything they told her.

But one thing kept her going. The memory of her very first story. She had betrayed Frank Thompson and it hadn't done him any harm. It had done them both a lot of good. It occurred to her that some of her contacts in advertising made a lot of fuss about nothing. After all, these precious secrets they went on about weren't a matter of life and death, they were all about business. A big bit of business was on the loose and they wanted a shot at it. If she put that in the paper, it wasn't going to ruin anyone. They'd still get a shot at it, as long as she didn't let on where the information came from. Frances thought about some of the other things she'd heard. The crooked television deals, the stolen accounts, the creative genius who was freelancing on the side.

All these things, if she printed them could hurt somebody and the person they could hurt most was the person who told her the story.

The solution was so simple, that when it came to her she wondered why she didn't think of it before. She could use anything she heard as long as she kept mum about where she'd got it.

She told Bill about her discovery and he nodded sagely. 'You're getting the hang of it,' he said. 'But I want you to remember one more thing. You're not Mata Hari. Everyone who talks to you knows damn well you're a reporter on this magazine, and what they're saying could end up in print. So stop feeling so damn guilty. You're not stealing anything and you're not betraying anyone who can't look after themselves.'

For the next few weeks Frances asked questions and listened hard. She told her news editor everything she had gleaned. Some of the information she gave him appeared in the magazine under her by-line and to her surprise there were no come-backs. Nobody wrote her an irate letter or complained about her behind her back because she protected the people who told her things. One or two of her contacts actually admired what she had written. And she didn't have the heart to tell them she hadn't done the stories at all. Bill had organised her tip-offs onto the news pages.

One day Frances discovered one of the other reporters working on a story that had originated from her. One of the top agencies was losing a huge account and the girl on the next desk to her was ringing around and putting a list together of who was going to compete for the business.

Frances went straight up to Bill.

'What's Patsy doing working on my story?' she demanded.

The news editor grinned broadly and leaned back in his chair.

'So you finally decided you want to stay here and be a reporter?'

'You bet I do, but you haven't answered my question. Why did you put someone else to work on the information I brought in?'

Bill looked Frances up and down.

'To make you angry enough to do something about it. I was getting sick and tired of writing up your stuff and seeing you sit back and let me get away with it. You're bringing in some decent yarns, it's about time you took responsibility for them yourself.'

Frances marched across to Patsy's desk and took hold of the typewritten sheets of information Bill had given her.

'Hands off,' she told her. 'That's my story and I'm going to write it.'

She pulled her weight after that. She wasn't the best reporter the magazine had but she was the hardest working one. There was nothing she wouldn't tackle. She went to marketing conferences, media workshops, creative jamborees, and no matter how boring the subject was, she threw herself into it as if she was covering the Olympic Games.

She was beginning to discover that writing about advertising was a kind of game with its own rules. If she wanted information, there were two ways of getting it. She could flutter her eyelashes and buy a round of drinks and people told her things or she could trade. It was the trading that fascinated her. It started with a piece of information. It could be something as big as a takeover bid, but usually it was the news that a juicy piece of business was up for grabs. Everybody stood to benefit from a story like that for it was the way most ad agencies won new business.

When Frances was new on the magazine she used to part with information like that. She'd drop it in over lunch as a sort of payment for being taken out. Then she got wise. She realised that this kind of story was too valuable to be tossed away over the *hors d'oeuvres*. She could use it to get more stories.

She first stumbled across trading when the creative director of McCann Erickson took her out to lunch. She had heard on the grapevine that a big toy account was on the move that week but she didn't know which one. She was sure the McCann's man knew, but when she asked him, she drew a blank. She tried prodding him to no avail. Finally in desperation she said, 'I was going to talk about a two million account I know is looking around, but I've changed my mind. You're not levelling with me, so I don't see why I should tell you everything I know.'

The effect was magical. The McCann's man lowered his voice and looked around him.

'If I come clean about the toy account,' he said, 'will you tell me about the two million?'

Frances was in business, and she was shameless about it.

She plied everyone she saw with her snippets of gossip and a lot of people told her to get lost but she lived with it. The men who played ball gave her enough valuable information to keep her busy.

Frances spent every free lunch hour and most of her evenings seeing her contacts. She loved industry gossip, because she loved seeing her name on the front page of *Campaign*. After eight months on the magazine, she discovered she had power. When she did something, people sat up and paid attention. At industry dinners when she opened her mouth, people listened and she realised she was valued at last. It was a different sensation to being needed.

Sam had needed her to keep his home in order. To look after him and to support him. Frances thought at the time it was enough to be needed like that, and now she knew it wasn't. She had become a person in her own right.

Richard was the first person to notice the change in her. They had fallen into the habit of seeing each other once a week. She knew him better than to expect any kind of permanent commitment, and all she was up to right now was a friendship with no complications, which Richard provided.

He knew she had changed when they stopped going to bed together. In a way he had taken that part of their relationship for granted because Frances had started it again. So when she put an end to it, he wanted to know why. It was tough getting it out of her. Since she had started working she had withdrawn into herself a little. Now she no longer confided everything. When Sam called her she often didn't mention it for days and when she did, she didn't always tell Richard what Sam had called for.

It was as if her hard-won independence had somehow

isolated her from the world. Frances existed now in her own bubble of privacy, and not sharing her body was part of that.

'It doesn't mean I don't like you any more,' she told Richard after he had pressed her. 'If anything I like you more than I ever did before. But liking isn't enough. When I sleep with a man I want better than that.'

He didn't understand.

'Do you want to move in? There's nobody else around, so you can if you want.'

Frances laughed and shook her head.

'I've got my own house now, and I like it that way. If we loved each other, it would be different, but that was over for us a long time ago.'

Richard looked beaten.

'Then what do you want of me?'

For a moment Frances felt compassion for this boy of a man. Then she reminded herself how he had cheated on her before, betrayed her trust, and she knew she owed him nothing more.

'All I want of you,' she said, 'is what you're capable of giving. Your company. Your time. The odd back rub. I'm not looking to fall in love.'

Richard accepted what she had to say, with one reservation.

'I'll stay around for now,' he said, 'but don't expect me to wait around for ever for you to get over Sam.'

Frances thought about it for days afterwards, for she had imagined she was cured. She certainly had no intention of returning to her husband and when he called her, as he did every so often, she avoided talking about the future. She was happy with her life in London, she told him. She was growing up at last. Finding herself.

'New York is lonely without you,' Sam said.

'How can it be?' Frances replied. 'You have your work. You have Louise.'

'No I don't,' he laughed. 'At least I don't have Louise. She works out of Europe as well you know.' He sighed. 'It seems both the women I love insist on living on the other side of the world.'

I'm glad she's in London, thought Frances. You can love her all you like. As long as she's tied to Europe, I don't give a damn.

Then one day a press release landed on Frances's desk and her whole world changed. The typed statement came from Kurnitz Tragos and Greene. It was a simple announcement.

'Louise Tragos, Chief Operating Officer of KTG is stepping down to return to New York. Her place will be taken by Nigel Farquharson, the agency's Managing Director. Miss Tragos will take up a newly created position with the parent company in Madison Avenue.'

A thousand dirty jokes came flooding into Frances's mind, all centring around the phrase 'newly created position'. I bet I know what she has in mind, thought Frances darkly. And when she's finished demonstrating it in bed, she'll be creating all sorts of other precedents. Like moving in. Getting married. The notion made her feel queasy. She could just accept losing her husband as long as there was nobody else to take her place. But Louise Tragos sneaking in behind her back. That was too much.

She had met the Greek girl just twice in her life. Once when she'd just met Sam and once when they were married. The second time stuck in her mind. Irritating her like a sore place. Somehow Louise had managed to make her feel like a mousy little housewife. It wasn't anything she said, but it was her attitude. Patronising and dismissive. As if coming from the wrong side of the tracks was some kind of virtue in New York. Frances had been made to feel like the outcast. The irony of it made her smile.

So Louise is going back to New York, she thought,

to take possession of my husband. A notion suddenly occurred to her.

I don't have to let her get away with it. The fact that she had any say in the matter came as a surprise to her, since throughout this affair she had stood by helplessly and let it happen. Louise was tougher than her. Louise had a big career. Louise was somehow more worthy of Sam. What could she do?

Now Frances thought, that's nonsense. Louise isn't anything I'm not, and if I want to, there's plenty I can do. For a start, I could go back to New York and when I get there, I could put up a fight.

I lost because I sat on the sidelines, she reasoned, while Louise was right at the centre of Sam's life. I won't let that happen again. I might not work for Sam but I can work in his business. With my experience there's bound to be a reporting job for me somewhere. She thought about the trade press in New York. There was *Ad Age*, *Forbes*, *The Gallagher Report*, *The Buzz*. Her mind centred on the last one.

The Buzz, a scandal sheet, was on the lookout for a reporter. Somebody on *Ad Age* had told Frances only last week and because she had had no intention of returning to America, she didn't pick up on it. She put in a call to her friend on *Ad Age*. If the job was still going, she wanted it. And she wanted it fast.

49

Louise had been home twelve days and already she felt different. London had been stimulating, there was no doubt about that, but she had been a big fish there. A big fish in a small pond.

Now she was back where it mattered. New York City, where the sharks had sharper teeth and tougher hides. Where the prizes were bigger. In New York you could shoot for the moon and every so often you got it. That's what she was here for. To shoot for the moon.

Kurnitz Tragos and Greene. Louise said it out loud, savouring the words. The agency had borne her name for just over a year now and she still couldn't get over the excitement of it. Was it really ten years ago, she wondered, that I walked these streets looking up at the fancy agency names. Young and Rubicam, Doyle Dane Bernbach, Acker and Stein. They were like another country to a kid from the Bronx. A country where only the privileged could walk. The privileged and the lucky.

Brian Elder came into her mind. Handsome, Waspy Brian Elder, the man with an itch that only she could satisfy. Louise remembered the things he used to make her do when they were alone. He might have been privileged, she decided, but I was the one who got lucky.

Now she was on top of the heap – or almost on top of the heap. She was a partner in an up-and-coming business. A business with potential, but a business that was yet to arrive. It's Sam's principles, Louise decided, that stop us from getting there. And it wasn't just the tobacco thing either. Every aspect of the agency was a casualty of his dreams.

Sam would tolerate only the best artwork, so they paid over the odds where other agencies added to their bottom line. What if the print was slightly sub-standard she thought. Nobody noticed except the poseurs who wanted to win awards.

I wanted to win awards once too, she recalled. Angrily she pushed the thought to the back of her mind. I grew up since then, she told herself. I took on responsibilities.

Then there was Sam's distaste for certain types of business: washing powders, toothpaste, discount stores. The big earners which went on selling year in year out with the same kind of advertising. Sam didn't want the big earners if he couldn't contribute something.

'They don't want your contribution,' Louise would tell him. 'They spend millions on research and that's what they run in their ads. The research. Why can't you just let them get on with it and take the money? Other agencies do.'

Sam was adamant.

'We're not other agencies. We have a reputation for fine creative work. Innovation. That kind of business would destroy it.'

Reputations are for college kids, thought Louise. College kids and dreamers. Businessmen, serious businessmen, thought about the bottom line. But she kept this opinion to herself. She had a lifetime ahead of her to influence Sam, to change his course, and she would do it slowly, insidiously, so he didn't even notice it was happening. She considered the evening ahead of her.

They were going to spend it quietly, just the two of them, in her apartment. Since she had got back they had travelled back and forth across town, commuting between their homes. On week nights she stayed with Sam because he was nearer to the office. Over the weekend he moved in with her. Neither arrangement was ideal. Sam's apartment had too many ghosts. He and Frances had been separated for a year now, yet every time she walked in the door Louise could feel her presence. The furniture, the awful modern pictures, even the china and the glass bore her stamp. This woman, this insignificant little dormouse, had pushed her personality over every square inch of Sam's space, and try as she might Louise was unable to relax there.

No, she couldn't live with Sam in his apartment, but neither could he live with her in hers. For it wasn't a home in the conventional sense. It was a pad for a bachelor. The long white living-room with its view over New York was designed with cocktail parties in mind. Parties and seduction. The area where the dining-room should have been was converted into a study and the closets in the bedroom were for one only. What we need to do, she decided, is to sell both our leases and move on to somewhere new. On our combined salaries, she thought, we could probably afford something in Trump Tower. Something ritzy and glamorous. Then she thought about Frances. I wonder how much alimony she'll demand?

Louise changed into lounging pyjamas by Donna Karan. It was the sort of outfit that looked as if she hadn't bothered, yet at the same time was perfect. The shirt that tucked into the pants could never come adrift the way shirts are apt to, because the shirt wasn't a shirt at all. It was a bodysuit and fitted snugly under the crotch with pop studs, and the pants were cut, so artfully, so cleverly, that Louise's size twelve bottom looked as lean as a boy's.

She ran a hand through her wild black hair so that it fell casually over her shoulders. She may be organised inside her head, but she didn't want Sam to know how organised.

He arrived late from a meeting in Minnesota and Louise was glad she had had time on her own before he got there. Tonight she was going to talk about the future. Her future. Their future together.

For an hour or so they talked about the business. It was

something they did more and more nowadays. They were, after all, partners as well as lovers, and the knowledge of just how closely their lives were intertwined made Louise feel secure. She knew just how much Sam earned, how much he had in the bank, which insurance policies he held. She didn't own him exactly but she was getting close.

She decided to press her advantage.

'We can't go on living like this,' she said.

Sam looked at her, waiting for what was going to come next. He had been half expecting this conversation, though she couldn't have chosen a worse time.

'Tell me what's on your mind,' he said.

So Louise told him, going into some detail about how impractical it was for them to live in two homes.

'There's not nearly enough room for you here,' she said. 'And your apartment's too full of Frances for me. I could never be happy living with you there.'

Sam was tempted not to tell her about his wife's imminent arrival. Then he thought the hell with it, she's bound to find out sooner or later.

'Any time now,' he said with a faint smile, 'my apartment's going to be too full of Frances for you to move in even if you wanted to. She's coming back to New York.'

The import of what he was saying hit Louise like a blow, catching her momentarily off balance.

'Is this your idea of a joke?' she asked, 'because if it is, it's in very poor taste.'

Sam rubbed his hands across his eyes in an attempt to wipe away the weariness he felt.

'I'm not making fun of you,' he told her seriously. 'Frances really is coming back. She's got a job with an advertising magazine. She called me and told me so a couple of days ago.'

'Then why didn't you say anything about it to me?' The smiling, composed Louise that greeted Sam when he came in was changing now. She sounded petulant and for the life of him, he couldn't blame her.

'I didn't raise the subject, because I didn't know how to deal with it. I still don't.'

'You're not going to just let her walk back into your life, are you? The woman deserted you nearly a year ago. She can't really expect everything to be the same now. Everyone changes. Everyone and everything.'

Sam hadn't anticipated Louise would be so harsh. It was tough on her, but she might have seen it from his point of view, or from Frances's.

'She is my wife you know – and anyway she didn't desert me. She went to England to sort her feelings out.'

'Oh, so we're talking about feelings now are we? Since when did you care about how Frances felt, or has something changed?'

Sam went over to where she kept the drinks and poured himself a stiff Scotch. In an effort to calm himself he swallowed half of it. Then he turned round to face her.

'Nothing has changed,' he said levelly. 'I had a difficult marriage which seems to be going through its final death throes. In a way what's happening is as painful for me as it is for Frances, but I can't just put an end to it. Not without hearing Frances out. It wouldn't be fair.'

Louise was getting back her cool now and as she did she set her jaw and started to smooth her hair behind her ears. Sam had seen her collect herself like this in client meetings and it made him feel uneasy. As if he wasn't the man who loved her, but somebody to be humoured and manipulated.

'I know it's difficult for you,' Louise said, 'but in the long run it's kinder to be honest. If you told Frances it was over and you wanted a divorce, it would be a blow, but at least she'd know where she stood. She could get on with her life. If you let her move back, you'll be prolonging the agony.'

Sam took a breath.

'You don't know Frances, and why should you? Laying it on the line like that would be the best way to destroy her. She's had a rough ride these past few years and she's only just coming to terms with it. She couldn't cope with me turning her out of her own home and I wouldn't do it to her.'

Louise looked at Sam, frowning. He noticed for the first time how masculine she seemed. Even when she was sad, Frances had some kind of warmth, and he hated himself for this small disloyalty.

'What are your plans?' Louise asked coldly. 'Do you intend to go on living with your wife while she's in New York or will you do the decent thing and move in with me?'

She was beginning to make him feel angry.

'You just told me your apartment was too small for the two of us. Or has it magically grown an extra wing now my wife is coming home?' Sam said.

Louise put down her glass of wine and walked up to where he was standing. Then she hit him across the face. It was a painful stinging blow. And she meant it to hurt.

'If that's how you feel,' she said, 'why don't you pick up your suits and leave now? There's nothing to keep you here.'

She turned on her heel and walked out, slamming the door behind her.

For a moment Sam stood there rooted to the spot, then the reality of the situation came through to him and he felt like a heel. It wasn't Louise's fault that Frances was coming home and it wasn't her responsibility either. It was an impossible situation and he hadn't made it any easier by yelling.

Sam's hand went up to the place on his face where Louise had hit him and he could feel the beginnings of a bruise.

'Louise,' he called through the closed door, 'come out from where you're hiding and we'll talk about it.'

There was no answer. He sighed heavily and made his way through to the bedroom where he found her crumpled up on the bed. She was lying face down with her black hair strewn all around her and he was put in mind of a rag doll.

He took her gently by the shoulders and pulled her up into a sitting position. He could see from her face that she had been crying.

'I'm sorry,' he said, kissing the places where the tears had been. 'I love you so much. I didn't want to hurt you. I'd do anything not to hurt you.'

'Anything but leave your wife.' The words came out in a muffled sob and Sam felt his heart turn over.

'I am leaving my wife,' he said desperately. 'It's just going to take a bit longer than I thought. That's all.'

'How long is a bit longer? A week? A month? A lifetime?'

Sam folded Louise in his arms, holding her close and stroking her hair.

'It won't be a week,' he told her, 'but it won't be a lifetime either. I've been married to Frances for five years now. There's a dead baby between us, and a couple of other things I can't go into. If I let go of her now, I'd never be able to live with myself. You have to understand that, Louise. You have to let me bury this marriage in my own time.'

She pulled away from him and looked into his face, willing herself to believe him.

'Do what you have to do,' she told him. 'As long as you love me, I'll try to be patient.'

50

It was strange being back home, and for Frances the apartment on 79th Street was home because she had made it so. In all the other places she had lived she had been a transient, just passing through. When Sam brought her here and married her it had been for ever.

She wondered if he felt that way this time round. He had given nothing away at the airport when he came to meet her. As far as he was concerned nothing had changed, and he had brought her back to unpack while he finished the day at the office.

Frances sat on the bed and looked at her cases. It would be so easy, she thought. All I have to do is hang up my dresses in the closet, tuck my nightie under the pillow, go out to the supermarket and make like a wife. Wasn't that what Sam expected her to do? She sighed. She'd changed too much since she had been away to go for the soft option any more. If she was going to save her marriage there would have to be some adjustments.

She got to her feet, went over to where her cases stood and pulled them out into the hallway and into the next room. It was the second bedroom. The small room with twin beds they kept for visitors. That's what I am now, she thought. A visitor. And that's the way I'm going to stay until Louise is out of the picture.

Half the problem, Frances realised, was that she had turned a blind eye to the existence of the Greek girl, as if pretending she wasn't there would somehow make her vanish. So now I stop pretending, Frances decided. My husband has a mistress. That's real. There's no point in pussy-footing around it. Only I don't have to go along with it. If Sam wants to screw Louise on his nights off, he's welcome to her, but I'm not going to take what's left over after she's finished with him. Frances had come to that decision while she was in London, but now she was standing in her home again, now she was actually unpacking in the spare bedroom she felt less brave. It was easy to make promises to yourself. Carrying them out was the hard bit. Then she smiled and relaxed. I gave up drinking didn't I? I found a job. I made something of my life. If I can do all that, I can get my husband back too.

When she had unpacked, she took a shower and made herself a cup of tea, then she started to prowl around the apartment. Nothing had changed. The pictures were all in the same places. None of the chairs had been moved. Even the *Vogue*s she had collected were still neatly stacked exactly where she had left them, and suddenly Frances realised that Sam had hardly used the apartment since she'd been in London. She had visions of her husband haunting the late night deli after the office or inviting himself to whichever friend would have him for the evening.

She had got him so used to being married and looked after that he had put his life on hold until she had got back. If Louise had been around it might have been different, but she wasn't, Frances consoled herself. So Sam hadn't come to need her.

Frances pulled herself up sharply. Sam needed Louise all right, but he didn't depend on her for everything. While that situation lasted, she still had a chance.

Sam was bemused at the new arrangements. He had offered her his bed and his body out of charity. Pity almost. Frances had taken his charity and thrown it back in his face. He was so surprised he found himself pleading with her.

'It's not sensible to camp out in the spare room,' he told her. 'It's lonely for me. Besides, if any of our friends find out, they will think there's something wrong with our marriage.'

Frances was immovable.

'There *is* something wrong with our marriage,' she said firmly. 'And until you put it right, I'm staying where I am.'

She wouldn't discuss it any further.

Sam had expected her to try and put things right. What he hadn't been prepared for was that she would demand it. This can't be Frances, he thought. It just isn't her style. But what was her style? When he had met her she had looked like Leah, his first wife. Girlish and vulnerable.

She had acted like Leah too until everything went wrong and she started to drink. He remembered the fat frowsy woman she used to be. She had needed him then. There was no way that Frances would have settled for the spare bed.

It occurred to him there might have been someone else. London had transformed her. It wasn't just that she had lost weight. There was a tautness he had never seen before, a kind of energy as if someone had lit the fires inside her, and it made him angry. Frances was his wife. If anyone was going to bring her back to life it was going to be him.

He was tempted to ask her what had happened while she was away but he kept his counsel. Once he started asking questions, it would throw the whole of their lives open to debate, and he wasn't ready for that yet. His plan, if he had a plan, was to sit out the end of their marriage and give it a decent burial. When it was over there would be confessions and recriminations. Until then it was safer to play the waiting game.

After a couple of weeks, Sam began to realise that he was the one who was waiting. Frances was doing nothing of the kind. She had started her new job and it seemed be keeping her busy. The magazine she was working for had hired her to run their gossip column and she was out till all hours seeing contacts around town and going to industry jamborees. The fact that she was having fun irritated Sam. He had expected dinner on the table, if not every night, at least once or twice a week.

Things may not be the way they were, but they were still married, damn it. She might try behaving like a wife.

Once or twice he told her so but it didn't seem to make any impression. Frances had lost her capacity for feeling guilt. She loved her job and the world she was being sucked into, the world of Madison Avenue. Before she joined it she thought it belonged to the likes of Louise Tragos and men like her husband. Now she knew better. The communications business was open to all-comers as long as they had something to offer. She didn't have a million-dollar account in her pocket, nor did she have the talent to write a world-beating advertising campaign. But she was bright and articulate, and she had found her niche. She commentated, and the business with its love of gossip and communication needed people like her.

Sam noticed his wife's growing confidence and it made him uneasy. So uneasy that he started complaining about her to Louise.

'She's behaving like a college kid home for the holidays,' he would say on the nights they saw each other. Since Frances no longer cared that he saw Louise he saw her more often. Sometimes he didn't even bother to come home. On those nights they would have dinner somewhere discreet, then they would go back to Louise's apartment and make love. It was the love-making that saved Sam. When he took Louise in his arms all the doubts and fears he had about his life seemed to melt away. He forgot about his wife, his business, his responsibilities.

He clung to her like a drunk clings to his last bottle and Louise didn't fail him. But when they got out of bed it was different. At least for Louise it was different. For she had more on her mind than Sam and his marriage. She had the agency to worry about. Her new responsibilities. And they were cutting her in half.

Her private self cared only for Sam and the life they were planning together, but the logical part of her, the ambitious part, pulled her in the opposite direction. Louise and her lover did not share the same approach to business.

She had known this the moment she had come back to New York and she thought that with patience and a little guile she could bring him round to her way of thinking. She had been wrong. Sam wanted to do good work. Louise wanted to make money. There seemed to be no middle ground.

Every time Louise tried to bring in a mail order account, Sam shouted her down with such force she thought he hated her.

'Coupons,' he would say disdainfully. 'They're for crass agencies. People with no reputation. Idiots.'

'But coupons make money,' Louise would protest. 'Isn't it worth getting our hands dirty once in a while if it makes our bottom line look better?'

'Never,' Sam would thunder. 'As long as I work here this agency doesn't touch coupons, washing powder or cigarettes. If you want to make money go work for someone else.'

Sometimes after these arguments they would go to their separate homes without speaking. Then one of them would weaken and ring the other, and they would meet and lose themselves in each other all over again. Until the next time.

In the end Louise confided her fears to Clay.

'Sam and I don't seem to be seeing eye to eye about the work,' she said. 'I don't know what to do about it any more.'

To her astonishment Clay understood.

'I've been having this problem with Sam for years,' he told her. 'Until you came along I kept quiet about wanting to make more money. He owned half the business and it didn't seem worth making waves. Now it's different.

'Look,' he told her, 'I'm going to level with you. I wasn't happy about having you in the business at first. I thought you'd be a liability, but you proved me wrong. You proved us both wrong. The way you handled the London operation showed me you were one hell of a smart lady. It also showed me that we needed you – not just in London, but here in New York.'

Louise looked him in the eye.

'I've seen the bottom line,' she said. 'We're making the same profits as we did last year. And that's not good enough. If we go on stagnating, we'll start to lose business.'

Clay lit a cigar.

'What do you think we should do?'

Louise thought about Sam and the last row they had. If they went on this way they were going to start hurting each other, and she didn't want that. Then she thought about the business and the loan she had taken out to buy her stake in it. She had guaranteed her apartment against it. That and everything else she owned. If the business went under, she went under. There was no choice.

'We're going to have to go on pushing Sam,' she said finally. 'If we both weigh in against him he'll have to see sense in the end, and if he doesn't do the logical thing, the right thing, then we'll have to talk again.'

Clay smiled and drew deeply on his cheroot.

'I knew I could count on you,' he said.

Towards the end of the summer, the agency lost one of its biggest accounts. White's Distillers, a small family concern, was taken over by one of the big conglomerates and the new marketing director announced he wanted a mainline agency to work on the business.

The loss deepened the disagreements within the agency and put Sam even more out on a limb. It also did something extra, it sparked off a whole new controversy about creative agencies. Lois Holland Callaway and Doyle Dane lined up behind Sam and his beliefs.

The press took the opposite stance and lined up behind White's. The issue was pulled into focus by the *New York Times*. On their main city spread they ran a page of Sam's best-known ads for White's. Opposite the work there was an interview with White's marketing genius. He damned Sam's efforts with faint praise.

'The creative community conferred awards on White's advertising,' he said, 'but were they deserved? Surely the acid test of all creative work rests in the sales figures. Sales of White's products were up, this can't be denied. But were they up enough? And was the rise due to Kurnitz's brilliance, or the excellence of the product?'

The White's man went on to stress that money should be spent not on good advertising, but on research. Only when the research was on target could the advertising start to make any impact and then it had to be based on research findings, not on creativity.

The day the *Times* came out with the report, Sam shut himself in his office and refused to talk to anybody. Then he went home early, a copy of the offending article tucked under his arm.

When he got in, he flung the paper on the dining-room table and started to work his way through a bottle of bourbon. Ten minutes later Frances let herself into the apartment. The moment she saw Sam's face, she knew what was wrong.

'I saw the piece in the office,' she said. 'For what it's worth, I think White's have got it all wrong.'

'What the hell do you know about it?' Sam exploded.

Frances didn't answer him. Instead she handed him a

copy of *The Buzz*. It was the new issue, out that day, and Sam flicked through it taking note of the items he hadn't seen in *Ad Age* or *The Gallagher Report*.

'It's a bright sheet you work on,' he commented. 'You managed to pick up three major moves nobody's got wind of yet.'

Frances looked impatient.

'I know all that,' she said. 'Two of them are my stories, but that's not what I want you to see. Keep on to the centre pages.'

But he'd got there already. Frances stood stock still, not daring to breathe until he'd finished reading. When he looked up she found her voice.

'Did you like it?' she asked.

Sam rubbed the side of his face.

'You didn't have to defend me like that,' he told her. 'I'm a big boy. I can take care of myself.'

Frances looked exasperated.

'I wasn't defending you. I was defending the advertising business. You're not the only creative genius in New York, Sam. There are quite a few in your class and once people like White's start putting down great ads, it's bad for everyone.'

Sam sighed and Frances noticed there were worry lines around his mouth that she hadn't seen before.

'I'm sorry,' he said. 'It's a great piece and I agree with every word of it. I just wish some of the characters I work with felt the way you do.'

Frances looked at him sharply.

'Don't they?' she asked.

Sam sighed. 'Not all the time.'

He motioned her to come and sit down and when she did he put his arm round her.

'Clay and Louise think my standards are too high, or rather they think they are unrealistic. They'd like me to sell out and start thinking of the bottom line.'

'You didn't say anything about it before. When did this all start happening?'

Sam put his head back, considering. He had never told Frances his problems before because he honestly didn't think she cared, but that was before he had seen her article. Now he told her what was bugging him, and in a way it was a kind of release.

In the past Sam had always confided in Louise, but in the past they had been on the same side. Now, in some subtle way, she had gone against him and Sam could see no end to it.

Frances broke into his thoughts.

'Will you do what Louise and Clay want,' she asked, 'or will you over-rule them?'

Sam laughed without humour.

'I can't do that,' he said. 'Together they hold the majority vote. No, what I plan to do is play for time. I'll take on a little mail order business, maybe I'll even agree to a washing powder. But it will be small beer – nothing big enough to tilt the balance of the agency.'

'What if something big comes along?' Frances asked. 'Something like Abner's business?'

'I don't know,' Sam said. 'I guess I'll face that one when it happens. At least I don't have to worry about Abner any more.'

'Because of what I did?'

He stroked her hair.

'Not because of you, though I have to say you were splendid. No, what finally put an end to the whole drama was Clay discovering what his wife was up to. Apparently Tiffany and Abner were having some kind of fling and Clay found out and hit the roof. He thinks he's put an end to it now, but obviously the idea of Abner as a client has lost a lot of its appeal.'

Frances remembered the lunch she had with Tiffany a week or so ago. Richard Gregory had told her about the affair in London but Tiffany wanted to talk about it, so Frances let her have her say and she realised that Tiffany, her girlfriend, had been at the bottom of the whole plot. She was the reason Abner wanted to put his business with Sam's agency.

As the realisation dawned Frances looked anew at the woman who had been her first friend in the city and she judged her.

She had always been dazzled by Tiffany: her clothes, the way she carried herself, her vast circle of friends, was something she aspired to. Now she knew she had been wrong all along. The woman sitting opposite her was a phoney, from her dyed hair to her lifted face. How come I never noticed before? she asked herself. We saw enough of each other. I even went to the same hairdresser as her.

She remembered what the hairdresser had done and she knew, even as she sat there, she had been taken for a fool. I was so unsure of myself, she thought, that I let this woman walk over me. Worse. I let her make me over. She looked into Tiffany's overpainted face with its arched, surprised-looking eyebrows and crimson mouth.

She doesn't feel a thing, Frances thought. No warmth. No concern for my feelings. She doesn't even care for her husband. All Tiffany wants is success, and to be on the top of the heap. She'd sell her soul for those things.

As if on cue, Tiffany started telling Frances how she was deceiving Clay. She went on in detail about the afternoons in hotel rooms and the lies she manufactured. Suddenly Frances knew she didn't want to listen to this woman any more. Tiffany had done her best to ruin her life and she'd nearly got away with it. This time she wasn't going to get a second chance.

She called the waiter over and asked for the bill and when her friend protested about how early it was, Frances invented an urgent reason to get back to her office. Then she got out as fast as she could.

They hadn't seen each other since then, and now as Sam was telling her about Clay putting an end to Tiffany's affair, Frances was tempted to bring him up to date on the matter. All she needed to say was, 'It's still going on. In hotel rooms all over the city.' Then she thought, what's the point? What do I gain by it? If Tiffany wants to go to hell, she can do it in her own way. I'm not going to help her.

She got up from the sofa and regarded her husband.

'Would you like me to get supper?' she asked. 'There's not much in the icebox, but I can rustle up a steak.'

'That would suit me fine,' Sam said and he watched her walk into the kitchen. He thought of other suppers they had eaten together here. Relaxed easy meals where they had talked of nothing in particular, and he realised he liked Frances and he had missed her.

Maybe we'll be the exception, he thought. Maybe we'll be the one couple who can be friends with each other after the divorce. We'll have to be discreet about it though. Louise would never understand.

51

Every now and then the advertising industry liked to congratulate itself. It did so by admiring its own work and giving awards to the advertisements the judges decided deserved it that year. In their way, Madison Avenue's bunfeasts could be compared to the Oscar ceremonies, but instead of taking place in a cinema, they were held in the ballroom of a plush hotel and everybody sat and ate dinner while the prizes were being given out.

That year Sam won a Clio award for his work on White's Distillers. It was something of a consolation prize, but it did much to save his face. The agency took a whole table for the dinner dance at the Plaza, but Frances wasn't on it. Louise accompanied him that night, and although a few eyebrows were raised, he had a good excuse. Louise was his partner at the agency. She had a perfect reason to be there.

He nearly got away with it. If Frances hadn't decided to turn up, he would have got through the evening without comment, but Frances had no intention of melting into the background. She was part of the business now, as much a part as Louise, and if her husband didn't want to escort her, then there were other men who would.

She accepted an invitation to the Clio awards from one of the creative directors of Doyle Dane Bernbach. He was handsome in the dishevelled fashion of the Eighties with a dark layer of designer stubble round his chin and a mass of dark blond hair. While everyone else that night wore their tuxedos in the traditional way, Milton Goldman, Frances's date, broke the rules. He teamed his dinner jacket and ruffled shirt with blue jeans and instead of looking silly, he looked original. As if the way he wore his monkey suit was the right way and everyone else was out of order.

Frances was pleased she had gone with Milton. He knew she was married, but he didn't make a big deal about it. As far as he was concerned she was an attractive woman and he was going to do his best to make sure she had a good party. Doyle Dane had taken three tables that night, and because of the agency's reputation they were the three best tables. Over on the other side of the dance floor, tucked in a corner was Sam's table. Frances couldn't even see it from where she was sitting and she thanked her lucky stars. She wouldn't have missed this party for the world and she was more than upset that Sam hadn't had the decency to take her, but she didn't want a fight. Her differences with her husband were a private matter to be argued over only in private. Tonight all she wanted to do was have fun.

The presentations took up a good part of the evening, taking place at the end of dinner just as coffee was served – before the dancing and the table hopping got underway.

Gerry Della Femina was giving out the prizes and Frances leaned back in her chair and gave him her full attention. In his day, Gerry had been one of the brightest creative talents in the city and his way with words had made him rich.

Frances reflected on her husband and the problems he was having with Clay and Louise. I hope he holds out, she thought. If he loses it will be a terrible waste.

She looked up and saw Sam come striding towards her. He was on his way to get his Clio and he had to walk past her to get to the top table. She felt embarrassed.

Milton Goldman was whispering something in her ear as Sam approached, a joke that was doing the rounds about Della Femina, and before she could stop herself she giggled. Sam was about a yard from her when it happened and the expression on his face told her everything. He was furious.

Good God, she thought, he probably imagines Milton is my lover and she wanted to stand up and tell him then and there that he was mistaken. It wasn't the way it seemed. But she couldn't, and afterwards it was too late.

Sam accepted his award with a stony face and without looking in Frances's direction again, marched back to his table. For the first time in a year, she wanted a drink. Really wanted one. I'll wait till the presentations are finished, she told herself. Then I'll ask for a brandy.

Half an hour later the speeches were all finished and the dancing started. She turned to Milton.

'Do you think I could have something to drink?' she asked.

The creative man seemed surprised.

'You haven't touched alcohol all night. Don't tell me the sight of your husband has driven you to the bottle.'

'How did you know I was on the bottle?' Frances snapped sharply. Too sharply.

Milton looked penitent.

'I was joking,' he said. 'I had no idea. Really.'

She smiled.

'It doesn't matter. Anyway it's better I don't start drinking again. I'll only make a fool of myself.'

He moved in and looked at her closely.

'You won't do anything of the sort. Not while you're with me.'

Then before she could reply, he stood up and pulled her to her feet.

'Come and dance,' he said.

Because it was an evening dress occasion, there was old-fashioned dancing: waltzes and foxtrots, and Milton, in spite of his unusual appearance, was surprisingly good at it. Frances guessed he was older than he looked, maybe thirty or even thirty-five, and she wondered if he would ask her out again and if he did, whether or not she would go.

The band slowed down into a waltz and Milton took

hold of her and pulled her close. If they had been dining in the ordinary way she would never have let him hold her like that. She hardly knew him. But this wasn't just any dinner. This was an industry jamboree where cuddling up to an attractive stranger was perfectly in order as long as it was on the dance floor.

For the second time that night she saw her husband. He was coming across the floor and Louise was nowhere in sight.

As she followed Sam's progress across the floor, she realised he was heading in her direction. She pulled away from her dancing partner feeling guilty. As if she had been caught doing something wrong. Then Sam tapped Milton on the shoulder and Frances knew she was in for trouble.

'Forgive me,' Sam said, 'but I think this dance belongs to me. My wife promised.'

Milton looked at Frances with a question in his eyes and for a moment she was tempted to deny her husband. Then she thought better of it. She had vowed to herself earlier that evening that her quarrel with Sam was a private one, so she smiled and disentangled herself.

She squeezed Milton's arm. 'I'll see you back at the table. I won't be long.'

'How do you know you won't be long?' Sam asked, taking his place on the dance floor. 'I might keep you here all evening.'

'I doubt it,' she said, 'not with Louise around.'

She suddenly became aware of how she was dressed. At home she wandered around in jeans and a sweatshirt and when Sam saw her going to the office in the mornings she was always in a trim little suit. But there was nothing workmanlike about her tonight. She was wearing one of the dresses she had bought in London. A Jean Muir in clinging silk jersey, long in the skirt and low in front. It made her feel vampy and with Milton she had been happy to feel that way. Now she merely felt self-conscious.

'Louise doesn't own me,' Sam said sharply. 'I'm free to dance with whoever I like.'

Frances looked at him from under her lashes.

'Even your wife,' she said.

She couldn't resist it, but as she said the words, she regretted them.

'I suppose you're trying to make me feel bad about bringing Louise tonight,' Sam said. 'In this situation what else could I do?'

Frances was irritated. It was bad enough that Sam was doing what he was doing, but to make excuses for it was too much.

'In this situation,' she said stiffly, 'you might have consulted me first. We're still married to each other you know.'

Sam scowled.

'So you finally noticed,' he said. 'I thought you were too busy with your toy boy to bother with a detail like that.'

Frances felt herself go hot with embarrassment. She lost her step and would have stumbled if Sam hadn't caught her round the waist and whirled her closer.

'He isn't my toy boy,' she protested. 'Apart from talking to him tonight I hardly know him – and he isn't a boy. He's more grown-up than he looks.'

'I'm sure he's just dying to prove that to you,' said Sam. 'If I hadn't cut in when I did, he would have proved it right here on the dance floor.' He paused for a moment and looked at her.

'It's the dress that's the problem. It's too tight and you shouldn't wear anything so low-cut.'

Now Frances was really angry.

'Who are you to say what I should or shouldn't wear,' she stormed. 'I bet you don't tell Louise where to go shopping. You wouldn't dare, would you?'

She noticed how hard Sam's face looked and when he spoke again his voice was low and deadly.

'Louise is nothing to do with it. I'm not married to Louise. I'm married to you and . . .'

He was about to go on when his attention was caught by something. Frances followed his gaze and saw Louise, the girl they were arguing about, standing on the edge of the dance floor. Frances had always imagined her to be tough and in control, but tonight she looked neither of those things. She seemed to have lost weight since they last met and it didn't suit her. She had scraped that lush black mane of hers into a twist at the back of her neck and Frances thought it made her look older, almost mannish.

'You might not be married to her,' said Frances, 'but I think you should go back and join her.' Then she added, 'She is your partner after all. Whatever that means.'

Before Sam could reply, she had slipped out of his arms and disappeared into the mêlée of dancing couples. Sam made his way slowly to where Louise was standing. Before she could speak he took her arm and guided her back to the table where they were sitting. When they got there he sat down heavily and poured himself a glass of wine.

'I tried to make her see reason,' he said to no-one in particular. 'But it was no good. Frances is incapable of seeing anyone's point of view but her own.'

'It's probably the young man she's with,' said Louise. 'I hear he's got quite a reputation with the girls. If you ask me, I think it's gone to her head.'

Sam turned round to the Greek girl, and for a moment she thought he was going to hit her.

'Nobody asked you,' he said.

On her way home in the taxi Louise tried to identify the emotions coursing through her. She felt first furious, then disappointed, and finally let down.

She had felt this way before in her life. When Sam first walked out on her it had been like this. She cast her mind back to a time she would rather forget. The time Brian

510

Elder plundered her body. She knew why she felt the way she did. She had been used: first by Brian, then by Sam, and now by Sam's wife.

How dare she walk into the awards dinner the way she had tonight? How dare Sam allow her to? Everyone there knew that Louise was his girl now. That soon, when the formality of his marriage was over, they would be together permanently. Though when Frances made her appearance in that indecent dress, the marriage didn't look like such a back number.

Louise recalled the look on the faces of the men sitting at their table. She had seen the same look on furtive little boys back in the Bronx. Sexy and lecherous and knowing. They all thought Sam was still sleeping with his wife, and they all knew Sam was sleeping with her. She had never been so humiliated in her life.

She told Sam what was on her mind before she walked out.

'I'll let you run home to your oversexed little wife,' she had said. 'You know you're just dying to. From the way you were dancing with her you obviously couldn't keep your hands off her.'

Now going home in the taxi she wished she hadn't said it. The evening had been a complete shambles as it was. She didn't have to add to the chaos. The taxi drew up outside her building and she paid off the driver and hurried down the canopied walkway.

Sam was standing just inside the door with the collar of his coat turned up and it was clear he hadn't seen her yet, for he was hunched over and troubled and his hands were clenched up inside his pockets.

Love and yearning welled up inside Louise, and with it forgiveness. She put her head down and pushed her way through the heavy glass door.

They didn't say very much to each other. They didn't have to. They had quarrelled too many times, and made

511

it up too many times for more explanations. They simply held on to each other, and when they came out of the embrace, they walked over to the elevator and went up to her apartment.

She made him a drink as she always did after they had been out. Bourbon and water. For herself she poured a glass of dry white wine, cold from the fridge, then she kicked off her shoes and threw herself onto the sofa.

They sat and talked about the evening, carefully avoiding any mention of Frances and by the time they made their way through to the bedroom, Louise was starting to warm up to Sam again.

She put her arms round him and started kissing his neck, behind his ears, then his hands were on her breasts and she found his mouth. She began to feel excited but it was a curious excitement. A stirring that had nothing to do with love. And suddenly she understood why. He had humiliated her earlier, in front of all their friends. Everyone in the business. And now her body demanded that he humiliate her again.

I can't do this to Sam, Louise thought desperately. He knows nothing about this part of me. He could hate me for it. But her body wasn't listening.

She found herself walking over to the bureau and rummaged around in one of the drawers until she found what she was looking for. Then she had it in her hand. A long black cane with a springy tip. She swished it back and forth remembering the pain it could inflict in the right hands and as she did the delicious excitement she always felt before she was punished started to flow through her.

She turned round now and faced her lover. Then she handed him the cane.

'This is for you,' she said bluntly. 'I want you to finish off what you started this evening.'

Sam looked at Louise standing before him in her underwear. A wisp of lace was holding her breasts in place and she was wearing the tiny briefs Calvin Klein had made so popular. He had always desired her like this, only now he felt his need for her ebb away.

He looked at the shiny black instrument in his hands.

'You want me to hit you with this?' he asked. 'Why?'

Louise looked angry.

'You know damn well why. You're not a little boy, Sam. You've been round the tracks the same way I have.'

He exhaled slowly.

'So that's how you get your kicks. Why didn't you tell me about this hobby of yours before? I feel I've been missing out on something.'

It was then she realised she should have listened to herself.

She had finally shown Sam who she really was. She had put all her frailties, all her weaknesses on display, and he had no idea what she was doing. It was worse than that. Not only didn't he understand, he was repelled by her.

She went towards him and took the cane out of his hands.

'Forget this ever happened,' she said. 'It was a bad idea to start with.'

But Sam wasn't letting her off the hook.

'I think it's time you told me the rest of the story,' he said. 'If we're going to have a future, that is.'

Louise started to cry. Slow miserable tears dripped down her cheeks and she wiped them away, streaking her mascara as she did so. Then she pulled herself together and went into the bathroom. With deft hands she wiped off her ruined make-up and shrugged herself into a terry robe. Then, her mind made up she went back into the bedroom to face her lover.

'The whole thing started out as a joke,' she said. 'A sort of lark to spice up our sex life.'

She went over and took his hand pulling him down to sit on the bed. Then she curled up beside him. 'I was having

513

a few drinks with the girls in the gym,' she said. 'You know, the crowd I usually work out with, and one of them had got hold of one of those sex magazines. It was real porno. Lots of pictures and detailed instructions. We all started talking about our sex lives.' She paused. 'Without mentioning names. I guess we got kind of carried away. Anyway one of the crowd was absolutely convinced that all the tricks and perversions were a real turn-on. She said she tried some of the things out on her husband and they drove him out of his mind. I thought it might be fun to do the same to you.'

Sam looked at Louise. She's not telling the truth, he thought. The story is too elaborate, too out of character. This woman doesn't go in for hen sessions in the showers and she doesn't get that close to other women either. She has no use for that kind of relationship.

He sighed.

'You're telling me this is the first time you ever tried this kind of thing?'

Louise nodded, and looked nervous.

'None of your other lovers used a cane on you? I find it hard to believe.'

Sam picked up the instrument she had given him and started slapping it lightly down on the bed.

'This isn't the sort of thing you buy as a joke,' he said. 'Whoever acquired this, be it you or someone else, knew exactly what they were about. I may not go in for these kind of games but I've known people who do, and my guess is you're one of them.'

Louise started to fall apart. It was as if her face that had been tightly held together for so long could no longer make the effort and it screwed up and crumpled like a little girl's. Sam's first emotion was to walk out and leave her where she sat. Walk out for ever. But he hesitated for a second too long, and in that instant he was overtaken by another emotion. Compassion.

He felt pity for Louise. Pity and responsibility. He remembered feeling the same way about Frances when she was drinking too much. My wife and my mistress, he thought bitterly. I thought they were so different. Such opposites. Yet they end up being interchangeable.

He looked at the woman sitting in front of him and after all the years of knowing her, all the years of loving her, he finally saw her for what she was. Human. Vulnerable. Damaged beyond his understanding.

What did they do to you, he wondered, the lovers who came before me? How did they hurt you? He was tempted to prise the rest of Louise's secrets from her. In this mood she would tell him anything he wanted to know, but he decided not to press her.

Instead he put his arms around her.

'Are you going to leave me?' she whispered fearfully.

Sam stroked her hair.

'No,' he replied wearily. 'I'm not going to leave you. I've loved you too long for that.'

52

Living with Frances was becoming increasingly difficult. Half the time she wasn't there and Sam had no idea where she had got to. When she was around the apartment was unkempt. Sam had never thought the girl he had married was untidy. In all their years together she had given him no clue to this, and now he felt betrayed. Duped. Conned. Every time he saw her tights hanging up to dry on the rail over the bath he felt like shouting at her. Every time he found dirty dishes and unwashed coffee cups in the sink he wanted to strangle her. Except he couldn't, because by the time he came on her transgressions she had usually flown the coop.

He was reminded of his days in Tel Aviv when he had been serving in the army and sharing an apartment. Then he had a succession of room-mates, all of them messy – some of them downright dirty. But they had been men and he had made allowances. Men couldn't look after themselves. Not all men. Anyway Sam hadn't been married to any of them.

That was another thing that pissed him off. Here he was married to a woman. Paying the bills. Toeing the line. Or if he wasn't toeing the line, at least he was keeping up the appearance of toeing the line. And Frances was doing nothing at all. It had started after the night of the awards dinner. It was as if his escorting Louise signalled the end of something. After that Frances behaved as if he wasn't a husband at all. To her he was the guy who lived down the hall. Someone to whom she wrote little notes like: 'We're out of milk. Could you get some on your way home?' Or: 'I urgently need my silk trousers. Could you pick them up when you pass the cleaners?'

He blamed this new behaviour on Milton Goldman. He was her new lover, that was obvious, and he was teaching her bad habits. The whole thing filled him with fury. Sam started sneaking around the sort of bars he had quit when he was a junior copywriter. He was on the hunt now, looking for gossip, trying to find a juicy item that would forever damn the creep who had made off with his wife.

He finally found what he was looking for. A drunken art director who had once worked with Goldman filled him in. It seemed the creative director had once been married but it hadn't lasted very long due to Goldman's temperament. According to the art director he liked getting high then beating up his wife.

Sam treasured the information, hugging it to him like a priceless nugget of gold. Then one night when Frances was at home he sprang it on her.

'Your new boyfriend's not all he seems,' he said casually.

Frances, who was making herself a cup of coffee, looked up.

'How do you mean?' she asked.

Sam waited for a moment, wondering how best to break it to her. He decided on the blunt approach.

'The man takes drugs. He smokes pot and he injects. The last girl he was married to left home because of it.'

Frances looked at him blankly and went on stirring milk into her coffee.

'Who says?' she asked.

Sam started to feel ridiculous.

'A guy I met in a bar. An art director he used to work with.'

'You're making it up to put me off him,' Frances said crossly. 'But you're not going to. Milton's fun and he believes in looking after me, which is more than you do.'

Then she put down her coffee cup and flounced out of the kitchen. Sam didn't attempt to go after her. Whether or not the story was true was immaterial. It was Frances's reaction to it that mattered, and the way she stated her case. She had more or less told him she'd found someone else. Someone to replace him. Now it was just a matter of time before she moved out and ended the marriage.

I had it coming, he told himself. I didn't stop seeing Louise. I didn't even talk about it to Frances when she moved into the spare room. I just accepted the situation and hoped things would work themselves out. Now they had, he had only himself to blame.

He stopped his train of thought right there. Why am I blaming myself, he wondered. I should be celebrating – calling Louise and making plans. Only he wasn't, because he had started to think twice about building a future with Louise.

They hadn't been getting along so well since she had been back in New York. The work that had always united them seemed to be driving them apart. London had changed her in some way he couldn't define and for the hundredth time Sam wondered who had taught her the games with the cane. The sex games.

Since he had known what she really liked and what turned her on, he had felt inadequate. Not that their sex together had been bad. It was just different, with Sam behaving warily, half expecting, half dreading that she would spring yet another surprise on him.

Women, he thought wearily. If I could I'd do without them. Life would be simpler. Or at least more peaceful.

Sam sighed and looked at his watch. He had spent the evening alone at his apartment, putting the finishing touches to a client proposal. It was nearly midnight and he thought about turning in.

I'll put the chain on the door and lock up, he decided. Frances probably won't be coming home now. Then he heard her key in the front door. She wasn't alone. He heard a man's voice in the hall and supposed it was Milton. He saw he had guessed right when they came into the room. They had been out to dinner and probably a club as well for they were discussing the merits of Aretha Franklin.

They didn't see him at first and he didn't announce himself. He was curious to see how his wife behaved when she was with another man. She didn't flirt, he noticed. There was a confidence about her that went beyond coquettishness. She was wearing a wrap he hadn't seen before, a light flimsy thing made of some silky fabric, and she gave it to Milton to put somewhere.

The intimacy of the gesture appalled Sam. Frances was used to handing her wrap or her coat or anything else she didn't want to wear any more to this man. He remembered with a stab of pain that she used to do it with him. When did that stop, he asked himself. When did she stop depending on me for the little things like carrying her wrap or pouring her a drink?

Frances interrupted his reverie.

'I didn't see you sitting there,' she said calmly. 'Have you been in all evening?'

Sam nodded, then he remembered his manners.

'Can I get you a nightcap?' he asked. He looked at Milton. 'Both of you I mean.'

The younger man had tried with himself that night for he was all buttoned up in a velvet dinner suit and his shirt had ruffles at the neck and wrists. He smiled at Sam a little self-consciously.

'Mine's a bourbon-on-the-rocks, if it isn't too much trouble. I think Frances will have mineral water.'

'I know what my wife drinks,' Sam snapped. 'Grant me some knowledge of her.'

Sam looked at Frances standing nervously a pace or two behind her escort and he regretted losing his cool. I'm behaving like a heavy father, he told himself; treating

Frances like a wayward teenager who's stayed out too late with her latest suitor.

To hide his confusion he went over to the drinks cabinet and made Milton his drink, then he made one for himself. This situation required a little Dutch courage.

It was Milton who eased things, taking his drink over to the sofa and sitting down. He started a conversation about the latest government advertising campaign, asking Sam's opinion and taking care to agree with what he said. For the next twenty minutes the three of them sat around making small talk and feeling uncomfortable.

Sam permitted himself a smile. It's nearly midnight he thought and I'm sitting in my own apartment with my wife and my wife's lover, and we're all being so damned civilised about it. If the situation was different, he wondered, if Louise was sitting here instead of Milton, would Frances be as tactful as I'm being?

He remembered the ultimatum she had given him. There's something wrong with this marriage she had said. Put it right or I stay in the spare room. Well two could play at that game.

Sam stood up suddenly, surprising his wife and her guest.

'It's time we both went to bed,' he said. 'I've got an early start, and Frances never sleeps once I've woken her.'

Milton looked nervous.

'I thought . . .'

Sam didn't let him finish the sentence.

'Whatever she told you, I wouldn't be taken in by it. Frances likes to tell attractive young men that she doesn't enjoy a normal married life but it's all bullshit. My wife is a very demanding woman.'

He paused, holding the astonished young man in his gaze.

'Believe me,' he said, 'there's no way any man could live under the same roof with Frances and not share her bed.'

There was a silence while the three of them looked at each other. Frances had gone very pale and the muscles of her jaw were tightly clenched. She's furious, Sam thought, but if she says anything now it's going to look like protesting too much. In the end Milton was the first to speak.

'It's time I was on my way,' he said. He looked at Frances.

'You and your husband have got a lot of talking to do,' he said. 'When you've managed to work things out you might give me a call. But take your time. I don't want to be caught in the middle of anything.'

When he had gone, Frances turned on Sam.

'Just what do you think you were doing?' she demanded.

Sam went over and poured himself another drink.

'I was staking my claim. You don't really think I was going to let go of you without putting up some kind of a fight.'

Frances was gripped by several emotions, the strongest of which was to wipe the satisfied smile off her husband's face.

'You selfish bastard,' she whispered. 'You don't want me but you don't want anyone else to have me either.'

He put his drink down and reached for her.

'Who told you I didn't want you?'

Frances hadn't been this close to her husband for a long, long time and she had forgotten how attractive she found him. There was something male about Sam, something that made men like Milton seem almost inconsequential.

She felt him reach around to the back of her dress and start to undo the zip, and she felt weak. I shouldn't be doing this, she thought. He's got someone else now. We've both got someone else. But he was kissing her. Sweet demanding kisses and she couldn't concentrate. She felt her dress slipping down around her waist, then she felt Sam's hands move to her breasts, teasing and caressing them so that the nipples stood on end. And she was lost.

Sam picked her up and carried her over to the hearth-rug, and sinking down beside her he took off the rest of her things – her bra, her tights, the stretchy lace panties. Then he undressed himself.

'We shouldn't be doing this,' Frances protested. 'Think about Louise.'

'You think about Louise,' Sam said roughly, 'I've got other things on my mind.'

His hands were all over her, stroking, exploring, reclaiming a territory he had once thought was lost. And everywhere he touched her, the tips of her breasts, her navel, the moist opening between her legs, seemed to be made of fire. Frances felt her hips move in the old rhythm she had once known with him, and he took it for a signal and climbed on top of her.

She was used to him behaving gently with her, the way he had when she was bruised, but the moment had made him forget her fragility and he parted her legs and thrust himself into her with such force that she screamed out.

None of her protests could stop him. It was as if he was consumed with the need to conquer her and he ground into her again and again until he found the response he was looking for.

Something inside Frances caught alight, something she had always known was there but was too frightened to acknowledge. Now she recognised it there was no stopping her. She felt like a primeval animal, full of lust and the need to devour. As she looked into the eyes of her husband she saw another animal just like her, just as greedy as she was, and she rejoiced in it.

So this is what it's all about, she thought. This is why he left me for Louise. This is what he was looking for. They made love half the night on the carpet in the living-room, then Frances got up and took Sam to bed. Her bed in the spare room. And made love to him again in ways she had never dreamed existed. Then she slept close up against him so that his warmth enveloped them both.

In the morning she rose and made breakfast while Sam slept, then she woke him gently, setting the coffee beside him.

Frances watched him for a long time as he drank it before climbing back into bed beside him and putting her arms round him.

'I've decided to move back into your bedroom,' she told him firmly. Then she took a deep breath.

'I know you're still seeing Louise, and I hate it. But I can't keep away from you any more. Not after last night.'

53

Sam felt as if he had been jogging along in a groove, a hole he had dug for himself, and now it was Christmas and he had to take a decision. Did he spend the holiday in New York and see Louise for part of the time, or did he take Frances away to the Caribbean?

The Caribbean had been Tiffany's idea. Frances had been felled by influenza at the end of November and despite taking two weeks off work she still wasn't well.

'Why don't you take your wife off to the sun?' Tiffany had suggested one night over dinner. 'A friend of mine has a house in Barbados, right on Gibb's beach. She's not using it this Christmas, it's yours for the price of a phone call.'

Sam looked at his wife. She could do with a couple of weeks in the sun. He hadn't seen her so pale since she lost the baby, but there was more to it than that. He wanted to take her away not because she needed it but because he needed it. Ever since the night he turned her boyfriend out, things between them had changed. We are actually closer than we were before, he thought, but it's different now.

For now Sam had to court Frances. Just because she was sharing his bed again, it didn't stop her from living her own life. She went to parties on her own and she dated. When Sam wanted to see her, he had to ask her if she was free. The fact that she made herself free for him had nothing to do with it. She was independent, and he knew if he didn't do something about the situation, and give up Louise once and for all, Frances would get bored and leave. Or she would meet someone else. Both eventualities were inconceivable to him. Sam turned to Tiffany.

'Barbados sounds like a good idea,' he said. 'Give me your friend's number and I'll follow it up.'

That had been a week ago and he still hadn't done anything about it. If he did, he knew it would precipitate some kind of crisis with Louise, another quarrel, and he couldn't face it. Why don't I just end it, he thought. Why don't I just make a clean break and have done with it?

In a way he had been working up to it. He and Louise saw each other less now, and when they did meet there was a tension between them. Yet for all the fights and differences they still needed each other. There was a bond between them. A bond that went back over the years. A bond that increased its hold the day Louise became a partner in the agency. Sam knew without being told that he still got his own way at the office because of Louise. More and more these days Clay was standing against him. Clay had made no secret of the fact that he wanted mail order and even cigarettes on the client list. If Louise had cast her vote with him, there would have been no more discussion. Sam would have had to accept a radical change in direction whether he liked it or not.

He sighed. Right now he was stuck with Louise. And the situation.

The phone rang and Sam picked it up, absentmindedly. It was Frances.

'I won't be home till late,' she informed him. 'A big story just broke and we're all going to be here till midnight sorting it out.'

'Don't worry,' Sam soothed her, 'I'll wait up for you.'

Frances didn't say anything for a minute or two. When she spoke again she sounded worried, as if she was trying to hide something.

'Don't do that,' she said. 'I'll probably go and eat something after I get away from the office. I might stay over with one of the others here.'

Any normal husband wouldn't take this nonsense, Sam

thought. Any normal husband would order her home the minute she left work. But he wasn't any normal husband. He had a mistress. A mistress everyone knew about. And because of her he had to defer to Frances.

'Okay,' he agreed quietly. 'I won't wait for you tonight, but I want to talk to you. So will you have dinner tomorrow night? I've got a surprise for you.'

Frances said she would, then she kissed Sam down the phone and rang off. Sam sat and thought, then fumbled in his pocket until he found the scrap of paper he was looking for. On it was scribbled a phone number belonging to the friend of Tiffany's who owned the Caribbean villa. The sooner he called her and organised a Christmas holiday, the sooner he'd have a surprise for his wife.

Bloomingdales was all lit up for the season. In the main windows right in front of the store was a fat Father Christmas surrounded by a dozen or so mannequins. All the other displays that season were of elves and fairies, but Bloomies didn't want to miss out on sales, so their mannequins wore designer dresses. Instead of fairy spangles there were Donna Karan dresses and pant suits by Michael Kors.

Louise was half amused by the display and half irritated. The American way, she thought. We always put commerce first and the hell with the sentiment. Then she laughed and jostled her way past the crowds into the main store. Sentiment, she decided, was definitely on hold for the festive season this year.

When Sam had told her he was going away to the Caribbean she had let rip. The bastard had waited till the very last minute to break the news. He had let her buy the Christmas tree, put up the decorations. He even went along with her plan to spend Christmas Eve together. So of course she had got in provisions: a fine plump goose with chestnuts specially imported from France to stuff it, three kinds of green vegetable, crystallised fruit, plum pudding and brandy butter, mince pies. The works. She had even hiked all the way to New Jersey to buy caviar that had been smuggled in half price by a Russian sea captain.

It had all been for nothing. Last night over supper Sam had told her there had been a last minute change in plan. A villa in Barbados had come into his possession. A friend of Clay's wife was looking to lend it out and Frances had grabbed it.

'She hasn't been well since November,' Sam explained. 'It would have been cruel to let her go on her own.'

Louise saw red.

'What about me?' she asked. 'I've been working my socks off since the summer to keep the agency afloat, to keep Frances in dinner parties and expensive jewellery for Christ's sake. You don't think she makes enough to live on at that scruffy little trade paper she writes for? Now, after killing myself on everyone's behalf, you announce you're skipping off to the sun.' She mimicked his voice.

'Frances hasn't been well. The poor girl needs a rest. What the fuck do you think I need? Or didn't you remember me when baby-blue-eyes sweet-talked you into going along with her?'

Sam stared down at the tablecloth. This was going to be more difficult than he thought.

'It wasn't like that,' he said quietly.

'Then what was it like? Or don't you want to go into that.'

Her eyes were blazing now, and for a second Sam thought she was going to lash out and hit him. He made to leave, but she pushed him back into his seat.

'Don't go all blank on me,' she said. 'I asked you a reasonable question. How did your wife get round you about Christmas?'

'Frances didn't get round me. She didn't have to. Look,

I am married to the woman. I can't just abandon her to suit your whims.'

Louise looked at him with an expression very similar to hate.

'That isn't what you said at the beginning of the year,' she said bitterly. 'Back then you were waiting for this legal commitment of yours to die a natural death. It didn't did it? Something changed. Was it Frances, I wonder? Or was it you?'

'Nothing's different,' Sam said wearily. 'How many times do I have to tell you that? Look, it's Christmas time and like it or not, I'm tied to a woman who's got no family in this town, or this continent come to that. What do you want me to do with her? Tell her to spend the holiday on her own?'

Louise stood up and lit a cigarette. Then she threw the lighter down on the table and sucked deeply on her Marlboro. This smoking was a new habit of hers, one she had acquired in London and it got on Sam's nerves.

'You don't have to tell Frances to spend Christmas on her own,' Louise said sweetly. 'Just tell her to spend it in her own bed.'

It was the first time she had let on she knew he was still sleeping with his wife and he geared himself up to protest, then he changed his mind.

'That remark's not worthy of you,' he said. 'It's also none of your damn business where my wife chooses to sleep.'

Louise sat down again, heavily. She took her cigarette and stubbed it out in the remains of her dinner. It was a sluttish gesture, a gesture she had brought with her from the Bronx and only performed in private.

Only now she didn't bother to disguise it. There didn't seem any point.

'So you *are* sleeping with Frances,' she said. 'I suspected you were. I didn't ask you, because honestly I didn't terribly

528

want to know.' She took a deep breath. 'Where does that leave us?'

'Where do you want it to leave us?' Sam asked.

Louise pursed her lips.

'Don't answer a question with a question. You know exactly what I'm asking you. Now you're sleeping with that air-head you're married to, is there any point in us going on as we are?'

Sam got up and went round to her side of the table. He took hold of her shoulders and turned her round so she faced him.

'Louise,' he said. 'We've been at each other's throats for the last six months now and we can't seem to make any sense of things. Maybe it would be better if we did give things a rest for a while. We need a cooling-down period, you and I, and Christmas is as good a time as any.'

Louise started to interrupt, but he wouldn't let her.

'Look, I'm going to the West Indies for two weeks – maybe longer if the business can do without me. While I'm away I intend to do a lot of thinking. You should do the same. It's your life too that's being messed up. Maybe you deserve better than the deal you're getting right now.'

Louise looked at him and there was sadness in her eyes.

'You're damn right I deserve better,' she told him. 'Whether I want better is a whole other discussion.'

After that there was nothing else to say. If they had had a fight it would have been different. He would have shouted. She would have hit him, and they would have ended up in bed the way they always did.

Now we don't do that, Louise thought bitterly. Now he wants a cooling-off period. He wants to go to the West Indies with his wife.

She sat down in the middle of her bachelor girl apartment and for the first time in her life she felt defeated. For she *was* defeated. The man she had loved for so long had finally told her goodbye.

She felt the tears prickle behind her eyes. When did it start to change, she wondered. When did Sam stop loving me and start loving Frances all over again?

A small knot of hopelessness started to form in the pit of her stomach and as she sat and surveyed the debris of her life she felt it begin to grow. Now it wasn't a knot at all, it was a tidal wave, a flood of grief surging through her. She let it come, surrendering herself to the emotion, bathing herself in hot tears. Yet all the time she was doing it, a small cool voice in the back of her head told her she was deluding herself. At first she didn't listen to it, she was too busy feeling bad, but as the tears receded the voice became stronger.

Louise forced her mind back to the time when Frances returned to New York. Before then she was ahead. Sam was hers. Nearly in the bag. If Frances had just stayed away for a few more months he would have filed for divorce, and she wouldn't be sitting on her own now.

With a sudden clarity Louise realised Frances hadn't been the fool she'd taken her for. She'd hurried back to New York just weeks after she did herself because she knew something was up. Louise wondered why she hadn't caught on to her. It was a classic scenario – wronged wife fights back – only she didn't think Frances was a fighter. She always seemed so pathetic.

I have to wait with her, Sam had said. Hold her hand until the marriage is finally over. And Louise had gone along with it.

The tears had stopped entirely now and a voice, which she recognised as the voice of her reason, dominated her thoughts. I behaved like a fool, she thought. Love weakened me. And while I was in that state I let Sam's wife, then Sam himself, do what they damned well liked.

She remembered the awards dinner when she first saw

Frances after her homecoming. She was dancing with some pretty young creative director, and she was looking good, so good that Sam had to go over and cut in.

I must have been blind, she raged. Blind and dumb and stupid not to have seen it coming. That night Sam wanted Frances more than he wanted me, and I had to pick that moment to hand him a whip and ask him to beat me.

Louise started to feel angry now, and this new emotion cleansed her and made her feel strong. When I loved, she thought, I never felt like this. At that moment she realised that love was something she could do without.

She concentrated on her anger now, fuelling it with images of Sam and Frances cuddling in each other's arms, laughing at her.

They won't get away with it, she thought. They can't turn me into the discarded mistress all used up and worn out.

She got up and fluffed her hair out around her shoulders. I'm Louise Tragos she told herself. I'm tough and I'm smart and I'm more than a match for either of them.

She knew now that she had to avenge herself, but she had no idea how. All she did know was that she didn't want to waste any more energy, any more grief until she had a plan. So she went to bed and before she turned out the light, she put her feelings on hold. They would remain that way, she decided, until she had figured out what she was going to do.

The next day she went out shopping.

Someone had given her a birthday present a couple of years ago, an embroidered cushion bearing the legend: When the going gets tough, the tough go shopping.

Louise had always thought it was a cliché, and had put the cushion away in a drawer. Now, in Bloomingdales, she was living out the cliché and it gave her little comfort. She bought five pairs of Dior tights, some gold hoop earrings and a belt with a silver buckle in the space of half an hour. Then she took the elevator to the second floor and made her way to the designer departments. There was something aimless about the way she shopped. Something self-destructive. She bought a tweed jacket from Donna Karan, a pair of silk pants from Calvin Klein. Then she stopped off at a new department where they were selling a range of Italian shoes and picked up a pair of lizard skin boots.

The moment she paid for them, she knew she would never wear them. They were too impractical to wear. Anyway there was nothing in her wardrobe that went with them. For a moment she was tempted to buy an outfit to go specially with the boots, but she rejected the idea. Where would I wear it, she thought. I'm going nowhere this Christmas. Nowhere except my apartment.

The thought of the holiday stretching ahead of her filled her with depression. She supposed she could get in a stack of videos, and there was some work she had to catch up on. The thought of the office reminded her of something. She did have somewhere to go. It wasn't anything particularly exciting, just Clay and Tiffany giving an annual cocktail party for the office staff.

All the stenographers would be there in their party dresses, which would be discount glitz. She shuddered. The party was tonight and right at this moment all the girls would be sitting in the beauty parlour having their hair teased. Louise had visions of how it would be. Pimply little boys from the accounts department making time with all those refugees from the beauty parlour. What do I need with it, she thought. Then she visualised her apartment with its decorated Christmas tree, its rows of cards from all the art houses she did business with, its bulging refrigerator full of goose and caviar. She had made her apartment festive for Sam and now he had gone somewhere else without her. Worse, he had gone somewhere else with his wife and she was left to celebrate on her own.

Suddenly she couldn't face it. Clay's party wasn't much, she knew that, but it was better than nothing. Better than going nowhere. Maybe I'll find myself someone, Louise thought. A little art director perhaps, or a young copywriter. She'd recruited little boys barely out of their twenties before when she had been in London. They weren't what she wanted, but they filled in the gaps, and saw her through the lean times. When life got interesting again, they could be dropped without too much trouble.

Louise struggled her way out of Bloomingdales and managed to grab the only cab left in this city bent on celebration. She checked the time on her gold Rolex. It was coming up to five o'clock. If she took a fast shower and washed her hair, she could be in Westchester by seven-thirty.

Abner Morris nursed his highball and contemplated getting drunk. Not merry, not amusingly high but falling down drunk. He had had enough of the festive season to last him for several decades and it was only Christmas Eve. Why did I ever get it in my head to have an affair with a married woman, he asked himself? I should have known right at the start she wouldn't be there when I needed her. Married women are never around for public holidays or Sunday afternoons. They're with their husbands or their families. And me, the married woman's lover, is stuck making do with second best or worse, getting drunk and feeling sorry for myself.

He had been at the party for around an hour and as yet he had only managed to grab five minutes of Tiffany's time. If she wasn't answering the door or filling people's glasses, she was looking over her shoulder at her husband the whole time. Abner suspected Tiffany was frightened of Clay. She had never actually admitted to it, and she strived to give the impression that hers was an easy going, happy-go-lucky kind of menage. But Abner thought otherwise. Clay was tougher than he looked and whenever he was with his wife, he got the impression she was on a very tight rope. Tiffany could jump through all the sexual hoops when she was with him, but deep down Abner knew she was only out on loan. She would never leave the fat little advertising man she was married to.

He leaned across the bar and asked the man behind it to fix him another drink. And that's when he saw her. There were plenty of women there that night. Most of them younger than she was but when it came to style none of them could hold a candle to her. There was something special about her. A kind of aura that said 'I'm exciting and I'm as difficult as hell, and if you get anywhere near me, you'll get your fingers burned.'

Abner had to meet her. He walked away from the bar and the freshly poured drink and negotiated his way across the room until he ran into Clay. The fat man was deep in conversation with one of his media men, but Abner cut in.

'Who's the girl?' he asked.

Clay looked out on to the sea of glitz and cleavage.

'Which one?'

Abner started to get impatient.

'The dark, horny looking girl in the black dress. The one with the "fuck you" smile. Do I have to draw a diagram?'

'Okay, okay, don't get excited.' Clay put out a hand to steady Abner who seemed to have taken leave of his senses.

'You're talking about Louise Tragos, and she's not just any girl. She's my third partner in the agency and she's spoken for.'

It didn't cross Abner's mind that she would be anything but free, because he wanted her to be. More than wanted. Insisted.

'Where's her husband?'

'She doesn't have a husband,' Clay said.

Already it was starting to sound better.

'Where's her guy, then, and who the hell is he?'

There was a short silence during which Clay considered what to do next.

Sam was his partner from way back and he owed him some loyalty. On the other hand, Sam was away in the sun with Frances. And what he didn't see, he wouldn't miss.

'If you want to know who Louise belongs to, you'll have to ask the lady herself. All I can tell you is that tonight she's alone.'

Abner started to smile. It was the well-groomed smile he usually wore but underneath it there was steel and more than a hint of danger.

'Introduce me,' he instructed. 'And make it fast.'

Close to she was even better. Her skin was taut across her cheekbones and her eyes were almond-shaped, like a panther's. She wasn't just an assembly of interesting features, though. There was more to her than that. The arrogance Abner had spotted when she first walked into the room was what stopped him. She wore this attitude the way other women wore perfume, and he knew that whatever happened between them that night he would be unlikely to forget it.

For a while they made small talk. Circling each other like gladiators. Assessing strengths and weaknesses. Calculating the options. Finally Abner made his move.

'Clay tells me you're spoken for. Does that count for tonight?'

She looked at him.

'That depends on what you have in mind.'

If I told you, thought Abner, you'd either smack my face or you'd take your dress off. With Tiffany around I can't afford to take the risk.

'What I had in mind,' he said slowly, lying through his

535

teeth, 'was to get out of here and buy you some dinner. I don't know about you, but I'm starving.'

Even if he hadn't eaten a late lunch the last thing on his mind was dinner but it would do for a start.

Louise looked around the room, then she consulted her watch.

'It's not even nine yet. Won't our hosts be offended if we take off?'

Abner thought about Tiffany. Earlier she had promised him she would slip out of the house for an hour or so during the party. The plan was to drive down to the beach and use the time creatively, but that would have to wait. He could have Tiffany any time. This girl, he suspected, wouldn't wait around for him or any other man.

'There are a lot of people here tonight,' he said guiding her towards the door. 'Nobody will even notice we've gone.'

He drove back to the city at top speed, breaking every limit. There was something suburban about Westchester. It was a place where happy families, husbands and wives spent Christmas and weekends. He wasn't in that class at all and nor was the woman sitting next to him. The sooner he got back to his home ground the better.

He took her to a little French restaurant. In reality it wasn't a restaurant, it was too chic to take just anyone from off the street. Nadia's was a members only club, and to belong you either had to be descended from the Pilgrim Fathers or you had to be very rich. Abner was both.

The moment they arrived, they were ushered into the small bar, only it wasn't a bar. It was a drawing-room with a roaring fire and instead of drinks being served across a counter, the members were able to pour their own from the decanters sitting on top of a Georgian bureau. Louise asked Abner for a glass of dry white wine and looked around her.

She'd heard about Nadia's from friends of hers but she

536

never imagined she would actually find herself having dinner there. It was too top drawer, too old money for her. To the naked eye no-one could tell where she came from. She looked tough, successful, international, but buried deep inside her there was a frightened girl from the Bronx. An immigrant who had made it to the city on her wits and her sex and as long as she lived she would never cast that girl out of her soul.

She surveyed the man who had picked her up that evening. She hadn't been looking for anyone like Abner. What she had in mind was a little boy, nice-looking and biddable. This character with the black hair and the tough face was another story. She sipped her wine and wondered what she was going to do about him.

They ate dinner around ten-thirty. It was late and the food was delicious but neither of them was hungry. They both knew the fancy restaurant and the vintage claret were steps on the way to where they had been heading all evening.

In the early days, when she started dating, Louise played the courtship game by the rules. You drank together, you dined together and during those activities you talked a lot and got to know each other. When she was younger it was important that any guy who got serious shared her politics and understood her ambitions.

Now it was different. She had all the friends she needed. Her business associates took up the rest of her time. If it was love she needed, there was Sam. And for sex there were plenty of boys.

The problem with Abner Morris was that he came from no known category, so she didn't know how to deal with him.

Around midnight they finished dinner and her whole body tensed while she waited for him to ask the inevitable. Will you come back to my place for a nightcap? She wanted him. She was too old to lie to herself about that. But she didn't want to be just another easy woman passing through his life. So she took the initiative.

'Don't worry about seeing me home,' she said. 'I can find my own way.'

He looked at her with evident amusement.

'What brought this on?' he asked. 'You're behaving like a teenager.'

'I don't want to go to bed with you,' she blurted out. 'Not tonight.'

He patted her hand.

'If you want to wait till tomorrow, it's okay by me, but it seems an awful waste of time.'

Louise leaned back in her chair. Her companion was playing with her. She was about to get angry when she realised what he had just said.

'Were you asking me to spend Christmas with you?' she asked.

'Of course. What else?'

'But don't you have friends, plans, a woman somewhere waiting for you?'

For a moment Abner looked serious. Then he said, 'Louise, I'm doing my damnedest to impress you, so I suppose I should lie and invent a social whirl that's going to take me away over the holiday. But I'm too old for that. There are any number of parties I can go to but they're tacky affairs, full of married men and little tarts. I can do without them.'

She sat regarding him for a long time.

'You didn't tell me about the woman.'

'There's nothing to tell,' he said gently. 'It's common knowledge I've been seeing Tiffany Greene for the past couple of years, just as the world seems to know you and Sam Kurnitz are an item. But I don't think either of them are going to get in our way over the next few days.'

Her head came up.

'Who told you about Sam?'

'Nobody. It was easy enough to work out for myself. Clay told me you were spoken for but the man wasn't around. So I had to assume he was married. Then you told me the rest. You're probably not aware of it, but you mention Sam far more than any business associate ever would. You quote him so often that I can almost see the man looking over your shoulder.' He paused. 'Also I have an unfair advantage. I happen to know the guy. So I'm aware his wife isn't the only woman in his life.'

Louise felt crushed and it wasn't a feeling she was comfortable with. In all her relationships, even with Sam, she was the one who was in control. Now this stranger seemed to have taken the reins out of her hands and she couldn't even work out the next move. Abner seemed to sense this, for he got to his feet and led her out of the restaurant. Then, before she could suggest anything else, he hailed a taxi off the street and gave the driver his address.

When they got to the building where he lived, he helped her on to the sidewalk and hurried her through the double glass doors. She stopped when they got inside. A look of panic on her face.

'What's the problem,' said Abner. 'Didn't any man ever try to get you into bed before?'

She laughed, releasing her tension.

'No,' she said. 'I was always the one who did the seducing.'

He put his arm round her waist and shepherded her into the elevator. It was the gesture of a man who was used to women and who didn't take them very seriously.

'That's what you think,' he said.

When they got into his apartment, he didn't ask her if she would like a drink. Instead he got her one. A glass of dry white wine. She was fascinated to see that he had chosen the same Bordeaux she had been drinking at Nadia's.

'I can guess where you get your supplies,' she told him.

He shook his head.

'Wrong,' he said. 'The club gets its supplies from me. I set them up in business in the first place.'

They talked about Nadia's for a while, then Abner told her a little about setting up his own operation. He was as interesting about the Macho Clubs as he was about his tobacco business. And at some point, she knew not how, she found herself talking about the agency. She only ever talked advertising to Sam or the people she worked with and she found it liberating to discuss it with somebody outside the business. Abner understood her problems, but he wasn't involved with them, so he could stand back and take the long view. She realised, with a start, that she was totally relaxed.

She had come into this man's apartment frozen up with fear, terrified he would pounce on her the minute they got through the door. Here they were at two o'clock on Christmas morning arguing about the profitability of some of her smaller accounts.

'What we really need,' she told him, 'is that cigarette business of yours the agency turned down last year.'

He came over to where she was standing and took her by the shoulders.

'We can talk about your business requirements tomorrow,' he said. 'Right now what I need is you.'

He pulled her close and started kissing her and she felt herself respond to him, opening her mouth to receive his tongue, relaxing her shoulders so the spaghetti straps that held up her dress slipped down.

He pushed her away from him. Then they started to undress each other slowly, letting their hands linger in all the private places. When they were both completely naked, he took her by the hand and went through into the bedroom.

She cast her eyes over him, taking in the lean exercised body, the penis coming slowly erect. Then she went towards him, her arms outstretched. Once again he pushed her away, but this time there was nothing gentle in his touch and she found herself stumbling across the carpet.

'What did you do that for?'

He didn't answer and she saw him walk over to one of the closets that lined the room and rummage through it. He found what he was looking for and he pulled out one of the uniforms the Macho waitresses wore in the club. A black mini-skirted dress with a tiny pinafore.

'Get into that,' he told her. 'And don't bother about putting your knickers back on.'

She still didn't know what was going on until he produced the whip. Then she started to remember. And to get excited. Quickly she put on the tiny indecent dress.

'How did you know?' she asked.

'Don't be naive,' he said coming towards her. 'It was written all over you.'

54

Louise had rehearsed exactly what she was going to say.
I had time to think while you were away over Christmas,
she would tell him, and I realised it wasn't working for us
any more.

I realised Abner Morris was better for me than you are.
Better in bed. Better in every way. No she wouldn't say
that. Not to his face. She'd let him find out about Abner
gradually. It was more satisfying that way.

She thought back over the long lazy Christmas. The
turning point in her life. Before then she had always settled
for second best. She had been chief executive of her own
agency but the agency had been in London, not in New
York. She had loved the most talented man in her business,
but she had had to share him with his wife. Now she shared
her man with no-one. Tiffany had got her marching orders
the moment the holiday was over. The next candidate for
the hit list was Sam. It will be such a pleasure to send him
on his way, Louise thought. And the pleasure was double
edged. For she was not just planning to kick him out of
her life. If things worked out the way she had carefully
arranged, she would be kicking him out of his business
as well.

The plan had taken shape somewhere between Christmas
and New Year's Eve. She and Abner had spent the time
together. Mostly alone, for neither of them felt the need for
anyone else's company. Abner had their meals sent in from
Nadia's. There was a private cinema in the Macho complex
where they caught up on all the new movies. They swam
in the Macho pool. They made love. And they talked.

Louise mostly talked about Sam, and when she'd got

him out of her system, she talked about the agency, which brought the discussion back to Sam and his refusal to accept the commercial aspects of the business she was in.

Abner understood, naturally. He had had the same differences with Sam himself.

'I like the guy, and I more than like his work,' Abner said. 'All I wish is that he would grow up. He's setting himself up as some kind of moral conscience for the ad industry. "Smoking is a killer habit." I know that, but alcohol kills if you drink too much of it and I read the other day that carrots kill if you eat a ton of them. None of that has anything to do with selling. Sam Kurnitz is an advertising man. His job is to sell products. Not to judge them. That's the province of the preachers and the politicians.'

Louise sighed.

'If you knew how many times I tried to tell him that. Not just me, but Clay as well. There are times when we're both frightened his attitude will bring the business to a standstill.'

Abner regarded his latest mistress. She was exactly what he had been looking for. Tough, sexy and independent as hell. She didn't have designs on him the way Tiffany had done because she wasn't looking for a man to give her security. She had that all on her own. And the name of it was Kurnitz Tragos and Greene.

He smiled. I wouldn't mind settling for this one, he thought, because she doesn't need me. She doesn't need anything except her own success.

'How would your agency survive without Sam?' he asked.

Louise thought for a moment.

'Some of the business would walk right out the door,' she told him. 'There are clients who are in love with what Sam can do for them. They get excited when their ads attract attention and pick up awards. But there's another kind of business that isn't interested in fancy accolades, and that's the stuff that brings in the money.'

'Do you think you can attract that kind of client?'

Again she looked pensive.

'If we didn't have Sam, I could do it,' she said seriously. 'But it's a big step to take – a huge gamble, and I don't know if I'm ready for it yet.'

Abner left nothing to chance.

'Would a sixty million cigarette brand make you ready?' he asked.

Louise smiled at him, and she looked so sleek, so feline that any minute he thought she would purr. She had been looking for vengeance, and now it had fallen right into her lap.

She had gone to Clay with the proposition directly after the holidays. Sam wasn't due back from the West Indies for another week, so she had time to make the plan watertight.

Clay had gone for it, as she knew he would, though his conscience troubled him for a day or so. He and Sam had started the agency together. They had been friends as well as partners.

'I was Sam's friend as well,' Louise told him. 'More than his friend. But in this situation it's either friendship or survival. Look,' she continued, 'we lost one of our biggest clients just over six months ago and the bank have already started to kick up. If we don't take the business Abner's offering we're going to be in trouble.'

Clay frowned.

'If we do take the account there will be trouble of another sort. I wouldn't put it past Sam to walk out over this.'

She was glad he said it first. That way, Sam's leaving the agency didn't look as if it was entirely her idea.

'So Sam walks out,' she said, 'he isn't the only creative talent on Madison Avenue. There are lots of other writers.

544

Not as famous as Sam, of course, but the potential's there, and they won't be as difficult.'

Clay wasn't happy with the idea but in the end when Louise ran the figures past the accountant he was convinced. Sixty million dollars in billing would turn the agency right round. It would also give them breathing space. With the new business they could afford to lose Sam's clients and replace them with the kind of business that gave them a faster return.

The agency would change, it would lose its creative profile, but they were half way through the Eighties now and clever advertising wasn't as important as it was. There would always be an audience for good work, just as there would always be people who watched channel thirteen. But Kurnitz Tragos wasn't going in that direction any more.

Sam got back to the office a week after Christmas. His holiday had clearly suited him for he was tanned and relaxed and whenever Louise looked at him, he seemed to be smiling.

It was the smile that finally made up her mind. She was going to take him to one side and explain the situation so it didn't come as a surprise when she and Clay voted together to take the cigarette business. But the smile stopped her.

This new happiness is all about Frances, she thought. The little flake didn't waste any time when I was out of the picture. I bet she dreamed up all sorts of ways to get round him on those long, hot tropical nights. The thought of Sam and Frances in bed together added to Louise's fury. I'll wipe that stupid expression off his face, she thought. When I've finished, he'll regret he ever chose her. Better than that, he'll regret he ever met her.

She called a meeting of the board to discuss the agency's finances. In the past agency meetings were at Clay's instigation and took place in gyms and Turkish baths. Now Louise had joined everything was more formal. The three of them hired private rooms in uptown restaurants when they wanted to talk turkey. For this meeting Louise had organised a room in Nadia's.

Using the club had been Abner's idea and she had gone along with it, because she had plans for him. If Sam resigned, as she suspected he would, there would be a vacancy on the board of Kurnitz Tragos. Abner would fill it to perfection.

She smiled as she filled her briefcase and got her secretary to organise a taxi across town. Abner wouldn't be a full-time partner. She had no intention of being upstaged by her lover. She'd done that once in her life and once was enough. No, Abner would be her sleeping partner. The man in the background who held the purse strings. With his support she would run the whole show.

On the way to Nadia's, Louise thought about the name on the masthead. The agency had started as Kurnitz and Greene. When she joined the board it had changed to Kurnitz Tragos and Greene and now it was going to change again. She ran through the combinations. Tragos and Greene. Tragos, Morris and Greene. She shook her head. Neither of them sounded quite right. Then she tried a third way and she leaned back in her seat and sighed with satisfaction. Of course, she thought, why didn't it occur to me before? As she drove through Manhattan the name finally became clear in her mind. The new agency would be called Tragos and Partners. It had a satisfying ring to it. A confident ring. A permanent ring.

55

The minute Sam walked into the meeting, he knew something was wrong. Weeks later he asked himself what exactly had made his hackles rise, but no matter how hard he tried he couldn't put his finger on it. There was no single thing that shrieked out a warning signal. Instead there was a combination of little things.

Clay, who normally didn't make an effort with his partners, was wearing a dark suit that day. A dark suit and a starched white shirt and a tie pin with a diamond in it.

'What's all this for?' Sam asked as he took his place behind the table Nadia's had set up for tea. 'You look as if you're going to a funeral.'

Clay flushed, and Sam noticed beads of perspiration break out on his forehead. He's expecting something to happen, Sam thought. Something he's not happy about.

His eyes moved to Louise. She was all dolled up in padded shoulders and a short tight skirt. Nothing unusual there. Her spell in London had turned her into one of those women executives who dressed for power. For a moment he thought of Frances and how she didn't go in for that kind of thing any more. He felt a stab of guilt. He should have told Louise the moment he got back from Barbados that they were finished. Except he hadn't had the chance. Every time he tried to get her alone, she was off somewhere doing something. She seemed to have been frantically busy these last few days, and in the end he left it. Now as he saw her avoiding his eyes, he regretted not coming clean. There was unfinished business between them and he feared it might get in the way of their real business.

One of the club servants came in bearing a silver tray

laden with an assortment of little sandwiches and cakes. He set it all down between them and Sam fought down a feeling of irritation. There was something pretentious about this tea-time ritual. Something phoney. He remembered Clay sweating in the hot room at Zilli's when they talked over whether or not to take Louise into the business. We didn't need dark suits and cream cakes and fancy restaurants to make up our minds then, he thought.

It was at that moment he realised that something had changed. In the old days when one of them had something on their mind they said it, straight out. Without hesitation. Now it was obvious something was up, but nobody was saying what it was.

Louise poured the tea for the three of them, making a production of it. Like some dowager duchess receiving her family. Or her underlings perhaps? Sam had the uncomfortable feeling she knew something he didn't. Something important. Suddenly he wanted to get this farce over with and go back to the office and do some real work.

'Tell me,' he said without preamble, 'what are we doing here? It's got to be something pretty momentous to drag us all the way up-town in the middle of a busy week.'

There was an uncomfortable silence and Louise and Clay started to speak at once. Sam motioned Clay to be quiet.

'Ladies first,' he said.

Sam had the impression he had put her on the spot, but she swallowed hard and took the stage.

'We've been offered a big new account,' she said. Her voice had gone up an octave or two, and he realised the business had a problem attached. If this was something to celebrate she would have said, 'We've got Martini', or 'The Chrysler business fell into our lap'. Instead she stuck to a speech she'd been rehearsing, enumerating all the accounts they put on in the past year and noting everything they lost.

'What's the spiel for?' asked Sam roughly. 'This is our

business we're talking about. We know what the bottom line looks like. Get on with what you have to say.'

He hadn't meant to sound so tough, but Louise's executive lady act was beginning to rub him up the wrong way. She'd been a full partner for less than two years and already she was acting as if she owned the place. He decided it was time he and Clay sat down the way they used to and talked things over man to man. Getting involved with Louise had confused things not just with his wife, but with his partner as well. The sooner he could straighten his life out the better it would be for all of them.

He swung round to face Louise, who was looking frozen and slightly twitchy. Board meetings clearly weren't her forte.

'I said earlier we had been offered a new account,' she said nervously. 'Actually it's not as new as all that. We were asked to handle it some time ago, only Sam turned it down.'

Realisation began to dawn. So that's why she's jumpy, he thought.

'You know I don't work on cigarettes,' he cut in. 'We've been through all that before.'

'You didn't go through it with me,' said Louise. 'When Frisco presented itself last time, I was away in London and you only told me about it when you'd turned it down.'

Sam was surprised.

'I kind of assumed you'd go along with the general consensus. There didn't seem any need to haul you in from London and put it to the vote.'

A stray tendril of hair had escaped from the neat coil at the base of Louise's neck. She tucked it back briskly, impatiently almost, and Sam noticed how hard she looked with all her curls scraped back. Her responsibilities are changing her, he thought. She's not the same girl any more.

'You assume too much,' she told Sam. 'I thought a

cigarette account was a damn good idea the first time round, and I still think it's a good idea.'

Sam looked at Clay who was staring at the tablecloth.

'And what do you think?'

With an effort the fat man pulled himself together.

'I agree with Louise,' he said. 'I might not have been convinced once upon a time. But we lost White's Distillers last year and we haven't replaced it. If we don't do something fast we're in danger of trading at a loss.'

'Since when did that bother you?' asked Sam. 'We've had our lean times before and we've always come through. Our work is what sets us apart from the run-of-the-mill shops. Our work and our principles. If we take the Frisco account we'll be like all the other dross that call themselves agencies. We'll go down to their level and we'll be lost.'

Louise sat up and lit a cigarette.

'It depends what you mean by lost,' she said slowly. 'If you mean we'll come into line with the rest of the business, I don't think that's such a terrible thing. Other agencies our size deliver far bigger profits than we do, because they're not so fussy about what they take on. Okay, so they don't pick up so many awards but I never noticed a Clio making any difference to our bottom line.'

She turned to Sam.

'When the push comes to the shove,' she said, 'nobody really gives a goddamn about beautiful advertising or sounding smarter than the next man. In the end what really matters is making money. Clients respect that. Other agencies respect it. Only people like you think putting the dollar first is a little bit dirty.'

Sam regarded her for a long time without speaking and it was as if he saw two people. There was the Louise he had loved. Passionate and vulnerable. And there was this other Louise. The calculating ball-breaker. She's been talking to Clay, he thought. Not just the other day either. She's been bending his ear for months now to bring him in line with her ideas, and I was so in love with her, I let her get away with it.

He sighed. He had thought earlier he could straighten things out with his old partner. Now he knew Clay was a lost cause. If Louise wanted the Frisco business the fat man would side with her to bring it in. Nothing he could say now would change that. And he knew he only had one option left.

'If Frisco moves into the agency,' he said, 'then you know where I stand.'

Clay pushed back his chair and got up.

'Don't do it, Sam. I beg of you. It's not worth it. We've both worked too hard for it to end like this.'

Sam looked at his old friend and he felt sad. He had once thought Clay was tough and streetwise. Now he knew he was neither of those things.

'You can't play both ends against the middle,' he told him. 'Either you do things Louise's way or you listen to me.' He saw the agony on Clay's face. 'Don't have a heart attack,' he said. 'I know which way you'll swing, and in the long run it will probably make sense for you. You never did have the courage to stand up and be counted. Lunatics like me go for that option. But then liking myself always mattered more than the fast buck.'

He turned to Louise.

'If I've read you right, you already arranged for someone to put up the money to buy out my shares.'

For a second Louise's confidence seemed to leave her, and Sam caught a glimpse of the girl he used to know. Then like a mirage she vanished into thin air and Sam was left wondering if she had ever existed.

'You guessed right,' she said crisply. 'Abner Morris is putting up the ante.'

So that's what she's been up to, he thought. I thought the whole thing looked too slick. So Abner's got into the act at last. The bastard's tenacious. I'll say that for him.

'What does Abner get for his money?' Sam asked. 'A share in the agency, or a share in you. Or are they both the same thing?'

Louise bit her lip.

'That's fighting dirty,' she said.

Sam stood up and started to pile things into his briefcase.

'I'm entitled to fight dirty,' he replied, 'it's what you've always done. You used Brian Elder to make your name in the business. Then once you were a force to be reckoned with, you wanted more. So it was my turn to be used. Now Abner's in line. He'll give you what you want, Louise, don't worry about that. We all do in the end.' He paused. 'There's only one last thing I want to know. When you've got it all, when you're sitting on top of your own agency, making a big fat profit. Where do you go from there? You're getting well into your thirties now and you're starting to look it. By the time you've got to the top, wherever that is, I can't see you settling for a husband and children, and I can't see any man wanting to make a home with the kind of woman you're becoming. Even Abner Morris wouldn't have the stomach for that.'

For a moment Sam thought Louise would advance on him and attack him with her bare hands. Then he realised the old Louise would do that kind of thing. This new girl sitting in front of him was cooler than that, and more in control.

'Get out,' she said tightly. 'Get out before I have you thrown out.'

He looked at her, and this time he let his pity show. And his disgust.

'Do you know something, Louise? I really think you would.'

56

For days afterwards he walked around as if he was submerged beneath the sea for there was a curious silence all around him. Sam was used to people demanding things of him. In the army there were places he had to be, routines he had to perform. At work there were meetings, clients, deadlines. Now there was nothing. It was as if his life had been a film, speeding forward. And somebody had frozen the frame. Not somebody, he thought bitterly. Louise had done the freezing. In one short day she had managed to cut him off from all his ties. The following morning when he picked up the phone to his secretary she wasn't there. Further investigation revealed that his entire office, his desk, his files, the work he had in progress had all disappeared.

He got hold of Clay and demanded to know what was going on but his former partner was cagey with him. He kept mentioning Louise's name when Sam asked him a direct question and in the end he gave up and called his lawyer.

It took forty-eight hours to arrange Sam's departure from the agency he had created. All the negotiations were done third hand through lawyers, and at the end of the game Sam took away half a million dollars for his shares, a view of the Chrysler building George Lois had painted for him and an original Eames chair. Both items had been in his office for ten years and Clay had them sent round in a taxi.

Sam looked at them in the middle of his apartment and a feeling of utter hopelessness enveloped him. I spent twelve years of my life building a business, twelve years of late nights and junk food on the desk, twelve years of dreams, and all I have to show for it is a lousy chair and a picture of New York.

He thought about the money that had been paid into his account the day before. It was more capital than he had ever laid hands on but what could he do with it? If he wanted to take a trip around the world it would pay for that. Except he didn't want to go round the world. He had just come back from the West Indies and he didn't need a holiday. Besides he liked New York.

He thought about setting up another agency but he knew the money wouldn't cover it. He would need a backer or a loan from the bank, and his chances of getting either were slim. The publicity surrounding his departure from Kurnitz Tragos and Greene had seen to that.

He wondered when Louise had spoken to the trade press and the *New York Times*. Was it before the fateful meeting in Nadia's? Or did she move like lightning two minutes after the event? Either way she'd done for him. To the advertising community he looked like a prize patsy. A fall guy who had been thrown out of his own agency by a woman. A few insiders had known about the relationship between them and within hours the news had spread around town. Louise Tragos had screwed Sam Kurnitz in every sense of the word.

Sam kept quiet throughout all of it. Now wasn't the time to tell his side of the story. If he answered back now he would only add weight to the cloud hanging over him.

No, he would say nothing until he found a new job, or a new partner.

In the next few weeks he was offered things. Doyle Dane wanted him to fill a creative director's spot, he would be one of five. Sam turned it down. Twelve years of calling the shots had changed him. Today he was no longer capable of standing in line and waiting for judgement. Grey offered him the top creative slot and he said no to that as well.

The agency wasn't his style. He was approached by several people to set up businesses. He saw all of them and discovered he had nothing in common with any one of them for they had nothing to offer except for their stake money. They didn't understand Sam's kind of advertising and they didn't share his beliefs. All they wanted to do was make a fast buck out of the reputation he had built, and he wasn't going to be bought. Not until he had tried all the alternatives.

At the end of six weeks he had followed up all his leads and come up with nothing and the self-pity that had been dogging his heels threatened to overwhelm him. Louise did this, he raged to himself. If I'd never met her I'd still have my business. My wife would have suffered less and my child would have been born.

He was standing in the main room of the apartment on a February afternoon. Outside the sky was grey and overcast and added to his gloom. If he had been looking out on to a storm, the bad weather would have lent dignity to his mood, but there was no drama in drizzle and gusty wind filled with debris from the streets.

Sam turned away from the window and went into the kitchen to get a cup of coffee. Frances was there leafing through a magazine. She had finished work early that day and was wondering where to go for supper when she saw her husband's face.

'What is it?' she asked. 'Something's getting to you. Eating away at you. I don't like it.'

He told her about Louise and the bitterness he felt. It was a long tirade. The diatribe of a disappointed man. Frances was shocked, though not at what had happened – she knew about that and had felt her own rage. What stopped her dead was what this whole business was doing to her husband.

She had known other men who had suffered worse blows than his recent one and who had carried on undefeated. She herself had suffered yet when things were at their worst she had not given way to despair. She hardened her resolve. Louise had not destroyed her, she'd hurt her and though Frances had changed, she hadn't gone under. Her husband wouldn't either.

'I think it's time we forget about Louise,' she said quietly. 'There's too much going on in our own lives to waste any more energy on her.'

'What's going on with us that's so terrific?' Sam said harshly. 'I've got nothing and you've got next to nothing working for that trade rag.'

Frances's head came up.

'For Christ's sake snap out of it,' she said. 'I know you haven't been offered anything you want but it's not the end of the world. We've got half a million dollars in the bank. There's got to be something we can do with that.'

'Like what?' he asked her. 'It's not enough to set up another business if that's what you're thinking.'

Frances thought for a minute. Then she turned to Sam. 'How much more would you need?'

'Another three hundred thousand minimum, and nobody I want to do business with is coming through with that kind of money. Even the bank won't stake me.'

Frances got up and walked through into the other room and she looked around it as if she was seeing it for the very first time. The sofa and the glass-and-ceramic coffee table had been chosen by her at the very beginning of her marriage. She ran her fingers across the terrible modern painting over the mantel Tiffany had made her buy. Even that had memories. Then she finally looked through the long plate glass window that was the central point of the apartment and she marvelled at the view of the city she saw spread out before her. This town will always remind me of the time when I was young, she thought. When I could still be innocent enough to dream.

She set her chin. Dreams die, she thought. And we

all grow up. She walked back to the kitchen and her husband.

'I've got your stake money,' she told him.

He laughed at her.

'You're crazy,' he said. 'What are you selling?'

She didn't smile.

'Rephrase the question,' she told him. 'Ask me what we're selling.'

'Okay, what are we selling?'

The words came out in a rush, as if she had been keeping the news to herself too long and now she had to share the burden.

'We're selling the apartment,' she said. 'One of your old friends from Benton and Bowles made us an offer on it when the story about you broke in the press. Apparently he'd always been after it but you never wanted to sell.'

Sam looked amused.

'The guy who wants the place, he's not called Mort Shulman by any chance?'

Frances sat down.

'How did you know?'

'Because he rang me about the same time as he called you. He wanted to make sure we both knew about his bid. I told him to get lost.'

She looked at him levelly.

'I told him we'd be interested,' she said. 'More than interested.'

'Why did you do that?'

Frances kept up the cool determined gaze she had worn since she came back into the room. She had fought with her husband once before, and won. Now she was going to win again. This time for both of them.

'I did it,' she told him, 'because the guy was offering over a million dollars and I knew even then we were going to need all the money we could lay our hands on if you were going to come out of this mess holding your head up. Look,' she continued, 'we don't need to live here any more. Who have we got to impress? Clay and that dingbat he's married to? Clients you haven't got any more? Abner Morris? The people we need to convince right now, my darling, are marketing directors who are looking to give their business to a brand new agency. And those characters aren't looking to come to candle-lit dinners at your home. They're going to turn up at your brand new ultra-modern offices. So you'd better make sure you've got the money to pay for them.'

Sam put his hand up and took hold of her then pulled her down so that she was sitting on his lap.

'Tell me something,' he said, smoothing the hair out of her eyes. 'As you're suddenly the big expert on real estate in the city, where exactly are we going to live now you've sold the roof over our heads?'

Frances rented a loft in the SoHo area of New York. It had once been used as a warehouse and the shabby dark painted walls still betrayed its origins, but despite its run-down appearance, the place suited her purpose.

The area was central so Sam could get to and from the city in a hurry and the space the loft gave them was big enough for all their furniture and possessions. They might have come down in the world, but that didn't mean they couldn't live like human beings.

Frances took the loft the first moment she set eyes on it. Decent places were few and far between in Manhattan and she didn't have time to spend traipsing around.

She looked around her at the peeling walls and the cracked floorboards. What this place needs, she thought, is a gang of workmen with me in charge of them. Then I might get it into some kind of shape. She felt panicky. When am I going to do all this, she wondered. The office is already kicking up about me taking days off to find somewhere to move to. They'll go crazy if I tell them I want another three weeks to fix up the new apartment.

She thought about Sam's plans for a new agency. The pair of them had spent every night till the early hours going through papers, figuring out how many staff they needed. Seeing job candidates. Imperceptibly Frances had become another pair of hands for Sam, typing important documents on her portable, running around to see offices he couldn't get to, making calls he was too tied up for. Now she needed to take even more time out so they would have a place to live. I can't do it, she thought. I can't make our new life together and hold down a job.

She gave the janitor the down-payment on the loft and took the subway back to the magazine. Then she went in and saw her editor.

'There's not enough of me to go round,' she told him, 'and my husband needs me more than you do. So I'm quitting.'

They gave her a terrific send-off. The reporters clubbed together and bought some decent Californian wine and with the money left over they went to the local deli and got a cheesecake. It was her parting gift. That and a list of all the movers and shakers on Madison Avenue, complete with their private telephone lines.

'Keep it by you,' her editor instructed. 'If you or Sam needs to get to anyone in a hurry, you'll find it useful.'

She took it and there were tears in her eyes.

'What's the matter with you guys?' she asked. 'I thought the least you could do was come up with a client or two.'

Sam found offices on Lexington Avenue. They were on the tenth floor of a new modern block and the moment he walked into them he knew they were what he was looking for. There was a clean, bright reception area big enough for a dazzlingly pretty receptionist and a battery of telephones. The walls were freshly painted and cried out for

Sam's ads to be displayed all over them. But the best thing was the working space. It was a big open-plan area, newly carpeted. There were no cubby holes where anyone could hide away and hatch plots. In this agency everyone worked together. If they needed a meeting of staff, they could hold it right there out on the floor. If somebody wanted to talk about a new campaign, they could wander over to where Sam was working and go right ahead. Nobody will stand on ceremony here, he thought, because there's no place to do it.

He went home that night and told Frances he was ready to go into business. All he had to do now was hire himself some bodies.

Junior staff was easy enough. Headhunters provided art directors, traffic men, media experts, account men. What Sam needed now was a classy new business act. There were half a dozen top men on Madison Avenue he would have jumped at. They were all booked. He took his time interviewing the second division but after five days, he saw nothing he liked. Then Brian Elder walked into his brand new reception area. Sam was coming out of his office when he saw him standing there and he recognised the client supremo on sight. He was still the city slicker he remembered from the old days when he was still working for Acker and Stein. He still sported his Westpoint tan and his suit was the best Brookes Brothers were making that season. But the man was frayed round the edges. It wasn't an obvious thing. Elder wasn't losing his hair, and he didn't seem to be sporting any new wrinkles, but there was something tense about him. An edginess that communicated.

Sam wracked his memory. Where was Elder working nowadays? The last report he had on the man was that he was up at McCann's and doing well. So what was he doing here, sniffing around an agency that wasn't even started? Sam decided to go and find out.

Elder did his best to appear casual.

'I heard on the grapevine you were setting up again. So I decided to come round and see if you needed any help.'

Sam went to the cupboard and got out a bottle of Scotch. There was something about Elder he didn't like. He was good at what he did, that was for sure but there was something fly about him. Something tacky.

He poured the drink into two glasses and waited for Elder to make his pitch. For a while they talked generalities. Elder wanted to know how Sam had set up the agency and why he hadn't gone into partnership with any of the men who had approached him. He even had a list of their names.

'Why didn't you go for it?' Elder wanted to know. 'Why didn't you just take the dough and ask questions afterwards?'

Sam took a deep breath and swallowed half his Scotch.

'Because I would have been lumbered with a partner I didn't like. I would have had to live with him and I've done that once already.'

Elder started to smile.

'You're talking about Louise.' His eyes took on a far-away look. 'The reason she got out of hand, if you don't mind me saying so, is you didn't understand her. She's a tough girl, that one. Treacherous as hell. I knew it the first moment I met her, which is why I kept her under control.'

Sam looked at the too tailored, too confident man sitting in front of him drinking his Scotch and he wondered why he was wasting his time listening to him.

Except, there was something about what he had just said, something about keeping Louise under control that intrigued him.

'Louise is too devious to be pushed around,' he said. 'Nobody could ever control her the way you just described.'

'I didn't describe it,' said Elder, 'but if you like I will.'

He took the bottle of whisky and poured a hefty slug into his glass. Then he settled back into his chair.

'When I first ran into Louise she had just escaped from the Bronx. The kid was a real slum bunny. She dressed like a beatnik. Her hair was all over the place, and she was rough round the edges, but she had something even then. Her visual ideas were better than anyone else's in the department and she was as ambitious as hell. If I'd asked her to turn cartwheels down Fifth Avenue in the nude she would have done it. And that gave me the clue to her. You see, she was ready to be trained. If she'd been around longer I couldn't have moulded her the way I did. But she knew nothing. So I started to teach her a few tricks and she caught on fast.'

Sam started to feel slightly queasy.

'What sort of tricks?' he asked softly.

Elder laughed and finished the best part of his Scotch.

'I didn't give her a course in marketing, if that's what you're talking about. What I taught that girl, I taught her strictly out of office hours. A minute ago you told me she was devious. I spotted that in her right away, but I wasn't going to let her practise her little games on me. So I showed her other games: I taught her that pain was a fine and a beautiful thing and that if she behaved herself her master would administer it. I controlled Louise because I controlled her pleasure. Her body belonged to me.'

Sam shuddered, remembering how Louise, broken and shamed, had handed him a cane to beat her with.

'So you were the bastard who did it to her, you were responsible for her corruption.'

The elegant huckster from the East Coast preened himself.

'I did her the world of good,' he replied. 'I'm sure Abner Morris is applauding the job I did on her. It's not every chick that has her repertoire.'

Sam got up from where he was sitting. He didn't offer his hand.

'I think we're just about done,' he said. 'In spite of your business record there's no place for you in this agency.'

Elder didn't move.

'Stop being emotional,' he said. 'You've hocked yourself up to the eyeballs for this set-up and you haven't pulled down any business yet. Right now I'd say you need me more than I need you.'

Sam should have thrown him out there and then but there was one question left that still puzzled him.

'Why the hell do you want to join me anyway?' he asked. 'It can't be for the money or the prestige, that's for sure.'

Elder passed a hand over his chin, and considered for a moment.

Finally he said, 'I want to even the score. I want to show Louise she isn't as smart as she thinks she is. I owe her that for the way she got out from under all those years ago.' He set his face. 'Listen to me. With my expertise and your talent we can grab most of her business before she knows what's hit her.'

Sam believed every word he said. Brian Elder had just the right touch to bring in any account he set his heart on. With him on the team, the new agency would prosper from day one. But he knew he couldn't take on this man and live with himself. He walked over to the door and held it open.

'It's been interesting talking to you,' he said, 'but don't hold your breath waiting for me to call.'

57

In the end Sam settled for quantity, rather than quality.

He hired two medium-weight account handlers who were on the loose. They weren't major talents, either of them, but they were solid and they knew what they were doing. If any potential client wants flair, Sam thought grimly, he can look towards me. That's what I made my name on.

He released the story that he was in business again to the trade press. The magazine Frances had worked for ran the announcement on the front page. Everyone else relegated it to page three or page five. Sam Kurnitz was no longer a hero on Madison Avenue. If he was to merit headlines again he had to pull in a hell of a lot of business. Either that or rob a bank.

The press reaction was reflected in the attitude of his old clients. They liked Sam and they admired him, but before they started rocking the boat they wanted to see if he was going to make a success of his new agency.

Sam was undeterred. If anything, having his back against the wall made him sharper. He went after everything in town. If a tampons account was up for grabs he was there first with a finished up campaign when everyone else presented roughs. Sometimes he didn't wait for an account to look around for a move. If he heard the slightest whisper that a certain client wasn't quite happy with the climate of his agency, he was on the phone offering his services. In his first three months of business Sam had travelled the length and breadth of the States showing his credentials to anyone who would see him, but nobody bit because nobody wanted to stick their neck out. In the public's mind Sam was a loser. A fall guy. Samson to Louise's Delilah.

'What we need right now,' Frances told him one weary night when they were totting up their losses, 'is a breakthrough. If just one client was willing to take a chance on us, everybody else would follow.'

Sam nodded.

'But where is he?' he asked. 'I've been chasing my tail for months now looking for just a sniff of business, even a development project, but nothing seems to happen.' He looked anguished. 'Is there something wrong with me suddenly? Has my work gone to pot?'

Frances poured him a drink, then sat down beside him.

'Nothing's the matter,' she said calmly. 'Everybody who starts on their own comes up against this problem. It's only a question of time now. Somebody will start the ball rolling.'

Frances had been telling her husband the same story every night since the agency opened its doors. Half the time she didn't believe what she was saying. Most of the time she felt like bursting into tears and throwing in the towel. But something stopped her – or rather someone stopped her. Louise Tragos.

Ever since she had relaunched her business, she had dominated the media. Women's magazines carried interviews of her talking about how to succeed in a man's world. *Ad Age* ran a profile of her and the city page of the *New York Times* quoted her as saying that the day of creative advertising was dead.

'People don't want to be entertained by a campaign. They don't want to be made to think. All they want to know is where to buy the product,' she pronounced. 'I tell my creative geniuses to print the brand name big, at the top of the page if necessary. Then I leave the rest to the public's need.'

Frances threw down the paper.

'Can you believe this latest rubbish from Louise?' she asked her husband. 'Was she always like this?'

Sam shook his head.

'No,' he said, 'this is a recent departure. When I first hired Louise she was full of dreams and talent. I know you hate her and I don't blame you, but believe me, she wasn't always the monster you see today.'

'What changed her?'

Sam sighed, remembering her at the last meeting of the agency he once had a stake in.

'She got greedy. She wanted to make a lot of money without putting in any real work and she thought she could do it by bringing in huge clients and manipulating them behind the scenes.'

Frances looked at him.

'Like American Tobacco?'

Again Sam sighed.

'Like American Tobacco. But it can't work, not in the long run. Sure, she'll be rich for a few years, as long as she and Abner go on making music together. But the moment that relationship goes sour and the business walks out the door, she'll have nothing to fall back on. Nobody will say, let's give Tragos and Partners another chance because what have they got to offer? The ability to run a sixty-million dollar account? Any agency can do that. The reason business moves in this town is because of the advertising. If it's innovative, if it sells, if it alters the way people see a product, then clients are interested. I've always lived by that credo. I did it when I was up and I'm still doing it. No matter what happens I always will.'

Frances thought about what her husband had told her and picked up the paper again.

'I wonder what Clay thinks about this,' she said. 'Now Louise is grabbing all the attention I bet he isn't feeling too comfortable.'

Sam set his face.

'I wouldn't shed any tears for Clay,' he told her. 'The stupid klutz brought it on himself.'

The breakthrough they needed came just as their stake money was running out. After paying rent and salaries, Sam calculated he could only manage to keep going for another three months. After that he would have to start laying off staff and once he did that, the game was over.

Sam was working out what to do next, when a call came through from the Bank of Ontario. The marketing man on the end of the line told him they were launching a new credit card and the bank wanted Sam to pitch for the business alongside two other agencies.

Sam hesitated. To go after this kind of business would take a big bite out of his capital. Instead of three months' grace, he would be lucky if he could get by for another four weeks.

'How much is the account worth if we win it?' he asked cautiously.

There was a pause while the man from the bank went through his papers. He came back on the line.

'We reckon to be spending around three-quarters of a million in the test market. When we go national, the figure could go up as far as twelve.'

Sam did some fast thinking. This was the piece of business he had been looking for. It was spending enough to put him on his feet and it was prestigious enough to attract other clients. But could he afford the gamble?

Before he took that decision, he needed to know what kind of competition he was up against.

'Who are the other agencies in the race?' he said.

The marketing man started to get flustered.

'We don't normally give out that kind of information. Why do you want to know?'

Sam's voice had an edge to it.

'It's simple,' he said. 'If I don't stand a good chance

of winning this pitch, then I'm not interested. There's too much at stake to go after something just for the sake of it.'

'That's not what I heard. According to my contact in the trade, you've been going after everything that moves.'

'Things change,' said Sam briskly, 'so if you won't tell me the names of the other agencies, we'll end this conversation now.'

There was a silence on the end of the line and Sam mentally crossed his fingers. He was sticking his neck out, he knew that, but he also knew he'd rather take his chances now while it didn't cost him anything.

When the Ontario Bank's man came back, Sam detected a new warmth in his voice.

'Because I admire what you're doing, I'll tell you who else is in the race. But you've got to promise to keep this information to yourself.'

Sam said he would. Then he heard the news he was waiting for: he was pitching alongside Benton and Bowles and Norman Craig and Kummel. He let out a sigh of relief. In Sam's opinion they didn't have a creative record that could even come near his. He gripped the telephone receiver harder than he intended.

'We're on,' he said. 'Take this as a formal notice that Sam Kurnitz Advertising will present for your business.'

The next three weeks were spent in a frenzy of activity. The Bank of Ontario wanted a press campaign and a poster campaign. As well as that they needed to know how competitively the agency could buy space in newspapers and magazines. They also wanted a marketing plan based on existing research.

Sam put his whole team to work on the pitch. One of his new account men pointed out that at least two people should be handling general enquiries and seeing what other prospects were around. Sam disagreed.

'We've wasted enough time following up leads that go

nowhere. Let's concentrate all our efforts on something real for a change.'

Many men in Sam's shoes would have shown signs of flagging but, if anything, the toughness of the situation turned him on. He knew this was his last chance. If this failed, he'd had it. The knowledge didn't diminish his energy or his flow of ideas.

At the end of one week he came up with three concepts for Canada-Card. Then, without putting it to the vote, he threw out two of them and developed the third to finished artwork.

His unerring sense of style told him he had settled on a winner. The whole campaign was based on one simple premise. The majority of people are terrified of their credit cards, because they think it will turn them into spend-thrifts. Sam's advertising was designed to overcome that resistance, by taking a lighthearted approach. In one press ad he divided the page in half. On one side he showed the Canada-Card with the signature, Dr Jekyll. On the other card was signed, Mr Hyde. The headline asked, 'Are you worried that your Canada-Card will bring out the worst in you?' Underneath, the copy was simple and showed a sympathetic understanding of people's worries about owning a credit card.

Everyone in the agency agreed it was the best thing he ever did but he didn't relax until he had shown it to Frances. Through all this she had been the one person he could be certain of for she never lied, and she didn't agree with him for the sake of it. If she hated an ad, she told him. Sam was prepared to ditch all the work on Canada-Card if she said it was wrong.

He needn't have worried. She was as sure of it as he was.

'Have you no criticisms?' he asked. 'Our whole future rests on this.'

She smiled and squeezed his hand.

'I trust you,' she said. 'You wouldn't throw our money away on a no-hoper.'

Sam and a team of three key men flew to Canada to show their wares to the Bank of Ontario. They were the last agency to present and by the end of the meeting, Sam was convinced they had the business. The committee who received them didn't say anything specific but he had been around long enough to read the signs.

If an agency isn't going to land an account, the meeting generally finishes one minute after the agency has made its pitch. The managing director of the bank kept Sam and his team talking for three-quarters of an hour after they had seen everything. They wanted a breakdown of how much it would cost to produce the press ads. They even wanted to know which print houses Sam was going to use. Finally they promised to be in touch the following week.

Sam arrived home weary but jubilant. 'If things go the way I think they're going,' he told Frances, 'we could be out of here in a couple of months.'

She looked around the loft she had spent months getting together and felt few regrets. Everything from the uneven floorboards to the view of the tenement from the back window depressed her. She'd done her best with the place. She'd painted the walls and thrown brightly coloured rugs round the awkwardly shaped rooms, but the place still looked shabby.

'It can't be soon enough for me,' she told him. 'I'm not looking for Park Avenue, I'd settle for far less, but there has to be some place we can live where I'm not scared of getting attacked every time I step into the hallway.'

Sam went across to the dresser and refreshed his drink. 'The hell with it,' he said, 'we're living dangerously as it is, so why not take one more chance? Tomorrow morning I want you to go talk to the realtor and tell him to find us a decent apartment.'

He knew it was a crazy idea the minute the words were

out of his mouth but he had had enough. When he came back from Israel he hadn't been rich but he had always lived as if he was and now he was damned if he was going to change his habits.

Frances looked nervous.

'What if we don't land this business?' she asked him. 'What happens then?'

Sam took a big slug of his bourbon. 'What happens then is I put myself back on the job market. I'm still capable of earning enough to keep you in some kind of style. We've done quite enough of slumming it for one lifetime.'

'But the agency,' Frances said. 'All the hopes we had.'

Sam finished his drink and stared out of the window at the crumbling brickwork opposite.

'Don't worry about the agency,' he told her. 'Let me worry about it for a change.'

Four days later Sam heard from the Bank of Ontario. They sent him a letter signed from the managing director, Elton Kavanagh.

'Dear Mr Kurnitz,' it said. 'We very much regret to tell you that the bank has withdrawn its plans for Canada-Card. We apologise for putting you and your colleagues to so much trouble and, in the event, wasted effort. If we revive our plans for Canada-Card in the future we will be in touch.

Yours
Elton Kavanagh.'

Sam threw the letter down on the table and put his head in his hands. Of all the things that could have happened, this was the one he least anticipated. The factor over which he had no control. It's so unfair, he raged, this was my last card, the one gamble I couldn't afford to take and I was cut down. Not by a competitor, or an enemy or anything

I could understand. What finished me off was some joker at the bank who decided to pull the plug.

He was overwhelmed by despair. He had put so much into this agency. His money, his reputation, even the roof over his head. Now it was all for nothing. Once he'd paid everyone off, he'd be left with just enough to put a down-payment on a new apartment. And damn it, if he did nothing else, at least he could do that. At least he and Frances could start to live like human beings again.

He sat up at his desk and wondered what to do next. He could call Frances and tell her the news or he could put in a call to Judy Wald. He decided on the headhunter. If Judy came through with the possibility of a job, at least he would have something positive to tell his wife.

He went to pick up the telephone but it rang before he got to it. The voice on the other end stopped him dead. It belonged to his old partner, Clay Greene. This was all he needed. Clay crowing at his misfortunes.

'I'm busy right now,' Sam told him. 'Can I call you back?'

'No,' said Clay. 'I'm not calling from the office. I'm in a kiosk.'

What on earth was Clay doing on the street at ten in the morning, Sam wondered.

'Is anything the matter?' he asked. 'The agency hasn't burned down, has it?'

His old partner attempted a laugh. It sounded hollow.

'Tragos and Partners is still standing,' he said. 'But it's standing without me. I quit ten minutes ago.'

I can't cope, thought Sam. First I get the news I'm ruined. Now Clay rings me up and tells me the same story.

'If you're looking for a shoulder to cry on,' he said, 'you've come to the wrong guy. I've got too many troubles of my own to be much use to anybody else right now.'

'That's what you think. Can I come and see you?'

Sam sighed deeply. He was in no mood to listen to a

catalogue of Louise's crimes. 'Didn't you hear me the first time? I'm not interested in going over old ground. Go home and kvetch to Tiffany. She's your wife, she's got to listen to you.'

He was about to hang up, when Clay started to shout.

'Would you change your mind if I told you I could bring some business into your new set-up?'

Sam felt his brow break out into a sweat.

'What business?' he spluttered.

'Louise's business. The business that used to belong to us.'

Sam stared at the telephone he was holding. If Clay had called five seconds later he would have been hassling Judy Wald for a job as a creative director.

'How soon can you get here?' he asked.

58

The moment Clay got to Sam's office, he did a quick circuit of the premises, pronounced them suitable, then suggested they take their meeting somewhere more relaxing.

Sam groaned. He had endured Turkish baths and high-tech gyms with Clay. What on earth did he have in store for him now? He found out ten minutes later when the taxi deposited them at the front of the Carlton Hotel on the upper east side.

'If you wanted coffee,' Sam said, 'I could have rustled up some at the office.'

Clay shook his head vigorously.

'We're not going to the coffee shop. We're going to the swimming club on the thirty-fifth floor.'

Wordlessly Sam allowed himself to be led into the elevator and as it made its way upwards, he wondered when Clay would put his proposition. In the changing-room? In the pool? Under the shower? The possibilities, instead of irritating him, made him smile. They had been in business together nearly twelve years. They had had their fights and their disagreements but they had always been on the same wavelength. So I have to listen to marketing strategies under the shower, Sam thought. At least the man will be talking my language.

He was wrong about the shower. Clay had no intention of discussing his business there.

He felt the Jacuzzi would be more appropriate. The Carlton Swimming Club occupied the entire top floor of the hotel. As well as an Olympic-sized pool, there was a steam room, a sauna and a large marble whirlpool bath. The first two services were hidden away in a separate section of the Club. The Jacuzzi was out in the open at the far end of the pool.

There was something hedonistic about the whole set-up, Sam thought. Most New York health clubs had a spartan feel about them, all shining white surfaces and scrubbed pine. The Carlton was the antithesis of this. The entire pool area was paved in mosaic. Turquoise mosaic into which were set tiny glittering stones so you had the impression you were walking on a moving sea. The same turquoise mosaic covered the walls but instead of the shining stones, there were intricate frescos of old Egyptian kings holding court in their palaces. By the side of the pool, running the length of one wall was the bar. If Sam had expected health drinks, he was in for a surprise for the swimming club served the same kind of refreshments as the 21 Club. Hard liquor and char-broiled steaks.

'Who on earth comes here?' asked Sam. They had changed into swimming trunks, which the club provided and were making their way towards the steaming and mercifully empty Jacuzzi.

Clay grinned.

'Arabs come here,' he said. 'And fat businessmen like me who like the atmosphere of a health club, but don't want to take any exercise. I've had it with exercise,' he added, 'that gym I took you to nearly finished me off.'

Clay led the way up the tiled steps to the hot tub, but before he got in he shouted across to the bartender, 'Bring me a bourbon.' He turned to Sam. 'What will it be?'

Sam settled on a beer then he got into the water. If Clay wanted to play Arab potentates, it was fine with him so long as he got down to cases. This he did when the waiter came across with their drinks.

He identified five sizeable chunks of business that the pair of them could move out of Tragos and Partners with no trouble at all.

'There's just one problem,' said Sam. 'My severance

agreement. The agency paid me half a million bucks on condition I don't approach any of the clients for a minimum of two years. I can't see any way round it unless you set up on your own and use me as a consultant.'

Clay looked doubtful.

'I don't like the idea,' he said. 'You and I have always operated as a partnership. I can't see it working with one of us on the outside. Too many factors could get in between us.'

'Like they did last time, you mean.'

There was a silence, while Clay threw back his drink. Then he heaved himself round in the water until he faced his former partner.

'Look,' he said, 'I know you don't want to discuss Louise, but unless we do, we're never going to be able to have a sensible conversation again.'

He signalled the bartender for another round of drinks, then he let Sam have it.

'You know, you were just as responsible for the split between us as Louise was,' he said. Sam started to interrupt, but he wouldn't let him.

'The moment you landed that big catfood account, things started to change. And that was years ago, before Louise had even gone to London. I figured something had happened between the two of you when I couldn't get you to listen to me any more. You were too busy for me suddenly. I'd ask you for your opinion on our building society business, or the new breakfast cereal we were launching and the answer would always be the same. "Can't you see I'm up to my ears on this Kitten Catfood commercial or this Kitten press ad." It was as if you'd suddenly turned off to everything to do with the agency that didn't directly concern Louise.

'Why do you think I let her get involved in our other business to the extent I did? It was a way of attracting your attention. I knew if Louise was interested in a project, you would be too.'

Sam sighed deeply. 'I didn't know I was that obvious.'

'Obvious,' Clay laughed. 'If you'd announced it to the whole agency, it couldn't have been plainer. Louise was your lover, girlfriend, mistress . . . Whatever you wanted to call her, it was clear she virtually owned you. During office hours, at any rate.'

'It must have come as a great relief when I called it quits,' Sam said.

Clay looked questioning.

'The first time round you mean? Sure, it was a load off my mind. At long last I could involve you in the running of the agency again. It didn't last of course. The second she came back to New York, it was back to the old ways. She would talk and you would listen, and I might as well have not existed. Only it was worse the second time round because Louise was a full partner by then and she had every right to weigh in with her opinions.'

Sam picked up his second beer and found the steamy atmosphere had warmed it through. He called across to the bartender for a Perrier water, then he concentrated on Clay.

'When did it go wrong?' he asked. 'When did you start to talk to Louise and not to me?'

'Not for a long time,' Clay replied. 'Not until you and Louise started quarrelling and by then I was so worried about the agency's future, I would have talked to anybody who was making some kind of sense.'

Sam picked up his water and drank it out of the bottle. The heat and the Jacuzzi were getting to him. Why can't we have this kind of discussion in restaurants like everyone else in the business, he thought.

'Are you saying I wasn't making sense?' he asked.

Clay nodded.

'That's exactly what I was saying. Somewhere along the

line, the woman had scrambled your brains. Oh, you were still doing great work. Nobody could take that away from you, but your judgement was shot to pieces. I couldn't reason with you any more and after a bit I didn't want to.'

'So you voted with Louise against me.'

Clay pulled himself to his feet and started to climb out of the hot tub. He was rosy pink all over and Sam was reminded of a giant lobster. He sank down by the side of the bath fanning himself. Then he changed gear.

'Look,' said Clay, 'you made a big mistake with Louise and so did I. If it's okay with you I'd like to call it quits. We have business to discuss and right now I think that takes priority.'

Sam made a wry face.

'If you insist,' he said. 'Though how we're going to go into any kind of partnership when I can't approach my old clients, I don't know.'

'I know you can't go for your accounts,' said Clay, 'but there's no law that says your accounts can't go for you.'

Sam looked up in surprise.

'I don't see how,' he said, 'I never see them.'

'I've got a plan to change all that. Let's go into the shower and I'll tell you about it.'

But Sam had had enough. He'd endured the Jacuzzi, warm beer and Clay's half-baked excuses. Any further conversation would have to be on his terms.

'I'll do a deal with you,' he said. 'I'll buy you lunch at the 21, if you promise to keep quiet about your idea until we get there.'

Clay nodded assent. The 21 was as good a place as any to plan a come-back.

'What I have in mind,' said Clay toying with his steak tartare, 'is a gamble that could close you down tomorrow if it fails.'

Sam sighed. Why was nothing ever straightforward in

his life? If this had happened to anyone else, five pieces of business would have walked through the agency door and that would have been that. Instead he was facing ruin for the second time that day. All of a sudden he didn't care. He'd lost everything he ever had. What else can anybody do, he thought? Kill me?

He turned to Clay.

'Okay,' he said, 'tell me about it.'

His companion looked dreamy.

'I'm planning to throw a party,' he said. 'Not a run-of-the-mill white wine and canapés party, but a big bash, a lavish bash with champagne and caviar and flunkeys dressed in white tails. The kind of affair that Donald Trump would throw if he wanted to launch a new hotel.'

Sam put his fork down.

'Where do you intend to get the money for it because I haven't got it.'

'Yes you have,' said Clay. 'I checked with your accountant before I rang you. I told him I was speaking for the landlord of the building and I was enquiring how much more rent I could expect. Your guy must have been feeling pretty insecure, because he told me right off. You've got six weeks left. Six weeks' rent, six weeks' salaries, six weeks' lunch bills. Listen to me, I'm willing to match your six weeks' money with the same amount out of my savings account. That way we can more than afford my party.'

Sam started to shake his head.

'Why should I do it?' he asked. 'What possible reason do I have to throw away the rest of my running expenses on a party?'

Now Clay looked cunning.

'You won't be throwing your money away,' he said. 'You'll be investing it. My plan is to invite every one of our ex-clients to this party. Them and all the other guys who can give us business.'

Sam tried to interrupt, but Clay wouldn't give him the chance.

'The mistake you made the last time you went chasing after business was you looked too needy, too anxious. Well, this time you're not going to come on like a loser. You're going to make like the guy who broke the bank at Monte Carlo.

'You're going to look so busy, so damned affluent, that people will be falling over themselves to give you their business. In this town people like success. They respond to it. If you tell any client, even a multi million dollar client, you're not sure you have time for him, he'll beg you to take him on. Look at Abner Morris. You told that guy in words of one syllable you didn't want to know from cigarettes and he was on his knees pleading with you to give him a chance.'

Sam started to laugh.

'It's way over the top of course. No-one in their right mind would ever fall for it.'

Clay shook his head. 'Not true,' he said. He indicated a group of dark-suited executives sitting around a table. 'Recognise any of them? Between them they run a couple of billion dollars' worth of business. Yet they all got conned in a Wall Street scam six months ago. Nobody falls for a worse deal than a salesman and the better the salesman, the harder he falls. The guys you need to impress are so used to giving it out, that when they get it back they can't see it coming. I promise you Sam, if you put on that party – if *we* put on that party, we'll be back in business before the evening is over.'

Sam pushed away his half-eaten steak. It could just work, he thought. He remembered all the time he'd spent putting on elaborate presentations. He'd gone without sleep dreaming up award-winning ideas. And for what? For people like the Bank of Ontario to tell him they'd canned the idea of a new credit card. They weren't going to do business after all.

'Okay,' he said, 'count me in. I've tried to get off the ground all the ways I know. Let's try something different for a change.'

59

They sent invitations out to everybody. Marketing directors, managing directors of public companies, heads of rival agencies. And they didn't just ask the top brass: they invited junior brand managers and copywriters too. They were setting out to look like they'd made it on Madison Avenue, and for that they needed the applause of the whole world. As an afterthought, Sam put Abner Morris on the mailing list. If he turned up it would worry Louise. And he wanted her good and worried. He wanted all his enemies nervous as hell.

Somebody had once told Sam that when you're making your name, a good enemy is worth two friends – because they can be guaranteed to talk about you. Tonight everybody was going to be talking about him and if it wasn't him they were gossiping about, then Clay was going to be on the tip of everybody's tongue.

Sam's split with Louise and Abner had made headlines in the advertising press. Clay had kept his mouth shut about the reasons for his own departure, but speculation was rife. It was well known in the business that Louise and Sam had fallen out over the creative product and now history everyone assumed had repeated itself with Clay. Louise had done her best to deny any differences, but when Clay announced he was going back into business with Sam, his motives were obvious.

The two of them had played the story like the professionals they were. They held a press conference at the Plaza where they told the world they had pulled in a raft of new business but beyond that they refused to go into details. They only said that it was business as usual for Kurnitz and Greene and anyone who wanted to know more had better put in an appearance at the party to celebrate the re-launch of the agency.

Although Clay knew what kind of party he wanted, he had little idea of how to go about it and in the end Frances had to step in and take over. She did it knowing it would be the last party she would give for a long time, for Frances was pregnant again. She had suspected it for some weeks and the doctor had finally confirmed it the day Clay came back into their lives.

She had been tempted to tell Sam there and then but something told her not to. He was so distracted at the moment, so absorbed by his business, that nothing that didn't directly concern it was going to make any impression.

No, she thought, I'll let him have his party first. Then when it's all over and he and Clay are back in business, I'll let him into my secret. It will be better that way.

She put it out of her mind and got on with things. Her first act was to hire a specialist catering firm. These were the people that visiting rock stars called in when they were launching a new record, and they were much in favour with the young British Royals because they knew how to turn it on. The party could be held in a palace or Grand Central Station and the guests could come from almost any walk of life, but the end result would always be the same. It would be the most glittering, the most talked about, the most fun occasion in the city that night.

The first thing the planners did was to clear the agency. All the functional pale wood furniture was moved against one wall, the typewriters and business machines were put away, and all the office chairs disappeared. In their place padded white sofas and tiny gilt stools appeared.

Into this background they brought flowers. Armfuls and armfuls of white roses, white orchids and pom-pom chrysanthemums appeared all over the agency. The organisers set them up on frames, wove them around windows and trailed them across the polished floors.

Sam was put in mind of a wedding, or a gala and he added his contribution to the party by bringing out all his old ads. Campaigns that had won awards and hadn't seen the light of day for ten years or more were produced out of cupboards. This was the work that made Kurnitz and Greene a force to be reckoned with in their heyday.

The party people clapped their hands together and agreed with him about the ads. They were the point of the festivities after all, but they wanted to put them in silver frames and when Sam told them not to, they insisted on hanging garlands of flowers round them. In the end he had to put his foot down.

'This is something you don't have to dress up,' he told them. 'The people I've invited know damn well what they're looking at and if they're not interested, all the glitter in the world isn't going to help.'

In the end he got his way, but they made up for the austerity of the ads by bringing in strings of fairy lights and huge, vulgar chandeliers which they hung in every room.

By five o'clock they were finished and even Sam had to admit that the place looked like the setting for the best party he had ever given. When Frances walked in and saw it, she felt a small moment of panic. This represents everything we've got, she thought. All our savings, and I haven't even told Sam about the baby. With an effort she pulled herself together. So we fail, she thought. So what? The worst thing that can happen is we don't get rich overnight.

Sam can still find a job. We've still got enough strength between us to start all over again. Then like her husband, she put the idea of failure behind her. Tonight she was playing to win.

The first guests started to arrive at five-thirty. Most

of them had come straight from their offices expecting a run-of-the-mill agency party, but from the moment a waiter in white tails pushed a glass of champagne into their hands, they rapidly changed their opinions. As the crowd grew excited a buzz started to emanate from it. It was the kind of noise Frances had heard on successful first nights on Broadway and her heart rose.

She wandered round the room, eavesdropping on people's conversations.

'. . . must be making a bomb,' she heard a grey-suited executive say. 'He has to be to put this on.'

A copywriter with crazy hair was confiding to a colleague, 'The bastard gets all the good business nowadays . . . now he wants to rub our noses in it.'

Two balding men were standing in a corner holding a whispered conversation.

'I thought I saw Harv Menzies a second ago. What's he doing here? We're still handling all his business aren't we?'

Slowly she started to relax. So far the party planners had managed to fool the crowd. Now Clay and Sam had to do their bit. She cast a worried eye in her husband's direction. He was talking to a fat balding man in a shabby tweed coat. What's he doing wasting time with some out of work art director, she thought furiously. He should be concentrating on some of the big spenders we've invited tonight. They were all there: Heinz, American Home Products, NBC, Canadian Pacific, Texas Oil, Ford Motors, Western Union, Johnsons, Campbell's soups, and many more.

Frances stopped one of the agency's traffic men on his way to the bar.

'Who's that man talking to Sam?' she asked.

The traffic man peered shortsightedly through the crowd. Then he smiled with evident delight.

'That's Mel Pringle,' he told her. 'He only runs Corn-flour products.' He looked dreamy. 'Right now he could be talking to Sam about biscuits or spaghetti or soup or just anything.'

Frances squeezed his shoulder.

'Thanks for the reassurance,' she said.

She went and got herself a glass of orange juice, and started to mingle with the guests. Frances was talking to a man from Volkswagen when she saw her. How does she have the bare-faced nerve, she thought.

If I was Louise Tragos I wouldn't come within ten miles of the place. I'd be too bloody ashamed. But Louise didn't look furtive or even slightly worried. She was holding the arm of Abner Morris and acting like she owned him.

Frances couldn't resist it. Picking up her glass, she made her way over to where Louise stood. Close to, she looked older than she had imagined. Her high-domed brow was criss-crossed with parallel furrows and there were deep indentations around her mouth.

'What brings you here?' Frances asked pleasantly. 'I'd no idea Sam had invited you.'

Louise seemed to freeze as she saw her and Frances realised she wasn't cool and relaxed at all. It was a pose. A calculated act to cover her nerves.

'I came here with Abner,' she said. 'We wanted to see how Sam and Clay were making out.'

Frances kept her smile intact. It took considerable effort.

'And what do you think about Sam's – I mean the agency's success?'

The other woman looked wary, as if anything she said might incriminate her.

'You look like you're doing a bomb,' she said finally. 'It must be a relief for all of you.'

Frances pulled herself up to her full height.

'Not really,' she said. 'We always knew we'd succeed. You don't really think either of them would walk out on you without some guarantees?'

She thought she saw Louise grow pale, though it could

have been a trick of the light. The woman had plastered herself with so much make-up it was difficult to tell.

'I didn't know anything about guarantees,' she said. 'None of my clients have mentioned anything about moving.'

She looked up at Abner and in that second Frances saw fear in her eyes. She pushed her advantage home.

'Louise,' said Frances very slowly. 'Sam told me you were a sophisticated woman who'd been around the business, so I'm surprised at you. Do you really imagine if your business was looking to move, they'd tell you? I always thought the losing agency was the last one to know.'

Then she turned and walked away before Louise could answer her.

Abner looked worried.

'What was she talking about?' he asked. 'I thought you had everything at the agency sewn up.'

Louise pasted a smile on her face. It took a great deal of effort.

'I have,' she answered shortly. 'The woman doesn't know what she's talking about.'

Then her eyes did a quick circuit of the room. Clay was in some kind of conference with her ovenware client and Sam was chatting to Kitten Catfood. Doubts started to nag away at Louise's consciousness. She had come here tonight to gloat at a failure. Because she knew Sam and Clay so well, she could see right through their plan. They were giving a party to look like something they weren't. What she hadn't counted on was that the plan would succeed.

She turned to Abner again.

'People are such fools,' she said. 'They really think that just because Sam Kurnitz is throwing around a little free champagne, he's suddenly got a lot of business.'

She heard someone come up behind her.

'Who says I haven't got a lot of business?' She swung round and found herself face to face with Sam and for

587

a second she froze. He was looking well, better than she expected, and there was an air of confidence about him. As if he'd just heard some very good news.

'I hate to disappoint you, Louise,' he said, 'but a man across the room has just asked me to handle two million dollars' worth of his business.'

'Anyone I know?' Louise asked.

Sam smiled and took hold of her hand, then he raised it to his lips, lightly kissing the fingertips.

'No-one you should worry about,' he told her. 'Not while you have Abner to look after you.'

She pulled her hand away.

'I can look after myself,' she said roughly. Then she whirled round and headed towards the door. She had no intention of standing there while her former partners tried to make off with her business. Her common sense told her that one or two accounts would follow them. They had to. But the important business would stick. American Tobacco would stay with her.

She reached the swing doors and was about to push her way through them when something Sam had said to her once flashed through her mind.

'I can't see any man wanting to make a home with the kind of woman you're becoming. Even Abner Morris.'

He had told her that at the last meeting of Kurnitz Tragos and Greene, before it became Tragos and Partners and she had put the remark down to malice and hurt feelings. Now she started to have doubts. What if Abner fell out of love with her? How would her brave new agency fare then?

She turned round and reached into her purse for her lipstick. It was the dark red Paloma Picasso she always wore.

Then she hurried across to the mirror in the reception area and began re-applying her mouth. When she was satisfied with the way she looked she retraced her steps and Louise came back into the party just in time to see

Abner with his arm round Tiffany. The dark woman, she noticed, had a hungry, available look on her face. Oh, no you don't, she thought pushing her way through the crowd. Abner Morris is the one client at this goddamn party that's taken.

For Frances, the rest of the evening passed in a blur. Sometimes she saw Sam with a client she knew, then she saw Clay with the same client. First Tiffany, then Abner, then Louise whirled towards her, then floated away in their own separate directions. There were so many people at this party she had put together, so many faces she had seen and met and forgotten. Sam introduced her to a man called Brian Elder and his face gave her a jolt, but she couldn't for the life of her remember why.

Her old friend Bernard Glenn was there, arm in arm with a guy who used to work with Louise. For a moment she wondered if anything was going on between them. Then she didn't care. Nothing anyone did to anyone mattered any more. Nothing anyone said could make any difference now. It was past ten. The party was winding up. The die was cast. Either they had made it or her baby would be born poor.

When everyone finally left, the agency looked as if a bomb had hit it. Champagne bottles stood empty on the hired gilt tables and the carpet was covered in broken white flowers.

I wonder what happened, Frances thought. For a moment she toyed with the idea of slipping out of the door and going home to bed. She was too tired to waste any more energy on her husband's business. Another life claimed her now. A more demanding one.

Then she saw Sam across the room. He was standing in front of one of his old ads, and he seemed in a kind of trance, as if he was re-living the thought process that went into the creation of the piece of work.

I never knew he cared so much, Frances thought. It's as

if every campaign he ever wrote came straight out of his heart. Like the child growing inside me. In that moment she understood the man she had married better than she had ever done before, and she knew she wouldn't leave the agency until she had found out whether or not Sam's gamble had paid off.

Before she could get to him, Clay loomed up in front of her.

'I suppose you want to know how we did,' he said.

She nodded. Clay threw himself on to one of the padded white sofas and started to tell her.

'Four of the old clients are begging to come back, but that's not the whole picture. What really clinches things is the new business. Accounts that walked in tonight and got fooled by the expensive glitter.'

Frances stopped him right there.

'The glitter didn't fool anybody,' she said. 'How could it? What clinched it for you was the work.'

She indicated the walls around them.

Every surface was covered with posters and press ads and storyboards for commercials. There was the new campaign that Sam had devised for Canada-Card. There was everything he had ever done on Kitten Catfood. There was even the ad for office copiers that Sam had threatened to jump out of the window over.

Clay looked at them and sighed.

'You're right,' he said. 'What everybody needed was a little reminder of what we could produce when we were trying.'

Frances sat down beside Clay and linked her arm through his.

'Tell me about the new business,' she asked. 'Tell me what you and my husband managed to hustle tonight.'

He grinned, held up his hand and started ticking things off on his fingers.

'As of tonight,' he told her, 'we have a development

project from Campbell's soups, a mortgage broker, a Californian baby food and the man from Ford has been talking to Sam about launching a new car.'

She felt a mist rising up in front of her eyes and she grabbed a chair.

'How much does that add up to?' she asked.

'With the car or without the car?'

'Tell me both,' she demanded.

Clay did the sums on his fingers again.

'Without Fords we've got thirty million dollars in turnover. We can just about tick over on that. With the motor corporation, we're tipping a hundred million.'

Frances put her hand up to her forehead. Nothing was real to her any more. Four hours ago she was sending her unborn baby out with a begging bowl. Now it looked as if they could all move back to a penthouse.

'When will we know about the car?' she asked.

Clay ruffled her hair.

'You'd better ask your husband that. He was talking to Ford's managing director.'

Frances looked up and saw Sam walking towards them. He was holding himself in the way he always did when he was riding high. Straight and proud with his head up and his eyes told her that tonight he had fought all his battles and won them.

'We got it, didn't we?' she asked. 'The man from Ford said we could have the car account.'

Sam nodded.

'Of course he did. If you're going to start having babies we have to find some place decent to live. And that takes money.'

Frances shook her head.

'Did I hear you right?' she enquired. 'Were you saying something about me being pregnant? How could you possibly know?'

Sam took hold of her hands and pulled her out of

the sofa where she was sitting. Then he held her very close.

'You seem to have forgotten something. I've loved you for many years now, and I've known you as intimately as any human being could know another. If you so much as put on two pounds I can tell. So don't think I haven't known about our baby for at least a month. I probably spotted it before you did.'